TOGETHER

WE BURN

ALSO BY ISABEL IBAÑEZ

Woven in Moonlight

Written in Starlight

Rogue Enchantments
(short story in *Reclaim the Stars* anthology)

ISABEL IBAÑEZ

TOGETHER

WE BURN

WEDNESDAY BOOKS
NEW YORK

First published in the United States by Wednesday Books,
an imprint of St. Martin's Publishing Group

TOGETHER WE BURN. Copyright © 2022 by Isabel Ibañez.
All rights reserved. Printed in the United States of America.
For information, address St. Martin's Publishing Group,
120 Broadway, New York, NY 10271.

www.wednesdaybooks.com

Designed by Jonathan Bennett

The Library of Congress Cataloging-in-Publication Data is available upon request.

ISBN 978-1-250-80335-1 (hardcover)

ISBN 978-1-250-86562-5 (international, sold outside
the U.S., subject to rights availability)

ISBN 978-1-250-80336-8 (ebook)

Our books may be purchased in bulk for promotional, educational,
or business use. Please contact your local bookseller or the Macmillan
Corporate and Premium Sales Department at 1-800-221-7945, extension 5442,
or by email at MacmillanSpecialMarkets@macmillan.com.

First Edition: 2022

10 9 8 7 6 5 4 3 2 1

For Mamita and Abuelita Consuelo,
you both are the passionate and stubborn YA
heroines I've always looked up to.

In Loving Memory of
Teresa Díaz de Beccar

GREMIOS DE HISPALIA
GUILDS OF HISPALIA

GREMIO DE DRAGONADORES
Dragonadores, Dragon Hunters and Tamers, Arena Owners, Dragonador Instructors

GREMIO DE MAGIA
Magos and Brujas

GREMIO DE SANADORES
Healers, Botanists, Apothecary Owners

GREMIO DE COMERCIANTES
Merchants, Lenders, Traders, Carpenters, Blacksmiths

GREMIO DE LOS SASTRES
Textile Workers, Seamstresses, Laundresses, Tailors

GREMIO DE ANIMALES Y VEGETALES COMERCIALES
Butchers, Hunters, Farmers

GREMIO DE LAS ARTES
Painters, Sculptors, Dancers, Actors and Actresses, Singers, Writers, Weavers

GREMIO DE NOTICIAS
Writers, Printers, Publications

GREMIO DEL MAR
Fishermen, Sailors, Shipbuilders, Navigators

GREMIO DE EJÉRCITO
Patrol, Guards, Army

GREMIO GENERAL
Open to the General Public

DRAGONES DE HISPALIA

DRAGONS OF HISPALIA

CULEBRA
Four legs, resembles a serpent. Small wings, flies short distance.
Stays close to the ground, emerald scales. Shoots poisonous liquid.

LAGARTO
Swimmer dragon. Drowns victims before devouring.
Shimmery, iridescent scales sold as jewelry.
Found along the coast of Valentia.

RANCIO
Golden scales, red irises. Emits a gas that can rot whatever it touches.

MORCEGO
Black dragon with ivory horns. Breathes short bursts of fire.
Great bat wings. Body shape resembles a bull.
Preferred dragon for arenas.

RATÓN
The rat of the skies. White scales and gleaming red eyes. More common than rodents.
Squat in length, round in the belly. Easy to overtake and kill.

ESCARLATA
The elusive and legendary red dragon. Believed to be near extinct and difficult to domineer.
Ruby red scales, immense wings.
Breathes fire for up to half a minute.

TOGETHER WE BURN

PROLOGUE

My mother died screaming my name.

Papá and I had traveled with her to La Bota, a theater outside Santivilla's ancient round walls. I remember it was near an orange grove that tartly scented the air like a thick lemon wedge flavoring tea. Her performance was in celebration of the recent capture of the Escarlata, the legendary and elusive breed of dragon with scales the color of chili peppers. It was known for its fury and volatile nature, for the fire hidden deep in its belly. Only one or two are successfully brought down alive each year. We were all excited to see one, bound in iron.

We sat in the front row surrounding the circular stage, built a hundred years ago and where many flamenco dancers came to perform. It was Mamá's favorite place to dance, out in the open, surrounded by the tangerine-hued mountains to the east and the ocean to the west.

Flamenco was born in Santivilla, the capital of Hispalia, and there's nothing quite like it anywhere else. The blend of the guitarist's strumming, my mother's castañuelas, and the citrus-scented air makes what we in Hispalia call the perfect ambiente.

We all should have been safe. The red dragon was in chains and ready to face the Dragonador.

Papá handed me a plate piled high with toasted almonds, perfectly salted anchovies, and soft cheese, and I munched happily as we waited for Mamá to perform as the opening act for the fight. Off to the side, the bald guitarist was already settled on a sturdy wooden chair. Surrounding us was a tremendous crowd sitting on the stone benches, and together we were all drinking and merry to be under a cloudless blue sky, even if the heat was remorseless, making my embroidered dress stick to my sweat-soaked skin.

It was the beginning of spring, just days after we celebrated the death of winter. It was too hot for my mantilla, and instead, I left my arms and shoulders unprotected under the metallic sun, hanging straight over our heads.

"I forget, Zarela," Papá had whispered in my ear. I squirmed away from his thick beard, still black and without a touch of silver. "Do you know this dance?"

I nodded. "Mamá taught me last month."

When Papá smiled, he did so with his whole face. His dark eyes crinkled, the dimples on both cheeks deepened, and the scruff of his beard moved with his mouth as it reached for his ears.

The guitarist started strumming his instrument, and he was truly excellent, because within moments he made the guitar sing and cry and roar, and the music rode the wind until my body thrummed with each note. Then there was a sudden silence. The crowd surged to their feet, stomping and whistling as Mamá climbed onto the stone stage.

My breath caught at the back of my throat.

She stood in the center, arms curled high above her head, and the fabric of her tight, flaming red dress hugged the curve of her back and fluttered in long ripples around her legs. Still, my mother wouldn't move until she found the beat, counting in her head.

Her hip dropped and she twirled her wrists. The notes propelled my mother in circles, her strong legs stomping on the stage, fingers twisting high in the air. Her dark, curly hair whipped around her face—she refused to braid it at the crown of her head like most flamenco dancers, because according to her, what's the point of whirling in tight circles if you can't feel the wind in your hair. The expression of joy on her face was clearly visible, mesmerizing.

I hated taking my gaze off Mamá when she was preforming, even for a moment, but I did it anyway because there's only one thing better than watching her on stage: the look on Papá's face. He was bending forward, elbows on his knees, slack-jawed, and dark eyes intently focused on Mamá. He knew every step of this routine, every turn her head made. She danced the way she loved: steadfast, gracious, wildly, and slightly aggressive.

The musician ended the song with a flourish, and Mamá's performance finished with her back arched and her left foot giving one last, loud stomp. I jumped to my feet, clapping and roaring along with Papá and the hundreds of spectators who threw gardenias onto the stage. Mamá grinned and found us, her arms stretched wide as if reaching for the ends of the earth. Her glittering, dark gaze landed on mine and she whispered, "te quiero." I mouthed it back to her, and Papá dragged a heavy arm across my shoulders, pulling me to his side. He smelled like chicory and tobacco and the orange he'd devoured earlier.

We beamed at her, and she bowed, facing her familia.

She swept off the stage. Papá remained to save our seats, and he merrily waved as I left him to join Mamá in the changing rooms next to the stage. She gave me a hug and kiss on the temple, asked me to fix her hair while the Dragonador entered the arena. I remember the sound of applause as the Escarlata was let loose, and the fighter began his dance with fate. I hurried to pin Mamá's hair back, eager to rush back to our seats in order to see the death of the red dragon. Even Papá had only killed the breed just once in our arena. It was sure to be quite a match, and I didn't want to miss it.

Mamá turned to me and tucked a gardenia in my hair.

That was my last moment with her.

Bloodcurdling screams bellowed from the arena. Mamá immediately shoved me inside one of the curtained-off areas where performers could freshen up before their event and asked me to stay hidden, told me that she was going to find Papá.

Then she was gone.

I didn't want to stay behind and hide. The yelling grew louder, the sound of fire blasting from the monster became incessant. I rushed out of the dressing room and raced to the ring, my sandals smacking against the hot stone. I remember my breath freezing in my chest at the sight of the Escarlata racing around the arena, its wings having some-how escaped their iron binding.

The monster was free.

It wasted no time in launching itself from the hard, packed sand of the arena. The red dragon flew around stage, its bloodred scales glint-ing horribly in the sunlight, and a terrible, frightening stream of fire erupted from its mouth in one long gust. It scorched parts of the crowd, the stage, the poor guitarist still clutching his instrument. Mamá was not even ten feet from where he stood. My gaze met hers.

"Go back!" she yelled. "Zarela!"

The tunnel of flames swerved and she was engulfed, and a guttural scream ripped out of her as her body burned. The heat from the blast was thick, and I choked on the smoke and scent of singed hair and flesh. The crowd ran in every direction, someone slammed into me and knocked me off my feet. The gravel stung my cheeks, and my hand bled from the shards of someone's plate. I pulled a jagged piece from out of my palm, hissing loudly.

The Escarlata opened its jaws wide, readying to let out another fiery blast.

Papá found me on the ground and pulled me to my feet, and then yanked me away from the dragon ring, from the sight of my burning mamá. We ran for the orange grove, kicking dust in our wake, and hid under the thick leaves. I gripped Papá, sobbing against his chest, and the sound of his heart hammered against my cheek. He pulled me deeper within the tree's canopy. The branches scratched my bare arms. The blossoms smelled like rotting fruit.

I never ate another orange again.

UNO

Underneath my feet, the dragon waits.

Almost unconsciously, my attention drifts to the cobbled ground. I picture the dungeon below this tunnel, the horrid damp smell, the shadows crowding the corners and swift turns, and the row of cages where the monsters are kept under lock and key. In my mind, the beast moves restlessly in its cell, waiting for the moment the iron bars lift so it can bolt into the arena, searching for flesh, for a glimpse of the color red. The image incites a riot in my blood.

The trapped air inside the tunnel glides down my throat, fills my belly. When I exhale, some of the fear goes with it. My mind clears as I quicken my steps, following the curved wall made of craggy stone.

I have minutes before my flamenco routine.

La Giralda's iron bell triumphantly heralds the start of our five hundredth anniversary show, and the sound carries to every corner of Santivilla and sinks into my skin, rattling bone. It's a siren's call, promising the best entertainment you'll see all week, for the not-so-bargain price of twenty-seven reales. Outside the arena, there's a long line curling around the building of those keen on still entering.

But there's not an empty seat left in our dragon ring.

We're the best at what we do, a set of familial skills passed down for centuries. Papá is descended from a long line of Dragonadores, famous for their courage in the ring. This building made of stone and brick and sweat is in my blood. The most prized possession belonging to the Zalvidar name, and one day it will be *mine*.

I walk along the underbelly of the ring, my wooden heels slapping against the stone corridor that leads to the arena, famous for its white sand that glitters under the sun. It's brought in from the coast, carted on dozens of wagons pulled by several pairs of oxen, an effort well worth its price. There's nothing quite like the look of spilled blood against something so pure.

My tomato-red flamenco dress swishes around my ankles, and I run my fingers along the craggy walls. I approach the entrance, and the roar of the crowd booms loud and insatiable. The sound skips down my spine, and a pleasant shiver dances across my skin. I almost forget about the dragon waiting to be unleashed.

Almost, but not quite.

Lola Delgado gently nudges me. "Are you worried about the dragon, the dance, or both?" She tugs impatiently at her wild dark hair. Lola gives up stuffing loose tendrils into her bun with a sigh. The light from the torches casts flickering shadows across her deeply tanned skin. She narrows her hazel eyes at me, understanding the reason behind the tight set to my mouth and why my knuckles turn white around my mother's painted fan.

"It was one of my mother's newest routines. An instant classic."

Lola's a head shorter than me, but even so, she manages to curl a protective arm around my shoulders. "The crowd will love you. They always do." She drops her voice to a whisper. "Even if you perform one of *your* dance routines."

She's willfully forgetting about the last time I tried to do one of my own creations. The crowd was expecting to see a traditional routine of my mother's, but I gave them one of mine. It still unsettles me—how quickly their cheers turned into disappointed shouting and insults.

I had finished the moves with my chin held high, even though I wanted to lie down on the hot sand and cover my ears so I couldn't hear their yelling. I've never forgotten how little the people of Santivilla think of me.

But what truly destroyed me that day was the bitter gleam of sadness in Papá's eyes, his thin smile that told me that even *he* wasn't interested in seeing anything but my mother's routines.

"They want Eulalia Zalvidar." People want her brilliance on the dance floor, the luring sway of her hips, the way she could make you feel bold and inspired, all from watching her stamp across the stage. This is why I dance steps that belonged to her first.

She frowns. "Zarela . . ."

"It's fine." I straighten away from her, ears straining to hear the music that'll signal my entrance. "Estoy bien, no te preocupes."

"I do worry about you," she says. "And it's not fair. You're the responsible one."

"Just tell me I look presentable." I lift up the skirt, letting the ruffles skim my ankles. "How does the dress look?"

She reaches forward and rearranges the collar so the pleats lay flat. As one of the maids of the household, she's responsible for making sure I look the part. "Estás guapísima."

"Thanks to you," I say with a small smile.

She grins and her round cheeks flush prettily. Anytime we talk about clothing, her eyes light up. Had her circumstances been different, she could have apprenticed at the Gremio de los Sastres, the guild of tailors and textile workers, but her family couldn't afford to send her. Now she works alongside our housekeeper, Ofelia, helping with the cooking and cleaning. But over the years, I've hired her to design and sew new dresses for my flamenco routines.

Her talent ought not to be wasted on dirty linens.

"Oh, I *know* I did a fabulous job with the alterations."

"Your humility moves me."

She continues as if I haven't spoken. "And that dress is doing marvelous things for your—"

I narrow my gaze. "Let me stop you right there."

"What? I was only trying to say that the fabric drapes in all the right—"

"*Lola.*"

She winks at me, and I resist hitting her with my mother's fan. She's trying to distract me, but my nerves roar to life despite her outrageous flattery. The crowd's cheering is insistent, demanding to be entertained like a child. The sound envelops us in a fiery rush. Lola winces. I lean forward, unable to keep the smirk off my face. "Did we drink a little too much manzanilla last night? The sherry always gives you a headache."

"Ugh," she mumbles. "I resent your horrid, smug tone. To think I came down here to make sure you were fine—" She breaks off, swaying on her feet.

"You came down here to see Guillermo," I cut in with an arched brow. "Admit it."

She looks away, biting her lip.

"What happened to Rosita?"

Lola rolls her eyes. "She was too wild."

"But *you're* wild," I say laughingly.

"Exactly. I can barely take care of myself. I'm too young to worry about anyone else."

I gently push her behind me, as I desperately fight a laugh. "You're a menace. Go find a seat."

"If you see him," she says with a sly smile. "Tell him I like the way his pants fit."

"I will never say such nonsense to him or anyone, ever."

"What?" she asks innocently. "He's entirely too handsome for someone so studious. Someone ought to let him know."

Personally, I don't understand Guillermo's appeal. As a member of the Gremio de Magia, he spends most of his day bent over chopped-up dragon parts: pulled-out teeth, sawed-off ivory horns, and eyeballs stored in vats of oil. Guillermo is here now, somewhere in the arena, waiting for Papá to kill today's monster so that he can pay for the remains and take them back to the Gremio in order to concoct more potions.

"I'll tell him you say hello," I say finally.

"That doesn't sound like me in the slightest."

"I'm not going to do your flirting for you. Not even if you ask nicely."

Lola pouts and then stumbles away, and I let out a little laugh. I turn back around. I have to concentrate on my performance and not think of anything other than the steps and the music. I focus on my breath as it catches in my throat, and on my body coiled tight and ready for the show.

The entrance is an arched doorway, lined with cobblestone in varying hues of clay and the tawny sand outside the walled city of Santivilla. On the other side, patrons wave their sombreros in the air as they catch a glimpse of me, dressed as my unforgettable mother, wearing her flamenco dress and shoes. The outfit is endlessly bold, with ruffles adorning the off-shoulder neckline and hem. Lola altered the costume to fit my smaller frame perfectly.

But while I may style my black hair like she did, wear the same color rouge on my lips, and line my eyes in charcoal the way she liked, I am not my mother. I am the forgettable village next to her metropolis.

What she did was miraculous. I merely worship at the same altar.

Nerves grip my heart and squeeze. It's always this way before I take the stage. I'm holding up my father's name and my mother's legacy. I inhale deeply, allowing the crowd's cheering and sharp whistling and the sounds of the strumming guitar coming from the center of the ring to remind me of who I am: Zarela Zalvidar, daughter of the best performers in all of Hispalia.

I damn well better act like it.

This is the most important show we'll ever put on, our five hundredth anniversary spectacle, covered by the national paper, *Los Tiempos*, and watched by wealthy patrons and prominent guild members from all over Hispalia. They've come with their velvet drawstring purses, lofty connections, and dreams of being entertained extravagantly in a city as beautiful as it is dangerous.

The crowd hushes at the sight of the guitarist settling onto his stool above the platform. Pressure builds in my chest. My shoulders are tight, and I roll each side. I inhale again, holding air captive deep in my lungs.

I exhale, and I imagine my fear riding my breath, leaving me behind. I throw my shoulders back, my spine straight and proud like La Giralda's bell tower, and I march toward the raised wooden platform in the middle of the arena, arms outstretched to meet the hundreds of spectators sitting around the ring. I keep my chin lifted high, and my grin wide enough for everyone to see. Five hundred spectators stomp their feet to the rhythm of the guitar, clapping their hands at a fast clip.

Ra-ta-ta-ta-ta-tat.

It's a drug, that dizzying rush as people scream louder, wanting a part of me. Papá stands at the other designated entrance for performers, with a gleaming smile. He's with his childhood friend, Tío Hector, a fellow Dragonador who owns a popular dragon ring across town. He's not really my uncle, but I've always called him one for as long as I can remember.

The throng hushes. I close my eyes and wait for the beat. When I find it, I slowly stomp on the stage. The soles of my black leather shoes smack against the wood like a battering ram. The sound is the base of my performance, and the noise anchors me to my mother.

I sway my hips as the guitarist strums faster and faster, fingers moving quickly up and down the instrument. I spin and twirl, bending backward as I whip out my fan, flinging it open with a snap. The cheering starts anew, and I smile as I stomp and clap along to the rhythm of the music. I lay my fears to rest. In this moment, I relish the dance and the way the music glides along my body as I position my legs and torso into strong lines.

Grief has made me a better dancer. I command the stage and offer this tribute to Mamá, to her adoring fans who scream her name even now. It's why I've stopped Papá from introducing me ahead of my performance.

The song ends at a slow crawl, and I move with the dying notes, bending forward in a traditional Hispalian bow. Sweat slides down the back of my neck, and my breath comes out in great huffs. Every dance is a fight against the ground, and my legs shake from the effort to win. Flowers rain, dropping dead at my feet. I straighten, wave at the patrons and their fat purses, and sashay to Papá and Hector where they wait by the second tunnel entrance, quietly proud. Papá carries an enormous bouquet of gardenias, the stems tied tightly with a gold ribbon, fluttering in the breeze like a banner beckoning me home. I take the flowers as Hector leans forward to fix the adornment in my hair, smiling broadly.

Papá curls a strong arm around my waist. "Preciosa. Just like your querida mamá."

He studies my face, searching for my mother in the curve of my cheek and the fire in my eyes. But I'm not her. I can't say the words out loud—he'd be crushed, so instead, I say what he needs. "Para Mamá. So we never forget her."

A small smile tiptoes across his face, but I'm not fooled. He might convince a stranger that he's happy, but I've seen what a real smile looks like, and that's not it, though I've grown accustomed to this version.

Hector guides me backward, farther into the tunnel where the white sand no longer covers the ground. He yanks on a pocket iron bar door, dragging it forward until it slides into the gap on the opposite wall. Papá remains on the other side, closest to the arena. I reach between the slots, wanting Papá's hand. I try to remain calm, remind myself that my father is the best Dragonador in all of Hispalia.

But the risk never fades.

Any fight could be his last.

Last week, a dragon wearing ribbons and a necklace made of flowers gored a fighter in the stomach in one of our rival's arena. The man had died in front of hundreds, including his wife and two small children.

Papá strides to the center of the arena where the stage has already been removed, and all that's left is the hot sand. His snug jacket encloses his strong arms, and his patent leather shoes are polished to a resplendent sheen. The ensemble he wears is startling white, stitched with red thread and adorned by a thousand beads in a burst of chaotic color, handmade and designed by Lola. It had taken her months of painstakingly sewing each sparkling piece onto the Dragonador costume, known everywhere in Hispalia as the *traje de luces*—suit of lights.

His broad shoulders are proud and straight enough to measure with, and his hands grip the golden handle of the red banner that bears our family name. Every step Papá takes adds flair and drama to the fight. He is a consummate entertainer and charmer. Born to please and impress. Passionate, quick to anger, and fiercely loyal.

In the arena, he is the most like the Papá I remember.

The lone iron gate rises. The crowd sits, quiet and expectant. Hundreds of fans open and snap in the sweltering heat, fluttering like bird wings. My heart thuds painfully and Hector pats my arm reassuringly.

"He'll be fine," he murmurs.

I barely hear him. From within another dark tunnel—there are three leading out of the arena—the Morcego races forward like an enraged bull. Its ebony body shines bright, glowing with energy. Two ivory tusks trailing golden ribbons protrude from its toothy mouth, and its eyes are bright yellow and mesmerizing. Around its neck are flowers, fluttering delicately against the scales that are stronger than armor.

I can't take my gaze off the beast.

I clutch at the cobbled tunnel wall of the arena entrance, fingers digging into the grooves. My chest is on fire, rising and falling too fast. The dress is a fist around my heart.

Hector leans close. "Zarela?"

I nod and breathe deeply, fighting to regain my composure. The dragon is wider and taller than Papá, but there's determination in the flat line of his mouth. He's never feared them. I thought he'd turn away from dragonfighting after Mamá died, but her death only made him angry. Instead of one show a month, we now host two. I worry Papá won't stop fighting until all the dragons of Hispalia have been hunted down and dragged in front of him.

The dragon snaps its great jaws and rushes forward, shiny claws digging into the sand. Papá sidesteps the attack, and the capote's fabric curls around the wind like a beckoning finger. The beast's attention is on the red flash of cloth, and Papá knows it. He pulls a long, thin blade with his free hand, while launching the banner high into the air. The dragon jumps, jaws snapping, trying to reach for it. But its wings have been clipped, and it can only jump so high. The Morcego lands on the ground with a furious roar, and as the dust rises and then settles, Papá makes his move.

The banner hits the ground.

Papá's blade sinks into the back of the dragon's neck, at the tender skin unprotected by scales. The beast lets out a deafening howl and slumps sideways while the crowd jumps to their feet. I sag against the wall. He's safe. Papá raises both hands in triumph, and then he bends forward, sticks out his left leg, and moves his right arm in a wide arc high above his head. A traditional Hispalian bow. The famous bell rings again, heralding Papá's victory.

The show is a success.

I can see it in the smiles of our patrons, I can hear it coming from Papá's adoring fans, stomping their feet. Duty beckons, and I turn away from Papá and walk down the long tunnel and back into the prep room. A few of Mamá's dresses are kept here, safe in an antique armoire. Every time I change, I'm greeted by a veritable rainbow of sequins, ruffles, and lace, each tied to a memory of my mother. Sometimes I can smell the gardenias clinging to her hair, feel the hot flash of her temper, see her quick smile. I decide to remain in her red flamenco dress to send off our patrons instead of changing.

Paying customers will stream into the main foyer, twittering with excitement and the rush of seeing a live dragon up close. They'll want to meet Papá and me, and I hurry to the main hall.

Heat floods into the great receiving room from the open entrance to the avenue and sweat glides down the back of my neck. Dozens of fat, squat candles delicately scented with gardenia petals illuminate the wrought iron chandelier. Servers carry trays laden with thinly sliced jamón and hard goat cheese, bowls of roasted marcona almonds, and olives marinated in olive oil, thyme, rosemary, and lemon, and porcelain pitchers filled with summer-touched wine, flavored with thick slices of golden apples and strawberries.

The tall, wooden double doors are flung open, perfectly centered to the grand red velvet staircase that splits halfway to the second floor, and then leads up in each direction to a balcony overlooking the foyer. The second floor has several entrances opening to long corridors wall-papered in red velvet that lead to the stone benches encircling the arena.

Once the dragon has been carried off to be butchered and Papá is done with charming the crowd, everyone will come down the stairs and I'll be waiting for them, wearing a gardenia and a smile. I grab a glass of sangría and enjoy several sips, doing my best to ignore the sound of the mob protesting dragonfighting outside La Giralda. They march up and down the avenue with their banners and self-righteous attitudes. As if dragons don't attack the cities of Hispalia, as if the monsters don't ter-rorize people on their journey from one town to another. Traveling to the coast isn't simple for Hispalians, not when we have to bring guards to fight off a potential attack from the skies. I take another long sip and pull an apple slice into my mouth when a sudden noise startles me.

Bloodcurdling screams enflame the air.

I whip around.

It came from the arena.

I rush from the doors, full skirt swirling, and race back the way I came. The guards are at my heels, swords drawn. More screams ring loudly in my ears, the sound reverberating and crashing against the stone walls. My hands are sweating by the time I make it to one of the arena entrances. I don't recognize the people rushing past—blurs, all of them, some finely dressed, others in simple tunics and trousers. Their faces are carved in stark terror.

I clutch at a man's sleeve. "What's happened?"

He spins to face me, dark eyes frantic. A bloody gash mars his fore-head. "Get away from the arena!"

"¿Qué? Señor, por favor—"

He yanks free and follows the crowd. I scramble away, shoving people as if I carried a sword and not a delicate fan, until I finally reach the arched entrance. I stop at the sight before me, sand kicking up at my heels.

On the pale floor of the arena, bodies lay in bloody heaps, staining the ground a deep rose red as people frantically try to flee the ring. My stomach lurches, and acid rises at the back of my throat.

Above, our dragons fly free, swooping and diving, claws out.

DOS

My hands fly to my mouth. The monsters are everywhere—racing between the rows of seats, chasing after patrons rushing out into the arena. They ought to be locked in the dungeons. I press against the curved wall, needing the strength of the stone to keep me upright.

¿Dónde está Papá?

I can't see him anywhere, not through the mess of people fleeing into the tunnels, pushing and shoving. Others are trying to drag the wounded away from one of the Morcegos. I search for our five dragon tamers.

I know they're out here; they have to be.

Except everyone is covered in sand, in blood, in ash. Faces blend together, features hard to distinguish. At last my gaze snags on one of our tamers—Marco—dressed in black leather from head toe, wielding blades and whips. He fights off one of the beasts, but the dragon roars and whips its tail, crashing against his chest. The force of the hit sends him flying, and he smashes against the arena wall with a sickening crunch.

"¡Aquí!" I yell to the person closest to me. "Follow me!" I guide whoever I can to the nearest tunnel, the hem of my dress caked in bloody sand, when I stumble over something.

No, *someone*.

I fall to my knees next to a child-sized body, burned crisp, my nose and mouth full of smoke and fire. Pandemonium reigns in every corner of the arena.

No sight of Papá or Lola anywhere.

The deafening growls coming from the beasts make my head spin, as if I'm on a too-fast carriage ride, tumbling down a hill, spinning wildly and out of control. Someone knocks me sideways. I land on my stomach and sand blasts my face, creeping into my eyes, the corners of my mouth, and up my nose. I sneeze, spit out what I can, and then wipe my face with the ruffled collar of my dress. It's beyond ruined.

Quickly, I scan the arena. How many monsters have escaped their pens? Dragon one—the Culebra—flies low near the opposite entrance. Dragons two and three—both Rancios, crawl thirty feet from me, emitting an awful stench, like spoiled milk. In the distance, I catch sight of three more, our newest, soaring into the air.

We hadn't bound their wings yet.

The sand around my hands darkens, the heat of the sun momentarily blocked. Warm gusts of air whip at my hair. I slowly glance up. Through the curling smoke a shadow looms from above. My stomach lurches.

The Morcego.

The deadliest dragon we own. Great bat wings, shiny black scales, and the ability to breathe fire, furious like an enraged bull readying to charge. Two great horns are on either side of its nostrils. His jaw opens, and the telltale crackling noise follows.

"Zarela!" someone roars. Papá's face hovers inches from mine, his lips twisting in horror. He drags me to my feet as the beast blasts us with fire and smoke. Papá whips me around, and I feel him shuddering from the scorching hit. He screams into my ear as his clothes, his flesh, burst into flames. We stumble into the corridor, away from the carnage and the roiling mess of people facing a terrible, furious death. The scent of his charred skin makes acid rise up my throat.

It hurts to talk. My mouth is dry and filled with smoke. "¿Estás bien?" My steps fumble. I want to see how badly he's hurt.

"Don't slow down, hija!"

We race along the tunnel, the small space thick with the sound of people yelling for their loved ones. Everyone is dusty, covered in grime and stained with blood. Guilt slams into me, followed by a profound sense of shame. We're responsible for all these people. How did this happen?

How will we survive this?

Dread pools deep in my belly as we get to the main foyer, filled with patrons. Time seems to jump forward, crosses miles in the space of a blink. Ticket holders flee La Giralda, rushing out the front door and escaping to safer ground. It takes everything in me to hold it together.

Beside me, Papá drags his feet. His olive skin is nearly bleached of color. He sags against me, coughing loudly.

I stumble from his weight. "Papá!" He pitches forward, and my body shudders in alarm. "Papá!"

He crashes to his knees. I'm barely fast enough to keep him from breaking his nose. I grip his tattered jacket and slow his descent to the ground. Tears blur my vision. Slowly, I peel away the fabric and he groans. The upper right portion of his back and shoulder is a mess of bubbling and seared flesh. The blast missed his heart, but the wound is severe, blackened and smoking in some areas.

The roar surrounding me seems to drop to a hush. All I can hear are the sounds of my breathing; all I can see is my father's unconsciousness. Dimly, I hear someone yelling my name.

"Zarela, gracias a Dios," Lola exclaims when she reaches me, dropping to her knees. Her face turns ashen when it lands on my father's wounds. "I'm going to send for the Gremio de los Sanadores. We need healers." Her gaze wanders over my shoulder, taking in the many people moaning and begging for help. "Lots of them."

I look around, despair rising. There's still so much to do. All these people need to be moved out of La Giralda and taken to the Gremio de Sanadores, the local hospital run by healers. How many of them will survive? How many of them died?

I'm afraid of the answer.

"I'll ask them to bring members who can help transport the wounded," Lola adds, and then grimaces. "Those who *can* be moved, anyway."

She's right. Some people are too injured to be moved and will have to be treated here.

"Go, and hurry." Everywhere I look, people are huddled into themselves, in shock, covered in bloody gashes and sooty clothes.

"I'll be as quick as I can," Lola says, jumping to her feet. Dirt and sweat stains streak her tunic, and her leather sandals are caked in sand. Someone steps in her path before she can leave. He's tall with dark hair bound in a messy knot at the nape of his neck, his rich black skin shines with sweat, as if he'd come running. Warm brown eyes latch on my maid. He wears the typical all-gray ensemble preferred by the Gremio de Magia, the only flash of color coming from the vibrant embroidered patch sewn onto his long tunic, depicting an intricate crest made up of a wand and a grouping of stars.

Guillermo, the aspiring mago and apprentice at the Gremio de Magia.

"Do you have something I can give my father?" I ask him. He tears his attention off Lola and glances past me to Papá.

His lips twist in horror at the sight of my father's mangled body. "Lo siento—I'm no healer—"

"Is there nothing you can do?" I know it's unfair to ask him. Wizards and witches specialize in different kinds of magic, and some work closely with healers to create tinctures and tonics that push the body toward miraculous healing. The spells are costly, rare, and hardly ever on the market. Not unless you have connections.

Guillermo thrusts his hands into his tunic pocket and pulls out a thin wand. The wood has been dipped in a magical potion and has enough power for one use. Snap it in half, and the spell is released.

"All I have is a cooling spell," he says. "I get so hot waiting for the fight to end—"

He must see my disappointment written all over my face because he breaks off.

"Your father needs a healer," Lola says. "I'll run now—"

"I'll go with you—" Guillermo interrupts, clearly relieved.

She rushes away, the apprentice at her heels, both nimbly skirting around the wounded.

My mind crowds with one worry after another. The questions I crave answers to make my neck tighten. How did the dragons escape? Where are they now? What will happen to La Giralda?

"Señorita Zarela," someone says from behind me.

It's one of the housemaids, holding out a bottle filled with pressed aloe vera. Every arena must have supplies in case the worst should happen, stored in the required infirmary on site. Over the years, my parents have needed various treatments due to some scrapes and ailments while dancing under a hot sun or fighting dragons. Nothing serious, but the room always has bottles of tincture to help with minor burns, sore heels, and the like.

I blink as realization dawns. There're blankets and cots in that room, and a few potted herbs too. "Gracias, Antonia," I say, taking the medicine. "Will you please direct the staff to hand out as much of the supplies as people need?"

She rushes off to do my bidding.

"There you are!" Hector's booming voice calls as he strides forward, arms spread wide. Relief blooms in my chest. I dart into his embrace, pressing my cheek hard against his fine jacket. He stiffens, and I step back.

Sections of his jacket are scorched. "You're hurt."

"Not terribly," he says. "Just don't squeeze me too hard."

"Tío," I say. "Mi papá—"

Hector's eyes widen in alarm.

I gesture toward the ground. "Look at him."

Hector's lips thin to a pale slash. Then he beckons to someone sprinting past us, asking for help to move Papá to the infirmary. The other man agrees, and together they gingerly carry my father to the small room adjacent to the prep room. I move to follow inside, but Hector shakes his head. "Zarela, you must take care of the others. I have your father now."

"But—"

"Let me help you," he says quietly.

I look past him, at the prone figure of my father lying on his stomach. He's still but for the gentle movement of his back, rising and falling. "I'll send a healer to you as soon as they arrive."

Hector sends me away. My footsteps are heavy against the cold stone floor, and it's taking everything in me to keep my back straight, the guilt heavy on my shoulders. As soon as I return to the grand foyer, I hear my name coming from every direction, people needing salves and bandages and healers, but my mind narrows onto one blinding thought.

How did this happen?

Dragonadores die frequently in the fights—but the dragon is quickly captured and killed by tamers. It's what should have happened today—but there were too many monsters to contain, and our tamers died trying.

Hot shame rises, enflaming my cheeks.

I run around, handing out supplies and small jars of expensive burn ointment. I hand out whatever we have left on our shelves, cost be damned. Sweat beads at my hairline as I walk around the foyer, sidestepping the dozens of blankets and cots strewn everywhere.

"Señorita Zarela?"

The voice at my elbow jerks me from my thoughts. I turn to face Benito, one of our dragon tamers, his protective mask off, and his black leather ensemble half covered in dragon blood. He has an angular, sharp face with deep, weathered lines forged by years in the sun and taming beasts. "¿Tienes un momento, por favor?"

"Give me an update, Benito."

The lines at the corners of his eyes tighten. "I don't have an accurate number on how many people were injured, señorita. My guess is close to fifty, perhaps up to seventy." I wince and try to swallow, but my throat thickens painfully. He shifts on his feet, clearly ill at ease. "We've lost thirteen patrons, including an eight-year-old boy and a senior member of the Gremio."

My lips part. I turn over his words as if they're a nightmare and I'm desperate to wake up.

Benito clutches his leather whip tighter. "With your permission, I'd like to order most of your guards to help the wounded home."

"Of course," I murmur, surprised I can hear his words at all over my roaring heartbeat.

"As for your dragons—" He pauses, and I brace myself for the worst. Dragons are expensive investments. "Three dragons never left their pens," he says, counting with his fingers. "The last three are restrained and bound in the arena, while three others have flown."

My stomach swoops as a sudden, horrifying thought slams into me— the dragons that flew away will wreak havoc over Santivilla, scorching people, burning homes. "Is there any way we can retrieve them? Can you arrange a group of our tamers—" My voice breaks off at his crestfallen face.

"I am the only surviving one, Señorita Zarela." His next words are kind, kinder than I deserve. "At this point, there is no way to know where the beasts have gone. Would you try to find a pet bird that's escaped its cage? The dragons flew high and away from the city center. They might never return. I believe the best course is for me to remain with the other dragons down below."

His logic is sound, but I can't help worrying about an attack on the city. "Benito, how did this happen? How did our other dragons escape their pens?"

He frowns. "I found something strange. I think—"

"Zarela!"

Benito and I turn as Lola runs up to us, hair windblown, tunic untucked from her ruffled skirt. Dirt smudges both cheeks, and her eyes look wild. Guillermo isn't with her.

She stops abruptly, panting, and then clutches her side. "I am not built for running."

"Lola," I say, fighting to keep my voice calm. "What is it?"

"I've brought the healers, and they're with your father." Her next words come out shaky. "They said to come quick."

TRES

Years ago, my mother and I were practicing one of her routines, until the sun had dipped far under Santivilla's skyline. She demanded a lot, and I gave her everything I had for the chance to be like her. Mamá could have danced all day and done the same all over again on the next, but I struggled to keep up with her energy, her vitality. Her routines always stole my breath. Made my legs shake, and my chest rise and fall too fast.

Lola's words send me into the same state.

She seems to understand, because she immediately grabs one of my arms and helps me take the first step. Since the day Mamá died, I circled around my father, trying to protect him from any and all imagined dangers that might take him away from me. But he refused to quit the one thing I feared the most. Being a Dragonador has claws that have sunk deep into his flesh.

I gave up fighting him months ago. Foolish, deadly mistake.

"Will he live?" I ask through numb lips.

She squeezes me gently. "No lo sé."

Of course she wouldn't know.

We walk through the mess in the foyer, the iron chandelier lit with guttering candles, illuminating the room in a soft glow. I didn't realize the sun had gone down. The wounded who couldn't possibly leave La Giralda are situated on cots and blankets, surrounded by their friends and family—friends and family who glare as I stumble along to our infirmary. I feel their anger as if it were a blade in the back. It's no less than I deserve.

A healer waits outside the door, impatient, booted feet fidgeting. She's austere and grave, but I detect something else from that awful twist to her mouth. She's petite with deep black skin and a no-nonsense gaze, and wearing a simple blue tunic and skirt, her healer's linen clothing stained with far too much blood.

Papá's blood.

"Señorita Zarela." The healer nods once. "I'm Eva."

I lick my dry lips. "How is he?"

"He's awake," she says. "And raving. He's refusing my assistance, ordering me from the room. I can't work on him like this."

Relief courses up and down my body. Papá is alive. "Let me see him."

"There's more," she says. "The wound near his upper shoulder is deep, and I'm worried about infection. I must remove all the blackened skin." She hesitates. "It will mean that he'll no longer be able to move his arm higher than the level of his heart."

I blink, understanding dawning.

"I'm sure that's fine. Right, Zarela?" Lola asks. "Better to remove the"—she blanches—"dead skin?"

It's not the least bit fine. Without full mobility, my father will not win a fight against a dragon.

His Dragonador days are over.

It's what I want. And yet . . . Being Santiago Zalvidar the Dragonador is more important to him than anything else. More important than being a husband or a father. Papá will never forgive me if I don't do everything I can to help him hold on to his dream.

And I don't want to live in a world without him in it.

"Find another way," I say in a hard voice. "Find the right procedure. I don't care about the cost. Bring in a wizard if you have to."

Lola shoots me a look, dark brows rising.

"There is none," the healer says coolly. "If I don't remove parts of his shoulder and arm, he'll succumb to infection. He'll die in a matter of days."

There's a horrible silence, and I'm perfectly aware I have to fill it with my answer, but the words are stuck at the back of my throat.

"I can't proceed without permission," she says. "I'm dealing with a member of the Gremio de Dragonadores, and I fear retribution for permanently ending the famous Santiago Zalvidar's career."

Finally, I'm able to speak, even if it's hardly a whisper. "I'll speak with him."

I untangle myself from Lola and enter the infirmary, quickly shutting the heavy wooden door behind me. Papá lies on his belly on the narrow bed, and at the sight of his scorched back, my stomach lurches. It's a mess of bubbling skin, and mottled, dying flesh the color of night.

He acted quickly and saved me. His reward will be to lose his arena, his inheritance, a profession he loves, and maybe his life.

What is La Giralda without its famous Dragonador?

Papá raises his head and spears me with a heated look from his bloodshot eyes. He's been crying. My proud father, who's fought over one hundred dragons, lost the love of his life, reduced to tears.

"Zarela," he says hoarsely. "Don't let them ruin me. Do you hear me?"

I take a step forward. "Papá—"

His expression darkens, the lines across his forehead deepening. "Do not let them touch me."

"I can't do that," I say, fighting to keep my tone measured. "Papá, you must let her do the work."

"There has to be another way!" he roars, and I flinch as the sound whips around me, trapping me in his fury.

"You'll die if she doesn't rid the dead flesh." My voice breaks. "Do you understand?"

"Find a bruja." Papá slams his fist against the cot and he howls—in pain, frustration, I can't tell. He's panting, breaths coming in and out too fast. "That hurt, Dios."

"Papá," I say, rushing forward, but by the time I've reached his side, he's passed out again.

"Eva!" I yell.

The door opens with a snap, and she strides in, two others at her elbow. "Do I have permission?"

I swallow hard, unable to look away from my father. His lips are bent into a grimace. Even while sleeping, the pain won't leave.

"Señorita?" Eva asks, this side of impatient. "I have to move quickly if I'm to save him."

"I must pay a visit to the Gremio de Magia. Perhaps they might be able to help him with an encanto."

"A spell?" Eva repeats. "A custom spell that will cure him will take days to prepare. Your father doesn't have that kind of time."

"Are you sure?"

She regards me in offended silence. I thread my hands through my messy hair, breathing hard, knowing what I'll say but dreading it. He will hate what I've done when he wakes up. I can live with that. I can't, however, live without him.

I lift my chin. "Do what you have to do."

Lola follows me as I make my way back to the foyer. I'm about to veer toward the kitchen when a shout comes from the direction of the great double doors. Lola and I turn in time to see a black, four-wheeled carriage pulled by six horses stop in front of La Giralda. I stiffen against her, dread sinking into the marrow of my bones.

"Dragonador Gremio members," I say under my breath. I walk up to the entrance, head held high and wait for the group at the top of the marble steps.

I hope these are Papá's friends, and I pray the Dragon Master hasn't shown up himself. This is one man my father hasn't been able to charm.

But my prayer is dashed in the next instant.

A tall, broad-shouldered man climbs out of the gilded carriage, the moonlight casting him in a delicate silver hue. His olive skin is stretched and weathered, resembling a leather hat left too long in the sun.

Don Eduardo Del Pino.

Nothing escapes his attention. I lift my chin as my knees start trembling. This man holds our fate in his hands—and he can't *stand* my father. Papá has never explained why. He rarely comes to our arena. Mamá was still alive during his last visit.

I swallow hard, fighting to keep my panic at bay. Something of this magnitude can't be postponed.

Papá and I have much to answer for.

"Do you want me to stay with you?" Lola asks.

I shake my head. "Will you find Ofelia? Ask her to prepare bone broth for the wounded."

"What about a torta instead?" she asks with a hint of a smile.

I sigh wearily. "Yes, I think we all need cake."

She's gone before I can tell her I didn't mean it. I don't deserve cake.

Slowly, I turn and look down at the Dragon Master, accompanied by two other Gremio members. The three caballeros march up the marble steps to greet me. They're all dressed in matching, somber black trousers and coats, embroidered with white thread in the shape of various dragons. Their boots are adorned with brass buckles, and the worn brown leather almost reaches the knee. Around their necks is an unwrapped linen scarf the color of blood, stitched with the name of the Gremio. An ornate brooch, gold and shaped into a crest with a pair of interlocking dragons, completes the ensemble.

I incline my head toward the Conde. "Hola, Don Eduardo."

"Señorita Zalvidar." He has the kind of voice that could send children running. A hard rasp, filled with smoke and snarl, and hard-earned from years of fighting monsters. "One of your patrons notified me of today's disaster."

There's clear reproach in his tone. I should have sent word to the Gremio, but I'd forgotten.

The Dragon Master brushes past and stops under the doorframe. The others quickly follow with sharp exclamations. Seeing the wake of destruction through their eyes brings the experience of it fresh to my mind. The flames. Mauled, burning bodies. Bloody sand everywhere.

"How did this happen?" the Dragon Master demands.

I shake my head, numb. "I don't have a suitable answer. It's been chaotic—"

"That is unacceptable."

I fall silent, my cheeks flushing. Humiliation burns.

"¿Y tu Papá?" one of Eduardo's companions asks, scanning the room. He's shorter than all of them, with a round belly. "How is he?"

I hesitate. "He's with a healer."

Don Eduardo studies me for a moment, leaning more heavily on his black cane with the head of a dragon. "Will he live?" he rasps, voice yielding not an ounce of sympathy.

"Con la ayuda de Dios," I say.

"With God's help," he says. My father is the most respected Dragonador in all of Hispalia, and the Dragon Master can't offer a glimpse of concern. "Qué tragedia," he says. "And the arena?"

In the smoldering ruin that once showcased our imported white sand, the stone is scorched, and deep fissures have left their permanent mark. Huge chunks of the sand in the arena are a bloody, congealed mess. Three dragons are bound by a massive chain.

"Where did you get them?" one of the members asks.

"From the same place as the other rings in town," I say stiffly. These dragons can be found anywhere in Hispalia, in the desert plains to the north, in watery caves to the east. Like cockroaches, they multiply without any constraint, invading even the most unlikely of places. They're easily hunted and kept in ranches where they can be purchased for dragonfighting.

"We have to kill the line," the Conde says grimly. He half lifts a finger. "All three of them must die for what they've done, along with their mothers."

I flinch. Six dragons, six investments gone in one afternoon.

There's been too much death on this day.

The Conde strides forward and unsheathes his long blade. He sinks the sword deep in the muscle at the back of the neck, piercing the lungs. The deaths are quick. Over and done with, but the sound of their choked cries slams into my body like a physical blow to the face. Puddles of blood reach across the arena like gnarly tree roots.

The guild members regard the destruction of the building in silence for a long moment. They're grim and disapproving, and their sudden quiet sends a flicker of unease down my spine. The guards have brought down the victims, and they lie next to the opposite entrance, covered in sheets. Tomorrow, I'll arrange for their families to retrieve them. I make a note to send money for the funeral arrangements.

The Dragon Master regards the dead.

"The Gremio will stand with us, won't they?" I ask, unable to help myself. We are the most popular ring in Hispalia. Five hundred years of success and fame and legend. We've never had an incident before now.

No one responds to this, and my face drains of all color.

Eduardo sheaths his sword. His feathery white brows pull into a tight frown. "This event will not go unpunished. I'll send a summons for your father. Don't let him miss it."

"What's going to happen to La Giralda?" I ask, worry edging into my voice.

The Dragon Master levels me with a stern glare, and then he walks off, the other members quickly following. They leave me standing in the middle of the bloody arena, amidst the scorched stone and death.

CUATRO

I don't know what I'd do without Lola. For the hundredth time, my mind dwells on the moment when she'd first arrived to La Giralda. Short and skinny, her hair wild and unbound, nails ragged and shoes so dirty they were beyond saving. My mother had gone back to the city of her birth, Valentia, a coastal dwelling made up of fishermen and shipbuilders and marinas, to visit old friends, and when she came back, she'd brought three girls, all around my age. Three girls destined for hard manual labor and married off far too young.

"They need better work," Mamá explained. "I'm finding positions, but for now, they'll stay with us to help with La Giralda's upkeep."

Right after, I was trying on a new dress when Lola had walked in, carrying a tray with the coffee Mamá had requested.

Lola took one look at the dress and said, "That's the ugliest thing I've ever seen, and Zarela really ought not to wear pastels."

I gasped, but Mamá stepped back and tilted her head.

"You're right," she said.

Lola stayed.

She's here with me now, and even though I've been a crying mess, barely able to speak coherently, she listened to every halting word with the kind of patience she doesn't like to admit she has.

"Tell me again," she says.

I wipe my dripping nose with the heel of my hand. "I hate crying."

"I know," she says in a voice that feels like it's been dipped in honeyed tea. It works like a balm against my fractured heart.

More infuriating tears slide down my cheeks, and I angrily attack them with my tunic sleeve. "Eva—the healer—managed to rid his shoulder of all the dead skin, but she's still worried about an infection. She says some of the skin might poison his blood. Papá has a fever, and he's in so much pain."

Lola makes soothing noises and rubs my back. I'm too upset to tell her to stop fussing. We're both propped against my wooden headboard, tangled in the lavender quilt adorning my double bed. It's the middle of the night, and the staff are finally resting, while the rest of the wounded have gone back to their own homes.

"So, it's serious," Lola says gently. "Will he recover?"

"The healer made no promises. She's sending someone in the morning to help with his care." And Dios, please let him survive. I can't take another empty seat at the dinner table.

"What are you going to do about La Giralda?"

"Papá can't go back into the arena anytime soon. Or ever, I should say. He'll never fight another dragon," I break off, wincing. "I'll have to hold auditions and hire a new Dragonador." I bury my face in my hands. "Who's going to want to come back to La Giralda after this?"

At least we have plenty of money in our safe. Mamá always insisted on having reserves. And not all of our dragons were lost; we still have a few in the dungeons.

"Everyone loves the Zalvidars," she says. "Your family is an institution in Santivilla. There are streets named after your ancestors! A statue of your father is in the main plaza. You just need a plan."

I tip my head back, my gaze focused on the stone ceiling. "Let me think." Lola gives my shoulder an encouraging squeeze. "I've never hired a Dragonador—"

"That hasn't stopped you before," she says. "You didn't know how to manage ticket sales, but you learned."

"Hiring someone to survive in the arena is slightly different." Another thought streaks through my mind, terrifying and unsettling all at once. "The Gremio isn't pleased with us. You should have seen their faces—especially the Dragon Master. What if they threaten to shut us down? They've done it to other arena owners before."

"La Giralda?" Lola scoffs. "After five hundred years? Don't be hysterical. I'm the only one who gets to be that dramatic."

I shoot her a withering look. "I'm never hysterical. He doesn't like my father."

"Why? He's the hero of Santivilla."

"Papá has never said why."

She pulls at her bottom lip with her teeth. Worried, but trying not to be. I don't blame her—her place here is just as fragile as mine. Without her position, she'd have to move back to the obscure corner of Hispalia she hails from. "What if you sell the arena before the Gremio can exact any kind of punishment?"

I'm already shaking my head. "Papá would never let that happen. This is our home."

"It was just an idea." She lays her head on my shoulder.

The idea of selling our arena sits like a heavy lump at the back of my throat, impossible to swallow or ignore. But how will we survive without Papá performing? I could carry the show with my dancing for a while, but the people of Hispalia want to see dragonfighting. They travel to Santivilla for that reason. Our city thrives on the tradition.

Selling is not an option. La Giralda is our ancestral home. It's the last place my mother lived, this hallowed ground where I first learned to love flamenco. Now I understand why nations go to war to protect their land and their people. La Giralda is my beating heart, and I will fight to protect her.

No matter what it takes.

"You know you don't have to pay me for designing new costumes," Lola says softly.

"You should be apprenticing at the Gremio de los Sastres," I tell her for maybe the hundredth time.

It's an old argument. Most guilds take in children when they are six or seven years old to begin their training. Lola is seventeen, one year younger than me. Unless she has a lot of money, there's really no incentive for a Master at one of the guilds to bring her on.

"Why would I work for someone else when my employer here is perfectly willing to model anything I create?" Lola's exasperated smile fades. "Let me design something new for you. It will be a gift."

I glare at her. "I'll always pay you for your work. Artists should be paid, especially by friends. Don't ever say that to me again." I look down at Mamá's soiled dress and wince. This was one of her favorites, and now it's gone forever. My eyes burn.

Even if Lola makes me another dress exactly like it—and she could, she's that good—it wouldn't be hers. All of Mamá's clothing are my most treasured possessions. Each tie me to a specific memory, filled with details I otherwise would have lost. The way she looked, how she danced, the orange blossom in her hair, and the expression of unrivaled joy when she stepped out on the stage.

Time is the worst kind of thief, sneaky and effective and gone before you realize what's been taken.

Sometime in the yawning morning light, I climb out of my bed, careful not to wake Lola. I slip into my favorite mint-green silk robe and matching slippers and pull the heavy wood door to my room open, glancing over my shoulder, Lola's snores filling up the room.

Yes. She snores. She's loud even in her sleep.

I walk to Papá's room and quietly push the door open. The darkened chamber prevents me from seeing him clearly, but his quiet, steady breathing tells me he's profoundly asleep. Eva gave him a potent sleeping draft that will keep him resting for the majority of the day, and I'm thankful for it.

When he wakes, he'll realize what I've done to him.

I shut the door and tiptoe down the hallway leading to the grand staircase. My slippers are light against the stone floor. When I reach the balcony, I peer over the railing and into the foyer, three flights of stairs below. The gray morning light casts the room in shadows. Soiled sheets cover the smattering of empty cots cluttering the main area. Rolls of bandages, empty bottles of snail tonic, and dirty bowls litter most surfaces. The staff have their work cut out for them.

I creep down both flights of stairs, heading for the kitchen, where I know Ofelia will be brewing coffee and preparing breakfast for everyone. But the shouting coming from outside distracts me. Frowning, I walk to the front entrance of La Giralda, the noise climbing higher and higher. The sound deafens me the moment I push the door open.

I let out a strangled gasp.

Dozens of people march in front of my home, carrying banners and screaming their protests. All of them wear scarlet ribbons around their wrists—members of the Asociación, people against dragonfighting. It's typical to find them outside most arenas, a group made of perhaps ten to twenty yelling at the top of their voices.

But that's not what this is.

One of them, a woman with graying hair and broad shoulders turns to face me, lowering her tapestry. She has startling blue eyes and wears a red tunic, the color of rage and blood, and around her middle is a leather belt and scabbard.

"Murderer!" She stands ahead of everyone else, as if to protect them from my advance. "This is your fault," she snarls. "This is what comes with keeping wild animals in cages, bred for violence."

I open my mouth to protest—families are ripped apart and destroyed by the dragons routinely attacking Santivilla—when someone's spit shoots toward me, splattering my cheek. I flinch and wipe the sleeve of my robe against my face. These people have stolen into my home while we slept, have stalked and harassed Papá around the city, for years. They've sent us letters wishing we'd die slow and terrible deaths.

Someone clears their throat.

I tear my gaze away.

Lola places a firm hand on her hip. "Señorita Zarela—your father requests your presence."

My father must have taken a turn for the worse. "¿Papá? Está—"

"Ven conmigo." She strides back up the marble steps. I obey her and follow, the shouting resuming in my wake. *Murderer! Dragon lady!* I glance over my shoulder.

"You can't run from this!" the blue-eyed woman screams.

Lola shuts the door after me and gives me a pointed look. "I had to get you away from them," she says. "Nothing good was going to come from that conversation. I can't believe *I'm* the one who has to tell you that."

I blink. "What about Papá?"

"He's still sleeping."

"Lola," I growl as I attempt to march back out there and—

She makes exasperated noises and pushes me in the direction of the kitchen. "Go eat something. You are at your worst when hungry."

The scent of desayuno hits me the minute I walk inside the kitchen. This room always smells like a blend of coffee and rosemary, olive oil, and garlic. I inhale deeply, glad to be away from the dark gloom of the foyer. My mouth waters at the sight of pan-fried tomato slices piled on thick, crusty bread, topped with jamón and a generous drizzle of olive oil. A blazing fire roars in the great hearth, and our cook and housekeeper, Ofelia, grinds coffee beans at the wooden island. Dried herbs hang from the ceiling, and morning light spills into the room from the tall windows lining the walls.

"Buenos días," I say.

Ofelia looks up from the island, a slight frown on her lined face. She's a round-shaped woman, with a face like a hazelnut, motherly in her fussing. "Is it? You look terrible."

I can also count on her to be honest. "Thanks for that."

"Is Lola still sleeping?"

"She's awake," I say, in a mildly defensive tone.

"Hmph."

Ofelia can act like she doesn't care about Lola's well-being, but I catch her giving my friend brand new sketchpads and charcoal pencils for designing clothing. She sets a porcelain cup and plate on top of the six-foot wooden island and looks over to the fire. "Tomato slices are warming in the pan," she says. "You're not eating enough."

I pinch my nose.

"I'm worried," Ofelia says, while forcing me onto one of the stools. She bustles around the room, and while I watch her work, an idle thought bubbles to the surface. Ofelia has been with our family since before I was born. There isn't much that goes on in La Giralda that she doesn't know or have an opinion about.

"Have you seen the copper kettle?" Ofelia places one wrinkled hand on top of her head. She spins around the kitchen, eyeing the shelves. "I could have sworn I left it hanging above the fire."

I shake my head. With a sigh, Ofelia marches over to a basket filled with wands. She rummages through until she finds one labeled "encanto de recuerdos." A powerful remembering spell. These were a gift from Papá—who got tired of hearing Ofelia bemoan the latest thing she'd lost.

She breaks the wand in half, and a sliver of smoke, tinted a pale blue, swirls high, and she inhales deeply, shutting her eyes tightly and waiting for the spell to do its work.

"Did you see anything out of the ordinary yesterday?" I ask.

Ofelia opens her eyes, her expression clear, and then walks to a low cupboard. She rummages around, eventually letting out a triumphant cry as she holds up the lost kettle. Then she looks at me, and I repeat my question. "I don't think so. Why?"

"I'm trying to understand how our dragons could have escaped their pens."

"There was a lot going on." She brings the jug of milk to the island. "La Giralda was full of people and workers. Perhaps one of the tamers was distracted, left one of the cells unlocked?"

"Three of them?"

"Señorita, everyone was moving fast yesterday. I had several guards in here helping me load up trays for the feast after the show."

I look around the kitchen. "Is the food all gone?"

"There's not much left. Enough for a meal tonight, anyway."

"Papá can't have any of it. The healer said bone broth." Ofelia sets the food in front of me, and I load up a slice of bread with the tomato and ham and take a bite.

She makes a face. "Oh, he'll love that, I'm sure." She watches me eat for a few minutes. "The staff will want to be reassured. They're worried about their place here."

I set the toast carefully on the plate. We have many workers maintaining the great house attached to the arena. Ofelia manages the maids, but there's also guards and stable hands. And then, of course, our five dragon tamers.

But now we have just the one, I remind myself.

"La Giralda will recover. I'll be hiring a new Dragonador, buying new dragons." I don't mention the Gremio and their eventual summons. "For now, please tell anyone not to worry."

"And Señor Santiago?"

"My father needs rest." I stand. "Thank you for breakfast."

She gestures to my dish. "You barely ate."

My stomach is too much in knots to eat another bite. I'm steps away from the entrance when her soft voice makes me pause.

"You'll be running La Giralda now, señorita."

There's a note in her voice that makes the ground tilt under my feet. It sounds like trepidation. She doesn't think I can manage the responsibility, or maybe she's worried about her own fate. I try to imagine how La Giralda will survive without my father in the arena, with me in charge when all I know how to do is dance and twirl my mother's painted fans. My pulse thunders against my throat, and I have to clench my jaw in order to keep my panic locked inside where it belongs. I don't have time for it.

I face her with a smile. "Everything is under control."

Ofelia wipes her hands on a dirty cloth, and then she gestures to a little end table underneath one of the windows. "A missive came for your father."

My gaze lands on a small silver dish where a roll of parchment bound by a black ribbon sits against other notes of correspondence. The black ribbon detail makes my knees tremble. A summons from the Gremio de Dragonadores. I pick up the note and carefully unroll it.

> *Señor Santiago Zalvidar,*
>
> *Please present yourself to the Gremio this morning before noon. A fine of four hundred and fifty reales must be paid today, according to the breach in conduct expected of every arena owner. Your arena must also return payment to every patron who bought a ticket. The Gremio de Dragonadores will manage reimbursements.*
>
> *Bring all monies to the meeting.*
>
> *Don Eduardo Del Pino*
> *Conde de la Corte*

I glance at the wooden clock standing by the kitchen door. Papá has to leave in two hours to make the meeting. He won't be able to travel, so I must go. I've never stepped foot inside their building. While there have been a smattering of women Dragonadores, it's not encouraged.

The world of dragonfighting is run by men.

I reread the letter and silently fume at the implication that we won't return our patrons' ticket money. Why else would they request the payments and want to handle the situation themselves?

Ofelia stands in front of me, brow raising to her graying hairline. "Well?"

The amount we owe is staggering, but fortunately the money is tucked away in Papá's safe, thanks to my mother's insistence we always keep reserves. I'm more worried for La Giralda and Papá's position within the Gremio. I fold the parchment, creasing it horribly, my cheeks burning as if I've stood over a roaring fire. "Everything is fine."

I'm incredibly proud that my voice doesn't waver.

"What are you going to do today?" Ofelia asks, her attention dropping to the message from the Gremio.

"I need to have a conversation with Benito," I say. He can tell me which dragons we have remaining in the dungeons; if they can fly or have poisonous breath or scales as thick as shields. Any Dragonador I hire will want to know what kind of monster they'll be facing in our arena. "Then I'll be out for the rest of the day, running errands. Papá needs to rest, and the healer will be coming by in the afternoon."

I set off for the underbelly of La Giralda. One of the maids has already lit the candles, and they illuminate the way to the entrance: a formidable-looking door bracketed by large torches with an immense iron lock. I've only been through once, well before Mamá's death. It was years ago, maybe when I was twelve. I remember the horrible smell of sweat and dragon saliva, the craggy walls and dim lighting. At that age, I thought dragons were fascinating, mysterious and awe-inspiring legends.

But Papá didn't think it was appropriate for me to be down there because of the potential risk. If he'd had a son, perhaps he might have felt differently. At some point, I lost interest in dragons. They became fixtures in Papá's world, separate from the time I spent dancing with Mamá. Papá never seemed to be afraid, and so I didn't worry.

All of that changed when Mamá died.

I can't look at a dragon without seeing my mother's last moment on this earth—her hands waving in the air, face contorting in pain, lips twisting as she screamed.

The dungeon door is before me. It's heavy and made of dark wood, carved with the words TAMERS AND FIGHTERS ONLY. BEWARE. We lost six dragons, and with only three remaining, it means our opportunity to recoup our losses has severely diminished. But I'll worry about that later. For now, our investments are locked and secured in their pens. I tug on the heavy cast iron handle and venture inside. The damp, musky scent of wet stone fills my nostrils. A sharp chill descends onto my skin, and when I glance down, I'm surprised to see I'm still in my dressing gown and slippers.

Stone steps lead into the bowels of La Giralda, and I slowly make my way below, sputtering torches illuminating my trek. The utter quiet disarms me. There are no sounds of the dragons' harsh breathing, great gusts of air escaping from their slitted nostrils. No sound of them moving restlessly.

I trace my fingers against the jagged wall and press on. "Benito?"

The silence lengthens, twisting and tilting in the dark. Strange.

A shaky breath drifts from my lips as I reach the bottom. I approach the long row of cells, each with its own massive door, fortified by a powerful encanto. The top half is made of glass, the bottom cast iron.

In the five hundred years since the first stone was laid, no dragon has ever escaped their cell. Once captured and brought down into the cellar, they've never left La Giralda alive. Papá once told me that nearly eighty dragons die every year in Santivilla. I used to think it was a high number, but after Mamá died, that changed.

Now I think that number will never be high enough.

I peer into the first cell and wait for my eyes to adjust to the darkened cage. Cavernous walls enclose the shadowed space, and I can just make out the blurry shape of one of our remaining dragons. Next to the iron bar is a sign nailed to a wooden post: MORCEGO DRAGON.

"Benito?" I repeat, glancing around, before stepping closer to the door. My breath fogs the glass. The beast lies on his side, spiked tail curled around his plump, scaly body. He sleeps, blithely unaware of my presence. Papá once told me their teeth have a serrated edge in order to help tear up flesh. There are forty-four of them lining its massive gums.

I step away, fear rearing its ugly head until it's a distinct boom, ringing in my ears. And then something odd catches my notice.

It's not moving.

Shouldn't its chest rise and fall? Shouldn't there be puffs of air coming from its nostrils? I lay my hands flat against the glass and lean closer, squinting into the dark.

The beast remains motionless.

I remove my hands and the door follows my movement, swinging forward and then back, gently tapping against the iron frame.

Someone left the cell door open.

With a gasp, I scramble back until I hit the opposite cavern wall. My heart hammers painfully against my ribs. I curl my arms around my chest, fighting to control the sudden blast of fear wreaking havoc in my body. I can't just leave it unlocked. It isn't safe. Where is the damn key? Benito ought to have it. He needs to be down here.

"Benito?" I whisper.

I don't take my attention off the unlocked door. I'm surprised I'm still alive. Maybe the dragon doesn't know it can escape. I inhale deeply and creep toward the pen. Sharp pebbles poke my skin through the soft fabric of my slippers. I tug the iron handle of the door toward me, my arm trembling. I wait for the fire I know is coming. But still the beast doesn't move.

A feeling of unease gathers deep in my belly. Something isn't right.

I yank one of the torches free from its place on the wall. Then I step inside the cell and hold my breath, daring not to make a sound. I wonder where I get the nerve to stand in the same space as a dragon.

Still no movement.

And where the diablos is Benito?

I take another step forward, sure that any moment the dragon's eyes will open, and it will laugh at my own stupidity. Any moment the creature will rise to its full height and loom over me. Another step, and another, until at last, I'm standing next to the Morcego. Something wet seeps into my slipper, and I jerk my gaze toward the stone floor.

I'm standing in a puddle, tinted red from the light of the torch.

My breath catches at the back of my throat. A long slide of blood crawls down the dragon's throat from a wound at the base of its neck. I tighten my hold on the torch and race out of the cell, frantically running to the next one. That door's open too, and there's another pool of blood. There's a wailing sound as I bolt to the last cell—I don't realize it's me until I crumple to my knees.

All our dragons are dead.

CINCO

I lurch to my feet and stumble away from the lifeless dragon, blindly shutting the door behind me. The sharp clang reverberates in the dungeon, the sound roaring in my ears. Who came down here and killed our dragons? Murdered them while La Giralda burned upstairs.

Goose bumps flare up and down my arms.

Where the diablo is Benito?

It's odd that he isn't down here like he ought to be. I straighten away from the iron door, fingers curling into fists, and I glance toward the steps. My body coils tight as it prepares to run all the way up and not stop until I reach the Gremio de Dragonadores.

I bite my lip hard to keep myself from screaming. Then I lift my foot, readying to bolt away from this awful dungeon and the stink of death. But something catches my eye.

A dark shadow in the damp corner of the dungeon.

The shape is bulky. I narrow my gaze, squinting, trying to discern its edges. The shape slowly transforms, becomes clear as my eyes adjust.

The bulk becomes human.

"Benito," I say in horror. "*Benito.*"

He's slumped against the wall, clutching his chest. I rush forward to see if he's breathing. But there's no movement, no breath comes out of his open mouth. His eyes are staring blankly toward my slippers. There's no blood or sign of a struggle. His face and his hands are free of bruises. He wears the same filthy clothes from the day before—covered in clumpy sand and dirt.

Something sour rises at the back of my throat, faintly tasting of tomatoes. I rub my eyes, hoping to rearrange the sight before me.

Benito is dead. Dead like our dragons.

My conversation with the tamer had been only yesterday. It was right after the dragons wreaked havoc in the arena. The moment after my whole world changed. He said he'd stay down below to look after the remaining three beasts.

And sometime between then and this morning, he died.

Dios. Bile rises in my throat, but I swallow it down, shuddering. My hands shake as I lean forward and run my hands along his leather vest and tunic, searching for any wounds.

But there are none. Whatever killed him wasn't a weapon made of steel.

The dungeon's walls seem to close in around me like a tight fist. I have to get out of here. I stumble away from poor Benito, and run up the stairs, my blood-soaked slippers slapping against the stone. I reach the grand foyer, as if navigating a great wind, near toppling over. I'm in shock, and I never want to come out of it. Because maybe there will be someone else who will step in with answers and solutions. Papá will know what to do. With a start, I remember how sick he is.

There's only me.

The ramifications of what I've seen make themselves all too clear. Yesterday was no accident, and someone didn't just forget to lock up behind them.

The dragons had been set free.

And someone had gone down into the dungeons after the attack and killed off the rest of our investments. Perhaps Benito got in the way, and they killed him. Benito who tried to tell me something the day before. And fool that I am, I didn't remember to seek him out to ask him. All of my thoughts line up and form one crystallized suspicion in my mind that robs me of my breath: someone is out to ruin us.

A memory races through my mind that sends a sharp chill down my spine. During yesterday's massacre, there were protestors outside our front door.

They wanted dragons to be left alone, to be free to roam the skies— destroying families and villages, killing anything in their path. Is it mad to suspect one of them of setting our investments free—damn the consequences?

It's the kind of twisty logic characteristic of their behavior.

I think hard, discarding one idea after the next. If my suspicion is true, then I'd have to figure out how they managed to release the dragons. The dungeon door is always secure, and each cell has its own lock. Without a key, there's no way inside.

My heart lurches.

The keys.

There are three. My father and I have one, and Ofelia has the last. Quickly, I race to the kitchen, immediately veering toward a pot where I know Ofelia keeps hers hidden. I reach inside, my fingers brushing against iron, and relief skips down my spine. One down, two more to go. My heart hammers against my ribs as I take the steps of the grand staircase two at a time, running for my room.

My key is exactly where it ought to be, tucked inside one of my drawers. I've never used it, but Papá insisted I have one in case something happened to the others.

Only one left.

I dash up to Papá's room where he's resting. His is on the nightstand, but he usually loops it around his neck on a leather string. I sag against his chamber door, frowning, while watching the steady rise and fall of Papá's chest.

None of our keys are missing.

How, then, did someone sneak into the dungeons? The door is made of impenetrable wood, and I would have noticed any scratches or signs of forced entry.

Someone might have used an encanto.

Spells are sold in the Mercado de los Magos, a legendary market where anyone can purchase a wand dipped in a variety of potions. Ofelia buys enchantments on a weekly basis. So does Lola, for that matter. The number of wands she has in order to create shimmery effects on the fabric she works with is obscene.

I make my way down to the grand foyer, shoulders tight. Every emotion I'm trying to hide knots deep in my belly. The pressure of saving La Giralda, terror that I'll lose Papá, worry about the families who lost someone, and our ruined reputation. Everything feels urgent, but all I want to do is scream until I have nothing left.

Two servants are sweeping and cleaning the grand foyer, putting away cots, throwing out used bandages. When they see me, they immediately still. Their gazes latch on to the blood staining the hem of my robe and my ruined slippers.

Lola comes barreling out of the kitchen, carrying a tray, presumably for my father, but one look at my face and she stops cold. "What's happened?"

"Benito is down there," I say through numb lips. "He's dead."

The tray crashes to the ground.

Dimly, I'm aware of the approach of one of the guards standing by the front doors of La Giralda. He catches my last words and takes off running toward the dungeon entrance. Lola stands among broken dishes, and one of the maids clears the mess, while the other darts to the kitchen in search of a wand to repair all the pottery. Lola moves forward, reaching for me, but I hold up a hand, knowing that if she hugs me, I'll only break down.

Which is the last thing anyone needs right now.

I hold myself still, fight to keep my voice steady as I fire off my questions to Lola and the two maids. No, they didn't see anyone approach the dungeon door. No, they hadn't heard anything suspicious, and no, they hadn't caught any talk about visiting the dragons. Throughout the entire conversation, I keep my face neutral, not wanting to alarm them. But inside, my scream of frustration waits. Maybe this is only a nightmare, and I'll wake up tomorrow on the day of the show, except everything goes right.

Thirteen people never perished.

The dragons remain in their cages.

My father isn't sick.

The sight of Lola regarding me critically brings me back to reality. "Leave us," I say to the other two maids. They quickly leave, darting nervous glances in my direction.

"What do you need me to do?" Lola asks.

My heart is a frightened bird, fluttering against my ribs, frantic wings beating wildly. "Send word to Guillermo and invite him to take home the bodies of the dead dragons. Make sure he pays you." My lips twist. "Three monsters in one day. I'm sure he'll be pleased."

"Zarela," Lola whispers, her tone faintly scolding.

"And then please ask the guards to have Benito buried in the family cemetery." My voice cracks. "He's been with us for years. I think he'll like that."

"¿Y su familia?"

I shake my head. "He only has us."

Lola grabs the sleeve of my silk robe. "How did he die?"

My lips try to form the words to describe how I found him. Cold, alone, pressed against the dirty dungeon wall, mere feet away from puddles of blood. No wound on his body. "He was murdered."

She gasps.

"Please do what I've asked," I say.

"Should I send word to the Gremio de Dragonadores? They'll want to know."

"I'm heading there now."

I want to stay here with her, and we could hide underneath my bed. But that's not what my mother would have done. No, she'd arrive at the meeting with the Dragon Master dressed in her finest, her chin lifted high. She'd demand help in discovering the culprit.

Don Eduardo will have to launch an investigation.

There's foul play at La Giralda.

Every Gremio handles crimes within their own establishment. No one from the magia Gremio can be tried or punished in the Gremio de Dragonadores, and vice versa. A necessity considering the latent animosity between the two guilds. If an offense has been done against one of our own by a member of another Gremio, a formal complaint and request is sent over to the Master responsible for the offender. It's a system meant to protect each paying member from unwarranted prosecution and to promote fairness and restitution. Anyone who does not belong to a specific trade Gremio is required to join the Gremio General. People like Lola, for example, who come from poorer families that can't afford to send their children to be apprentices.

I'll have to handle this very carefully.

Accusing nonmembers of a crime is serious and requires evidence. Without the full support of Don Eduardo, I'd be doomed from the start. But if I dutifully show up with the earnings from yesterday's show, he might be inclined to help me—despite the animosity he feels for my father.

I sip the warm air, fighting to clear my head, to slow my rapid heart. I come up with a plan. I'll dress for the day, collect the coins from the safe, and take the carriage into town.

Having something constructive to do calms me.

By the time I'm on the right floor, I feel more like myself.

The iron box is in Papá's office, hidden in a secret room behind a tapestry depicting a dragon fight. It's been the hiding place of our family's treasures throughout the centuries. Papá's study is still and quiet, save for the chiming of an old wood-framed clock on his desk. I have an hour before the money is due to the Gremio de Dragonadores, and I'm still not dressed, still wandering around in a blood-stained robe. If Mamá could see me now, she'd shudder. By now, she'd be dressed for the day with a cup of café con leche in her hand.

Another reminder that I'm not her.

The curtains are drawn, and I'm thankful for the dark as I pull an old key hidden within the tenth stone to the left of the window, counting upward from the ground. It's black and heavy, and it immediately makes my hand smell like La Giralda. Secrets and smoke and iron. I walk across the study and pull away the tapestry, revealing more of the same stone, except there's a hidden switch that makes the wall give and slide into a pocket door. There's enough money to cover all of the costs: the fine, hiring a new tamer and Dragonador. The buying of more dragons.

Not to mention Papá's care.

I peer inside and my breath hitches.

Instead of encountering piles of money, there's only a smattering of silver reales scattered among the safe floor. There ought to be linen bags filled with gold jewelry outfitted with rubies and emeralds, pearls and amethysts and diamonds as big as my eyes. None of it is here.

Nothing except the bag of coins from yesterday's earnings.

Understanding dawns as a memory slams into me.

When my parents argued, their voices carried to every corner of La Giralda. They usually fought about money. My father loves pretty things, always wanting the best for his family. Expensive fabrics, new tile for the grand foyer, imported white sand from the coast, costly jewels from the best joyerías in Hispalia. It was Mamá who pulled him toward practicality. After she died, so much of Papá had gone to sleep. As time went on, different parts of him woke up, and this was one of them: his ability to spend without restraint.

"Damn it, Zarela," I whisper. I should have seen this coming, could have been the voice of reason. But I guess parts of me were sleeping too.

Now there's nothing left.

Yesterday's earnings feel insignificant in my hands. The smattering of coins we have left over will barely cover groceries for the month. I slam the safe closed, the sound ricocheting in the small, stone room, but I barely hear it. Too many thoughts dance across my mind. They riot in my mind, loud and disruptive and overwhelming.

I need to sort through all the disorder.

I stalk to Papá's desk, painfully aware of the dwindling amount of time I have left to get ready, and pull a fresh sheet of paper, dip the quill in the ink, and scribble every expense down. I estimate the cost of running La Giralda for another month, the repairs, paying the guards, Ofelia and Lola, and a handful of servants, and groceries. Then I tally the cost of hiring a new tamer, Papá's care, and the Gremio fine.

All told, the total comes to around five thousand and two hundred reales.

That's only an estimate. How will I keep Papá and our home alive? If my despair were a place, it'd be the cold floor of an oubliette, where everyone I ever loved slowly forgot my name. I drop the quill and rub my tired eyes. I can't arrive to the Gremio empty-handed.

An idea takes root and blooms in my mind.

Something terrible and near unpardonable.

Papá would never forgive me, but what choice do I have? I leave the study and make my way down to the dressing room. Mercifully, no one is cleaning the chamber. The ornate armoire stands against the wall, an antique displaying dignity and style like a well dressed condesa. I yank open the heavy, gilded doors. Mamá's immortal dresses hang in a tidy row, her favorites that we kept after donating the rest to the Gremio de las Artes. Every week, they're taken out and spritzed in Mamá's favorite orange blossom perfume, and then carefully put away. Looking at them now, I'm reminded of her tart, citrus scent.

Like the city of Santivilla in the summer.

Mamá wore these dresses for notorious performances, for festive bailes held by Rey Alfonso and his wife, Reina Mercedes of Hispalia. I've danced in them during shows, and for fiestas hosted by my father for Mamá's cumpleaños, a tradition we've continued in order to honor her memory. These dresses are my inheritance, an heirloom of the greatest importance, and a link to my mother.

Selling them would be a betrayal.

With shaking hands, I pull three down from the silk hangers, moving carefully so as not to drag the lace on the floor, and then drape the precious bundle on the back of a leather chair. Then I pull on the silk chord by the enormous fireplace.

Ofelia appears minutes later. I stiffen instinctively. A part of me is so afraid to disappoint her. It was Papá who raised me on soft words and candied fruit, but it was Ofelia who fed me the bitter brew of adulthood.

She takes one look at the dresses and swift understanding dawns over her proud features—stubborn jaw, fierce brows, and the narrowed gaze of someone accustomed to recognizing nonsense. "What are you doing with Eulalia's things?"

I lift my chin, even though I'm in no way ready to have this argument. "I'm selling them."

"No puedes," she says flatly. "You can't."

"I must." I pull the delicate bundle into my arms, avoid the resentful silence coming from her as if she were an open fire.

"But—"

I shut my eyes. "Don't fight me. Por favor."

She studies me, her frown a hammer driving a nail into my heart. Her disapproval is a discernible weight that presses down on my shoulders. She runs a soft index finger down my cheek, and I open my eyes.

"Some things aren't replaceable," Ofelia says. "When they're gone, they're gone."

Her dark eyes are drawn, as if reliving a painful memory. I know exactly which one. That horrid day when we came back to La Giralda without Mamá.

I step away from her. "She wouldn't want us to close the ring."

Her lips thin into a long slash. "Well. Put on your face and pick an outfit. Your red gown looks lovely with your skin."

I think about how I'll have to appease the Dragon Master. "I'll look angry."

"Aren't you?" She asks. "Don't accept anything less than five hundred reales for each dress. I told you not to donate so many of them to the Gremio de las Artes."

"Five hundred?" In my whole life, I've never held nor seen that amount of money. Patrons purchase tickets in silver helóns. Papá could exchange the coins into gold reales, but he rarely does since day-to-day expenses are mostly done with silver coins. Except when he's buying new dragons. According to Papá, the best breeds cost upwards of one thousand reales each.

"But these," Ofelia says as she grasps the bundle, "were worn by your mother. Her statue stands in the main corridor of the plaza."

I bend my knees until I'm level with her eyes. No amount of gold coins would ever be enough. "Ofelia, I will do my best to honor her. You know that."

She clenches the fabric for a moment. And then lets go, one iron finger at a time. She backs away from me, hooded eyes lowered, and silently leaves the room. The guilt feels like an indigestible lump at the back of my throat. Hard to swallow. Hard to breathe. Appeasing Don Eduardo is more important than a pile of stitched fabric. Mamá would tell me the same thing. I'll always have the memory of her dancing in these dresses, if not the actual dress itself.

I leave the room to change into a long, silk dress with a ruffled hem and a lower neckline. My face is done up, hair braided and coiled atop my head. No one would guess at the inner turmoil threatening to over-whelm me. Then, at last, I'm finally alone in one of our finest carriages, painted a scalding red with gold trim and adorned by ivory tassels.

This, too, will have to be sold.

Ofelia gave me instructions to go to La Cortina, a boutique in the center of Santivilla. But I have a better idea.

It means visiting a woman my mother hated.

SEIS

Señora Montenegro's home is a street over from the plaza. I say home, but the more accurate description is that she lives in a building located between several shops that her family owns, including the largest newspaper in Santivilla, *El Correo*. The shops and newspaper take up the entirety of one block, and all of them have their doors thrown open, with patrons coming in and out of the various establishments. As we pass, vendors yell out their wares on sale.

Great oak trees line both sides of the avenue, and they create a pretty archway of leafy branches covering the two lanes of traffic coming up and down the cobbled road. We pass small markets and a restaurant famous for their churros dipped in hot chocolate and leche frita, cold milk pudding enclosed in a crunchy fried shell. My mother would take me every year for my birthday. I avert my gaze away from the gold-and-green-painted entrance.

Our driver makes a right turn, and the air is infused with the rich spices and oils sold on nearly every block: pimentón and roasted garlic, olive oil and cayenne pepper. And everywhere at once comes the sweet scent of orange blossoms.

The smell tastes like ashes in my mouth.

I hit the roof of the carriage twice with my fist, and it immediately stops. I climb out, the bundle of dresses in my arms, and address the driver. "Park close by, por favor."

He touches the rim of his sombrero. "Sí, Señorita Zalvidar."

Dread climbs up my spine like ivy. I want to turn away, clutching my mother's clothes, and never part with them. But I force myself to take a step forward and then another.

Señora Montenegro's grand entrance looms before me, a solid gold half-moon knocker hangs square in the middle of the door. I know for a fact it's been stolen half a dozen times because every time it was missing, Señora Montenegro complained about it at one of her parties.

But why have something like that out in the open?

Shaking my head, I lift the heavy knocker and let it slam against the door. A moment later, it whips open, and a dour-faced butler greets me with a flat, "Sí?"

"Please tell Señora Montenegro that Zarela Zalvidar is here." The man frowns. He isn't impressed by my name.

"La señora de la casa está comiendo." His gaze drops to the bundle in my arms.

"This will only take a moment." I tuck the dresses closer to my side, protecting them from his prying eyes. "Por favor, I have another appointment in half an hour."

He sighs but opens the door wider to permit me entry. Polished marble gleams under my booted feet as I follow the man down a long hall lined with paintings of the Montenegro familia. We stop at another set of double doors, and he bids me to wait as he steps inside. Soft murmuring follows, and then I'm ushered inside Señora Montenegro's dining room.

The lady of the house sits at a long, rectangular table with an array of small dishes filled with diced cucumber, tomatoes, and onion, each in separate plates. Another larger bowl bears the rich orange of chilled gazpacho soup, and at her elbow is a large pitcher of red wine with thick orange slices floating near the top. That's only the starter.

"Why Zarela," Señora Montenegro says. "I'm surprised to see you. Will you join me for almuerzo?"

I shake my head and carefully lay the dresses on the back of one of the plush chairs.

"Then why are you here?"

I narrow my gaze at her. She's perfectly poised, black hair sleeked back into an elegant knot at the base of her neck. Heavy jewelry adorns her thick neck, and her rose-scented perfume wafts in the air. She hasn't once looked at the dresses, despite begging me to sell her one—a week after Mamá's funeral.

This is not going to go well for me.

I can see it in her dispassionate stare, in how she's remained seated, where before she'd leap to greet me with open arms and a charming smile for the famous daughter of Hispalian upper society.

Yesterday changed all that.

More food is brought in on silver trays, this time laden with croquetas de jamón, creamy mushroom soup topped with cheese and fried breadcrumbs, and a salad of roasted beets and Hispalian sheep cheese. She nods in approval as she's served, seeming to forget I'm standing three feet away from her.

"I've come to sell you three of Mamá's favorite ensembles," I say with a tight smile. "You've wanted them for years and—"

She noisily slurps the spoon. "Have I?"

"Unless I've been misunderstanding Spanish all these years."

My retort lands with an inelegant thud on the table. She regards me coldly, beady gaze traveling down the length of my body, no doubt finding fault in every curve. I wish I'd thought to bring Lola with me. She can charm a snake.

"I've heard the most unfortunate news about La Giralda." She delicately pats her lips with a linen napkin. "Quite the fall from grace. To think that I almost attended the show myself."

"Señora Montenegro," I say through gritted teeth. "Stop playing with me."

Her dark brow quirks in sly amusement.

I ignore it and press on. "If you're not interested, merely say so. If you are, please look them over."

She gently places the spoon on the table and pushes back the chair.

"There's no need for that tone." Coming to stand by my side, she reaches for the first delicate dress. "I remember this one. Seven years ago, wasn't it? Eulalia wore this for the birthday celebration of the Master of the painter's guild."

"That's right."

"Such a spectacular performance." She fingers the black-fringed hem. "I'll pay you one hundred reales for each dress."

"You've offered four times that amount," I seethe.

Her face is immobile as she stares into my eyes. "But the family name had more weight to it then. The only reason I'm even offering to buy them at all was because your mother was a dear friend of mine."

Mamá's real feelings about this woman invade my mind. I want to spit them out, ruffle that stony expression until I see something beneath that heavily lacquered veneer. How dare she offer charity? But I hold my tongue. I need whatever money I can gather, and it will not do to give the most industrious gossip in Hispalia more material.

"I'm sure my mother would be pleased by your generosity. However," I say, rearranging my face into an apologetic wince, "it just occurred to me that my mother wanted these dresses for Gabriela Asturias. Do you know her? How silly of me to forget such a thing! This black one is a particular favorite of hers."

Gabriela Asturias is the owner of one of the more popular restaurants in town. Her food is written about in *El Correo* every week, and all of high society dine in her establishment.

Señora Montenegro's gaze sharpens. "Oh?"

I play her in the same way my father rules over his guitar, beating it into submission. "I'm so sorry to have taken up your time. I'll just see myself out—"

"Wait a moment," she says quickly. "You know, dear, I've found I've changed my mind. I'll take them after all, and at the price I agreed to."

Ten minutes later, I'm fifteen hundred gold coins richer.

SIETE

The door slams shut behind me, loud and final, leaving me with a sour taste in my mouth. I wait for my carriage, ignoring the curious glances cast my way, and at the large bag at my feet. I lift my chin and stare almost unseeingly down into the street, the people becoming blurry. Señora Montenegro is a gossip, and by now, I'd bet piles of money—money I don't have—the horrid woman is writing letters to her friends, inviting them for afternoon tea in order to spread the worst kind of lies about my family name.

I will not have it.

The horses come into view, and I walk toward them, shoulders thrown back. She may think her words have hurt me, but nothing is further from the truth. I'll show her that our name isn't as flimsy as her character.

"Will you please bring down that bag?" I ask the driver, motioning toward the bulk at the top of the stairs. He nods and darts away, and I climb into the carriage, arranging the skirt of my dress away from the other bag of money I'd brought with me from La Giralda. The driver hauls the other sack and drops it next to my legs.

I have enough money to perhaps hire a new Dragonador.

But what about the rest of my expenses?

The carriage jerks forward and makes its way to the Gremio de Dragonadores. I leave the curtain of the window pulled back, and the sound of children peddling *El Correo* filters into the plush space.

"Massacre at La Giralda!"

"Thirteen perish in dragon attack!"

"Santiago Zalvidar left in disgrace!"

I clench my jaw, and it stays that way for the whole of the ride, until we arrive to the front door of the Gremio. I pick up one of the bags containing the gold coins. White marble steps lead up into an ornate archway with golden filigree designed to look like flames. At the base of the entry are statues of famous Dragonadores of legend, and as I walk past, I remember a conversation I'd had with Papá about how the guild was considering his likeness to add to the decor. It had been a proud day for Papá, and we'd celebrated with a roasted pig and freshly baked bread seasoned with rosemary and garlic.

One of the first happy days Papá had had after Mamá's death. He'd looked at me with a smile I recognized. Not even Don Eduardo's opposition to the statue stole Papá's happiness that day.

Ahead of me are handsome wooden doors, inlaid with golden swirls and loops, interlocking in the flame-inspired design. The Gremio headquarters is centuries old and has survived millenia filled with wars, dragon attacks, and scorching hot weather due to intricate and expensive encantos that took one hundred and fifty years to complete. Inside, magic is strictly forbidden, unless you have written permission from Don Eduardo. There is no love lost between the dragon and magic guild.

But Mamá had adored magic.

She loved going to the Mercado de los Magos, browsing spells that would change the color of her hair or rid her of sore feet. Papá humored her, and now that she's gone, neither of us complain when Ofelia goes to the Mercado to buy wands, despite the cost. Despite the fact that even the most powerful spell will not bring my mother back.

Attendants swing the door open. Bustling activity fills the round room with chatter, rustling papers, shoes thudding against the black, white, and golden checkered tiled floor. On the ceiling is a mosaic of shimmering red tiles depicting the Escarlata.

The monster who set my mother on fire.

To my right is a long wooden counter, and I march over to where a young man waits, dark brows rising. He's dressed in the traditional dark colors of the Gremio with gold stitching designed to look like flames accenting the hems of his sleeves. My dress curls and swishes against my legs, and I'm suddenly aware the noise in the room has dropped to a murmuring hush.

"Señorita Zalvidar," he says when I reach him. His manner is far from nice, but at least it can be called polite.

"I believe I'm expected."

He keeps his gaze firmly away from mine. "We thought to see Don Santiago Zalvidar."

"He won't be coming."

"¿Por qué?"

I bristle. "Is that any business of yours?"

He shuffles a stack of papers until they're neat and flush in his palm. "I'll take you up, then." The young man snaps his fingers, and from a back room another attendant comes to take over the front desk, wearing an identical dark tunic, hair smoothed back and polished so it shines like a mirror.

I stride alongside him as we head to the back of the great, circular room where more marble steps lead up to the second and third stories of the building. Overhead are wrought iron chandeliers that cast everything and everyone in a golden glow. From the corner of my eye, I catch sight of our family name written across one of the documents in his hands.

A smattering of goose bumps erupts up and down my arms. I point to the stack. "What are those papers?"

"Complaints filed against the Zalvidar family." He shoots me a quick look. "They've been coming in all morning."

My stomach sinks to my leather boots. I press my lips into a thin line and say no more until we've reached the third floor where the main offices are. At the top of the stairs is a loft area that overlooks the ground floor. Several worn leather armchairs are gathered around a low table, laden with mugs and books, and a pitcher of water. A leather ottoman sits in the middle, covered by a wooden tray holding various newspapers that declare the latest headlines.

The fall of the Zalvidar family.

Beyond the loft, there's a line of men waiting to enter one of the rooms in the corridor. They're all dressed in varying states of somber elegance. Dark jackets adorned with tassels and elaborate stitching, polished shoes the color of brandy and whiskey, and sombreros tilted just so. Dragonadores.

Only one of them doesn't look like the rest.

His clothing is rough, leather boots scuffed and dirty, beyond the help of even the most effective shoe polish. He leans against the stone wall, a creased newspaper in his dusty hands, his hat obscuring most of his face as he reads an article. The people around him give him a wide berth, and I instantly understand the reasoning.

There's something feral about this man.

The attendant leads us past the line of Dragonadores, and some send me admiring looks. The ragged-looking caballero, intent on his reading, ignores the appreciative whistling disrupting the quiet.

The attendant stops in front of the next door over. He knocks softly and a deep voice from within bids us to enter. My neutral and polite expression doesn't reflect my inner turmoil. I remind myself that what happened wasn't our fault. We were targeted, and I only need to provide enough information.

He will be fair and hear my case.

He *has* to.

Don Eduardo sits in a plush leather armchair behind a wooden desk, nearly as wide as it is long. There are journals and books piled high on one corner, and on the other is a small teapot and cup, the steam curling from the spout. A plush rug covers the middle of the herringbone-patterned floor. Three grand, arched windows overlook the city of Santivilla.

The Dragon Master pours water into the pot of an enormous fern perched on the windowsill. It's thick and vibrantly green, and the way he lovingly stares at the plant, you'd think it was his child.

The stack of complaints is deposited onto the desk. "I'll order more tea to be brought up."

"Excelente, Alberto." Eduardo sits and leans back in the chair, his fingers interlacing across his lap. "Como estás, Señorita Zalvidar?"

"Fair." My voice is as dry and flat as the desert lands north of Hispalia. Alberto helps me with my bag of reales and sets it in the corner of the room, and with a quick nod, he leaves the room. The Dragon Master motions for me to sit, and I sink into the available armchair. I brace myself for the Gremio's wrath.

Don Eduardo glances at the stack of papers. "Do you know what those are?"

I nod, my hands slick with sweat.

"Bien," he says coolly. "I prefer to deal in direct conversation. No sense in wasting any more time with insipid pleasantries."

Insipid pleasantries indeed. I've never liked the taste of tea, anyway. "I, too, would prefer to cut the nonsense."

I catch his lips flatten beneath his thick, pearly beard. I've startled him; he doesn't appreciate my tone.

"The situation is quite dire. Many Gremio members are demanding swift punishment. They are calling for the removal of your family from our membership and protection."

I slowly shut my eyes and imagine Papá's tormented expression. "Don Eduardo, por favor. My father's familia has been a part of this institution for centuries. I ask that you listen to what I have to say before you make any final decisions."

"Are you going to tell me that you're prepared to pay compensation for the patrons who lost a member of their family?"

"Qué?"

He regards me sternly. "I am demanding that on top of the fine and returning the money from ticket sales, you also compensate every family who lost someone."

It's more than fair. "I'll only need more time."

"We're concerned that many patrons will be wary of attending future dragon fights. Attendance might drop and that means less money for *all* Gremio members. Or did you think La Giralda's catastrophe wouldn't impact the other arenas?"

The world tilts under my feet. Tío Hector's face leaps into my mind. His arena might suffer, too. Shame rises up my throat. "It hadn't occurred to me," I say.

I don't have the money to pay for the compensation, the hiring of a new Dragonador, *and* more dragons.

"You have to make this right," Don Eduardo says in his hard rasp. "Families were torn apart."

"I understand, but you don't have all the information." I lift my hand as Don Eduardo opens his mouth to protest. "Con respeto, por favor escúchame."

"All right, I will listen."

"I believe someone is working to sabotage La Giralda."

He steeples his crooked fingers. "*Sabotage?* Why do you think such a thing?"

"Before the anniversary show, La Giralda had nine dragons," I say calmly. "During the attack three flew away, and three were executed by your hand. The remaining beasts never left their cages in the dungeon. I sent one of our tamers to keep watch, and this morning I found him and the dragons dead."

Don Eduardo's eyebrows rise.

"*Murdered.*"

He quietly regards me, stern-faced, the line of his long nose arrowed in my direction. "People die all the time and for many reasons. He might have died from dragon smoke for all I know. It's possible, if you're around dragons long enough."

I shift in the chair. "His murder seems highly coincidental when paired with the deaths of our other dragons. They were in the dungeon, not ten feet away from each other. Someone must have released our dragons into the arena and that same person killed our tamer and the other beasts."

"Was there a wound on his body?"

"No."

He eyes me skeptically. The door opens with a quiet knock and Alberto returns carrying a tea tray. He pours one for Don Eduardo and then one for me. I thank him, and he dips his chin before leaving as silently as he came in. The Dragon Master takes a sip.

I inhale, ignoring the flare of panic rising within me. "There's also the Asociación to think about it."

The Dragon Master scoffs.

I lift my chin. "They've protested against us for years. They were out there this morning marching outside our front door. There was a woman carrying a sword in front of my house."

"A woman. What woman?" he demands.

"Broad-shouldered with dark gray hair and pale skin and blue eyes."

"Martina Sanchez." He pauses. "She's the leader of the Asociación."

Now I have the name of the person working against me.

"Bring her in and question her. Her *and* her people are responsible."

"Martina?" he asks dismissively. "I highly doubt it. They gather outside of all the other arenas too. Their presence at La Giralda isn't special. We receive dozens of complaints every day about the organization. Martina and her ilk are hardly a threat."

"But they had means of entry in our arena—"

"And why is that?" he asks in a shrewd tone.

I lick my lips, not liking his pointed question. "The front doors are open to allow entrance for all of our patrons before the show. You can't fault us for that—not when everyone else does the same."

"Frankly, this conversation only tells me that you and your father are abdicating all responsibility," he says angrily. "The Asociación is a nuisance, no one is denying that, but historically they have never caused any real trouble—"

"What other explanation can there be?" I say. It's hard to keep my tone polite, not when I keep wondering if he's deliberately being combative because of his profound dislike for my father.

"Señorita Zarela," he says, laying his palms flat on the table. His veins are mountain ridges across the back of his hands.

"Did you not have hundreds of people present during the dragon attack? Any of them could have snuck into your dungeons and killed the monsters as an act of revenge."

Humiliation churns in my belly. We ought to have been better prepared—more guards, more spells to ward against outsiders from entering the dungeons. "Well, regardless, we won't know without an investigation."

The Dragon Master shakes his head. "Our first priority is to the families of those who have lost someone. An investigation will take money and effort, and I'm not interested in chasing a wild story when I have hundreds of people wanting your father's head," he says. There's no denying the subtle note of triumph in his voice.

I inhale deeply through my nose and fight to keep my blood from boiling red hot. The effort costs me and sweat slides down the back of my neck, gathers between my breasts.

"You won't consider any alternatives."

"This happened at your ring." The crescent-shaped lines bracketing Don Eduardo's mouth deepen. "People died under your watch. There are three more dragons roaming the skies. Someone has to pay, Señorita Zalvidar."

"But—"

"Be quiet," he says coldly. "It's your turn to listen. La Giralda is responsible for the safety of not only its staff and paying customers, but its dragons. If I were you, I'd find the gaps within your security. Someone wasn't doing their job."

My heart feels like it's taken a hit by an industrious blacksmith. Each beat rams against my ribs, one painful thump at a time. We are ultimately to blame for the disaster. Had we been better prepared, perhaps all of this might have been avoided.

"Now there's the matter of the fine, as well as sending a sum of money to the families who lost someone. I've consulted the Gremio board, and we believe fifty reales for each family is fair. As for the matter of La Giralda's membership and recognition as one of our dragonfighting houses . . . Out of *respect*"—he sneers the word—"for your father, you'll be put on a probation period—but only *if* you pay what's owed. Entiendes lo qué te estoy diciendo?"

Oh, I understand. "What is the total amount owed today?"

"The fine is four hundred and fifty reales. We'll take the ticket money *and* compensation and deliver it personally to all thirteen families."

"What will happen if I can't pay it?" I ask.

"As per the membership contract, the Gremio de Dragonadores is free to claim assets for their own in the comparable amount owed."

I slump against the armchair. "Assets? Do you mean—"

"I mean the Gremio is within its rights to seize La Giralda."

"*No*," I breathe.

"We may do as we please." His hard, raspy voice turns brisk. "Now, the tickets for a dragon fight cost how much?"

"Twenty-seven reales," I say mutinously.

"And your arena can seat how many?"

"Five hundred."

"That's right," he says, bending his head forward as his quill scratches against parchment. "La Giralda is the largest ring in Santivilla." He continues writing, while I sit in dread, waiting for the total. I lace my fingers tightly, hoping the amount doesn't take everything I have.

Don Eduardo glances up. "The total comes to one thousand and one hundred reales."

I swallow a painful lump at the back of my throat.

"Will you be able to pay the amount owed?"

"Sí." I gesture to the corner. "I have it in that bag."

"Excelente." He leans back against the leather chair. "I believe our business is concluded. If I were you, I'd be thankful that your family is still a member of this guild at all. No more mistakes," he warns. "Or your probation period is over."

His meaning is clear. One more misstep, and it might mean the loss of our membership.

"One more thing, Señorita Zalvidar," the Dragon Master murmurs.

I freeze, not liking the terrible calm in his voice. The quiet before the worst storm.

"As of today, Santiago Zalvidar no longer sits on our board. He is not allowed to vote on matters or be eligible for any high-ranking positions in this Gremio."

Don Eduardo can't hide the pleasure from saying these words to me. The loss of prestige and power, the respect of our name will devastate Papá. I stand, clutching the mug filled with scalding liquid. For a second, my hand wavers. And then I come to my senses.

He did say no more mistakes.

OCHO

I shut the door to Don Eduardo's office and sag against it, needing the strength of the oak to keep me upright. My knees shake under the weight of responsibility as the full enormity of my situation stares me in the face. Hiring a skilled, talented Dragonador will cost at least a hundred helóns a month. Without one, we can't compete with the other arenas.

The answer comes in a soft whisper.

As if Mamá stood over me, brushing the hair from my face. Her lyrical voice, full of strength and passion and confidence, rings in my ear.

Fight in the arena, Zarela.

The words press into me. I push against them with both hands.

It's the last thing I want to do. I hate the monsters, not just because of what happened during the show and of what they've stolen from me, but because with one look, I'm left weak and powerless. Unable to move, think, or talk. I hate how they make me *feel*.

Terror robs me of breath. Levels me to the ground.

La Giralda will not survive with only flamenco performances. From a business perspective, the idea of *me* fighting in the arena is a bold move, one to draw positive attention, *much-needed* positive attention, back to La Giralda. But for that to be done well, I'd need to conquer my terror of the monsters.

Papá lies tucked in bed, fighting for his life. La Giralda barely stands. There's no one but me to save them both. A fire burns in my chest, fueled by the love for family and home and legacy. I've finally been given a flaming torch and something to burn.

I will become a Dragonador.

I straighten away from the door and walk forward, my gaze trained on the ground, lost in the thoughts consuming my mind. I don't see the tall person coming out of the adjoining room until it's too late. He drops his stash of papers, and they flutter to the floor. I realize too late that I'm still holding the damn teacup. It goes flying, spilling its contents in every direction before shattering into pieces. Dark stains spread across the parchment littering the ground, swirling with wet ink and becoming a blurred mess.

"Lo siento!" I say, mortified, my knees bending.

"Carajo." The voice is deep, with a rough, serrated edge. He takes hold of my wrist, preventing me from sinking to the ground. "You'll cut your skin on the shards, you fool."

I stiffen, pulling my limb free. He lets me go easily with a huff of impatience, leather hat casting a sharp shadow on the bottom half of his face, revealing only the rigid line of his jaw.

"I was going to be careful," I say, rearranging my skirt, trying to keep the hem from getting wet, but it's no use.

I scoop up the soggy sheets, the china crunching under my shoes. Each sheet has a detailed drawing of a different dragon. The sketch is technical, without any adornment or flourish, but beautiful in its simplicity.

Guilt sweeps across my cheeks. "Are you the artist?"

He rips the papers from out of my hands, and they immediately turn into a disorderly pulp. Slowly, he lifts his gaze and levels a look of such impotent fury, it almost makes me want to run. He's the man I noticed earlier, the one who looks as if he'd been recently brawling. His clothing is dusty, unkempt and beyond the help of any pressing. A long scratch drags down the length of his arm, as if he'd gone toe-to-toe with a furious cat. His eyes are dark, and they burn against his olive skin.

Twin fires scorching anyone who dares cross his path.

My attention drifts to the open doorway behind him, where several people file in, holding similar sheets in their hands. My gaze flickers back to his, another apology waiting on my tongue, but I shut my mouth instead. His scowl is ferocious.

Embarrassment unfurls in my chest. "What's in there?"

"It's the dragon registry office," he growls. "Where I just wasted an hour of my life waiting for the paperwork to be completed." His voice climbs higher. "Which I'll have to do all over again, thanks to you."

I bristle at his furious tone. "I *am* sorry."

His appearance suddenly makes sense. The unkempt attire, sand embedded in his nails, the scratches on his arm. I don't have to touch his palms to know they'd be covered in calluses. He's used to carrying steel.

This man is a dragon hunter.

He drops the wet clumps of parchment, and it lands on the ground in a noisy plop. With another searing glare, he walks to the back of the line, tight fists at his sides. One of the men in line glances over his shoulder, a sneer bending his mouth. "Nothing seems to go well for you in this building, does it, Arturo?"

My gaze ticks back to the brawny dragon hunter. I'm surprised by the name. It belongs to a hero, someone who fights for the weak and downtrodden. Each syllable is a whimsical note meant to come out of the mouth of a herald.

"Of course, you've always thought you were better than all of us," the man continues.

Arturo ignores the jab. I consider apologizing again, but given his rudeness, I don't attempt it. He doesn't fit in with the other hunters, with their pressed tunics and embellished trousers. They all seem comfortable in this building while Arturo's rigid stance screams that he'd rather be anywhere else. My presence only seems to enrage the dragon hunter. He keeps his stony face averted from mine, the line of his jaw unyielding and mean. But then one of the men leers at me and lets out a low whistle as if I were a wayward dog.

I stiffen.

Arturo's head jerks upward and he directs a glower to the whistler. Then to *me*, he snarls a quiet, "Weren't you leaving?"

As if it were my fault that man couldn't restrain himself. My feet don't carry me away fast enough, the heels of my shoes crunching against the shards littering the stone. I hope I never run into this hunter again. A sharp pinch scratches my shin, and I wince. When I reach the loft, I sink into one of the high-backed leather armchairs, facing away from the staircase. The area is mercifully empty, but behind me, people walk up and down the hall, disappearing into the various offices lining the corridor.

I rearrange my skirt and look into my boot. Part of the shattered teacup snuck inside. Grimacing, I carefully pluck out the offending piece, revealing a small wound, bleeding profusely. With a muttered curse, I wipe at the gash with the hem of my dress. I toss the shard into the hearth and stand. My thoughts return to the conversation with Don Eduardo, and my jaw tightens. He wouldn't take me or my suspicions seriously.

I *know* the Asociación is responsible.

If I can get a hold of the complaints against them, I can prove their behavoir goes beyond marching and waving their banners. For that, I'll have to find the right office. I glance down the opposite end of the hallway, deliberating, until I see someone coming my way. The clerk I met from before.

"Alberto!" I call out.

He's shuffling paper in his hands but looks up at the sound of my voice. "Are you speaking to me, señorita?"

"I said your name, didn't I?"

He eyes me warily. "What can I help you with?"

"I'd like to write a formal complaint against the Asociación," I say, thinking quickly. "Where can I do that?"

"Bottom floor," he says with a frown. "Habitación número siete, a la derecha."

There are several people waiting inside room number seven, wearing identical impatient faces. Most of them are older men, though there are a few stately women adorned in elegant gowns, feathered hats, and silk slippers.

The room has the same patterned tile as the main foyer, and there are several paintings lining the walls depicting famous Dragonadores of legend. A long desk stands at the back of the room where several harassed-looking attendants sit on leather stools, sorting through rolls of parchment.

"If you'll just wait your turn, caballero," one of the attendants says. "We'll get to everyone, te prometo."

I position myself at the back of the line, when the person ahead of me draws my attention. He's a few years younger than me and clearly sent by his employer who couldn't be bothered to come down to the Gremio headquarters himself.

"Are you here to file a complaint?" the boy asks. His voice is whisper soft and shy. "The forms are up front." I look to where he gestures. Rows of shelving are situated next to the main desk, each one laden with piles of parchment, quills, and bottles of ink.

Someone senses my taking a step forward because they throw a disgruntled look over their shoulder. The room is long, but it's filled with people standing close to one another, and there's hardly room to breathe, let alone to grab the supplies I need to fill out an official complaint. I use my elbows to make space. People grumble and close in from all sides, but I manage to reach the forms. A swift glance behind the main desk reveals filled out complaints. With a surreptitious look around, I grab several ink pots and roll them into the crowd behind me.

A loud crunching noise immediately follows as someone steps on one of the glass bottles. The man jumps a foot and crashes against someone. Another bottle is broken, and then another. Dark liquid splatters and pools in every direction.

"¡Que—" someone bellows.

Pandemonium ensues as the throng of people mash together. The attendants leap off their stools and rush into the roiling crowd. I dart behind the counter, my heart racing. Gremio members hurl insults, and a brawl explodes behind me. I grab a large stack of complaints and stuff them in my bag until it's near overflowing.

Now to get out of this room.

Nimbly, I dart around swinging fists and screaming men until I burst through the door and out into the corridor. I race along the hallway until I reach the main entrance hall. It's only then that I notice someone is at my elbow, breathing hard.

Alberto.

"Why are you following me?" I clutch my bag tighter.

"Does Don Eduardo know you're still here?" he asks crossly.

"As a member, I'm allowed to issue a complaint," I snap, gesturing back toward room number seven.

"But you're not a member—your *father* is."

My mouth drops. "Excuse me?"

"The member fee was only paid for one person." He pauses. "Santiago Zalvidar." He gestures to an attendant standing by the front. "You don't have the right to issue any kind of complaint."

"Papá is unwell, and so I must do his business for him," I say, my anger rising. "This is ridiculous—"

"Please escort Señorita Zalvidar from the premises," Alberto says to the approaching attendant. "Inmediatamente."

My heart detonates against my ribs. The only thing that keeps me from exploding are the scrolls in my bag.

"I'll call for Don Eduardo," Alberto threatens.

The sly smile stretching across his face makes the hair on my arm rise. He senses a chink in my armor. Before the massacre, he might have extended courtesy and respect.

Now, he sees someone he can look down at.

I swallow my pride and lift my chin. A crowd gathers around us, and my cheeks warm. The attendant steps forward, but I ward him off.

"I know the way out," I say stiffly, and I walk out the front doors, my shoulders thrown back.

"Zarela."

I blink, my eyes adjusting to the glare of the bright sun. At the bottom of the marble steps is Hector's familiar, kind face. His shoulders sag and he grins. Relief smooths his brow as I rush forward, my bag smacking the back of my thigh. He appears to have come straight from bed, his tunic and trousers wrinkled, and his hair matted and dirty.

"You look terrible."

He rolls his eyes. "It's nice to know I can always count on your honesty."

I walk into his outstretched arms. Tired and unkempt as he is, he still manages to show up when I need him the most. It's so like him. When I was young, my parents used to leave me behind during their travels to neighboring cities and countries. It was Hector who stayed with me while they worked, looked after me, made sure the loneliness didn't bite. My arms wrap tight around him, and he winces.

"Careful," he says. "My back is still . . . crispy."

"Lo siento."

He waves me off when I try to straighten his tunic. "I'm fine, don't fret. Zarela," he chides, "why didn't you come get me for your meeting? I had to find out from Lola, of all people. She made it sound like you were heading to your execution."

"She's dramatic, you know that."

He regards me with an air of amusement. "Do you think I'd be standing here, calmly talking to you if I had believed her?"

No, if anyone would have hurt me, he'd have burned down the whole building. "I wasn't thinking—I should have written."

He sighs. "That's all right. I'm here when you need me for such unpleasant things, especially when it comes to Don Eduardo. He doesn't . . . think clearly when it comes to your father. How was it?"

The details come out rushed. I tell him most of it—the fine, the amount I had to pay to compensate the families, and the warning of not making another mistake. I leave out the decision to fight in the arena—he'd *never* approve. I also don't mention the rolled-up complaints in my bag, which I'll read the minute I'm on my way home. Best not to embroil him into my suspicions. He'd only give me a lecture and forbid me from courting any risk. He's always doing that.

I hate to deceive him, but there are some things I need to do on my own—without interference or questions.

"How much money do you have left?"

"Four hundred and thirty-five reales. There might be a way—" I falter and swallow back a painful lump. "There might be a way to get more. It depends on how quickly I can meet with buyers."

Hector studies me, a question in his warm brown eyes.

"We're selling our carriage, two horses . . . my mother's wedding and engagement dress," I explain softly. "They'll fetch an enormous sum. That might be able to tide us over."

Especially if I'm the one who will fight in the arena. I know Hector would offer on my behalf, but I can't accept. He runs his own dragon ring across town.

La Giralda needs its own Dragonador.

Me.

"¿Dónde en el diablos está tu dinero?" Hector demanded. "Where has your money gone? There ought to be a fortune tucked away—" He drags a hand down his face. "Santiago. The man can have no sense. What did he spend it on? Carriages? Enough silk shirts to wallpaper La Giralda?"

I let out a gasping, incredulous laugh. It's an old argument. The last time it was about Papá's extravagant wardrobe—did he really need that many velvet jackets? That many leather sombreros and custom-made shoes? Papá is a fan of textiles.

It's been worse since Mamá died, but I didn't know how much. "Don't be too hard on him," I say quietly. "Everyone handles grief differently."

"So they do." He thinks for a moment and comes to a decision. "I'll buy your mother's dresses," he says with a fond smile. "At five hundred apiece. I'll have it delivered to you as soon as possible."

"Tío Hector, no, I couldn't possibly—"

He holds up his hand. "I am your padrino, and I want to do this for you."

Tears drip down my face. I place my hands around Hector, softly and gingerly, as if he were made of the most precious silk. "Gracias, gracias," I whisper, though the words aren't enough. I'll never be able to show my profound gratitude. Guilt pricks at me for withholding my decision to become a Dragonador from him.

"Tío, that is so incredibly decent of you," I say, my cheek pressed against the cotton of his embroidered tunic.

He huffs out a deep laugh that makes his chest rumble. "I'm not that noble. I'm going to turn around and sell the dresses for a thousand reales each."

I step back, wiping my cheeks, and I let out a watery chuckle. He's always been ruthless when it comes to finances. "I expect you to treat me to a nice dinner."

"You know I will." He sobers. "And what about you? Are you all right?"

"No, I'm not, but there's so much to do. I have to keep La Giralda running—"

"You're still planning on running the ring? How? Your father can't possibly continue dragonfighting. The arena is destroyed. Why don't you sell?"

His questions grate my skin.

I was about to tell him about the slain dragons in our dungeon, of my suspicions that someone is intentionally trying to ruin us. But he'll push me even more to give up on La Giralda. "I will find a way to keep our arena running," I say firmly. Hector wilts before my eyes, and my next words are gentler. He's only trying to help. "I must leave you now. I need to purchase a dragon and hire a Dragonador," I add quickly.

"Forgive me, Zarela, but what Dragonador will want to work at a disgraced ring?"

I flinch, the truth in his words a sharp jab.

"All graduates will have contracts for the rest of the season with other arenas by now."

He's right, but I'm not in the market for a fighter. What I need is a monster to face. "Tío, can you just direct me to where I can purchase a dragon? Por favor?"

"How will you be able to afford a dragon and their upkeep?"

My patience thins. "I have a solution. No te preocupes."

"But I do worry." Hector studies me carefully. "If you insist on continuing operations, then I advise you to pay a visit to Esperanza Ranch. It's outside the city, deep in the desert. I don't personally know the ranch owner, Ignacio, but I've heard no complaints. Perhaps they'll have someone on site you can hire to fight in the arena. It'll be your best chance on finding an available Dragonador this late in the season."

"I've never heard of this ranch," I say, frowning.

"Because most people want pure breeds from discerning dragon owners," Hector explains. "Ignacio's dragons are wild and more dangerous and not bred in captivity to ensure pedigree. Of course, *some* arenas want these animals because of the dangers they pose for the Dragonador," he spits out in clear disgust. "Those beasts are unpredictable. But you may not have a choice, and it's at least a place to start while you get back on your feet. I can't say I agree with your decision, Zarela. I hate to see you stressed over something that really ought to be handled by your father. Would you like me to come with you?"

I shake my head. "I can do this on my own."

"But—"

"Tío—you're meddling like my great-aunt Eugenia. Remember her?"

He laughs, a sheepish smile on his face. "You're like a daughter to me."

A stab of guilt pierces me, but I keep my secret. The minute I tell him my plans, he'll try to talk me out of them.

And I can't change my mind.

NUEVE

The road to Esperanza Ranch is unfinished. It makes for a horrid reading experience. Craggy rocks mar the dirt path, and overgrown wild shrubs blur the edges of the lane. Every bump jolts me upwards, and I hold on to the velvet seating with both hands. I should have gone by horseback but decided to visit the dragon hunter immediately after leaving the Gremio headquarters.

The scrolls are scattered all around me, curling on the seat across from mine, and in a messy pile on my lap. Most of the complaints are exactly what Don Eduardo said they'd be—members of the Asociación marching in front of various arenas, creating noise and dirtying the street with their discarded pamphlets. There are a few that describe the mob entering the arena itself, waving their banners, and screaming their protests.

None of those complaints feel dangerous.

I need better proof when it comes to the Asociación.

I let out a sigh, and peer out the window, wondering if perhaps I haven't lost all common sense. A dragon hunter out here probably isn't licensed with the Gremio. There are only a handful of respectable dragon hunters in Santivilla, and most are caballeros with a long family history of heading into the wild. Often, they have a waiting list as long as I am tall. But the way Hector talked about this particular ranch owner made me pause.

What sort of dragons does he keep in captivity?

The landscape changes from the lush foliage found enveloping the city limit to a rough, pebbly terrain filled with sun-kissed sand and prickly shrubs in differing shades of soothing green, snips of parsley and fresh mint. The road climbs higher toward a lone, square-shaped building perched on a hill overlooking Hispalia in every direction. We are perhaps three hours from the city. I've never traveled this far without guards capable of defending against a dragon attack. Santivilla specializes in carriage design meant to guard against any threats, including monsters from the sky. But the magic wears off over time.

Traveling is always a risk.

Living beyond the round wall of the city is a risk.

Esperanza stands on its own, with no neighbors or visible armor. It may as well be a dish of raw meat. Why keep yourself isolated and helpless? The ranch looms ahead, a plain structure made of stone. Entire sections are scorched, and parts of the wall show large cracks.

I've seen that kind of damage before—dragon fire.

The carriage stops at the front entrance. I scan the afternoon sky with a practiced gaze before climbing out. Nothing flies near the ranch, not even the occasional vulture. There's only the still quiet of the day, with hardly a breeze to cool the skin or rustle the leaves. Sweat turns my skin dewy and damp, my dress heavy and hot.

I walk forward, expecting someone to have noticed my arrival. But no one ventures out of the building. No guard or game master or butler. The thick iron gate studded with spikes remains closed. There's no knocker, so I pound on the iron, hoping the loud rattling sound will summon someone. Five minutes pass, then ten, but still no one appears. I frown—it *is* a working day, surely?

I march around the building, and the sight of the burnt walls makes my stomach turn. The russet roof reveals missing tiles, confirming my suspicion. A dragon paid a visit to this ranch. Instinctively, I glance upward again. Mercifully, the skies are still clear of any threat. My walk leads me to the back entrance, opening up to a small, paved courtyard. Beyond, the ground slopes downward, and at the foot of the hill is a sandy field. Scattered in clusters are round-shaped fences made of cast iron, reaching a height of at least two stories.

Each pen has a dragon pacing within.

I've never seen so many. There must be at least two dozen. Fear grips my heart and squeezes. I inch forward, making my way to the bottom of the hill, until I'm mere feet from the closest locked-up monster.

Their immense size towers over my slight frame. Unease unfurls deep in my belly. The snarls rip from their mouths, and the hair on my arms stands on end. Somehow, I'm meant to kill one in the arena, a feat that feels similar to traveling to the sun on horseback. I may as well marinate in olive oil and present myself to the dragon with my compliments.

A hysterical laugh rises up my throat, and I ruthlessly smother it.

Several field hands run around with pails filled with raw hunks of bloody meat. My stomach turns at the overflowing, grisly mess. The bottom of my dress drags through the muck and muddy grass as I venture closer to one of the iron pens. My boots step on squishy dirt, and I pray to the heavens that I'm not marching through dragon shit.

No one pays any attention to me. I've never seen some of these breeds before—monsters with shimmering yellow scales, another protected by emerald-green armor, so thick I doubt a sword could cut through. Another ring holds a blue dragon, smaller than the size of a cow, with sky-hued eyes and iridescent scales that mimic lapping ocean waves. Yet another displays a beast with golden scales and red irises. Its tail curls against its body, adorned with ivory spikes.

But as different in size and color as they are, they all have one thing in common: every single one is enraged, breathing heavily through their snouts and thumping their tails on the ground, restlessly moving against the iron posts, growling.

All of their wings are bound.

I avoid staring into their eyes and the odd guilt I feel, arriving like an unwanted houseguest. Instead, I focus on finding the ranch owner amidst the people doing various jobs, some hollering at one another, others feeding the monsters as if they were pets. The smell of excrement assaults my nose, makes my eyes water. Dios! The scent is criminal. I stop and use the sleeve of my dress to wipe my eyes.

I take a few steps before catching sight of another pen at the foreground, slightly away from the rest. Inside is a dragon with ebony scales and immense wings taped to its side. The beast is the largest one on the field, prowling in circles, and routinely slamming its massive bulk against the iron fence, testing the strength of its cage.

I know this monster.

The bull-like Morcego.

An older caballero with graying hair and rich black skin approaches me, but I hardly notice. Outside the cell stands a young man with black shoulder-length hair, broad shoulders, and rich olive skin. He's wearing a dark tunic with a leather vest cinched tight across his chest. Afternoon sunlight glints off the round metal shield in his right hand, imprinted with an image of a dragon in the center. He's utterly calm. A force contained and controlled.

He makes a loud clicking noise.

The dragon snarls at the sound and immediately stops pacing. I'm transfixed by the sight of the beast and the tamer, whose face shows no fear. There's an arrogant lift to his chin, a confident line in his back. I'm only a hundred feet from the pair, and I feel every dangerous inch of separation. The young man slowly lifts the entrance of the cell and when the bar is level with his hips, he bends and rolls forward.

The bar slams down, splattering mud.

My breath catches at the back of my throat. A sudden pain draws my notice, and I realize my nails are biting into my palms. I unfurl them and resume watching the tamer, now trapped with the Morcego. He's upright, body straight and loose with his knees slightly bent as if readying to lunge should the dragon attack. There's something familiar in the way he holds himself.

Feral.

He has no blade. No other weapon but his shield. Shock loosens my jaw, and I let out a sharp gasp. The older man next to me holds out a handkerchief.

"Señorita, estás bien?"

I force myself to look away from the impending slaughter. The caballero is at my elbow, gaze flickering to the young tamer. "Someone ought to drag him out," I say. "This is beyond foolish."

He shoots me a smirk, weathered face crinkling across his brow and at the corners of his eyes. "Do you think so?"

An exasperated huff escapes me. Have these people no sense? Images of my mother's burning body flash across my mind. The scent of her enflamed skin. The sight of her hair on fire. Her bones turning to ash. "This monster is not to be trifled with."

The caballero's smirk turns into a wide grin, hooking his arm with mine, preventing me from marching over to the tamer, just so I can yell at him.

"Mira," he says with a warm twinkle glinting in his coal-gray eyes. "Watch."

Anchored by the weight of his hand, I return my attention to the young man in the cell. The dragon hasn't moved, its gleaming teeth bared. It watches the tamer with barely concealed rage. Angry huffs of air shoot from its snout in a furious bellow. The creature is near trembling, wanting to lunge, wanting to maim.

The caballero tightens his grip on my arm when I try to intervene. Several of the onlookers stand up straighter as the tamer slowly lowers his shield. He lifts his right foot, as if preparing to take one careful step forward—

The beast roars. The deafening sound shatters the quiet. The telltale crackling noise follows, and I flinch. Faster than I thought possible, the young man jerks his shield upward as he drops into a crouch, and he meets the sudden burst of flames. The fiery blast pounds the metal, but the man's grip never wavers. Deep lines fan out from the corner of his eyes, and his jaw snaps as he grits his teeth, holding the position.

I can't breathe. Can hardly think.

I wait for him to burn, to let out a shrill scream of pain—but it never comes. Once the stream of fire ends, the young man jumps to his feet, unharmed, his face smooth and calm. His stance is infinitely patient as if he has all the time in the world.

"Incredible, isn't he?" the caballero asks.

That's certainly one word for it. A few others come to mind. "That shield must be blazing hot."

"Not the handle," he says, softening the grip on my arm. "He came up with a design involving a clever strip of leather and an expensive encanto. He's smart, my tamer. It took him weeks to get inside the ring with that particular dragon. He's made much progress."

"Is this your only tamer?"

The elder gentleman points at the young man, beaming with pride. "The best worker I have on the ranch. No one quite has his touch with the dragons."

"And you are?"

"Ignacio Aguilar." He releases my arm in order to fully face me. "The owner of Esperanza Ranch."

"A happy coincidence, Don Aguilar," I say, with a quick dip of my chin. "I've come to handle business with you."

"Como te llamas, señorita?"

"Mi nombre es Zarela Zalvidar."

Señor Ignacio inclines his head, his gaze lingering on my dark hair and the curve of my cheek. "You look like Eulalia. I saw her perform once. In the south of Hispalia, I think it was. A passionate, beautiful woman. It was a spectacular show."

I hear this sort of thing all the time, but it never gets easier. "Gracias." My attention drifts back to the young man, an idea brewing. "Tell me more about your tamer. Has he been here long?"

He shakes his head ruefully. "Only for a year. He was an incredibly talented Dragonador, the best in his class. But he changed his mind about the career, and now he helps out at the ranch. Hates hunting the beasts, but there's no disputing his talent for training dragons."

"Let me make sure I understand you," I say, unable to keep the excitement from bleeding into my voice. "He hunts the dragons himself?"

The ranch owner nods.

"And he is both a Dragonador and a tamer? A man of many talents."

"No, señorita," he says, while shaking his head again. "He *used* to be a Dragonador. He only hunts and tames them now."

But perhaps he can be persuaded to teach me. Hope cascades around me as if I stood under a rushing waterfall. I have found not only a tamer but a former dragonfighter. This is it—the answer to my quandary.

"Señor," I begin, "I have to buy a dragon, and as it happens, I'm in need of a tamer as well. I'd like to ask for your consent to hire him for a season, if you'll permit it."

"Arturo," he says, almost laughingly, "doesn't let anyone permit him to do anything. He is Arturo and does what he pleases. But you're free to ask, all the same. Buena suerte, Señorita Zarela."

He lifts his cap and walks away, whistling.

Wait—*Arturo*?

My jaw drops. Did I hear him correctly? Surely, it's not the same man I saw earlier at the Gremio. Por favor, don't let it be—

I face the iron ring, and this time, the dragon is quiet as the young man clicks his tongue. The beast is hypnotized by the sound, as if against his will, but unable to quit his fascination with the odd string of noise. Arturo slowly backs away and, with his heel, lifts the bar. When it's high enough, he spins and nimbly exits. I yank up the hem of my long skirt and rush to meet him before he disappears. The crowd disperses, presumably to handle their duties, and I'm left alone in between two iron cages with the tamer. The rings are occupied with a dragon each, and both are restlessly moving inside, growling and digging their claws into the earth.

Arturo sees my approach, and his black brows climb up to his hairline. Recognition flares across his features, and his expression rearranges into one of profound dislike. His dark eyes fall to my long dress, and his lips bend into a pronounced grimace. I don't blame his disapproval—

utterly ridiculous to be wearing this ensemble out in the muddy field. But my day veered into the unexpected, and I hadn't wanted to waste time returning home to change.

Still, his arrogant perusal is annoying.

I return the favor and slowly cast a wandering gaze that starts at the top of his head and down to his muddy, knee-high leather boots. When I reach his face, I quickly catalog his features: strong jaw, near hidden by a scruffy beard, his eyes are a chilly gray that instinctively makes me want to reach for my mantilla, and as I draw closer, his height only seems to grow taller and taller. He's handsome in a rough kind of way. The same way wildflowers are beautiful where they stand in a meadow as opposed to being perfectly trimmed for a crystal vase.

Arturo lifts his shield, almost as if unconsciously wanting to ward me off. "What the diablo are *you* doing here?"

"Why didn't you carry a weapon into the ring?"

"Pardon me," he says flatly. "I'm asking the questions here."

"Clearly not." I frown. "How did you beat me here? I left the Gremio before you."

"I rode horseback." His gaze drops to my dress. "While you, I'm sure, arrived on a velvet cushion."

A deep flush warms my cheeks. I hate that he's right. I need to regain control of this conversation. "You could have been killed."

A snarl pulls at his mouth. "Who are you?"

"Zarela Zalvidar."

He stills, glower frozen in place. A muscle ticks in his jaw as he slowly straightens to his full height. "What are you doing here?" he repeats. "How did you know where to find me?"

I blink, confused. "Find you? I wasn't looking for you." Some of the tension in his jaw softens. "I didn't know I'd ever see you again. I'm here on business."

My words somehow make his frown loosen, until there's a little line between his brows, more curious than annoyed. "What kind of business?"

"I'm here to buy a dragon."

A scowl rips through his features. "For the great Santiago Zalvidar, the hero of Santivilla."

He says my father's name as if it were a swear word. My dislike for the tamer soars. I consider walking away, but I need him. Perhaps if I talk about his prowess in the ring, he might warm up to me. "Why didn't you have a weapon with you when you faced the dragon?"

"I entered the ring without a blade because I didn't need one," he says in a biting tone. "Satisfecha?"

I'm the furthest from satisfaction. "How could you have known you wouldn't need one?"

Arturo narrows his gaze. "How many questions are you expecting me to answer?"

"As many as it takes for my curiosity to be appeased."

"Well, I have work to do, and no one is paying me to talk," he says, backing away.

"Well, while we're on the subject of work, I'd like to have a conversation about hiring you."

Surprise flickers across his features. "You want to hire *me*?"

"That's right."

A long moment of silence follows. He stares at me, as if waiting to hear that I wasn't being serious. In response, I fold my arms across my chest. "When can you start?"

He glares at me before stalking off, his footsteps heavy against the sand, as his voice rings out, "Never."

DIEZ

The kitchen fire crackles loudly, devouring the newly chopped wood as I carefully remove the kettle. Lola rummages through the bread basket, searching for the perfect loaf, muttering to herself about the lack of butter. I pour hot water for the tea into two clay cups.

Ofelia is off for the night, and Papá rests upstairs, covered in blankets despite the heat. I throw a disgruntled look at his dinner tray, the bowl of bone broth untouched. He slept most of the day, with only a couple of bouts of wakefulness. He'd asked for me, but my errand to the ranch had taken longer than I anticipated. I had arrived after supper because the main road into Santivilla had been packed with travelers, and by the time the carriage had pulled up in front of La Giralda, it was well into the night. I'd missed having a conversation with someone from the Gremio de Sanadores, but Lola asked the questions I couldn't.

"The healer—"

"Eva," Lola corrects absently.

"Right," I say. "She said the only thing we can do is keep Papá comfortable?"

Lola plucks an acceptable loaf from the basket, long and perfectly golden. "Eva will send someone in the morning to change bandages and apply an ointment." She glances at me. "She also inquired about payment?"

My stomach tightens. "How much?"

"The bill is over there," Lola says, gesturing to a wooden end table along the wall. I walk over and find a single note. The parchment is plain, the handwriting simple and direct. It says I owe their Gremio ninety-two reales. I swallow a bubble of fear. I set the sheet down and then drag one of the stools over to the island.

"So when Arturo said 'never,' did he mean never *never*, or ask-me-again-but-nicer never?" Lola asks.

"How do you know I *wasn't* nice?"

"Were you?" She fishes a knife from within a drawer and starts slicing the bread at an angle. "Tell me you have jam, or this bread isn't going to live up to my expectations."

"We have mermelada de tomate. Somewhere." Lola's expression brightens and I smile. Ofelia only makes her tomato jam once a month. I take a sip of tea and consider the question. "It was a weird conversation. I might have been critical."

"Is he handsome?"

I roll my eyes. "What does that have to do with anything?"

"Ha! So he *is* handsome." She lifts the knife and points the tip in my direction. "He must be. Anyone who can say no like that has to be. Imagine being able to say no without feeling guilty."

"I say no all the time."

"That's you. We were talking about me."

"I thought we were talking about where I'm going to find a dragon tamer I can afford. And dragons."

"What do you mean?" She finishes slicing and then finds the pot of tomato jam on a shelf and generously spreads it onto the bread. "You've found one."

"Lola, I can't force him to work for me! Arturo said no. He said 'never.'" I press my lips into a thin line. I will not beg. If he doesn't want to work for me, then I'm not going to demean myself by asking him again.

"Are you feeling well?"

"Of course I am," I snap. "Why wouldn't I be?"

"I've never known you to back down after you've decided you want something. And you want this dragon tamer." She waggles her brows at me.

"Don't be ridiculous. I need the dragon tamer; I don't want him." I push away the slice of bread, the tomato jam dripping over the edges, and I wonder how much it will cost me to buy more tomatoes for the week. "This is way too much mermelada."

"You don't have butter," she says with a shrug. "I had to compensate. Have you figured out how you're going to pay him?"

"Ofelia sold two horses and one of our carriages, that money and the sale of all five dresses paid for the fine, settlements, and initial repairs on La Giralda. Plus, Papá's medical expenses. So the short answer is no, I don't."

"But you have five hundred reales left over, right?"

I nod. "I need to use that to buy dragons. There won't be much to pay Arturo. He'll be expensive."

There's a loud bang as Lola rummages through more drawers, and my eyes widen. "What are you looking for?"

"Chocolate. You need a giant piece." She holds up a bundle wrapped in wax paper. "Found it."

She cuts off a small chunk and hands it to me, which I immediately put onto my plate to save for later. I'm not in the mood for sweets. "Gracias."

Lola cuts a piece for herself and takes a big bite. I nibble the corner of the bread. "Papá has Mamá's jewelry stored in her wardrobe. But that feels like I'd be crossing a line. It feels too personal and deeply wrong to sell them."

"Stones are replaceable," she says, sitting on a stool. "Your father's life isn't. What about asking Hector for more money?"

"I can't do that. He's already bought some of Mamá's dresses from me." I shove the plate away. "What are we even talking about? I still don't have a tamer or dragons to worry about paying for!"

"Seriously? Any moment you're going to figure out that he's the answer to your problems—"

"I *know* that already."

"—and you'll figure out what you need to offer him in order for him to say yes to the job."

"I'm not going back there. I have my pride."

Lola mutters something to herself about my being an idiot. "I'm not saying you have to go back and grovel—I'm saying discover his weakness and use that to get what you want."

"What makes you think he'll reveal his greatest desire to me?"

"Have you met you? The Zarela Zalvidar I know can be very persuasive. There's not many people you can't charm."

"But I'm not charming."

"Nonsense." She waves her hand in the air. "Everyone likes you."

"No, they don't," I say, remembering the awful sound the crowd made when I performed one of my own routines. "They love my mother, and by default, they tolerate me. I know how to play the game. I know what they want me to say and how to dress. Very few people have seen the real me. I can be combative."

"Only when you haven't slept well and you're under enormous stress, all while dealing with a sick parent and trying not to lose your family home."

"So you're saying I'm being combative."

"You might have been with this Arturo person," she says with a small smile. "But go back up there and don't take no for an answer."

"By being charming."

She holds up her cup of tea and salutes me. "By being you."

Lola downs the rest of her drink and then comes around the island. She kisses the top of my head and leaves to finish the last of her chores. I stare blankly at my untouched dinner. There have to be more things I can sell. Items no one might notice are missing.

I leave the kitchen, thinking of Mamá and what she might have done in my place. She wasn't one to wallow or make decisions out of fear. She loved to dance, loved painting fans, and magic, but that was the extent of her whimsical side. Mother knew how to stretch an helón, was an expert in her craft, practicing every day for hours, and she ran our arena with a calm hand.

Papá was the wanderer, and Mamá was the safe harbor he always came back to.

La Giralda is quiet and dark except for the lone candlestick I carry through the foyer. I walk up the main staircase and head to Papá's room, the light from the small flame casting monstrous shapes onto the walls. There's a soft rustling noise, the telltale sound of rats scurrying across stone.

Next item on my list: buy several cats.

Softly, I creep up against my father's bedroom door and press my ear to the cool wood. His fever has been keeping him up, making him restless and unable to get comfortable. I squint into the dark hallway, straining to hear any indication that he might be awake. But there's only the deep quiet.

Mamá's jewelry is kept in her wardrobe, in an ivory box on the very top shelf. While we donated most of her personal clothing, Papá hasn't entrusted me with the gems he gave her throughout the years. Perhaps he isn't ready, or maybe he thinks *I'm* not ready. Whatever the reason might be, we don't speak of the things she left behind: her wedding band, the pearl bracelet from their tenth anniversary, and the ruby ring given during their first performance together, in front of thousands, on the day she agreed to marry him.

The story of his proposal traveled miles across Hispalia, shared in private opera boxes and public taverns, and reenacted for high society in their grand estates. The ring is my favorite of my mother's jewelry, a fiery ruby set in a gold band, ornately etched with delicate filigree. She always wore it off the stage and only around Santivilla, so terrified of perhaps losing it while traveling from place to place.

The ruby alone is extraordinary.

But because it belonged to Eulalia, it's priceless.

Papá might forgive me for selling Mamá's dresses, but he'll never look at me the same if I were to sell her engagement ring. But if I don't, where will I get enough money to survive the next month? Mamá's engagement ring could fetch a lucrative sum, enough to hire a new tamer and buy more dragons, to fully repair La Giralda, keep everyone fed, and care for Papá.

I slip off my boots and slowly push the door to Papá's bedroom. It swings open, silent and inviting. My gaze adjusts to the dark and immediately veers toward the bed where Papá lies on his stomach, softly snoring. Then I shift my attention to Mamá's wardrobe. I can't believe I'm about to steal it. I step inside with my bare feet and guilty heart.

Perdóname, Papá. Please forgive me.

I sell my mother's ring the next day for two thousand reales.

It's over and done with, and I'm back in my chamber hours before lunch. Morning sunlight warms my room. The curtains are open, and the day promises to be pleasant, with only wisps of clouds dotting the azure sky. I make sure the door is locked, and then I take the large cloth bag filled with reales and pour it onto the stone floor. The gold coins wink back at me as I count them out, separating them into three stacks.

I try not to notice how badly my hands tremble, and instead concentrate on counting out every coin. The largest pile will pay for the dragons and new tamer. The other two bundles are smaller but will finance the repairs La Giralda requires, and cover my father's care and medicine. With our arena closed, we aren't making any income. I count the money again and take a handful from the biggest heap. I set those aside for day-to-day expenses: Ofelia, our driver who doubles as our stable hand, and trips to the mercado for food. I pluck ten gold coins and reserve the amount for an emergency.

I stare at the five piles. That's it. That's all we have for exactly one month of living expenses. No matter what happens, La Giralda must open its doors in four weeks.

Will we be ready?

Will I?

ONCE

The carriage is stifling hot. Sweat slides down my neck and sneaks into my serviceable ensemble, dampening the fabric. I use one of my painted fans to muster a breeze, but it's woefully unsatisfying. I gaze out the carriage window, and I'm slightly cheered by the sight of Esperanza Ranch. We're mere minutes away, but even one more second feels too long.

I've dressed sensibly this time. A light linen skirt and shirt in pale cream, with a thick, worn leather belt holding everything together and in place. On my feet are my favorite pair of thong sandals, and I braided my long hair into a crown at the top of my head. Stubborn strands escape the coil, and I impatiently push them back into place. On the floor of the swaying carriage is a leather bag filled with reales from the sale of the engagement ring.

My transport mercifully comes to a stop. I grab the money and step out, the sun's rays making my eyes squint. The front gate opens, and Don Aguilar rushes into view, carrying a large canvas sack, and munching on fruit. His gaze widens when he sees me, but it's quickly replaced by a knowing smile.

"Back so soon?"

"Buenos días," I say. "I'd like to buy a dragon from you, but it seems you're away this morning?"

He shoots me an apologetic smile. "I'm traveling for business. However,

Arturo can handle the transaction for you if you feel comfortable with him managing the purchase?"

"I'm here to see him as well, so it works out fine."

Don Ignacio smirks. "I don't think Arturo is expecting you."

"He's not. Where can I find him?"

"He's the only one of my workers who lives indoors with me. I believe he's having his first meal. He'll be in a terrible state before his third cup of coffee," he warns. "Arturo gets up at dawn with the dragons."

Having known Lola in such a state, I'm confident I can handle Arturo's mood. "Lead the way."

"Would you care for a cantaloupe?"

"I'm sorry?"

He reaches into the pack and pulls out one perfectly round fruit. "It will be the best you'll ever taste in your life, I promise you. I'll have Arturo cut one up for you."

I raise a brow. "I'm sure he'll love that. While I'm curious about your cantaloupe, I really must not irritate him beyond what he can tolerate. It's best I stick to my personal business."

"Nonsense. You have to try some," he says before leading me past the iron gate and then to a flat, square-shaped home, made crudely of adobo and mud, and a plain wood door with iron brackets. The entry has cacti and feathery-looking grass adorning the exterior, and while the house is forgettable, there's something sturdy and simple about the structure. I can't help but admire it. *I'm honest*, it seems to say. A safe place where you'll be kept clean, but never pampered or flattered.

We walk inside. Don Aguilar stomps his feet on an old, threadbare rush, and I do the same, ridding the bottoms of my sandals of rust-colored sand. Inside, the home is as cozy as its outward appearance. The walls were left in their original honey shade, and tawny-colored Hispalian tiles cover the floors. Pots of desert flowers and cactuses line various entryways, and from everywhere at once comes the scent of treated leather, dusty pages, crisp linen.

I follow the old caballero to the back of the house, taking note of his stooped shoulders and wan expression. He moves slowly, as if life had challenged him to a duel and won. We reach the end of the corridor, and the old man sways, swinging his hand wide and reaching for the wall. I immediately make myself useful and offer my own arm.

"Are you all right, Don Ignacio? Please, take a hold of me and we'll walk together."

The man's thin lips kick up into a smile.

"I'm fine," he says. "Perhaps a little ill, but who isn't at this age?"

He leads me to a nice-sized room, clearly used as a library. Walnut shelves hold rows and rows of books in every color and thickness, bound in leather or cloth. At the foot of the room is a handsome desk, and sitting, with his legs propped up and a steaming cup of coffee at his elbow, is Arturo. A newspaper obscures his face, but I'd recognize that head of wavy, dark hair anywhere.

"Arturo," Don Ignacio says. "A very beautiful woman is here to see you."

The newspaper dips half an inch and a pair of gray eyes stare at me coolly above the edge. He flicks the paper upward, and it resumes blocking his face from mine. A dismissive gesture that makes my blood spike.

"I have no business with this person."

"Arturo," Don Ignacio says, half-exasperated, half-amused. "What have I told you about scaring off potential customers? Please try to be polite."

The newspaper is discarded, and Arturo leans back against the leather chair, his callused fingers steepled. His cool gaze flickers to mine. "¿Todo bien?"

"Quite well. Yourself?"

He ignores my question. "Are you thirsty?"

I narrow my eyes. "Not at the moment."

"Hungry?"

"I ate earlier."

"Astoundingly hot, isn't it?" he asks.

"It certainly is."

Arturo's gaze cuts to his employer. "I've exhausted all polite conversation. Was there something else?"

Don Ignacio makes an impatient noise at the back of his throat. He opens his mouth to say something when the clock chimes. He pushes his hands into his hair, threading it back until it lies flat. "I have to go; the carriage is all packed for my trip. Are you sure you can handle the ranch for a couple of—" Señor Aguilar cuts off at Arturo's pronounced scowl. "I was only checking. Will you cut the cantaloupe for Señorita Zalvidar?"

"She isn't hungry."

I bristle at Arturo's flat tone. "She can speak for herself."

His attention returns to me. "You already did. I'm merely stating what I heard from your own mouth."

"If you make this young lady cry," Don Ignacio says with a stern frown, "I'll be very upset."

Arturo drags the paper back toward him, evidently done with conversation. "In a half hour, I'll be heading back out to the fields. I'd like peace, therefore I have no intention of making anyone cry, least of all a willful society girl with questionable manners herself."

Don Ignacio shoots me a helpless look. "I'll walk you out."

"I'm not leaving," I say firmly. "But please don't let me keep you. Have a safe journey. The last time I cried, I had very good reason. This encounter won't leave me in tears, I promise you."

He smiles, eyebrows quirking. I've surprised him. "Arturo, if this formidable young woman somehow does the impossible and manages to convince you to work with her, please leave Joaquin in charge until I return."

The response from the tamer is a look of such withering scorn, I'm half-amazed Don Ignacio doesn't let him go on the spot. But the owner of the ranch merely laughs and then squeezes my shoulder.

"Buen viaje," I say.

"Don't let him intimidate you." He leans forward to kiss my cheek. "You're welcome anytime. Stay forever if you'd like."

He leaves with one last furtive glance at Arturo, who holds the newspaper, unopened, and watches his employer leave the library with a questioning quirk to his brow. He tallies something up in his mind and doesn't seem to like what the answer adds up to.

"What is it?"

"He's behaving oddly," Arturo says mildly. "Usually, if I've made clear that I don't like someone's company, he'll take preventative measures to keep us apart." His lip curls into a smirk. "He's throwing us together for a reason."

"What reason?"

He shrugs. "Romantic in nature, I'd guess."

"That's ridiculous."

"Obviously," he says icily. Arturo opens *El Correo* and resumes reading, as if I weren't standing on the other side of his desk like a dog waiting for a scrap of meat to drop from the table.

"Let's start fresh," I say with forced cheer. "Will you please lower that paper, so we can have a conversation? It will only take a moment."

To my surprise, Arturo complies, but not before I catch his eyes flickering toward the clock on one of the bookshelves. A sharp hiss of annoyance escapes me. "Clearly, our first meeting was disastrous—"

He snorts.

"But I'm sure we can move past it and start anew. First, you seem to think that I'm nothing but a spoiled aristocrat, which is categorically false. I'm the daughter of hard-working performers. La Giralda recently suffered from ... an unfortunate incident. I'm here to buy a dragon and hire you to train it for our arena. My father is unwell, and so I will be taking over his role as a Dragonador—and I'd like for you to teach me."

"Señorita," Arturo says with just a hint of frost to his tone, "I abhor the practice of slaying dragons for *amusement*. I'm not interested in the position. Buen día."

"But—"

"You know the way out, don't you?"

I see red. I can't stand his smug tone or the way he thinks he can order me around, dismissing me and my father's work. I slam my hands onto the desk. "Dragonfighting is a three-thousand-year-old Hispalian tradition. It's an art form and part of who we are and integral to our culture. Dragonadores are artists. My *father* is an artist. How can you abhor it?"

"Because it's wrong."

"I don't understand how you can think so when dragons routinely attack Santivilla, killing so many people year after year. Dragonfighting is living history, and it takes courage and grace and honor."

He leans forward, the newspaper forgotten. "It also takes murder. You call it history, I call it archaic."

"Then why do you hunt them?" I demand. "Why work *here*?"

He remains stubbornly silent. This conversation isn't going anywhere. I straighten away from the desk and pinch the bridge of my nose. Lola said to find his weakness. I begin pacing the length of the room, feeling Arturo's cold gaze as if he were blasting me with wind from the snowy mountaintop range to the north.

Then I recalled what Don Ignacio had said earlier.

"You're unhappy here," I say at last. "You must be. As a former Dragonador, you know, perhaps better than anyone, where the dragons come from. They're hunted and brought—"

"Dragged," he corrects with a snarl.

"They're dragged to the ring," I concede. "Where they're usually killed, unless they win the fight and kill the Dragonador. But then its mother is killed as punishment. And you're working in a ranch that specializes in hunting down the very beasts you refuse to fight in the ring. Explain that to me."

He leans back against the chair and folds his arms. "I have my reasons, and I can't remember where it says I'm supposed to share them with you."

"Humor me."

His features are stone.

"Fine." I sigh. "Perhaps you can't find a job anywhere else. After all, you've trained with the Gremio de Dragonadores, graduated from their school. It's too late to take up another skill with a different guild. You're much too old." A scowl rips across Arturo's face as his gray eyes bore into mine, one intimidating beat at a time. "So you're stuck here hunting dragons."

"Don Ignacio lets me take care of injured dragons," he snaps. "Those he allows me to set free back into the wild."

I eye him shrewdly. "But that's not enough for you, is it? You want to keep *all* of them safe, for some damned reason"—his eyes narrow dangerously—"but you can't, and meanwhile you don't have a prayer of making a respectable living. At least in Hispalia."

I swing my leather bag around from behind my back and pour the entire contents onto the desk. Three hundred and twenty-five gold coins rattle against the wood, piling higher and higher.

Arturo's gaze never leaves my face. But his shoulders tighten, and his fingertips dig into his forearms. Intuition flares and I roll the dice.

"Here's your chance to start over. Dream up a new business. And perhaps," I say softly, "you can buy a plot of land. Create a sanctuary for your dragons, kept free and safe from the ring. Protect them from the magic guild, from becoming chopped-up body parts for their potions and encantos."

His eyes drop to the money. "Damn you."

"Three hundred and twenty-five reales," I whisper. I wait as he stares at the money, expression remote and closed off, his demeanor as prickly and off-putting as a feral dragon.

"Take your reales and leave."

His words register, but I refuse to believe I have come to the end of the road. I might find someone else to train the dragons, to instruct me—but I'm done with things going wrong, with things happening to me. "I'm not leaving until you agree to work for me. It's the right move to make. For both of us."

He jumps to his feet, and the leather chair crashes backward. "Get out."

I do as he says, but leave the money on the desk, glittering with temptation and promise.

DOCE

I don't go far. In fact, I don't leave the property at all. I stand by the front gate, tapping an index finger against my lips, contemplating my next move.

I straighten my shoulders and march toward the fields. The dragon pens become visible, and a nervous flutter dances deep in my belly. The creatures are restless inside their cages. Dozens of different breeds that will be bought for the arenas of Santivilla. We are the only country who hosts dragonfights—everywhere else, they're hunted down and killed. For everyone else, it's about survival. For us, it's about control and creating art. What other artist faces death while performing? We take on the risk to prove victory is possible against monsters. I will never understand why the Asociación can't see why we need to fight back in a way that lifts up the courage of Hispalians living under the constant threat of attack.

The creatures growl at anyone who draws near, dig their claws deep into the earth, no doubt wishing it were flesh instead. Wings that ought to bring them freedom are useless. I ought to pity the beasts. But I don't, not after what they've taken from me.

I scan the field and find what I'm looking for. The round courtyard overlooks the dragons' rings, and it's at least paved, with an old wooden bench next to a leafy potted plant. I settle onto the bench with a private smirk. Arturo will use the back entrance to reach the fields, and he'll have to walk through the courtyard, passing the only available seat.

He'll have to walk past *me*.

The sun glides across the sky as I impatiently tap my foot against the stone. Sweat beads at my hairline, the sunlight makes my skin tingle, sharp pinpricks that dig deep into my flesh. The dragons watch me from the bottom of the hill curiously and hungrily with their cold, reptilian eyes. Several hired hands work the fields, ridding it of weeds, herding cattle, and watching over a small group of sheep. They, too, gaze at me with furrowed brows.

I look away and focus on the rolling desert hills. Not for the first time, I wonder why this dragon rancher decided to live way out here. I ought to have asked. Another half hour sweeps past, and my resolve weakens when hunger makes my stomach growl. Am I a fool to stay? Arturo isn't someone who's easily persuaded. What if we did switch to only flamenco dancing? I might be able to hire more dancers, come up with new routines—

Of course that won't work.

The people of Santivilla bleed for dragonfighting. Once again, I hear the crowd's disappointment when I performed my own dance routine. In their jeering, I hear their accusations: Do you really think you can outshine your mother?

The back door swings open, startling me. Arturo strides out, carrying the paper, and his coffee. He freezes when he sees me, lips parting, and the drink splashes over the rim.

I smile. "I'd love a cup."

He appears dumbfounded, opening and closing his mouth as if wanting to yell, but not quite finding the words. This might be the first time someone has openly disagreed or disobeyed him. He's used to having people and creatures listen to him.

Well, I'm not one of them.

"I told you," I say firmly. "I'm not leaving until you agree."

He finds his voice at last, and with every word, his volume rises to a near shout. "This isn't your property. You're on privately owned land."

"Well, it isn't your property either."

He scowls at me, finally understanding. "You don't think Don Ignacio will run you off his lands when he returns?"

I slowly shake my head. "I think he's rather taken with me. He did tell me I could stay forever."

"He didn't mean that *literally*."

"I'm going to sit on this bench until you say yes. Night and day, until you agree to train me."

His lips thin into a pale slash against his tan face. "I'm not going to change my mind."

"Neither am I."

He looks down at his feet, thinking hard. "Don Ignacio will sell you the dragons you need."

"Not enough," I say softly. "I need you."

He jerks in surprise, his attention still on the toes of his boots. His grip on the rolled-up newspaper tightens, and I'm half worried he'll tear it in two. "I'm not available."

"Everyone is. For a price."

He meets my gaze levelly. "The rain will come now that we're in the dry season. Even the dragons hate the downpour." He smiles slightly, calmer now. "You won't last the day."

Arturo strides off, confident of my failure. Little does he know that adversity only makes me that much more determined. I smile to myself. I am the daughter of the best dragonfighter in Hispalia. I don't scare easily. I kick off my sandals and allow the warmth of the stone to seep into my toes. The heat grounds me and the big potted plant offers a little shade.

Nothing will make me move from this spot.

I stare down into the fields, at the dragon rings at the foot of the hill. Arturo approaches the nearest pen, following one of the tight and twisted dirt paths, and comes to the entrance, raising the bar and nimbly rolling forward and straightening on the other side. Someone rushes forward with the shield, struggling with its weight and carrying it with both hands.

"Toma, Arturo."

Without taking his attention off the monster, Arturo reaches backward and accepts the large disc, needing only one hand to manage its bulk.

The dragon—an emerald-green one—stills, its massive head tilted, and slitted eyes watching Arturo. I lean forward, unable to keep my attention away from the serpentine beast. Its body resembles a snake's: long and with a forked tongue, the head diamond-shaped. My stomach riots with nerves, but Arturo's demeanor doesn't display any of the same angst. He's as calm as a baby drifting toward sleep, unhurried and safe. He is so like my father, it takes my breath away.

He is a Dragonador.

Arturo brings the shield slowly up to the level of his nose. The Culebra jerks back when it sees its reflection in the polished surface and bares its teeth. The confrontation seems to annoy the dragon, as if Arturo were a mosquito buzzing in its ear. It dips its great head, and huffs of air disturb the sand. With a snarl, the beast swings its tail around, aiming for the tamer's midsection.

Without missing a beat, Arturo ducks under the tail and rolls out of reach, the movement fluid and controlled. The viridescent monster smacks the ground with its tail and lets out a thundering roar.

Arturo brings the shield up and whistles. Once, twice, three times. The noise is shrill—punctuating the air with violent notes. The dragon half slithers, half crawls away from the tamer until its entire body presses against the bars. It screeches and claws at the iron grillwork. It doesn't like the harsh sound.

This continues for a long moment until all at once, there's a sudden silence. The Culebra pushes away from the barrier and charges at Arturo. I jump to my feet, heart in my throat. Ready to scream, to run for help. But the tamer races forward at the same moment and nimbly bends and runs between the dragon's squat legs. He's on the other side of the monster, upright, and grinning, with only the shield guarding him against death.

This marks the first time I've seen a pleasant expression on his face, and the smile transforms his entire countenance. He looks younger, boyishly happy to be facing death. It's the same exhilarated air Dragonadores give off when they confront a dragon in the arena. Thrilled for the fight. Eager for the challenge. Ready to defend their honor.

I will never be like any of them.

But I can learn the moves. I won't survive if I panic, if I'm too slow. I fold my arms across my chest, my resolve soaring. I can't leave until he agrees. Arturo lifts the bar and rolls under it and rises to his feet outside the ring.

The dragon spins, massive tail whipping wildly, looking for its prey. When it discovers it lost, the beast lets out a furious cry. The tamer turns his back on the monster and tucks the shield close to his side. He moves into the next iron pen, but not before darting a quick look in my direction.

The tamer sees me perched on the hill, with the sun's rays hitting me squarely in the face, and he scowls. I can discern his expression from all the way up here; it's *that* pronounced and severe. A dark slash dividing his face. A silent request that I leave the ranch and never return.

Nothing will change my mind.

The day passes much the same. Arturo works with the dragons—though what he hopes to achieve, I can't begin to guess. Every now and then, he shoots me exasperated, resentful looks which I'm sure are meant to drive me away. His annoyance only spurs me on.

I'm getting to him.

When the sun sets, someone rings a bell hanging by the outhouse, signaling the end of the day. The iron pens are firmly locked, and the hired hands depart from the fields toward the stables. Arturo walks up the hill, dirt smudged on both cheeks and across his brow, dark wavy hair damp with sweat. He strides past me, ignoring me entirely. Only the slam of the door tells me he knows I'm still here.

The turn of the lock makes me flinch.

I'm alone out in the fields, the darkness burying any shred of light.

With the sun gone, the air succumbs to the bitter chill sweeping through the desert. Goose bumps flare up and down my arms and legs. My thin cotton shirt and skirt do nothing to protect me from the night's stinging bite.

Arturo's form appears at one of the windows, and after confirming that I've remained behind, the shape stalks away. A half hour later, he returns and glares at me from behind the glass. I fold my arms, and smile.

Once again, he stomps out of sight.

The stars keep me company, twinkling against the inky darkness of the night. I try not to think about the monsters down below, try not to dwell on the iron locks keeping them trapped. Golden and red eyes stare up at me. Predators observing prey. I shiver and pull my sleeves down. Can't fire melt iron? It can, surely. Unless the cells have been enchanted. It would have been wise to ask.

I avert my gaze. Don't think about it. If the dragons haven't burned down their cages by now, they probably won't tonight. That's the story I'm telling myself, but my stomach tightens into a knot anyway. The cold seeps into my bones, fear glides into my heart and refuses to budge. For a moment, I deliberate between staying on the hill or heading back to the warmth of the carriage. But if I move from this spot then I'm setting a precedent. I don't want Arturo to come back to the window and see me gone. He'll think he's won.

I lie on my side, tucking my legs into my chest, and close my eyes.

I jerk awake. Someone leans over me, casting a shadow from above. I squint up at the shape, eyes blurry with sleep. The person moves away, and a thin ray of sunlight hits me square in the face. The awful cold from the night is long gone. Yawning, I sit up and stretch my sore muscles. It'd taken me ages to fall asleep, interrupted with the sight of Arturo returning to the window again and again. He didn't seem to have a good night's rest, either. The iron bench made a miserable bed, but there wasn't enough grass to lay on the ground. I drew a line at sleeping on cold and damp dirt.

The person, a young child, smiles at me shyly. She's a skinny thing, with dark brown skin, and in her hands is a clay cup, steam curling upward. My nose picks up a nutty, rich aroma.

She holds out the coffee, the sweet angel.

I accept the offering. "Gracias."

The girl stares at me while I take a sip. I smile at her, and she grins and then darts away, down the hill toward the outhouse where a long line of people wait. Someone must be cooking because the smell of smoked jamón rides the hot air kissing my cheeks. My stomach growls.

"No food for you."

I turn toward the voice. Arturo stands a few feet from the bench, and from underneath the brim of his leather hat, his lips are already set in that scowl. His gaze drops to the cup. Wordlessly he holds out his hand.

I look down at the coffee in dismay. "But I only got one sip—"

"Don't care. Give it to me."

"But I'm thirsty. And hungry," I add with a pointed look in the direction of the food.

"Then go *home* and eat." His palm is still outstretched.

It's a three-hour journey and I vowed I wouldn't leave the ranch empty-handed—not yet. With a sigh, I offer the cup. He takes the mug and walks off, but not before I catch him bringing the coffee up to his lips.

Bastard.

The line for food moves quickly, and soon everyone has a small tin tray, piled high with thick slices of bread and hard cheese and smoked ham. The bell rings, and the workers leave the cookware inside the outhouse where it presumably gets washed. I look around for a privy but find none. Perhaps there's one inside the outhouse. I leave my bench and head down, but at the entrance, I'm barred from entering by a rude attendant.

"What am I supposed to do?"

The man points a crooked index finger to a path that leads into a small grouping of trees and bushes. "Arturo says you're welcome to use the shrubbery."

I flatten my lips. "Is this really necessary?"

"Evidently," the worker grunts.

Nature demands I relieve myself immediately, but what I'd really like to do is argue the point with this man who won't even let me step a foot inside the outhouse. I glance over his bony shoulder and find a table laden with bowls and platters filled with leftover food from the morning meal.

"The dragons get the leftover food," a worker says before I can ask for a plate.

"Of course they do." I turn away and veer onto the path toward the enclosure of trees to take care of business.

When I make it up the hill, I stop short.

My bench is gone.

TRECE

I blink, surely the lack of food and water is getting to me. But no, the bench is really gone. Arturo got rid of it, just like how he thinks he can get rid of *me*. Soft footsteps coming from somewhere behind me make me stiffen. I don't need to turn around to know it's Arturo.

"You took my seat." I glance at him over my shoulder. His smile is a smug curl against his tanned skin. He actually thinks he's won.

"I felt like redecorating," he deadpans.

I turn around in a huff to stare at his retreating back as he makes his way down to the field. The dragons are awake and restless, searching for food, for freedom. For a moment, my resolve wavers. I could return home. Nothing would be easier. My carriage is still here. I can be on my way to La Giralda in moments. Away from the beasts, from the stubborn dragon hunter.

I straighten my shoulders.

His scoffing tone when he called me a society girl grates against my skin. Does he think I'm merely playing? I will not cave. If I go home now, I would have sold my mother's engagement ring for nothing. I stride to the front of the ranch where my carriage waits. The driver rests on the roof, legs dangling over the edge while the horses lazily pick at the weeds.

"Hola," I say.

The driver props himself up onto his elbows. "Lista? Are you ready to go home, Señorita Zarela?"

I shake my head. "I'll be staying here."

The driver's gaze widens. "Aquí?"

I nod once. "Please tell my father I'm securing dragons for the next fight and that I'll be home soon. Ofelia can manage the household, and Lola will help her as needed." I hesitate, wondering if I ought to ask him to bring me bedding, fresh clothes, and food. But if I make myself comfortable, Arturo can keep ignoring me. He'll look at my supplies, the velvet cushions from La Giralda, and walk past me.

If I stay the course, Arturo will have to acknowledge me.

"But—"

"Safe journey. Vaya con Dios." I walk away and march back to the fields, every step bolstering my resolve. I'll stand all day if I have to. I'm many things—stubborn and quick to anger and competitive—but I'm not a liar. I meant every word, and if he thinks he can scare me off, it's only because he's underestimated my determination.

Failure isn't an option.

Arturo has left the ranch for the day. I walk large circles at the top of the hill, round and round until the bottom of my feet ache and are dusted with russet earth. If I were to sit even once, I know I wouldn't be able to stand again. The workers bustle from one end of the field to the other, darting quick glances at me when they think I'm not looking. I'm on display, the flamenco dancer who has mysterious business with the dragon tamer.

The clouds thicken into a dour color, threatening a downpour. Before the evening bell rings, Arturo returns from his hunt, astride a reddish stallion and leading a procession of several riders dragging a large crate with an iron cage secured to the frame. Inside is a bull-like dragon with ebony scales—a Morcego.

These are the monsters I know. The beast has small bat-like wings that allow it to fly, but only short distances and low to the ground. The dragon snarls at anyone who comes near its cage, snapping its teeth and letting out an earsplitting shriek. I wince as I squint down the hill, trying to make out what kind of weapon the tamer carries, but I see none.

Naturally.

The Morcego roars again and batters the wall of its prison, rattling the iron bars. The crowd backs away, and only Arturo remains, feet crossed at the ankles, arms folded across his broad chest. He's utterly motionless as he studies the newest addition. His dark hair whips in the stormy wind, and when one of the ranch hands draws closer, Arturo snaps out a command. I can't hear the words, but I recognize the biting tone. Even the rough wind can't steal that away. Someone hands him a long pole wrapped in red fabric. The tamer slowly unfurls it and the cotton lengthens, becoming a bloodred cape.

The tool of the Dragonador.

Arturo gives the order to prop the entrance of an empty ring open. Then he has someone open the door of the Morcego's cage with a long hook. The dragon rushes out, wings unfurling, and charges immediately at the red cape in Arturo's steady hand.

What follows is a nimble dance of twists and turns.

The dragon rushes Arturo, who swerves out of the way at the last minute. He ducks when the Morcego tries to swat him with its tail. Jumps out of the way when the beast breathes fire and smoke. This continues until the tamer has somehow gotten the monster through the entrance of the vacant ring. He tosses the cape through the slits, and a heavyset worker quickly hands him the enchanted shield.

Arturo lets out a sharp whistle, and the door clatters shut. He's trapped inside with a feral, untamed dragon three times his size. I ought to be used to this sight. How many times have I seen Papá confront the same enemy? But sweat dampens my hands and my stomach roils like water at the base of a waterfall.

The tamer slowly brings his shield up to the level of his nose. The dragon's reflection startles the beast and it paces—but doesn't attack. Arturo clicks his tongue and takes a step forward. The dragon eyes him warily. Another click, another step forward. The reflection in the shield becomes larger. He's inching closer and closer to the smaller opening where he can duck under and through.

The dragon's frantic movements slow. Arturo lifts the bar of the small entrance with the back of his calf, all while maintaining the rhythm of the clicking. He's gotten near touching distance of the monster. Then he turns and rolls out of the ring, and the clicking stops. The Morcego jerks its head back and then lets out a bloodcurdling screech.

We all instinctively flinch. Even me, relatively safe on the hill. Arturo hands over the shield to someone waiting at his elbow, and then he shoves his hands into the pockets of his trousers, whistling a tune I don't recognize, and heads up the hill, more or less in my general direction.

The minute he sees me, the merry tune breaks off and his jaw tightens. As he draws closer, I catalogue his features: pulled-in brows that spell out his frustration, rigid shoulders, and his lips thinned to a pale slash. The long lines of his legs pound the hard earth.

He's in no mood to talk with me.

Arturo brushes past me where one of the ranch hands waits at the back entrance of the house. They begin speaking in earnest, and several times, the worker gestures in my direction. I can imagine what information he's relaying: how I refused to leave the ranch, how I sent away the carriage. Arturo hears it all, expression made of stone. He never once looks at me.

And then the conversation is over, and Arturo stalks into the house.

The bell tolls and everyone disperses; people find their horses, workers walk off the property to their respective homes. Darkness creeps forward, like the sea encroaching on dry land. I prepare myself for another miserable night. How many days will it take? What if Arturo *never* changes his mind? I cannot abide looking foolish, but I'm out of options. I have to at least have one more conversation with him.

Rain splatters on my shoulder. I close my eyes with a grimace as another drop smacks my forehead. Then another, and yet another. In seconds, the sky starts dumping water in torrential bursts. My clothes stick to my skin in a matter of moments. The ground turns to dark sludge, made thick by grainy pebbles and limp grass. I open my eyes and make my way to the paved courtyard, thankful to be at least out of the mud.

I face the ranch and glare at it. One of the windows brightens, lit from within. A lone figure materializes behind the panes. He stands motionless, a dark, nebulous shape against the warm light. I regard him steadily, the water clinging to my eyelashes.

We glower at each other for a long moment. The rain continues, coming down in gusting bursts, smacking every inch of my body. I set my shoulders in grim determination, folding my arms across my chest. The cold seeps into my clothes, and I rub my arms briskly in a futile attempt to shield myself from the wet. I stomp the ground to keep warm. What I wouldn't give for a plate piled high with smoked rice and perfectly crisp rabbit.

Home beckons.

My soft bed and equally soft bedding. A steaming cup of hot chocolate and Lola making me laugh as she regales me with impressions of Ofelia. I fight the persuasive voice from deep within myself telling me to knock on the door and ask for a ride back into Santivilla.

It is Arturo's continued refusal to speak with me that keeps me rooted to the spot. I dare him to come out and face me. But he doesn't, and at last, he turns away from the window. I stumble to the potted plant and sit under the leafy bushes. The hard pavement offers no give to my sore legs, but it's at least somewhat clean. I try not to think about the number of days I'll have to remain on this infernal hill, while my father gets sicker and sicker.

But I can think of nothing else.

The next morning is just as cloudy, gray and dour without a hint of warmth or sunlight. I push onto my feet, back sore and stiff, and limp down to the shrubbery in order to relieve myself. My clothing is damp and mud stains nearly every inch. Hunger makes my stomach loud and demanding. My hands are stiff from curling into fists all night, numb with cold, but I somehow make it back to my spot at the top of the hill.

The back door opens and Arturo appears, carrying his cup of coffee and the day's paper tucked under his arm. He looks refreshed and dry, respectable in his clean tunic and pants where I must look like a mud puddle.

He gives a cursory glance around the courtyard but then freezes at the sight of me. "I thought you'd gone."

"No," I say.

Arturo drags a hand down his face. Then he meets my eyes levelly, and I have a hard time reading his expression. His features seem to be at war. I detect the gleam of respect in his eyes, while his mouth is bent into its usual scowl. Nothing escapes his attention: my bedraggled appearance, the grime on my clothes, my dirty and cramped hands and feet. The way I'm still shivering from the cold night, even though the moon is long gone.

"Come in, then," he says shortly.

"I'm not leaving until we have another conversation."

I expect him to argue with me. But he merely walks off, sipping his coffee. I follow after him into the warm house with its soothing honey-colored walls and firm ground. He leads me to the office and gestures to the chair facing his desk. "Sit down before you fall over."

I sink into it, groaning.

"Do not move from this spot," he says in a flat voice, and then leaves the room.

I lean back against the plush seating and my eyes drift close. The rattle of plates startles me as Arturo returns, balancing a tray. On it are two cups and a plate of sliced tortilla, a kind of pie made of potato that's pan fried in olive oil. There's another small plate of diced chorizo and thick sliced bread, toasted and slathered with butter. My mouth waters.

Arturo places the food on the desk. I reach for the chorizo, but my hands are so stiff, I drop it. Arturo stands by my chair, focused on my cramped fingers. His lips press into a thin, disapproving line. He bends and picks up the chorizo and gently places it in my hand, asking in a stern tone, "Do I need to feed you?"

"Of course not." I eat the meat and then reach for a generous portion of tortilla. In seconds, I've cleared the plate. Then I grab one of the cups of café con leche. The first sip spreads warmth throughout my body, and I let out a delighted moan.

Arturo walks around the desk and sits in the leather chair. Once comfortable, he regards me with a stony expression. The air around him is steeped in quiet menace.

"Why are you doing this?" I ask.

"What, exactly?"

"Feeding me. You didn't yesterday."

"I don't want to deal with a corpse later."

I flinch. "It wouldn't have come to that."

His tone is an accusation. "So you say, but from where I sit, you look half dead."

I blink. I can't look as bad as all that, but I reach for a slice of bread and take an enormous bite. "You're being dramatic. Gracias por la co-mida y café."

"Don't thank me for the food and coffee. The only reason you're in here at all is because I don't want to explain your death to Don Ignacio when he returns from his trip."

"I expected him back by now."

"He'll be gone for a few more days. Why? Did you think to use him to convince me?"

I shake my head. "No, I thought it'd be nice to have a conversation with someone friendly."

"This can't go on."

I lift the cup to my lips and take another long sip. I've been waiting for this moment, but now that I'm here, I don't know what else I can say to convince him. Exhaustion clings to my edges, threatens to topple me over. Arturo knows where I stand. No sense in arguing further unless it's to discuss his hours. "I need you."

"It's bad enough to sell them to other Dragonadores," he says in a near whisper. "I can't train you. I can't go back inside a dragon arena. My life as a fighter is behind me."

"I'm not asking you to fight."

"Don Ignacio has me hunt them down. I train them, only to be slaughtered later. You're asking me to teach you how to kill them. That's where I draw the line."

"But you are still leading them to their deaths—"

"You think I don't *know* that," he says harshly. "That I don't hate every minute of it?"

"Then why work here?"

Arturo glares at me, folds his brawny arms across his chest. That's right, he doesn't like questions.

"My father is ill," I say. "His care requires money. We both have to do things we don't want to. I have to keep the ring open, and that means fighting dragons. If I could hire someone else, I would, but a close family friend has assured me that it's impossible this late in the season. There are no other suitable options."

He looks away from me. I follow his gaze to the sack filled with money propped against one of the bookshelves, shoved away and out of his line of sight. But no amount of will can keep a desperate man from a pile of gold. He knows that and so do I.

"You need the money," I say gently after finishing the toasted bread. "This is how you'll start over. Every coin in that bag belongs to you, and with it, you're that much closer to buying this ranch and turning it into whatever you'd like." I take in a fortifying breath and release it slowly. I know what more I can offer, but it's literally everything I have left. "I'll up your payment to five hundred reales. That's almost two hundred more than the original amount."

A person could live off that for two years. Well-fed and comfortable. I hope I sound confident, carrying myself as if handing over five hundred gold coins is nothing out of the ordinary. I clutch my shaking hands in my lap, force my face into a neutral expression, desperate to hide my panic. If he doesn't accept this, I don't know what I'll do.

Arturo returns his attention to me, studying my face, my eyes, and then he shifts in his chair. Weary acceptance takes over. A rush of hope takes flight within me, fluttering against my rib cage, yearning to be free. I lean forward, waiting to hear the words.

"Which dragon do you want?" he asks at last.

I have to restrain myself from leaping to my feet. It'd only annoy him, and besides, I'm too tired. "The Morcego."

"And the other?"

"Your pick. Whatever you think is best."

He raises a dark brow. "Do you think it's wise for me to pick out the beast you'll face in the arena?"

"You just admitted you didn't want my life in your hands," I say with a grim smile.

"Which is exactly what will happen anyway. It's my training that will keep you alive. Or not," he adds thoughtfully.

My smile vanishes. I'd spent all of my energy scheming and trying to maneuver the tamer into accepting the position. But now that I've succeeded, the reality of my situation hits me—in the shape of a black dragon with bat-like wings and a fiery rage.

The first rays of meager sunlight penetrate the dark room through the dirty panel windows. My clothes slowly dry, stiff with mud. I gesture to the worn tomes perched on the wood shelves. "Have you read all these books?"

Arturo remains silent. I'm genuinely surprised not to spot steam curling from out of his ears. He's dressed in his usual dark tunic, trousers, and scuffed leather boots that have seen many a dusty road.

"If we're going to be working together, might you at least try to be pleasant?"

His lips thin. "I said I'll do the job. This doesn't mean we're friends, and I don't owe you any civil words beyond when I need to tell you to duck."

"I hope you'll give more instruction than that."

He merely shrugs, and I pull my brows into a tight frown. Not exactly comforting. My gaze lands on the silk bag of coins again. Three hundred and twenty-five gold coins is a small fortune. And now I've offered him even more. All I have. "Are you happy with the compensation?"

His lips twist in disgust. Perhaps at the question, but maybe he can't stand the idea of me knowing how much he needs the money. "Yes."

I reach for another slice of bread. "I work best when there's a plan to follow. How many training sessions do you think I'll need before I'm ready?"

"Are you afraid to die?"

I lower the food from my mouth. "Isn't everyone?"

His dark brows lower, and his voice comes out grave and serious. "Above all else, before you step into the ring, make your peace with death. If you're afraid of the outcome, it will hinder your concentration and ability to focus on defeating the dragon. Can you do that?"

I glance away, my throat tightening. The memory of my mother's scream reverberates in my head until I wince. I picture facing a dragon, with its gleaming teeth, sharp claws, and scorching fire. They're monsters, incapable of loyalty or compassion. Fear curdles in my belly, and I swallow painfully.

"You said you didn't have any more options, but that's not exactly true," he says flatly. "You could marry."

I hastily set the cup onto the desk with a sharp rattle, cheeks flushing. My heart thuds loudly against my ribs. "What?"

"You could marry," he says again, and for the first time, his tone softens. My heartbeat returns to normal. For a strange, exhilarating moment I thought he'd been suggesting . . . but no. Instead, his voice holds a subtle note of pity and my jaw locks. "Find a wealthy husband willing to shoulder your financial burden," he continues. "You're pretty enough to tempt someone."

Easy for him to suggest something like that. To sign over my rights, become someone's property. Financial burden. An exchange in which I'd lose my self-respect, become someone I didn't recognize. Chattel. A porcelain figurine on a shelf. The lies that will spread from my one visit with her. The idea of marrying sends a cold shiver down my spine—of rushing to pick just anyone from the dwindling number of caballeros who might still consider it.

There might be someone out there who would treat me as an equal like my father did with my mother, someone who would know and love me and want a partner in life. I'd be stupid not to consider it. But I don't have the luxury of time, and if I rushed marriage now, it'd be far from the kind of relationship I've dreamed about. Being beholden to someone for the rest of my life would chip away at my soul, until nothing remained.

No fire, no heart.

That's not a life I want. I'd rather face a dragon.

"Not an option," I say. "What happens now?"

"We leave for Santivilla."

I glance at my grimy shirt, no longer the color of whipped cream. Not exactly the triumphant return I was hoping for. "I'm going to need a basin of hot water first."

Arturo shoots me a brittle smile. "I'm going to need you to ask me first, instead of telling me."

"You can't expect me to arrive at home with my face and hands dirty."

"Still not hearing a question."

I sigh. "Will you please fill whatever miserable basin you have with water? Hot water?"

"It's a lot of work."

"Yes, breaking a wand in half for the agua caliente encanto is incredibly tiring."

"We don't have any magic here," Arturo says. "Not one wand."

I gasp. "How do you get hot water, then?"

"The old-fashioned way," he says in a cold voice. "We boil it."

"What's wrong with using magic?"

He arches a brow. "Not everything has to be solved the easy way. I don't use it unless it's absolutely necessary."

There's an age-old animosity between the Gremio de Dragonadores and the Gremio de Magia—a feud brought on by the latter's use of dragon body parts for their spells and potions. They were the original hunters, killing the monsters by the hundreds. That's when the dragons fought back, attacking Santivilla until Dragonadores became a necessity. Now, magos and brujas visit arenas and collect the dead bodies to work their gruesome magic. No more hunting of the beasts, but it didn't matter. Dragons hold grudges and have long memories.

This is why the Gremio de Dragonadores is the favorite in Hispalia. We didn't start a war with monsters.

"Will you please boil water, then? Por favor?"

His dark eyes glitter in the brightening room. "No, I don't think I will. The only person responsible for your present state is you."

"But—"

He stands abruptly. "I'll prepare the dragons for departure. Meet me out front when you're done."

I swivel in the chair. "Your hospitality needs work."

The words barely make it to him as he quits the room. He's crossing the threshold, and yet his reply drifts back, scraping against my skin.

"You weren't invited."

CATORCE

Two wagons with iron bars latched overhead contain a dragon each. One is the Morcego I requested, the other is the blue dragon who seems out of place up here on the giant hill, surrounded by desert hills. Arturo has saddled his red stallion, and eight oxen are already in place to pull the beasts for the journey back into Santivilla.

A pair of guards travels with us, dressed in thick leather vests and knee-high boots with thick soles, and each carries a whip in one hand and a long bow in the other. On their backs are bundles of arrowheads plated in steel and shimmering in the sunlight, which means they've been enchanted to penetrate dragon hide. I understand the need for precaution. Dragons tend to attract more dragons, so the risk of an attack is much higher.

Arturo's only adornment is his leather hat and shield strapped to his back. My dragons are hostile, snarling and breathing fire at anyone who approaches the cages. Now I wish I'd come out of the house promptly, if only to see how the tamer had lured the beasts into their respective cages. But I'd been looking for water and a bar of soap and couldn't unearth either.

I brush the caked mud off my shirt. My sandals are ruined but at least wearable. The tamer checks the oxen, whose ears nervously twitch despite standing several feet from the wagons. Next to the cages are large chests, unlocked, and made of oak with sable leather accents.

"Can you ride?" Arturo asks in a brisk tone.

I eye the assembly of workers, dragons, oxen, and wagons. No carriage in sight. Of course I can ride, but not that well. "What happens if I say no?"

"I mentally prepare myself for a miserable ride to Santivilla." He points to his red stallion. "We're sharing the saddle. Meet my horse, Beto."

The horse eyes me warily and stomps his foot.

"There isn't another I can ride?"

Arturo doesn't bother to reply. He gracefully pulls himself up, the muscles of his back rippling. I *hate* that I notice. I climb up behind him, and it's impossible not to touch him. My thighs press against his legs, the strong line emanating heat. He stiffens when I place my hands around his waist.

"It's this or I fall off," I say under my breath.

He lets out a sharp whistle and digs his heels into the horse's side, and we lurch forward, venturing down the gravel path. It's a winding road traversing wide fields and loping hills edged by mountains, forests of desert plants and shrubs, and a smattering of small neighborhoods circling around one-street towns that aren't included on any map of Hispalia.

Overhead, the clouds have dispersed enough to allow slender shafts of sunlight to stream through, brightening patches of hard red earth, but it does nothing to raise the temperature. The dragons interrupt the sounds of oxen grunting and the occasional cry of a hawk. They snarl and rattle the iron bars of their cages. It's cooler up on this hill, and I tuck myself closer to Arturo, almost instinctively.

Mercifully, he doesn't comment on my proximity.

I tip my head back and study the sky. "What happens if we spot a dragon?"

"You're just wondering about this now?"

I poke his shoulder. "Answer me."

"We don't provoke the dragon," he says. "If it comes after us, we'll deal with it."

"But how?"

He doesn't respond. Someone never taught him how to carry on a conversation. I force out a deep breath. The tamer can barely stand the sight of me, fine, but being out in the open like this seems like a bad idea. At least in a carriage, I have the illusion of safety. The dry country-side steadily turns redder and hillier. Sweat gathers between my breasts, and my skirt is warm from the heat of the saddle. It doesn't help that the man in front of me radiates heat as if he were a roaring fire.

"Why do you live all the way out here? It's utter madness to invite so much risk into your lives. You'd be much safer in the city," I say after a long moment of silence. It might have been an hour. My legs are sore, and the saddle has no give against my skin. It's unforgiving and uncomfortable.

Arturo says nothing.

"That wasn't judgment," I say quickly. "I'm only curious. The ranch must suffer from frequent dragon attacks. It's the only large building in this area, vulnerable and without the aid of the bell to warn against an oncoming assault."

My statement is rewarded with more silence. I poke his back, and he grunts in response. When I poke him again, he angles his face down, halfway in my direction, so that I may see his snarling profile. "What do you *want*, señorita?"

"It's just plain rude to eschew conversation when someone is trying to engage you in it."

"*Is* it?"

"My mother would think so."

He stiffens and then grudgingly says, "Where and how we live isn't your business, but if you must know, the reason we're so far removed from gentle society is because the dragons come to us, more often than not, *precisely* because we're vulnerable."

Arturo snaps around, his back rigid. Conversation over.

Fine.

He doesn't want to be friends, or evidently friendly. I'm hiring him to do a job, best to remember that. We may as well settle the particulars.

"I want to confirm we're both in agreement in terms of what my money has paid for. I'm paying for two dragons and for you to train them for the ring. Further, you'll instruct me on all dragonfighting techniques. There's still the matter of your working hours. I suppose we can discuss that when we arrive." I hesitate. He's accustomed to sleeping at his place of work. It never occurred to me to offer the same. "I can provide sleeping arrangements."

"You've already given me your money. It's a little late to be going over the details, isn't it? You're stuck with what I choose to give you. Including my *hours* and where I sleep."

Stuck with what he gives me? That sounds like he'll do the bare minimum and maybe not even that. I'm paying him for the best instruction he can offer. His attitude doesn't fit with how I know Dragonadores from Hispalia behave.

Their word and character are paramount—above all else.

"Are you trying to tell me that you're not honorable?" I ask quietly.

Arturo pulls on the rein and the horse comes to a sudden stop. I lurch forward, barely catching myself from hitting his back with my nose. He halfway turns on the saddle and glares at me.

"For the last time," he says in a near growl, "I said I'll do the job. Do not question my honor."

"Then why the nasty tone?"

He leans forward, and the brim of his hat brushes against my forehead. "Because you ought to have gone over the details of the job and your expectations before handing me the money. Mistakes like that will cost you. I'm guessing the coin you gave me was hard to come by."

"Why would you think that?"

Arturo lets out a crack of laughter. "Why else would you spend the night outside of a stranger's home? No one does something like that unless they're desperate."

"Or stubborn," I say through gritted teeth. "That doesn't mean I'm short on coin."

He's quiet for a beat. "Maybe not, but the look of terror on your face when you paid me does."

A lump sits at the back of my throat.

"You're determined," he says. "I'll give you that. But you're going to need more to survive Santivilla without your family's name."

Weary resignation covers me like a well-worn coat. "You know what happened." Probably since the day the first reports circled in the city. Terrible news travels the farthest and quickest.

"I know what happened," he says grimly. "Disgraceful."

He turns around, and for once I'm glad to be facing his back. I pull my hands away from him, not wanting to touch him more than I have to. His words are a kick in the teeth. I want to poke him again and explain that it wasn't our fault, that we were sabotaged—but my fingers stay clenched around the saddle. My intuition flares as bright as a lit candle in a dim room. No matter what I say, he won't believe a word of it. Not without seeing the evidence for himself.

A shadow darkens my vision.

It's massive and grows wider and longer, blocking the sunlight. I glance up, and my breath traps itself in my lungs. A scream builds at the back of my throat, but I bite my tongue until I taste blood.

Dragon.

I shield my eyes from the sun and squint up at the monster circling, sure that I'll see La Giralda's colors—golden and red ribbons scalding the wind, but I don't. Its body is covered in scales the color of salt and bone. And now it's directly above us, wings stretched wide, allowing it to glide through the air.

Everything happens at once.

Arturo pulls on the reins, and the horse neighs loudly in protest. I slam forward, my chin smacking against the tamer's shoulder. He whips around in the saddle, makes eye contact with the guards as the beast lets out a roar.

The Ratón dives, claws out, bloodred eyes gleaming.

It's not one of mine. But it wants me all the same.

Arturo jumps off his stallion and then yanks me down. He pulls me to the wagon where the two guards have already opened the wooden chest. Arturo glances upward, gaze narrowing on the dragon as it lets out another roar.

"Hunting?" one of the guards asks.

Arturo nods grimly. "Protect the woman."

The second guard pulls out a cloak that's made of dried grass. It smells like it's come from the bottom of the river—fishy and damp. He hands it to me. "Put this on, señorita."

I look at Arturo, whose eyes follow the flying beast. "What is this?"

"Put it on," he repeats. "And then run a hundred feet from the wagons and hide beneath the cloak until I say it's safe."

"What about you?" I glance inside the chest, but there's no other weapon. No extra bow or sword. I don't understand how he can possibly protect himself.

He forces his attention away from the dragon. "Stop fighting me and do what I say."

"But—"

Arturo glances up. "*¡Ahora!*"

The dragon swoops, and I pull the cloak around me as I bolt away from the group. My feet pound against the russet earth, kicking up pebbles as I run. The long blades of grass tickle my nose and the pungent odor makes me sneeze, and I lose precious seconds when my eyes water and I have to slow down in order not to trip. A shadow materializes above me, and there's a loud crackling noise that rents the air.

"Señorita! The hood!" Arturo roars from somewhere behind me.

I snap the hood of the cloak in place as a burst of heat engulfs me. I drop to the ground and scream and scream under the cover of the dried grass, curling myself into a tight ball. Images of my burning mother fill my mind. I'm going to die just like she did. Tears stream down my cheeks, and my body winds itself in knots. It's unrelentingly hot. So, *so* hot. I'm locked in a furnace. Sweat drips into my stinging eyes. The smell of the grass intensifies with the frightening heat of the blast.

The pressure against the cloak eases, and then it's quiet.

I let out a shuddering gasp. My body wasn't burned to a crisp. I reach out and touch the grass. It's plain and dried with long blades the color of a dead, moldy lime. This is what saved me.

My ears strain to hear what's happening. Slowly, I lift the corner of the cloak to peer out and toward the wagons. The blades obscure sight, and I brush the leaves aside. The dragon lands on the ground at a run, racing for the tamer—who stands alone. He's brought up his shield to the level of his chin and his feet are shoulder width apart. Sunlight reflects off the metal, and it's hard to stare at it directly. I search for the guards, but they're nowhere in sight.

The dragon slows when he's a few feet from the tamer. It's three times the size of a human. Sweat coats my palms as I lift the cloak higher, the grass rustling. Arturo told me to stay hidden, but all I want to do is run for my life. The effort to remain motionless makes my legs shake. I lift the cloak higher, the dry grass rustling loudly.

The dragon jerks his face in my direction.

It takes a giant step toward me. Arturo slaps his shield with the flat of his hand, but the dragon has seen me, sees the smoke curling from the dried grass. It's confused I'm still alive. The dragon lets out a roar as it lunges toward me.

"Now!" Arturo roars.

The two guards jump to their feet from behind the dragon, hidden by knee-length shrubbery. Something long and thin blurs past and smacks at the soft flesh behind the dragon's neck. The beast shudders and a shrill cry poisons the air. Its wings flap, and warm air rushes toward me. Dirt is flung into my eyes. Then the dragon launches itself upward, blood dripping onto Arturo and the guards. Thick drops splatter everywhere.

I shove the cloak and stand as the dragon flies higher and higher, disappearing so fully I might have imagined its terrifying presence.

Arturo glares at me. "Why can't you do what you're told?"

I take a step back—from his expression, from his tone. "It attacked me!"

"I said to stay hidden, didn't I? You could have been hurt."

I can't bring myself to admit how badly I wanted to flee, to run for my life. "I wanted to make sure you were all right."

He wrinkles his nose in distate as if my words were nothing better than rotten eggs. "I had it under control—and because of you, there's a wounded dragon flying around near the city. Nothing is more danger-ous than a wounded beast. *Nothing.*"

"It's done," one of the guards says, picking up the cloak. It's scorched and near crumbling in his hands. "Your charge is safe, and you don't know what the dragon will do now. No sense in worrying."

Arturo scoffs, but turns away to check on the other beasts.

"What is that cloak?" I ask.

"It's called griminea," the guard says. "It only grows for three days in the mountains to the north. Fire-repellent grass—if treated and dried properly. Arturo spent years collecting it." The guard fingers the blades gingerly. "It only has one good use in it."

He drops the cloak and joins Arturo and the other guard near the wagons. I trudge after them, unable to stop thinking about that cloak made of grass and how the tamer had spent years making it.

And how he'd given it to me.

QUINCE

We arrive in Santivilla as the noon bell tolls from the cathedral in the main plaza, far away from the desert and hills, cloudy weather and caged dragons. The tamer hasn't said another word to me in miles and miles, and my legs are sore from the ride. As we draw closer to La Giralda, my stomach clenches. I'd left home days earlier, in a terrible rush and with my mother's engagement ring. Lola promised to care for Papá, and I left her plenty of coin to pay for the healer's services. Papá might still be in bed resting. Or he might be wondering where all the money has come from.

I hope he understands why I did what I had to do.

We turn a corner, and La Giralda looms before us, round and battle weary with scorched walls and chipped paint. Carriages fill the cobbled streets, barreling past our dragon arena without slowing down like they once did. There used to be rows of artists capturing La Giralda's likeness, paintings sold for good coin in the market. But they've moved onto landmarks that don't bear the stink of disgrace. It isn't only the artists who are missing—usually, foreigners love to stop and visit the ring of the most famous Dragonador in Hispalia. The main foyer is always open to the public where there are dozens of paintings showcasing our family's ancestors, as well as a chance to see some of Papá's old trajes de luces.

But the marble steps leading up to the great doors are empty. I've always thought our arena would outlast the ravages of time, but now I see how horribly naive I was to think so. This building isn't immortal, and if I don't do my part to save it, its name will turn to dust like the rest of us. I can't let that happen.

"Where are your stables?" Arturo asks.

I'm about to reply when one of the dragons lets out a tremendous howl. I whip around, turning so my body is half facing the beasts. The Morcego rams its body against the iron bars, trying to break free.

"Those cages are secure?"

When he doesn't reply, I poke his back and he grunts. Both dragons are now slamming against their prisons, snarling and shooting bursts of flame. Onlookers scramble away with shouts of alarm.

"I can't have another disaster right out front of La Giralda."

"If you're going to doubt me in *this*," he says sharply, pointing to the cages, "then I suggest we part ways right now."

"Will you stop growling at me? It was only a question," I mutter as he pulls up the reins in front of the arena. I climb down and turn toward the creatures. They're using their claws to scratch at the iron. "Why are they acting this way?"

Arturo hops off his horse. "They've never been around this many people before. They're scared."

The dragons let out another burst of fire, and a nearby stand of oranges bursts into flames. The owner of the produce glares at me. "*Scared?*"

"We need to get them off this avenue," he says, his attention on the slowing carriages. Curious onlookers poke their heads out the windows and point fingers at the beast. People strolling on the street stop to gape at the monsters, some rush away with alarmed yelps. But many more crowd several feet away from the cages to look at the wild drag-ons, without any adornment or clipped wings. Everyone has seen them flying, even more in the arena, but to see them on the street like this is highly unusual.

I ought to have known. Papá must use the street in the back to un-load them whenever a new shipment arrives. I've never been involved in that process; it was always Papá who sorted the dragons upon their arrival and assigned them pens in our dungeons.

"Stay back," Arturo snaps as the crowd draws closer. Many of them look twice at Arturo, at his unruly dark wavy hair, the hard lines of his shoulders, the sardonic curve of his mouth, and the feral gleam in his eyes. He is a gathering tempest over calm waters.

I scan the cluster of spectators, looking for our traveling companions, and as I do, my gaze snags onto a lone figure at the top of the steps. He's dressed in a fine suit, dark pants, and a crisp linen shirt tucked in, and even from here, I can see it doesn't fit him as well as it used to. The clothes hang off his thin frame. My breath catches as my eyes travel up to his face.

It's my father, a thunderous expression stretched across his features.

He's pale and wan but *standing*.

Relief hits me square in the chest, and tears gather in my eyes. I haven't seen him standing since the day of the massacre. It's enough to make my knees shake. Arturo follows the line of my gaze, and when he sees the most famous Dragonador in Hispalia, his reaction isn't what I expect. There's a subtle tightening of his shoulders, the slightest flare of his nostrils. When most people see Papá, they tend to stumble over themselves, wanting to flatter, to touch, to own a piece of him. I'm used to my father not belonging to me. His fans, his audience and supporters, all have roots, sprouting and tangling into our lives.

I've long given up carrying shears.

But this tamer doesn't exhibit any of the reactions I've seen all my life. I ought to be pleased that he doesn't want to rush over, ignoring me and everyone else, but instead, his indifference, the quiet dislike marking his face, sends a flutter of annoyance through me.

"He's a proud man," I say quietly. "I wouldn't disrespect him."

Arturo's gray eyes slide to mine, and in their depths, there is that awful look of contempt he carries like a shield. He despises who we are, what we do, and how we've chosen to survive. Papá's attention focuses on the tamer with an unrelenting stare. Even from where I stand, I can see his own growing dislike.

I look at Arturo as if for the first time, to see what my father is seeing. Papá will have to accept my plan for La Giralda, and that includes this dragon tamer. Every detail about him, from his dark clothing, the scowl carved against his skin, and his sharp tone, is meant to ward off anyone wanting to get close. Arturo is a walking fortress.

The dragons grow restless in their cages as Papá walks down the steps, shoulders straight, jaw set, and hands steady. My gaze narrows. The effort costs him. He's grown thinner, and his skin is pale and drawn with deep grooves marching across his brow. I've never seen him look so old in my life, not even when Mamá died, and terror reaches into my heart and squeezes. He shouldn't be out here, shouldn't be out of bed.

I rush to Papá once he reaches the cobbled avenue. He takes me into his arms, and I breathe in the scent of chicory, pressing my cheek against his soft tunic. "Papá, go back inside. I'm handling everything."

He squeezes me and then gently sets me aside to walk closer to the dragons. He studies them, his features somber and grim, before turning on the ball of his foot to face Arturo.

"I'd like to speak with both of you in my office." He takes my hand. "Ahora."

I let them go to the office first while I rush to the kitchen. Ofelia is busy washing dishes in the large wood tub, humming softly to herself. As soon as I walk inside the room, she lets out a harsh cry and rushes to me, her wet, soapy hands grasping my own.

"You said it was going to be a quick outing," she says in an accusing tone. "It's been days, Zarela! Lola has been useless with information, your father nervous, and we've suddenly had repairers walking in and out of La Giralda, carrying buckets of paint, ruining the carpet with their muddy feet. Where have you been?"

I squeeze her hands. "I can't explain now. Papá wants to see me in his study. Do we have tea? Coffee? Lunch?"

Ofelia gives me a disapproving look. "It's like you don't know me at all." She lets go of me and immediately pulls a wood tray from one of the shelves. "Who else have you brought with you? Here, slice this."

She hands me day-old bread, judging by its rough texture, and a knife. I start cutting. "I've hired a new tamer, and Papá is meeting him for the first time, and I need this conversation to go well."

Because I've already paid him, and we can't afford to find another. I don't say this out loud, though she must know the financial strain we're experiencing.

"Your father has been so worried," Ofelia says in a reproachful tone as she adds food to the tray: a bowl of green olives marinated in olive oil, slices of jamón and manchego, and a small plate of seasoned tomatoes. "He insisted on getting out of bed."

Guilt lances me. "But I sent word."

Ofelia waves her hand airily. "Vague information."

"What has Eva said?" I ask.

She gives me the tray. "His fever has gone down, but she's worried about a relapse. He needs plenty of rest, and he needs to be eating. Ask me how he's doing there."

I open my mouth to do so, but she starts up again.

"The only thing he'll eat is toast!" she cries. "Lola begged him to eat the oxtail I prepared, but he didn't have a bite. I don't understand. He loves oxtail."

"I'll get him to eat."

Loud pattering of feet draws closer, and I whip around in time to see Lola burst through the kitchen door. "You're back!"

She's breathless, carrying a bundle of sheets. Her hair is loose and wild, and Ofelia eyes it disapprovingly. The familiar dynamic warms my heart, tugs a reluctant smile across my face.

"What have I missed?" she demands, dropping the heap onto one of the stools.

Ofelia scowls. "Don't leave that there! Take it straight to the washing."

We both ignore her, and I hide my smirk as I catch sight of Ofelia throwing her hands up in the air. Lola pulls me into a tight hug. She smells like clean linen and coffee. A pang of regret pierces my heart. I'd left her to look after so much.

"I can't talk long. Papá is with—"

"The tamer," Lola finishes, stepping away. "I saw from the window. He has beautiful hair. I knew you'd get him to say yes to fight in the arena."

"Not exactly." I clear my throat. "He's going to be training me. I'm going to take my father's place."

Lola's jaw drops. She opens and closes her mouth, and then sputters, "But what will you wear?"

It's so like Lola to say exactly the right thing. Tension lifts off my shoulders and I laugh.

She looks at me serious and grave. "Leave it to me—I'll design the perfect outfit. Of course I'll have to order the materials from Valentia because Santivilla's fabric choices are just awful."

The coastal town, famed for its beaches and paella made of squid and mussels and fragrant saffron rice, and avenues paved in marble was the city of her birth, along with my mother's. Mamá's family owns a charter company specializing in taking well-paying customers out to the glittering blue waters hugging the coast in the hopes of catching a sea monster or spotting a sirena. Mamá always said she was never made for the sea and ran away to marry my father who promised to always keep her on solid ground. It's a fancy town, and my parents and I used to travel every year to visit my grandparents. Outside of Santivilla, it's my favorite place in the world.

Papá and I haven't gone back since Mamá died.

Ofelia stomps over to us. "Lola! The washing!"

Lola winks at me before picking up the sheets and darts away before Ofelia can lightly smack her with the nearby broom. She's been known to do that, especially when I sass her.

I take the tray and then climb up the stairs, thoroughly aware of the grimy state of my clothing and my hair hanging in dirty clumps down my back. For a moment, I contemplate changing, but angry voices drift down the corridor. I hold still, trying not to rattle the plates and cups, and lean forward, ears straining to catch their conversation.

"I want your word as a caballero," Papá says coldly. "You will not say a word to her."

The hair on my arms stands on end.

"Señor, I'm no caballero. My parents always worked, you see," comes Arturo's dry voice. "I'm as common as the dirt in the arena and no gentleman."

"Then swear on your honor," Papá says in that same winter-frost voice.

There's a long moment of silence.

"Why should I?" Arturo says at last.

"You'll be rewarded."

I clench my fingers around the tray until the knuckles turn white.

"With what money? La Giralda barely lives."

"Zarela must survive," Papá says.

An uncanny tingle skips down my spine. In the space of a few minutes, Arturo revealed my plan to fight in the arena—*to my father*. I groan loudly. This is *not* how I wanted him to find out. I was going to prepare my argument, confront the conversation logically, and reason with him.

"Then keep her out of the arena," Arturo says coldly.

Papá sighs. "You've met my daughter; you know what she's like."

My hands jerk in surprise, and the cups slide, clinking loudly. The talking abruptly stops.

The door flies opens, and Arturo leans against the frame, glaring at me. "How long have you been standing there?"

I bristle at his sharp tone. "Are you questioning my right to stand where I wish in my own house?"

"I'm questioning your manners since you've clearly been eavesdropping." He opens the door wider, and I breeze by with my chin high in the air. I wait for him to help me with the heavy tray, looking at him expectantly.

He does not.

"I don't know why you think you can speak to me the way you do," I say as I place the tray onto the desk. Arturo doesn't bother replying. I turn toward my father, who sits in his chair, a grim expression marring his features. I don't like the green cast to his skin, don't like the way he's slumped down into the leather chair.

And I don't like how he's looking at me as if I've betrayed him.

"Papá, I—"

"You and I will have words later, Zarela," he says, and while he sounds angry, his eyes tell me something else entirely. I've scared him.

"Someone has to," Arturo says in an undertone. He helps himself to a plate and settles onto one of the leather chairs facing the desk. I don't know why I thought hiring him was a good idea.

I clear my throat and address my father, though I'm unable to meet his gaze again. "Will you eat something?"

"I'm not hungry, tesoro," Papá says.

Tesoro. Treasure.

He used to call me that all the time whenever I was upset or had just had a fight with Mamá. The word worked like honey, sweet and golden, a balm against whatever had gone wrong that day. Usually a dance routine I had a hard time with, my mother wanting me to wear my hair a certain way or telling me to put on makeup to go to the market.

She'd know how to get him to eat.

I load a plate with food and set it in front of him with a cheery smile. "Have something for me, then."

From behind me, Arturo mutters under his breath, "The man said no."

I sit in the last available chair and glower at Arturo. "He needs to eat."

"He *needs* his daughter to listen to him," Arturo says, exasperated. "He said he wasn't hungry."

Papá continues to study us, and for some unfathomable reason, his brow clears. He settles back against his chair, and his mouth bends into a soft smile.

"No one but me and Lola stands up to my daughter," Papá says. "And sometimes I can't manage even that. She's had her way far too often, and it's mostly my fault. My wife never spoiled her, and now I'm paying the price. I believe you'll do fine at La Giralda, Señor Díaz de Montserrat."

My jaw drops. My father is usually charming with strangers. He can make you feel special and wanted, but the way he's treating this tamer isn't typical. He's just this side of polite, and a trifle too honest—the kind of honesty that doesn't paint me in a flattering light.

He never reveals anything private about our family to people he doesn't know.

The tamer pops an olive into his mouth. "Just Arturo is fine."

"Do you two know each other?" I ask finally, as Arturo continues eating and my father resists even a crumb of food. The realization that I'm clearly not wanted for this conversation hits me like a slap to the face. Neither replies to my question and my frustration rises, like the tide battering the seashore. After all, this was *my* idea.

Papá and Arturo ignore me. I reach for a plate and pile it high with olives and manchego, fighting resentment.

"So now you're hunting dragons," Papá says. His words are harmless enough, but his tone isn't. There's a strong current of disapproval.

Arturo dredges a slice of bread through the olive oil. I tally the cost to replace the nearly empty jar in my mind. "What of it?"

"Didn't you work for a season in Hector's arena?"

He shrugs.

My eyes widen. Arturo worked for my uncle? Interesting. And I can't believe his rudeness. Would it destroy him entirely to be civil? I half turn in my chair to face my father, fully expecting him to roar with outrage, but instead, Papá seems unbothered by this rude young person eating most of the food.

"Just to clarify, how do you two know each other *exactly*?" I demand again.

But neither responds, and instead, they exchange a silent communication that I can't understand or interpret. How do they know each other? There aren't that many Dragonadores in Santivilla—only the best graduate. It's possible their careers overlapped.

"From where did you study?" Papá asks quietly.

Arturo blinks, clearly not expecting the interrogation. I open my mouth, burning with questions, but Arturo quickly cuts me off. "San Jorge."

"The best Dragonador school in Hispalia. Why are you not fighting in the ring?"

Arturo shoots him a pointed look, loaded with meaning. "I will never fight again, not for anything. Fighting dragons should be a thing of the past."

I bite back my retort. Not this argument again.

"Why," Papá says, "do you think the tradition continues after three thousand years?"

"Money, why else?"

"A cynical person would answer me that way. Dragonadores exist to show the people of Hispalia that dragons can be beat. We can have victory against the formidable beasts. People are attacked every day, villages destroyed by fire, children murdered in their sleep. We fight to give hope."

Papá's passionate eyes shine brilliantly when he talks about his life's work. But that isn't the only thing I notice. There's more gray in his hair than I remember, more grooves fanning from the corner of his eyes.

"There are other ways to inspire hope than carrying on a tradition that broadens the divide between dragon and man," Arturo says quietly.

"I think traditions ought to be honored," I say.

"There's a way to respect where people have been while adapting and embracing progress."

"Except our reality is still the same as it was when dragonfighting began—we are still at war," I say.

"Only because we haven't attempted anything else," Arturo snaps.

"They aren't *dogs*," Papá says. "They will always crave human flesh, will always use their strength to destroy. They can't be trained."

Something flashes in Arturo's eyes, but it's gone in an instant. Papá doesn't notice, but I do.

"I believe you will teach my daughter well," Papá says after a beat. "She is my greatest treasure. You must see that she's prepared—I'm holding you responsible."

Arturo glances at me, and for once, that haughty scowl isn't on his face. He appears indecisive, as if regretting accepting the position.

"Remember the money," I say. "And what you'll gain."

"Remember," Papá murmurs, "what I'm owed."

My brows raise. "What has Arturo done to be in debt to you, Papá?"

"Old business from his Dragonador days," Papá says coolly. "That's everything for now, Arturo."

Arturo stands and with a curt nod, leaves the room. The sudden silence makes me squirm in my seat. I brace myself for the conversation coming.

Papá doesn't make me wait too long. He stares at me grimly, hands laced right in his lap, as if he can't bear to hear the words from the looming conversation. "Zarela, who gave you permission to fight in the arena?"

"I'm sorry for the way you found out," I say softy. "But I *will* become a Dragonador. It was the only decision to make."

"I don't believe that," he says. "Find someone else. Write to the dragonfighting school, ask them if they have anyone available—"

"Hector assured me that most Dragonadores are under contract somewhere else." I hesitate, not wanting to hurt him. I inhale deeply and prepare to stick a knife between his ribs. "La Giralda has lost all respect, and the chances of another Dragonador battling in our arena are low. Besides, we don't have the money to pay for one, even if there is someone. It has to be me, Papá. Your daughter, known as a dancer, but now a Dragonador. People will be curious." I squeeze my eyes shut, unwilling to see his face when I remind him of the truth. "And your Dragonador days are over."

My words are met with silence. I open my eyes to find him huddled deep in his chair, his face in his hands, shoulders shaking. "Your mother would never allow it," he says hoarsely, between his fingers. His face has lost its healthy glow, a stark contrast to his tanned hands. "What kind of father would I be to permit you to do this?"

"There's no other way forward," I say. The old ache rises and clutches my heart in a tight fist. "Mother isn't here."

"Where did the money come from?"

I take a deep breath and tell him the truth.

All of it.

Papá wilts before me, as if he were a flower beaten down by the sun's rays. My hands clasp tight in my lap, and I breathe deeply to fight my heart's battering assault against my ribs. We are mirror images of each other. Shoulders held straight, carrying heavy burdens, the both of us hurt, grieving Mamá, and with identical fighting spirits. I did the right thing. I know I did, and he knows it too, however much he may not like it.

"You should have asked me first."

"You were unconscious."

His dark eyes flash. "Zarela, you had *no* right."

"What else could I have done? You needed medicine, repairs must be made, our dragons were murdered, the tamers have died." I splay my hands. "Tell me how I could have done better."

His shoulders sag, and I reach forward across the desk and lay my hand out with my palm facing up. Papá's face crumbles as he grasps my hand, fingers trembling. "Perhaps you ought to go back to bed. You're still not well."

"Lola arranged for Eva to come today," he says with a grimace. "The pain is constant."

I can sense his frustration and the underlying terror he feels to have death so near, the wolf at the door in a room with no escape. I can see the way it makes his hands tremble. "Why haven't you eaten?"

He shakes his head, wincing. "Nothing sounds good."

A frown pulls at my brows. He shouldn't be out of bed, shouldn't be worrying about La Giralda. The stress won't help his recovery. He seems to be thinking along the same lines because his expression settles into weary resignation. "This isn't the Hispalia of my youth, hija. I never would have dreamed that someone would have snuck into La Giralda with the intent of hurting us. Setting the dragons free, murdering the rest. Poor Benito."

With everything else going on, I hadn't spent any time dwelling on who was responsible for the disastrous anniversary event. "We should try to find that person."

"It's too dangerous."

"But—"

"Zarela," he says, wheezing. "Look at me. I can't help you the way I want to. You're going to be fighting in the arena, and all of your focus should be on your training. At least until—"

"Until what?"

He flushes and averts his gaze. Whatever he's about to say costs him. "Perhaps . . . it might be time to . . ."

My mouth thins. I know what he's going to suggest, but even without the words hanging between us, my palms coat with sweat. "What, Papá?"

"Perhaps we ought to think about a suitable husband for you. You're eighteen years old. Truthfully, I should have started thinking about this much earlier. All the señoritas your age are married with babies on the way."

"Lola isn't," I remind him.

"That's because she has several older sisters, and her mother has too many to worry over. I have no such excuse."

I look at our joined hands. I think about all the reasons why his idea is a terrible one. I discard one thought after another, searching for a reason that won't hurt him. I can't tell him what I've seen and heard outside of La Giralda's walls. How we'd be lucky if our name brought in even a third of ticket buyers—let alone a *suitable* husband. I can't tell him the bachelors he'd like me to consider won't consider *me*, a señorita with a ruined last name and a legacy that's lost its promise. "I want what you and Mamá had. I won't settle for less."

"Zarela—"

"Give me time," I say. "Let me try to fix our situation my way."

"How long?"

"One dragon fight. If the sales aren't back to what they once were, I'll find a man to marry." The words nearly choke me. "Someone you approve of."

He nods, and the deal is made.

I can't help feeling that I'm taunting fate by even suggesting it.

DIECISÉIS

I settle Papá back in bed and force him to drink water, and then he drifts to sleep, his brow wrinkled and drawn. I smooth his graying hair off his face and then place a soft kiss on his cheek.

Papá snores softly, and I smile, happy to see him making noise. He's been too quiet, too soft.

The meeting with the dragon tamer gave me hope. Papá was out of bed—terribly weak, but *out of bed*, and holding his ground against Arturo and his curt replies and secrets.

My thoughts snag on the wild-rough handsome face.

Skin as rich and deep as polished amber, eyes frigid and gray like a gathering storm. I flush for a reason I don't want to name. What happened for him to choose another path? Once you're in a gremio, you can't just leave and start another life. It's a commitment that's supposed to last for the rest of your days. People of Santivilla don't look kindly to those who divorce from their gremios. It's a rule that isn't written down anywhere, but some rules are like that. They don't need to be official to be true. So then, why would he break it? Something must have happened to change his mind so drastically. I make my way down the grand staircase, intent on finding the mysterious tamer. I'm directed to the dungeons.

My steps reverberate in the cavern, and voices reach my ears. Sounds of people arguing, their words on fire in the dark. Arturo and one of my guards.

Our new dragons are in their cages near the entrance of the dungeon, locked in individual cells. The lit torches cast monstrous, flickering shadows against the craggy walls. The beasts pace restlessly in circles, bodies scraping against their pens and clawing the stone floor. The sound grates, and I clench my teeth.

Arturo abruptly stops talking to the guard—arrested by something he sees in one of the empty cells. He draws closer, squatting and analyzing something on the ground. He has a handsome profile. Proud nose and rigid jawline, dark hair softly curling across his stern brow. I'm immediately annoyed that I notice. Arturo rubs his hands along the craggy wall and then holds up an index finger to his mouth and sniffs. Then he swivels on the balls of his feet and unerringly finds my eyes in the dim lighting. He glares at me, holding up a finger, stained in a shimmering substance.

The man is always glaring at me.

"Someone's been using strong magic down here." He points to a faint squiggly line glittering in the shadowed room. "See the remnants of the spell? The ones with more expensive ingredients often leave a residue. The potions are thicker, not like the cheaper spells you can buy with two copper coins."

I look to where he's gesturing. "Perhaps a cleaning spell?"

He frowns. "Maybe. But the encanto smells costly. Nothing like your run-of-the-mill mopping spell." Then he points to the dark puddles in one of the cells. "Dragon's blood," he says. "What happened here?"

I wrap my hand around the cell bar. Terror sizzles through me. Virtually all of the wands in La Giralda are dipped in inexpensive, short-lasting spells. "Powerful magic? *Why?*"

"How would I know?" Arturo asks in a curt tone. "I'm only telling you it was done." He points again to the floor. "The blood?"

My mind reels. I look around the dungeon, remembering the slayed dragons in their cells, and Benito lying dead in the shadows under the shining streaks of magia. None of this is a coincidence. Someone used an encanto to carry out their plans. *Who?*

I thread my hands through my hair. I consider marching to the Gremio right now, but the memory of the Dragon Master's skepticism keeps me rooted to the spot.

Don Eduardo won't believe me.

"Señorita?"

I blink, dragged back to this dark chamber filled with ghosts. "Sorry, what was your question?"

His eyes miss nothing, and I'm worried he'll see the rampant discord marching across my face.

"I wanted to know about the blood," he repeats slowly.

I hesitate, the words waiting in my throat. Arturo raises an impatient brow, as if he thinks I'm being a coward, but it's hard to lay myself open. There are very few people I trust. "I'll tell you, but only if you reserve any judgment until I'm finished, and you've heard what I have to say."

He slowly stands, watching me for a long considering second, and then asks neutrally, "Well?"

"On the day of the massacre, someone came and let loose our dragons." I point to the other end of the cellar. "Down that way leads to the arena. The dragons burst into the stadium, set fire to everyone in their reach, and escaped. All but three weren't set free, and they were in their cages. By the next morning, someone had come down and killed them while they slept."

Exasperation crosses his face. "Your security is appalling."

The guard clenches his fists, and I shoot him a look to settle the anger edging into his bulky frame. Arturo leans against the jagged cavern wall, booted feet crossed at the ankles, sinewy arms folded tight against his chest. I clear my throat. "Our security consisted of five tamers—they were the best money could buy and busy helping the hundreds of people exit La Giralda safely. They all died on the day of the massacre, save for one."

"Were all these cells full?"

I nod. "Yes. One dragon in each."

Arturo counts the pens. "Five tamers against nine? You call that ample security?"

He's right, and we both know it. My shoulders soften under his scrutiny, and I unlock my clenched jaw. Shame bubbles like acid deep in my belly. Failure isn't easy to admit, and I have to pull every word from where it wants to stay hidden. Ever since Mamá died, Papá hasn't been himself. I ought to have stepped in long before disaster stuck. "I should have done better."

"Have you brought all of this to the Dragon Master?"

"Of course I did." My lips twist. "He didn't think much of my suspicions."

Arturo raises his hand and gestures for me to continue. "Which are?"

I avert my gaze—not wanting to have another conversation where someone dismisses my ideas outright.

"I can't help you if you don't tell me," he says quietly.

My brows raise, along with a strange fluttering in my belly that takes me by surprise. "Help me?"

"I'll be working here," he says. "I'd like to make sure I'm not in mortal peril."

Right—that's reasonable, and the butterfly in my stomach vanishes. "I thought perhaps the Asociación was behind the massacre. They came the next day, leading a mob of people to march in front of the entrance of La Giralda."

Arturo glances at the remnants of magic glittering on the wall, brow puckering. "You might be right, but they couldn't have managed this on their own." He holds up his index finger, the one stained by magic. "The most potent of spells cost a lot of money, and the people who run with the Asociación don't have it. Most of them belong to lower-ranked guilds or the Gremio General. People belonging to those don't have two silver coins to rub against each other. I find it more likely they are working with someone else. Or rather, being *managed* by someone else."

Another unseen enemy. Terror closes around me like a tight fist. "I hope you're wrong."

Arturo's chin lowers. "I noticed there's a lock on the entrance in here. Who has access to the key?"

"My father, Ofelia—our maid who has been with us since my infancy—and myself."

"And where are they kept?"

I swallow nervously. "Mine is kept in a drawer in my room. My father has his around his neck at all times. Ofelia keeps one in the kitchen, hidden in a pot."

"Why does she have one?"

"She directs the workers who routinely clean the cellars."

"And you've checked to confirm yours is in your drawer?"

I place my hands on my hips. "You must think me an idiot."

He quirks a brow. "I don't think about you much at all, señorita. Certainly not enough to dwell on your intellect."

Mortification settles into my skin, creating a riot in my blood, flushing my cheeks and ears. The space feels tight between us, the walls too narrow and not enough air to breathe between us. "That was rude."

He lifts a cold shoulder. "So it was."

Annoyance burns the embarrassment away, and without thinking, I shoot him an obscene gesture with my finger, something Lola taught me.

I expect his fury and brace for it—but Arturo lets out an astonished shout of laughter, and the sound reverberates down the length of the dungeon. I can't keep the answering grin off my own face. His laughter dims to a small smile, and he mutters something that suspiciously sounds like *damn*.

We are quiet for a long beat, drawing away from each other and resuming old battle lines. "What about the other keys? Are they accounted for?" Arturo asks in a determinedly flat tone.

"I searched and found all three keys the day after the massacre."

"And since then? Are they still there?"

I blink. "I haven't checked or thought to look. Since they never went missing, I assumed the culprit used other means of entering the dungeon. Besides, nothing has happened since then . . ."

"If someone is trying to sabotage La Giralda, as you suspect, then those keys need to be secured in a safe location at all times. How do you know the culprit didn't return one of the keys after they freed your dragons?"

"But why risk discovery when they returned it?"

"Perhaps to deflect suspicion," he says darkly. "If they took a key to begin with, it suggests they know where it's hidden. Someone like that would have to be connected to La Giralda. A disgruntled guard or an angry maid."

His interrogation only reminds me of how much I've let fall through the cracks. I ought to have made it a point to talk to Ofelia and my father. I ought to have scheduled another meeting with the guild and demand they begin the investigation.

I'm not doing enough.

My words are seasoned with the potent taste of shame. "I should have thought of that."

His expression softens. "Well, I can't leave without confirming these dragons will be safe here." He turns to the guard. "Stay here until I return."

"Where are you going?" I ask.

"To speak with Ofelia, of course," he says over his shoulder as he darts away. He disappears up the steps. A moment later he comes back down again, scowling. "Where can I find Ofelia?"

I don't attempt to be polite and do nothing to fight the amused smile tugging at my mouth.

Arturo growls impatiently.

I laugh. "This way, tamer."

I can feel his breath on my neck as we climb. His presence suffocates, taking up too much space and impossible to ignore.

"Do you have something shiny?" he asks.

I stop and turn around. I'm two steps higher and at eye level. "Shiny?"

"It helps the dragons sleep," he says. "Gives them purpose, a job. When they have something to guard, they're less restless."

All I have left is whatever remains of my mother's possessions. And I'm not going to let a dragon have it. "Are you asking me to place jewelry in there?"

He shrugs. "Candlesticks work—if they're silver or gold."

"No silver or gold," I say. "I would have sold it by now."

I regret the words the moment they're out in the open. They reveal *far* too much. Several emotions cross Arturo's face. Surprise. Confusion. Pity.

I whirl around. I don't want his pity. I'm not someone to feel sorry for. I am the daughter of the most talented performers in Hispalia, and I will find a way for us to survive. I'll just need to work harder, that's all. When we reach the main floor, Arturo quickly steps around me and blocks my path, and then opens his mouth—but then immediately closes it.

"What?" I ask composedly.

He shakes his head, as if thinking better of it. When he turns away, he mutters, "Not my problem."

I lead him to the kitchens, and we're met with the yeasty scent of baked bread. Ofelia sits on the stool, slicing cucumbers and tomatoes.

"Gazpacho?" I ask.

She glances up with a soft smile. Her gaze flickers to Arturo and her smile vanishes. "Who is this caballero?"

"Ofelia," I say calmly. "This is our new dragon tamer. He'll be teaching me to fight in the arena. And thanks to him, we have two new dragons in the cellars."

"You mean thanks to your mother," she says sharply.

Arturo looks between us, dark brows quirking.

"Right," I mutter. "We're actually here—"

But Ofelia isn't done with her lecture, or with dragging our private business out into the open and in front of the last person I want knowing any of it. "You had better be worth it, caballero. This family has lost too much for you not to do your job with excellence. Do you know that Zarela had to sell her mother's things to make do?"

Arturo's expression turns to stone. "Mi nombre es Arturo, señora."

"That's all you have to say?"

Arturo places both palms flat on the island. "No. Where's the key to the cellar?"

Ofelia drops the serrated knife and walks over to a plain ceramic pot on the shelf. She empties the contents onto the table and out comes an old iron key. Then she sits down, an air of suspicion curling around her.

Arturo glares at the key as if it were singlehandedly responsible for every known disaster in Santivilla. He slips it into his tunic pocket. Ofelia stands, the stool shooting backward. I meet the tamer's gaze and raise a single brow.

"This one belongs to me," he says in a tone that demands no argument.

I don't protest, much to Ofelia's astonishment. For all of the tamer's faults, I know he cares for the dragons. He won't let anything happen to them. Not until the moment they step into the ring and their fate is out of his hands.

"Our maids have to clean down there!" Ofelia says. "I'm the one who—"

"Now it'll be me," Arturo says. "I'll be here first thing in the morning to see to the animals and lock the door behind me at the end of the day. The cages can be cleaned while I train the dragons. Take me to the other keys," he says. "Is there a place we can keep the spares? I don't trust they'll be safe otherwise."

Ofelia gasps. "Who are you to talk to her that way?"

I ignore her indignation, somehow knowing we'd only be wasting time. Arturo will want to see the keys for himself and won't budge no matter how she loudly she might squabble. "This way, tamer."

He follows me up the grand staircase, silent and watchful. I don't want him in my room, filling up the space with his judgment, his scowl and loud opinions. But nor do I want him to think I can't handle his presence or suspect that his gray eyes make my heart thump. I am *not* pleased by my attraction to this tamer. I don't want to wonder what his hands would feel like touching mine. I don't want to think about the iron line of his shoulders, or the way in which he calmly faces a monster.

I don't *want* to be impressed.

But I am. Damn it, I am.

The corridor holds the sound of our silence, the soft thud of our boots against the stone. We reach my chamber door, and I use my shoulder to push the heavy oak. I stride in, careful to keep my posture nonchalant. To my surprise, Arturo remains at the threshold, both feet out of my room. He takes a quick look inside, eyes latching on to the painted fans decorating the walls, the bed covered in a handsome embroidered quilt.

He clears his throat, and a faint blush spreads across his cheeks.

"Don't tell me you've never seen a woman's bedroom before."

Arturo scowls and leans against the frame. "Just find the key, will you?"

The key is exactly where I told him it would be, tucked in a drawer, hidden between old journals, pretty quills, and used bottles of ink. I hold it up to him, and his gaze narrows. There's a speculative gleam in his dark eyes as he considers the iron key in my palm. "Do you ever leave your door open?"

"Maybe during the day."

He trails a finger against the rough wood of the doorframe. "Who regularly comes in here?"

"Sometimes Papá. Lola and Ofelia do regularly."

He makes a noncommittal noise. I remember what he said about someone close to La Giralda taking one of the keys, and I don't like what he's implying. "They *wouldn't*."

"If you say so." He pauses. "Did it ever occur to you that someone who works here might have ties to the Asociación?"

I refuse to believe it. "You'll want to locate the third key," I say coldly, handing him mine.

He nods. "Y dónde está?"

"Third floor. With my father."

"Vamos."

But he remains at the threshold, his attention snagging on the dozens of fans decorating the walls. My mother painted all of them, something she'd do to calm down after an argument with my father. She had one for every fight, every season, every mood.

"I recognize that one," he says softly.

I follow his line of sight. The fan is painted black with an intricate pattern of gardenias, the petal edges golden and shimmering. She'd given me the fan for my first solo performance. I was so nervous, until I looked to the arena entrance where she stood hidden in the shadows. There she had danced with me, every stomp, every twirl in harmony with me.

The memory clenches my heart. I avert my gaze, eyes burning, throat on fire, and fight to push through the sudden stab of grief. When my vision clears, I brush past him and shut the door behind me with an audible snap.

"Papá's room is this way," I murmur as I walk the way we came and toward the stairs.

"You haven't asked me how I recognized the fan," he says, walking alongside my brisk steps.

I throw him a sidelong glance. "That was my first on my own."

"You're a beautiful dancer."

The words are so soft, I almost miss them. My gaze veers to his downturned face, to the way he resolutely refuses to meet my eyes, examining instead the toes of his boots.

"Gracias."

Arturo shrugs, as if to say that his compliment isn't anything special, as if it didn't rob me of breath. He follows me silently down the corridor and up the flight of stairs. There's no question that he'll wait outside while I venture alone into the darkened room. Papá sleeps profoundly, mouth slightly open, and soft puffs of air disturb the quiet of his bedroom. I creep closer to his bed, thankful for the slant of light pouring in from the windows.

He's a restless sleeper. The covers lay tangled by his feet, and one of the pillows is half under the nightstand. Both of his arms are stretched out, reaching for the ends of the bed. He lies vulnerable, with sunken cheeks and clothes much too big for him.

I can't get used to this new reality. Papá is young—younger than most fathers I know. Vitality is part of who he is, the great persona that entertains thousands while in the ring. He can't be dying.

I can't lose anyone else.

I lean forward and search for the long leather strip holding the iron key. I squint in the dim light, and at last I find it, half-hidden under my father's arm. Gently, I pry it loose. He doesn't wake, even as I quietly slip out of his room, the sound of his restless sleep drifting in my wake.

Arturo leans against the opposite wall in the hallway, arms folded, and ankles crossed. "Well?"

I hand him Papá's key. "All three are accounted for."

The tamer doesn't say anything for a long moment, head tilted forward so that his long hair sweeps forward, covering half his face. "You said all of your tamers died in the arena."

I shut the door behind me with a measured click. "Everyone except Benito."

"What happened to him?"

"He was murdered." I fold my arms across my chest to guard against the sudden chill against my skin. "Or he might have inhaled too much dragon smoke," I add bitterly, recalling my conversation with the Dragon Master.

"What do *you* think?" Arturo asks.

I splay my hands. "I believe he was murdered. But Don Eduardo doesn't think so. They said it was a common way to die if you're around dragons long enough."

"It is." He tucks a long strand of dark hair behind his ear, revealing the sharp line of his cheekbone. "But your dragons were let loose deliberately, and the rest were murdered. If I were you, I'd be suspicious of everything and everyone. I know I am."

Everything about him is meant to ward off people from drawing near. The dark, formidable clothing, that improbable hard gleam in his gray eyes, and the set of his jaw, a line sharp enough to cut through bone.

"You don't trust anyone?"

His lips thin. "Very few."

There's a weary bitterness in his tone I find particularly interesting. "Seems lonely."

"Does it?" he asks coolly.

I say something incredibly stupid. The words are out before I can think it through, before I can stop them. "You can trust me."

Our eyes meet, cold gray against warm brown. I can't name the raw emotion that flashes in their icy depths. "Really."

I lift my chin. It's too late to back off now. "Yes, you can."

He leans against the corridor wall, ankles crossed, somber. "The dragons I'm leaving in your care aren't safe here. I have half a mind to take them and go."

I blink at the change of subject. The quick dismissal of what I offered—friendship. I take a step forward and jab my index finger against his chest. "I paid for those dragons, tamer. They stay here."

He jerks his gaze to mine and grips my wrist. His hold is firm, but it doesn't hurt. "I never wanted to be a part of this."

Arturo might be talking about training me. But he also might be talking about something else entirely. Warmth spreads to my cheeks, heats my palms. "Let me go," I whisper. We're standing far too close, and he must realize it at the same time I do because he releases me in an instant. He clears his throat and steps away from me as if I were an open flame that needs to be put out.

"Fine. They'll stay," he says. "But I'm holding you personally responsible if anything happens to them outside that ring."

More responsibility. I'm drowning in it. "What do you suggest? All the keys are accounted for and in your possession."

His face is grim. "It's your problem to solve, not mine."

"Why do you care if the dragons are in danger here?" I snap. "They're going to die in the arena anyway."

"You think so? You'll have to fight them first, and I'm not betting on your victory," Arturo says calmly.

"*Outstanding.*"

But he's no longer paying attention to me. He scans the corridor, noting the many windows, and then he steps forward to glance down into the foyer from the balcony. "You're incredibly exposed here. From here on out, assume you're being watched. Take necessary precautions. Always have someone with you, wherever you go. Lock every door and every window at night. Don't assume someone else has done it."

My mouth goes dry and a cold shiver drags down my skin, like the icy finger of death's touch. "Duly noted," I croak.

"I'll see you tomorrow morning for training. Eighth bell. Don't be late." He straightens away from the balcony and descends the main staircase. I move to the railing, watching him depart, and when he reaches the first floor, he lifts his chin, unerringly meeting my gaze. I'm too far up to read his expression, and anyway, he quickly looks away. He shuts the front door behind him, and the sound carries up to the third floor, where I remain, struck dumb by a sudden realization.

He said it was my problem to solve, but he gave me suggestions anyway. Warned me of the potential danger. Bade me to check all entry points into La Giralda.

It felt protective.

Before I go to bed, I do as he recommended and make sure all the doors and windows are shut tight. I check in on Papá and Lola and Ofelia, and everyone is where they should be, breathing and safe from whatever dangerous threat is circling my home.

But it doesn't keep me from lying awake most of the night, listening for sounds of someone breaking in.

DIECISIETE

The tamer is late.

The eighth bell strikes as I wait by the front entrance of La Giralda, enduring the incessant yelling of the protestors and awful banners insulting my family name. But while I see the usual morning traffic, Arturo is nowhere in sight. I braced myself all morning for his scowl and ill humor. Nerves wreak havoc on my body, anticipating the first day of training. I peer up and down the cobbled street.

Nothing.

I turn away from the entrance in a huff, refusing to look at the growing size of the crowd for a moment longer. A hundred people march in front of the arena, demanding the building to be burned down, demanding our heads, demanding justice for monsters. Interacting with them is out of the question. There's no rational conversation to be had with a mob.

Frustration slicks down the length of my back. I need a cup of coffee. I stride across the foyer, my boot heels thudding against the floor, my mood as black as an onyx stone. When I reach the kitchen, my nose doesn't catch a whiff of what I'm craving.

"No coffee?" I ask Ofelia.

She pauses in rolling the dough for tomorrow's breakfast. "All out, I'm afraid."

I'm about to ask her to brew another pot when Lola ambles inside, yawning hugely, but at least dressed for the day. She sits down with an indelicate slump on one of the stools at the island and bats her eyelashes at Ofelia, who remains stone-faced. I hide a grin behind my hand. Then Ofelia places huevos revueltos in front of Lola, and the plate makes a loud clanking sound against the wood.

Lola grimaces. "You know how I feel about loud noises in the morning."

"And you know how I feel about your staying out all hours of the night," Ofelia hisses. "You're late."

Lola yawns again, and I laugh. Ofelia glares at me. "And you're enabling her!"

I give her a sheepish grin and then watch my friend devour the smoking hot eggs. "I need you to deliver a message for me."

Lola pauses her chewing. "Where to?"

"I need a favor from Guillermo."

She lowers her fork. "He won't do it. He's such a stickler for the rules and won't risk the Gremio de Magia's wrath by helping you."

I bite my lip. I haven't any money to spare. "Then you might have to use your persuasive charm."

"He's totally immune," Lola says with disgust. "It's like I'm *invisible*."

I watch her closely. "Do you really care for him?"

"Yes," she says reflexively. Then her eyes widen. "I meant, only if *he* does."

"So he doesn't listen to you?"

She scoffs. "Hardly. He never agrees with me either. So strange."

Honestly, I'd laugh if she didn't look so miserable. But I was hoping she'd be able to talk to him for me. His input on the mysterious encanto used in the dungeon would be helpful. I think fast for a solution worth his while.

"Tell him he can have the next dead dragon for free," I say.

"It won't work."

"He might surprise you."

Lola rolls her eyes. "I'll try. What do you want me to say?"

"Ask him to come by in the evening," I say. "Without telling anyone."

She raises her brows, but nods again and finishes eating. With a quick wave, she leaves out the side door. Ofelia stares after her. "What about the beds? The washing?"

"I can make my own bed," I say, heading for the door.

"I can make more coffee," Ofelia grumbles. "It will be just a minute. I have to grind the beans."

I sigh. And how much will that cost me? But then her words sink in, and it stops me cold. "More?"

She drops the dough into a bowl and places an old rag on top. "Your tamer drank it all."

"My *what*?"

"He ate most of the smashed tomatoes and bread too. A good deal of jamón and olives, and several slices of the manchego. He came hungry."

"¿Cuándo?" I sputter. "When did he get here?"

Ofelia grabs a handful of Hispalian oranges and cuts them half. "He didn't get to the juice. I saw to that. Only a handful left, and I promised your father."

"Ofelia."

She squeezes three oranges into a small glass. "He was here an hour ago. I believe he went to check on the dragons."

I spin on the balls of my feet and head to the dungeon entrance. The guard from yesterday bids me a buenos días.

"Where is he?" I ask.

"In the arena."

Of course he is. I race along the same tunnel used by the dragons and burst out onto the hot sand, where giant sections are still stained with blood. I make a mental note to stay on top of the repairs, including ordering the same white sand my father prefers. I reach the middle of the arena, so distracted by what else I need to do that I miss key information. There's no sight of the tamer. I spin around, blinking under the morning sun, but I'm alone out here.

A low whistle cuts the quiet. Soft and insistent.

I glance in the direction of the noise, and there, sitting as casually as you please, is Arturo, up in the stadium amidst the cracked and scorched stone. He stands and carefully picks his way through the debris. The masons working on the seating ought to have started by now. He hoists himself above the perimeter wall, which stands shoulder height to my father, and leaps over and lands on both feet, as if he were a nimble cat.

"I don't like to be kept waiting," Arturo says.

This is his greeting. No hola or buenos días, just an accusation. And I know he's had café, so there's no excuse.

"I was at the front entrance," I say when he's within hearing range, because I'm not shouting to be heard, and especially not before I've had coffee. "Did you have to drink all of it?"

He considers my question. "Yes, I did."

"I was expecting you at the eighth bell, not the seventh."

He circles around me in the same manner a predator might when stalking its prey. I turn with him, instinctively not wanting to give him my back.

"Annoying, isn't it?" he asks mildly. "Having a stranger in your home when you least expect it?"

"Are we back to that? That was miles behind us. Literally."

He glances down at his fingernails. "You know, I find I'm still sore about it."

"Will you just begin with your training?"

He smiles to himself, a private smirk that I'm sure he wants me to wonder about. But I don't care what thoughts clog his mind. This morning, I woke with the strangest pressure in my chest. The first day to prove myself capable of saving Papá.

Saving our home.

Arturo leans forward with his smile that might be evil, but certainly mischievous, and his dark eyes glittering. "Then let's work."

A deep roar comes from the tunnel entrance. Scratching noises rend the air amidst someone else panting sharp huffs of air—two some-ones. Arturo's guards come into view, leading one of the dragons—the

Morcego—by long chains. The metal clatters against the stone until they drag the beast onto the bloody sand. It snaps its jaws and lets out another roar. Around its snout is a leather muzzle that keeps the beast from yelling too loudly—or from breathing fire. Each horn on either side of its trapezoidal head is a foot long, capable of goring anyone who dares come close.

I have to breathe through my nose to keep myself from fainting. The dragon's nearness makes the muscles up and down my body roll with tension. Dimly, I hear Arturo give his men orders, but the words are garbled and out of reach, like the elusive stars that only come out at night.

Fear takes root deep in my belly, and I rebel against it. I drag more air into my lungs. Slowly, my heart returns to its normal, steady beat. The guards stand on either end of the dragon, hands tight on the chains, their muscles straining against the writhing monster. They fight for a scrap of control against such a beast.

"The Morcego," Arturo says, coming to stand next to me. "What do you know about this animal?"

"Not much," I admit. "Traditionally used in dragonfighting for thousands of years, replacing the gladiators who fought in the rings by our ancestors. Their horns are deadly, made of ivory and quite valuable. After each fight, the horns are given as gifts to prominent Masters and members at other gremios."

"That's the tradition," Arturo says impatiently. "I'm asking what you know"—he marches closer to the beast and points at it—"about this creature."

"Breathes fire," I say, wanting to have that particular ability myself in this precise moment. "Short, bat-like wings, thus its namesake, despite its strong resemblance to a bull. A flier."

"Bien," Arturo says. "What else?"

I think hard and finally come up with something else. "If it drinks water, it can't breathe fire for up to an hour."

"That's true of all dragons," he says. "Even the spitting ones."

I splay my hands. "That's all I know about them."

The tamer turns fully to face me, leaving his back exposed and placing enormous trust on his guards and their ability to control the monster. "All dragons don't see color—except for the color red. We don't know why that is, but we do know that it was the first Dragon Master, Alvaro Baltasar, who deemed that all capotes, the capes used during the fight, come in that hue." He strides to the wall perimeter and picks up a rolled bundle of fabric. Then he hands it over, thrusting it at me. His fingers brush mine, and a jolt zips up my arm. "Have you ever held it?"

I shake my head. The capote is heavier than I imagined. Slowly I unfurl it, and the fabric catches the slight breeze, faintly rustling. It's another hot, blue-sky day in Santivilla, and sweat beads at my hairline.

"Hold it up and against whatever side of your body is the most comfortable," Arturo says. "It weighs fifteen pounds. It'll take some getting used to."

"Is using both hands all right?"

He gives a curt nod. "Practice waving it around, but never allow the cape to remain directly in front of your body. Always keep it moving from one side to the other."

The cape seems to have a mind of its own. The fabric swishes and dances in the air, and I struggle to maintain control. Arturo lets me fumble for a moment before coming up behind me to grasp the capote on either side of my hands. The weight in my palms lessens, now that he's helping me. It's manageable, but now my attention focuses on his whisper-soft breath at the back of my neck. His body is close to mine, radiating heat and confidence, and warmth floods my cheeks. I want to shove him away, to create enough distance between us so that I don't feel so affected by his nearness.

"Like this." His hand comes close to mine, thumb next to pinky. I resist the urge to pull away. Together we move the cape, using the breeze to force the fabric into a gentle arc, swaying at our command. The flow of the cape is oddly soothing and rhythmic, like dancing. An ache yawns wide in my heart, a wound I didn't realize was there. I miss dancing. The steps, the stomps, the rhythm. Even swaying like this fills the wound. I look over my shoulder and smile, blazingly happy. Arturo blinks, surprised.

It occurs to me that he's never seen this particular expression on my face.

A deep flush blooms in his cheeks. Abruptly, he steps away, and cold air rushes in where his body was. Once again the cape flaps uncontrollably in my hands. I hold it out in front of me, trying to fight the wind, the stretch of red rustling violently.

"Your cape is your shield. *Never* hold it out in front of you," Arturo repeats.

I keep practicing, trying to keep my motion fluid and graceful, but I only seem to succeed in bumbling along like a drunk looking for the next tavern.

"Do you have a capote you can practice with?" Arturo asks. "It looks like you'll need it."

I glare at him, and he flashes a quicksilver grin. It's there one moment and gone the next. The flash of amusement softened his face.

"Roll the cape," he says, "and leave it be for now. Let's study the Morcego and find out what we can about your animal."

I do as he says, and when I'm finished, we turn as one to examine the beast. It's monstrous, with gleaming teeth and claws, scales that are thick and nearly impenetrable. How am I going to defeat this creature? How am I going to survive? Fear and panic roar to life in my body, in my blood. They riot together, marching in the same parade.

Unaware of my turmoil, Arturo continues his lesson. "The first thing you need to do when facing a dragon is to look for its weaknesses."

"The mound of muscle at the back of the neck," I say promptly. I've seen Papá thrust his blade time and time again in that spot. "The morrillo."

"That's the obvious one," Arturo says in an impatient voice, evidently peeved I'd interrupted his lesson. "But there are more. Check for vision problems; most dragons have them. A way to tell is if there are any unusual head movements."

Arturo launches to the side, and the beast jerks its head in the same direction, following the quick walk with ease.

"No vision trouble," I say.

"Espera," Arturo says as he walks around the dragon. The beast follows his motion, its long neck craning and twisting until it can't anymore. Then it snaps around, but this time Arturo walks quickly, darting in one direction and then sidestepping to the other in an expertly performed feint. The dragon tries to keep up but roars in frustration when Arturo escapes its line of vision just long enough to create confusion.

The tamer rejoins me where I'm standing. "Overall its vision is fine, except when you're moving fast."

"All right," I say, frowning. "So what do I do?"

"Move fast."

I roll my eyes. "What's next?"

He points to the dragon's back, with its thick black scales and small patch of exposed skin at the base of the neck. "There are three stages in fighting a dragon. The first is the initial attack, meant to weaken the animal. This is made with the shorter lance. You must stab the dragon in the morrillo in order for it to lose blood. For the second stage, you'll be given three banderillas, the little sticks with knives on one end and—"

"Flags on the other; ours are red and gold to match La Giralda's banners."

Arturo stares at me with impotent fury. This man does not like to be interrupted.

"I know the different stages in dragonfighting."

"I'm pleased," he says, sounding anything but. "What happens next?"

"Once the three banderillas have been used, the death stage comes next." I swallow. It'll be a miracle if I reach this point of the dragon fight.

"Go on," he says in his flat tone. "What does that entail?"

"I'm given the sword—" I break off, my brow puckering. "I assume that will be you?"

His jaw locks. "If I must."

"You must." I can't afford anyone else. "I use the cape and the sword to finish off the dragon. By now, it ought to be exhausted, weak and easily conquered. That's it, isn't it?"

Arturo curls his lip. "Not quite. Never forget that this is a show." He throws both arms wide open and spins around. "It's a spectacle! A performance meant to entertain! You can't just *kill* the dragon as humanely as possible. No! You must enrage the animal by employing several passes, slowly driving it mad. Prolong the killing." He kicks up sand. "Make sure there's enough blood on the ground to satisfy your guests. You can't make it look too easy."

I swallow back a hard lump. "You think this is easy? None of it is. I'm terrified."

"You ought to be," he says, jabbing an index finger in the direction of the monster. "Dragons are not to be trifled with. They're wild and dangerous. Every year, dozens of Dragonadores lose their lives. Never forget only one of you will make it out of this arena alive."

"I'm surprised to hear you say that."

He lowers his hands. "What?"

"Sometimes when you're talking about dragons, it feels like you prefer them to humans. Like you're fond of them."

"Fond?" he asks faintly. "*Fond?* I respect them, and just because they're monstrous and uncontrollable, doesn't mean it's fine to hunt them down and murder them for entertainment."

But it isn't for entertainment. Fine, not *just* for entertainment. That's a part of it, certainly. Dragonfighting is an art form, a calling rooted in antiquity. It needs to be guarded and protected and honored. Art ought never to be erased.

I say none of this out loud. I'm clear about where he stands, and he knows my argument. But he may not know what we do with the dragons afterward. "The meat off their bones is cooked in our kitchen and given to the poor. The rest of its body is used for potions. No part is wasted."

He regards me coldly, visibly weighing how to respond. "And you think that makes what La Giralda does every month humane?" he asks finally.

"I think it's about honoring tradition," I say quietly.

"Some traditions ought to be done with," he shoots back in a curt tone. "Or at the very least, reexamined."

I open my mouth to respond, but the dragon snarls and I jump a foot.

Arturo makes an exasperated noise. "I don't understand you at all. Anytime a dragon is near, your skin grows pale and your body starts shaking."

"Don't throw that in my face," I say in a tone that's as sharp as the lance.

"It's true. Why do it, then?"

I lift up my chin. "Because I have to."

"No, you don't. Everyone has a choice. You're choosing this—why? There's something I'm not seeing."

"I fight for my papá. To make sure our name endures beyond this scandal. I fight for our place in Hispalia. I want to protect everything my family has built." I sweep my arms wide. "Without the arena, we'll have nothing left. No money, our reputation destroyed, and our ancestral home gone. Can't you understand?" I take a deep breath. "If I lose La Giralda, I lose *my name*."

I expect to see more of the same written across his face—disdain and contempt—but in the depth of his thundercloud-gray eyes, I catch something that almost knocks me over.

Respect.

"You keep surprising me," he says, and there's a particularly despairing quality to his voice that I find riveting. "I wish you'd stop."

Warmth spreads deep in my belly. It loosens my tense shoulders, makes the tight line of my jaw relax. His words work like a balm, sweet, healing honey, and it's strong enough I can almost taste the addicting sugar.

"Why?"

"Because I don't like how it makes me feel," he snaps.

"Don't tell me we're becoming friends," I say lightly.

A rueful smile tugs at his mouth. "That's not what I'd call it."

Then his face shutters, returns to its naturally grim state, all hard lines and unyielding jaw. "The lesson is over. I'll come back tomorrow at the same time. We'll go over the weapons in each stage."

He whistles to the guards, and they drag the monster back to its cage. Arturo leaves with them, and when he's almost out of sight, he yells over his shoulder, "Don't be late."

It's only me now, standing in the middle of the arena, and for the first time, I wonder if I'll actually succeed in killing that dragon, or if my father will be forced to watch me die in front of his eyes like my mother.

Guillermo squats in front of the wall and drags an index finger along the faint magical residue streaking across at eye level. Today he's wearing a red tunic with blue stitching that contrasts beautifully with his dark skin. I still can't believe he'd actually come to La Giralda, willing and ready to help. The Gremio de Magia and their strict decrees don't allow much room for social engagements. We watch him as he studies the shining powder, muttering something under his breath.

"What did you just say?" Lola demands.

He ignores this and slowly smells the substance. Then he places the smallest speck onto the tip of his tongue. He twists his lips into a sharp grimace.

Lola gasps. "Why would you do that? You could turn into a gorilla."

Guillermo glances at her, bemused. "A gorilla?"

"Or a *toad*," she says coldly.

"A toad," he repeats. "My word."

Lola opens her mouth, but I quickly step into the conversation. I've seen just how long they can spend an afternoon arguing. Hours and hours and hours. "What do you think?" I ask.

He straightens, head tilted to the side thoughtfully. "Traces of mushroom, horsetail, nettle, and cow's tongue. And dragon tears," he adds with a grimace. "With those ingredients, it's decidedly *not* a cleaning spell. You'd find more lemon peel and citrus."

I think of Benito—who'd died without a wound on his body. "Could it have killed someone?"

Guillermo frowns and looks down at the streak of magic. "It has the right color—a faint golden hue for a killing encanto. Tears of a dragon are the hardest ingredients to come by. They're incredibly costly and bothersome to use, but if done correctly, the spell could have created a poisonous mist. But there would have had to have been a lot of it floating around. The whole room would have been impossible to see through."

Guillermo pulls out a wand from one of the deep pockets of his tunic and cracks it in half. A shimmering white light spills from within, illuminating the dungeon. He glances down, and I follow the line of his gaze and gasp.

Speckled throughout the chamber are smatterings of golden magic, climbing up and down the walls, hiding in corners, and dotting the floor in the thousands. The magia is everywhere, so faint and tiny, but taken together as a whole, the place looks as if I were staring up at the night sky filled with stars. Lola meets my gaze, her lips quivering.

"There's your confirmation," Guillermo murmurs. "And the reason you can see the line on the wall clearer than the rest is because that's where the wand was snapped in half. That section of the wall was blasted with the initial release."

Benito had died from inhaling the noxious fog. A tremor moves through my body. This is it. Confirmation: Benito was murdered. Killed during the night while I slept.

"You need to go to the Gremio de Dragonadores," Lola whispers. "They need to know."

I nod soberly. "This minute."

Guillermo looks between us in alarm. "You *can't*."

I startle at his sharp tone. "Why not? This is the proof I've been looking for—"

He holds up a hand. "I don't want to know the details. It's not my business. I did, however, help you without following proper protocol. I had no idea what I'd find down here, and from the look on your face, I'd say you discovered something serious . . . *Murder*." He pauses. "You aren't allowed to contract a mago or a bruja for something like this. We'd both get in trouble should anyone find out."

"You?" Lola asks, brows raised. "You broke the rules? But why?"

Guillermo flushes and stiffly repeats, "We can't tell a soul."

The blood drains from my face. He's right—and I'm on a probation period. I can't step a toe out of line without facing dire consequences.

"Listen, I like to follow the rules as much as the next person," Lola says. "But even I know we need to—" Guillermo shakes his head once, and Lola breaks off. Then in a much softer and terrified voice, she asks, "So we do *nothing*?"

The light from the wand vanishes, and it casts us back into shadow. My eyes adjust enough to be able to see their anxious faces, and my stomach clenches. I dragged them both into this.

"Not nothing," Guillermo says finally. "You can take what you learned and prepare yourself." He levels me with a look. "If I were you, I'd take proper precautions and be careful of going anywhere alone. Whoever caused you harm might do so again."

DIECIOCHO

The next training session nearly kills me. I spend every minute trying not to think of the spell that was used to kill poor Benito. Arturo left me on the arena floor with a smug smile when it was over, my breath escaping in great heaving puffs. Every inch of my body hurt, as if I'd spent several hours dancing, without any breaks at all. No amount of hot water could have helped ease the tight soreness flaring up and down my legs.

Most of the maids have gone home. As has been my custom, I walk to every door and window to make sure Papá and I are safe. I send most of our guards down into the dungeon to watch over our dragons, blow out all the candles, triple-check the locks.

My stomach grumbles, rude and unladylike, so I make my way toward the kitchen where I know Ofelia left a plate of dinner for me. But when I step inside, the first thing I see is a folded-up note with my name scrawled on the outside. The letter is from Hector. I'd recognize his horrible penmanship anywhere.

> *Dear Zarela,*
> *Do you have dinner plans this evening? My cook has made too much food and I need help in the eating of it.*
> *I'd like to hear about Santiago.*
>
> *Yours, Hector*

I glance at the cold plate of toasted bread and handful of olives left for me. There's no decision to make. Dinners at Hector's are a lavish affair with scrumptious sauces and crispy meat and the best pan-fried potatoes. I quickly run up to my bedroom to change and pray Hector won't see any of the sand under my nails. And then I race back down and use the servants' entrance because it's lesser known and half-hidden by high stone walls on either side of the entry. A path curls around to the back of the building where most supplies are delivered. The stable houses our lone carriage. Once full of horses and other carriages, the stalls sit empty, gathering dust, and the driver—whose hours I've had to reduce significantly—reads the advertisement I wrote up for my dragon fight.

When he sees me, he tucks the sheet into his trouser pocket. "¿Dónde quiere ir?"

"I want to pay a visit to La Doña."

He opens the door of the carriage, nodding. "It's been a while since you paid Don Hector a visit."

Guilt pricks at me. Usually, I'm over for dinner at least once a week. I step inside the familiar velvet cage with its pretty golden tassels and plush seating. My mother loved this carriage for its simple elegance. We head off to Hector's famous ring, built sometime after ours, but just as memorable and beautiful. All dragon rings are circular buildings with a giant arena in the middle and stone seating overlooking it. But each flies a different colored banner, except for El Prado, which decorates using our colors. I hear they serve terrible food. La Giralda is far superior in every way to the other rings.

Well, it *used* to be.

I lean my head back against the cushion and idly observe the loud streets as we travel closer to the other side of town. People are out for the evening, eating dinner in the various taverns in the main plaza, or enjoying the live music on nearly every street corner. You can't go a block without hearing someone strumming the guitar, while people dance flamenco out on the cobbled streets. The notes ride the warm breeze, skip into open windows, and settle onto people's skin, caressing them like a lover might. The music draws people from out of their homes, has them swaying on their front steps, tapping their shoes against the ground while sipping sidra, a tart cider imported from the emerald coast of Asturion. My parents once took me, just so I could pluck an apple from the orchards blanketing the sloping hillsides.

Santivilla at night is one long fiesta—romantic, wild, and unquestionably alive. Not one city hosts a party like ours does. I've never liked going out with Lola—too often being mistaken for my mother, and when she died, I couldn't bear the thought of someone calling me by her name, even as a horrible mistake.

We draw closer to the Gremio de Magia building, an impressive structure shaped like a cathedral, with magical stained glass windows and an enormous bell tower. Next to it is the legendary Mercado de los Magos—the famous witch market owned and run by the Gremio de Magia—so named for the numerous stalls selling bundles of wands, ingredients for potions, and various bottles of brews. It's a riot of colors, the streets painted a lush purple, the stalls decorated with ribbons and flags in every color. Most of the products sold are imported from the cities surrounding Santivilla. Spices and dried herbs from Cantabria. Thick and luxurious fabric dyed in rich colors from the mountain town of Besalu. Musical instruments and gorgeous pottery from Santillana del Mar. The Mercado de los Magos is a glimpse from every corner of Hispalia.

I peer out the window, and as we pass by the street, I come across a familiar face. I slam my fist against the roof of the carriage. "¡Para, por favor!"

We stop immediately. I don't wait for the driver to assist with helping me down, but dash across the street, shouting a hurried, "I'll be right back!"

I reach the entrance of the Mercado, keeping my eye on a girl with wild, curly hair wearing a gorgeous pale linen ruffle skirt that swishes at her ankles and a mauve blouse patterned with delicate flower buds. Her own design, I'm sure of it. The man next to her is tall with rich black skin, dressed impeccably in a pressed charcoal-gray tunic—not a wrinkle in sight.

"Lola!" I yell.

She turns, and her mouth forms a little *O* of surprise. "Zarela! What are you doing here?"

"I'm on my way to La Doña," I say, glancing at her companion. Frankly, I'm astonished to see Guillermo with her. She's been trying for months to get him to go out dancing, with very little success. I've heard how the Master of his guild keeps a tight hold on all the members, with strict rules to never share anything that goes on behind their doors. Magic is a lucrative business, and if you have enough money, you can send your child to the school to become an apprentice and later a member of the guild. But once you're in, it's almost impossible to come out.

Their secret teaching of magic is much too valuable for big mouths. Or for nights out with chatty and charming girls.

But she can persuade the sky to turn another color, so I really shouldn't be all that shocked. "So, you finally caved?"

"Excuse me?" he asks.

Lola nudges Guillermo, and he winces. "I've finally convinced my friend here to join me for a night out."

He blushes furiously. "I have *not* been convinced, Lola. Please stop telling people that. The magic guild expects their apprentices to behave and not engage in . . ." He fumbles when Lola half glares, half raises her brows in a suggestive way.

"In the act of dancing on tables?" I supply, looking between them, my eyes narrowed.

He shoots me a grateful smile. "Right."

"Do you always have to follow the rules?" Lola whines. "No staying out past ten, no drinking during the week, no dating until you graduate. It's horrid. Can't you take off that silly badge for one night—"

He stiffens. "It's not *silly*, Señorita Delgado."

Someone elbows me in order to rush toward a stall selling wands capable of turning rats into hair balls, easier to be swept away along with the rest of the dust.

"What are you two doing here, if not dancing?"

Lola lets out a loud laugh, louder than is probably warranted. I keep my gaze narrowed at her and she squirms. I know all of her laughs, and this one is her high, fake one that I detest. She uses it around Tío Hector, who unfortunately thinks he's funnier than he actually is.

"We're shopping, of course," she says quickly.

I look around. There's not a bolt of fabric to be found anywhere. Instead, vendors yell out their wares at the top of their voices: dragon teeth for sixteen reales, hearts for ten gold coins, ivory horns for fifty. Vats of dragon blood sell for dozens of copper coins. The meaty smell of the market lays heavy in the air, with an afternote of various herbs. It makes for a pungent experience, and no way is Lola buying anything from this place.

"I'm looking for a particular mushroom," Guillermo says quickly. "Lola offered to help me look."

"That's nice of her," I say, not believing him for a second. He's always straightforward, unassuming, and honest. A stickler for rules and straight paths. But he's lying to me; I can sense it. What are these two up to? "Well, take care of my girl. She's squeamish around blood."

Lola grimaces. "Why do they have to sell so much of it?"

Guillermo lets out an exasperated huff of air. "Because it's the Mercado de los Magos. We need all these ingredients to make the encantos."

She shudders.

"I'll see you tomorrow," I say. "Be safe and try not to fall off anything."

Lola laughs and pulls Guillermo away. I watch them for a moment, trying to figure out what's between them, what secret they hold together. But it's a baffling knot in my mind. For one thing, theirs is an unlikely friendship, and not just because of their opposite personalities. People tend to mingle with members of their own Gremio. It's not a rule, but a practiced preference. And secondly, this is the first time Lola didn't invite me to go dancing with her.

She clearly didn't want me around tonight.

Por qué?

I return to the carriage. The whole ride to Tío Hector's, I mull over seeing the two of them tonight and what it might mean. But no matter how I examine it, I can't think of what they're up to. Unless they're wanting a romantic evening together.

I scoff.

A romantic evening surrounded by smelly dragon body parts? Unlikely.

The carriage comes to an abrupt stop, and I pull the curtain back and peer out the window. The immense gates of La Doña loom a few feet away, gilded and glinting in the moonlight. Hector's arena is very different than La Giralda. Ours resembles a medieval castle with its bloodred banners and golden detailing, caramel-hued stones and iron accents. This circular building looks to have been sprayed down in expensive champagne. The white stone gleams, and the golden gates seem to herald a great king into battle. Navy and silver ribbons flutter in the breeze from the four towers, each of which has a private box from where the nobility can view dragon fights without mixing with commoners.

Two watchmen dressed in white jackets with blue trousers lined in brass buttons open the gates, and the carriage moves inside. When I open the door, it's in time to see Hector bounding down the marble steps from the main entrance. Like us, his home is adjacent to the arena, connecting via a corridor lined by arches and statues of sirenas, a nod to his growing up in the seafaring town of Valentia. His home matches the exterior, white and polished with marble columns, azure velvet curtains, and expensive wood furniture. Even the door knockers, fashioned as the heads of Lagartos, swimmer dragons, shine from the moon's rays.

"Zarela!" he exclaims when he reaches me. "I'm so happy you can join me."

I grip both his hands. "Hola, Tío Hector."

He looks over my shoulder, and when he takes in my driver, his brows pull into a frown. "Where are your guards? Who else is with you?"

He lets me go and peers into the carriage. Then he turns, mouth agape. "You're alone? At this time of night?"

Blood warms my cheeks. If he only knew about my time spent at the ranch, hours from Santivilla, without guards or even a chaperone. He'd have a conniption. Around Hector, I always had another protector, guiding my first steps, keeping me company during Mamá's shows whenever Papá couldn't get away from the arena. My own father isn't as protective, and I indulge Hector because . . . sometimes I think he just likes having someone to worry over. He has no children of his own, and my parents and Hector's deceased sister were his only family here in Santivilla.

"Tío," I say. "I was perfectly safe."

He loops my arm with his and guides me to the main arched entrance, an immense wooden door carved with ornate wreathes and golden seashells hammered into the wood. Inside is a grand hall with a navy-and-white checkered marble floor and a ceiling showcasing an oil painting of dueling ships battling for a fair mermaid. An ornate crystal chandelier fashioned after coral hangs above our heads, lit by dozens of fat, squat candles. If the room were a few feet wider, it'd be a perfect space for a ballroom. As it happens, La Giralda's ballroom is a lovely chamber with high, vaulted ceilings and thick wooden beams, iron wrought sconces, and a custom plush rug in varying shades of red and gold. It hasn't been used since Mamá died.

The butler approaches, dressed to match the floor in blue and white, carrying two glasses filled with wine that's been sweetened by thick apple slices, plump cherries, and several sticks of cinnamon.

"Algo para beber, Señorita Zalvidar?" the butler asks. "Tinto de verano?"

"Gracias—" I break off when my stomach rumbles. Once again, my cheeks flush.

Hector drops a heavy hand on my shoulder. "Dios mío! When was the last time you ate a decent meal?"

"I've been busy," I say.

He makes soothing noises and ushers me into the dining room off the main hall. A long rectangular table laden with silver candlesticks stands in the middle of the room. The stone walls showcase several tapestries, all threaded with golden dyed wool. In between the artisan decor are paintings of Hector's long-dead family, dressed in their naval uniforms. Tío doesn't talk much of the family he left behind in Valentia, but I remember overhearing that some of his relatives worked as spies for the Rey and Reina of Hispalia. I peer around and see the painting of our sovereigns, finely dressed in silks and wearing matching grim expressions.

It's a massive room for one person, and guilt pricks me like a needle. I ought to have made time to see him. But I'm here now and so I smile hugely and he beams back at me. "Because I'm your favorite person, I'm going to sit right here." I pick the seat at the head of the table. "What's for dinner?"

He grins and pulls out the chair to my left. "You *are* my favorite person, and I'm a bastard for not coming to visit sooner. We've been struggling since—" He stops abruptly, face twisting. "Forgive me. I know every arena has lost business. It's thoughtless of me to mention it. I can't believe—"

I reach out my hand to grab the sleeve of his velvet green jacket. "I'm so sorry. How is La Doña?"

"We don't have to talk about this."

"Tío."

He sighs. "We can't fill the seats no matter how much I mark down the price. People are too afraid to watch a dragon fight. I've had to let some of my staff go in anticipation of leaner months." He meets my gaze fiercely. "But I'm setting aside money for you from every ticket sold. It's not much, but—"

I half rise from my chair. "Tío! I can't accept it. Please do what you must to keep the doors open."

He motions for me to sit. "You're like a daughter to me. Will you deny my help? I'm only this generous for you and your father. Let's call it an emergency fund."

I clear my throat, overcome. "Gracias, Tío Hector."

How like him to think of the future. Papá lives in a dream, and with Mamá's passing, he's been as inaccessible as if he were living in the clouds. I know he loves me, I know he's proud, but sometimes I wish he'd come back to me. I miss our conversations and his teasing and the adventures he'd plan for us. I miss *him*.

Three servers appear from a side entrance leading to the kitchens. One carries a basket of freshly baked bread with a thick crust and a bottle of Hispalian olive oil, and the others each have a handle of a heavy cast iron pan filled with golden rice, scallops, garlic mussels, and perfectly sautéed shrimp. Another attendant places a dish piled high with fried eggplants drizzled in honey and garnished with sprigs of rosemary. It's my favorite dish, and my mouth waters at the sight. I haven't had a meal like this in a long time. The butler returns with a pitcher of red wine, and I take an indulgent sip from my glass.

I glance down, ready to fill my plate, and I'm hit with a sudden wave of nostalgia. My mother and Hector's sister, Amalia, had picked out all of the cutlery and dinner set on this table. Beautiful porcelain plates hand-painted in a navy-and-white checkered pattern, to match the tiles she'd picked out for the foyer. The flatware is made of plated gold and the glasses are long and slender—very modern for Hispalia, who traditionally prefer goblets, with an iridescent shimmer that reminded Amalia of a mermaid's tail. Hector never could say no to either of them, and opened his silk purse for their extravagant purchases. Amalia and my mother had been great friends, but the former died in a carriage accident not long after she helped Hector turn La Doña into the place it is today. She barely got to enjoy any of her work.

Tío Hector is no stranger to death. It explains his fear of something happening to *me*.

He catches my eye, and we share a private, sad smile as the servers fill our plates. He'd taken my mother's death hard. We all did, but for Tío, I think it reminded him of the day Amalia never came home from her errand. On the day Mamá died, he left Santivilla and returned to his family's home in Valentia. When Tío Hector finally came back, the sea air clinging to him like a barnacle, he came straight to our home and helped my father run La Giralda for months, forsaking his own arena and adoring fans, never leaving our sides.

I don't know what we would have done without him.

The servers leave and we tuck into the food; I dredge thick slices of bread in the olive oil seasoned with flakes of pepper and salt. It's heaven in my mouth.

"Tío—"

Hector shakes his head. "Eat first. Then we talk."

"But—"

He points to the paella. "You've grown thin. I don't like what I'm seeing. I'm terrified to ask if you've been sleeping. And when's the last time you brushed your hair?"

I think about the nights I spent sleeping propped against a tree, or the days spent practicing under a hot sun, burning my skin. At some point, he's going to find out what I've been up to. I ought to let him know about the show, but this is the first good meal I've had in what feels like forever. I don't want to spoil the mood, or his dinner.

The paella's warm scent wafts into my nose, and I decide to overlook his mothering. He asks about my father and tells me stories about learning how to cook.

At last, when I've eaten every grain of rice off my plate, he falls silent and gazes at me expectantly.

"I think I'm in trouble," I say, hating how my voice wobbles. I draw in a fortifying breath. "I believe the massacre at La Giralda was the fault of someone intent on sabotaging my family." I break off and examine my uncle's face to see how he responds to this statement. But he takes my words calmly and waves one of his hands in a gesture meant for me to continue. I clear my throat and begin again. "During the anniversary show, someone set our dragons free and released them into the arena. Shortly afterward, I discovered the rest of our beasts were killed, along with our last surviving dragon trainer, Benito. He was murdered by a powerful encanto. The bodies were left in our dungeon."

He sets the glass on the table carefully. "Zarela, this is serious. How could you not tell me?"

"Everything happened so fast. After the show, I was called to the Gremio—which you know about—and my father is still terribly ill . . . and I didn't know what to do," I added. "I brought all of this to the Dragon Master, and he didn't believe my suspicions. I think the Asociación is somehow involved, but I can't prove it."

Tío Hector is quiet for a long moment, gazing down at the table, lost in thought. I recognize this expression—contemplative, ideas spinning. It's the look he gets when he's coming up with a new pass to use against a dragon. "I think there might be a way to prove the Asociación's involvement."

At first all I can do is stupidly stare at him, hardly registering his words. "You mean . . . do you believe me then, Tío?"

Hector glances up. "Of course I do, Zarela. You're no fool."

This is why he's family to me. Believing me without question or criticism. My *own* father didn't do that.

"I happen to be privy to some information discussed in the Gremio," Hector says slowly. "I have reason to believe the money you paid that's owed to the patrons never made it to them."

My jaw drops. "It hasn't? Then where has it gone?"

Hector hesitates. "What I'm about to tell you must not leave this room. Do you promise?"

I nod, breathless.

"There's been significant correspondence between Don Eduardo and the leader of the Asociación—Martina Sanchez." He stops and stares at me pointedly, waiting for me to understand.

That awful woman again. The one with the pale eyes and banner clutched in her hands like a weapon. I replay his words in my mind, and then realization dawns with a sudden clarity that leaves me reeling. "You believe the money might have gone to Martina and her followers. But why? The Asociación is against the Gremio—on every level. Why would Don Eduardo give them my money?"

"Perhaps for a service," he says quietly.

He waits for me to put the pieces together. I think hard, my mouth dry. A possibility reveals itself. I draw in a shaky breath. "A service like sneaking into an arena to free their dragons? Like using a powerful spell?"

I've never seen my uncle look so grim, so serious. Conversation like this could bring trouble and misery into his life. If anyone were to find out, he'd be kicked out of the Gremio. His reputation would never recover. "I believe it's possible."

"But why?" I cry out. "What possible reason could Don Eduardo have to sabotage my family?"

"The Dragon Master has been the Conde de la Corte for two decades, winning the vote every time," Hector says in a hushed tone, and there's no mistaking the fear creeping into his voice. "But he's older now, and it was common knowledge that your father would be recommended for the position."

"*Papá?* But he never said!"

Hector shrugs. "Perhaps he wanted to wait until it became official. Obviously, that's impossible now. No one will want a disgraced Dragonador as the Dragon Master. The Gremio will have to keep Don Eduardo—unless the committee thinks of another viable candidate."

I lean forward and dig my fingertips into my temples. "Don Eduardo could have sabotaged us to keep my papá from the most powerful position in Santivilla? Could he truly be responsible?"

Tío Hector hesitates, his gaze on the wineglass. "I don't want to say without being absolutely certain . . ." He lifts his eyes to meet mine. "But it *is* possible, Zarela."

"What can be done?"

Hector adjusts the left cuff of his tunic. "Zarela, I don't know if anything can be done. Going against Don Eduardo is dangerous. If he's capable of all this, what more would he do in order to silence you?"

Fire roars in my veins, burns a way to my heart. "But I can't just do nothing!"

"I'm not asking you to," he says. "Let me make inquiries. *Privately.* This situation must be handled with care, Zarela."

While I hear everything he says, I already know that I'm not going to listen to one word.

We are innocent.

And I'm going to prove it.

DIECINUEVE

My chamber is an absolute disaster. Piles of clothing scattered across my bed, in heaps on the floor. I can't find anything that will be suitable for tonight's foray into the main square. The idea came to me as I sat across from Tío Hector, as I told him I wouldn't dare pursue my suspicions further.

But I lied.

I'm going to sneak into the Gremio tonight and find the correspondence between Don Eduardo and Martina.

Just as soon as I find something appropriate to wear. Despite having never broken into a locked building, I'm nearly positive my sunny-yellow dress with its ruffled hem and embroidered collar isn't the best attire. I let out an exasperated huff of air, annoyed at the slim offerings my wardrobe has to offer for clandestine adventures. Why must everything I own be jewel toned? Oh, that's *right*—Lola won't let me dress in anything remotely morbid-looking, which includes the color black.

"Going somewhere?"

I spin around with a gasp.

Lola leans against the doorframe, dressed in her blue nightgown adorned with far too many ribbons and an amused smile on her lips. Her gaze wanders to the piles of clothes strewn everywhere. "Ofelia is going to love this in the morning."

A deep flush crawls across my face. "What are you doing home so early? I thought you'd still be with Guillermo."

She rolls her eyes. "He had to make curfew."

"Oh," I say lamely. "Well, I'm just getting ready for bed."

She looks around, the corners of her mouth deepening. "Are you having trouble deciding what to wear to the party your bed is clearly having?"

I throw one of my tunics at her. "Leave me be and go to sleep."

She steps inside and shuts the door behind her. "Not until you tell me what you're doing and why you haven't invited me. If you're going to a tavern, I promise I'll purchase your first goblet of wine."

I roll my eyes. "I'm not going out dancing—I'm going to sneak into the Gremio de Dragonadores."

She sinks onto my bed. "That doesn't sound nearly as fun."

"I need to pull together a darker-hued ensemble." I take a deep breath. "Will you help me find something?"

Lola thinks for a minute and then leaves the room. I resume tossing each of my clothes around, searching for something suitable, until she steps back inside, carrying a dark skirt and tunic. Pieces without fashion or ornate detailing, and utterly forgettable. The clothing she wears while she's working during the day. It's only when she hands me everything that I realize what she's also wearing. Out of her nightgown and straight back into a similar dark skirt and simple cotton tunic.

"You're not coming," I say in alarm.

"Well, of course, I'd rather find a new place to dance," Lola says. "But if anything were to happen to you, who do you think is going to run for help?"

I pull her into a hug. "Gracias, amiga."

She sniffs. "Just as long as I'm not running several blocks."

We argue about how many wands to bring and at last settle on three each. I take one repairing and transformative spell and one for healing minor injuries. It's a cheaper potion, only meant to last for ten minutes. If someone were to stab me through the heart, I'd be done for. I don't ask Lola which wands she picked because by then, we've started bickering whether to walk or travel by horseback. Lola insisted the Gremio building is too far to walk, which is probably true, but it's easier to hide while walking along the darkened streets of Santivilla at night. Mostly because there are crowds of people doing the same, ambling along to one tavern after another until the sun comes up.

"If we run into trouble, wouldn't we want to escape rather quickly?" she asks when we're outside of La Giralda.

"But we'll have an easier time getting lost in a crowd if we walk," I counter.

She pouts but cedes the point. We set off, carefully traversing the cobbled road that meanders into the heart of Santivilla. The night is cool, and everywhere are the sounds of people walking up and down the streets, searching for the next stretch of entertainment.

We reach the Gremio, the imposing facade staring down at the pair of us, forbidding and immense. There are two sentries standing at the front of the doors and another walking the perimeter.

Lola looks at me. "I hope you have a plan."

I don't—not really, but my eyes land on the row of windows on the bottom floor. Each is cased in thick wooden trim that juts out nearly half a foot. Perfect for climbing, particularly because Don Eduardo's private chamber is located on the second floor. I only have to find the right window. I nudge Lola to follow me around to the side of the build-ing, venturing after the sea of people walking up and down the avenue that fronts the Gremio entrance. Drunkards half standing, supported by friends and shouting nonsense to anyone drawing near.

I sneak around the corner and peer down the tight row of shrubbery lining the building next to the path. Tilting my chin up, I catch sight of a potted plant—Don Eduardo's voluminous fern. His window is the fourth one down, I'd bet anything. Lola follows close at my heels—and then I grip her hand and point to a row of trees brushing against the edifice, long branches twisting outward toward the upper story windows.

Lola's lips twist. "I'm not climbing. Think of the insects."

"You don't have to," I say and walk toward the tree closest to the Gremio.

"Well, of course I do," she mutters behind me. "But I demand the right to complain about it."

I laugh softly and reach for the lowest branch and haul myself up. Lola follows suit, grumbling. It's dirty, slow work—finding the right branch, clutching the rough wood, and feeling the sandy grit coating every inch. I finally reach the correct height, and I cautiously sit and then scoot outward toward the Dragon Master's chamber. The branch is far enough away from the building for it to be scary. I swallow back my fear and keep moving.

"Sentry below," Lola hisses.

The guard rounds the corner of the building and walks right underneath my dangling feet, my skirt rustling in the wind. I hold my breath and draw up my legs so they're covered by the bushy leaves.

"Don't fall," Lola says.

I look over my shoulder and shoot her a glare. "Helpful advice."

"People tell me all the time I'm incredibly helpful, actually," she says. "Scary watchman is gone now."

She's right. I resume scooting across and then reach for the overhanging ledge. I'm a foot too far. Carefully, I bring up my feet and position myself to jump the rest of the way like a frog—a graceless one.

"You can't reach? Oh, well. Let's go find sangría."

I ignore her and take a deep breath and jump. My fingers latch on to the upper overhang and my knees land clumsily onto the window ledge with a loud smack. I wince in pain. That's going to bruise.

"You're mad if you think I'll be able to aim for that window."

"Shut up."

"That's not polite."

I pull out one of my wands, check the gold lettering to make sure I grabbed the right one. Transforming. Perfect. The trick with breaking the wand is making sure the snap happens as close to the middle as possible. Which turns out to be harder while perched on a window ledge barely wide enough to support my frame. I lean against the glass to secure my balance and bend the wand in half, muttering, "hammer," under my breath.

The spell leaks out in a pale shimmery swirl of mist, coating only one half of the wand, and it transforms into a thin, rusted hammer.

"Damn this cheap magic," I hiss. Which is entirely my fault as I hadn't wanted to spend more than we absolutely needed to.

"Zarela!" Lola says. "The guard!"

He's just rounded the corner. I press myself closer to the window and actually suck in—despite it doing nothing to help my situation—and bring my legs as close to my body as possible.

I keep my breath locked in my chest until he's turning out of sight. Then I smash the window, making a large enough hole for my hand to slip through. One quick twist and I've unlocked it, and in the next breath, I'm inside.

Lola follows suit, jumping with a cry louder than is wise, sounding like a wounded bird, and then falling spectacularly in a lump onto the stone floor.

"I could never be a thief," she says wonderingly, lying on her back and staring up at the ceiling.

I help her onto her feet, and she pulls out a wand for a simple illumination spell. The tip of half a wand lights up like a small candle. She hands it to me, and I peer around, making sure I was right about this being the Dragon Master's office. The leafy fern is perched on the sill, and the room certainly smells like Don Eduardo, all fire and smoke and stubbornness. The room is hot and stuffy, as if a fire blazed from a nearby hearth.

I hand Lola my wand that was dipped in cheap repairing potion. "Will you fix the window?"

His desk is nearly the length of a respectable dining table, all straight lines and perfectly sanded and polished wood. There are several drawers, large stacks of rolled parchment, nearly empty bottles of ink, and a marble container filled with handsome quills. I sift through the parchment first, unrolling several and quickly skimming the contents.

Several receipts for expensive wands, filled-out applications begging for consideration for admittance into the guild from recent graduates, more complaints about my family, which I promptly set on fire.

Lola snaps the repairing wand in half, and the window is stitched together—but not perfectly. Tiny veins of glass thread outward like a spider's web.

I groan. "Don Eduardo will notice."

"But he won't know it's us." Lola walks to the desk. "What are you looking for?"

"Correspondence between Martina Sanchez and Don Eduardo. Anything that mentions payment for a service rendered."

"Right. Where's your hammer?"

I toss it to her, and she slams the locks on the drawers. We rummage through each and find gold coins, several more receipts—the repairing of the Gremio roof which evidently costs quite a lot of gold for that kind of magic, but necessary as it deflects the fiery blast of a dragon. There are several letters between other Gremio Masters, and a leather book detailing his schedule. Lola flips through it, page by page, and at some point she snaps one of her wands. I glance at her as a cold breeze wafts around the room, gently curling the edges of the parchment.

"You seriously brought a cooling encanto?" I hiss. Ofelia buys these by the dozens as it gets murderously hot in the kitchen while she cooks.

"It's stifling in here," she says. "So clearly I was the one better prepared."

I roll my eyes and resume the search, fingers gliding over the smooth surface inside the drawer when my fingers scrape against one small parchment tucked in the back.

I unroll the parchment, hoping it's a letter from Martina.

It's not.

Eduardo,

By the time you read this, I'll be gone. The healers have run out of solutions, and I fear the worst is near. Do not trouble yourself by rushing to the estate. Instead, I must beg you to do something else for me.

Do not give up on him.

I beg you.

Hortensia

I frown, rolling up the missive. This isn't what I was hoping for in the slightest, but I can't help the pull of curiosity.

"Have you checked that drawer?" Lola asks, gesturing toward one. "I've looked inside the four on this side."

"Lower your voice," I say in a hushed tone. "And no, I haven't." Only two more to go. I'm just settling into the first of the pair when—

"What the hell is going on with that fern?"

I whirl around and gasp. Don Eduardo's beloved plant has grown. By several feet. Long tentacle-like vines erupting from the pot, slithering toward our ankles.

I leap away, just barely managing not to accidentally drop the lightened candle. Lola runs around the desk, her mass of curly hair fluttering behind her.

"His damn fern is enchanted," I snarl. "And it's blocking our exit."

"I dare you to shove it out the window."

"Because *that* won't look suspicious."

The pot shakes as the plant grows and grows, long serpentine coils forming around the desk and reaching for us.

We back away until we're at the door. I yank on the knob and pull it open—only to see a pair of sentries patrolling the corridor on the other end.

"Why aren't we leaving?" Lola asks from behind me, her tone threaded with panic.

"There are men outside in the hallway, standing watch."

"Carajo."

"My sentiments exactly." My mind chases one idea after another. "I have a healing wand. Please tell me you brought something useful."

Lola dips her hand into the pocket of her skirt and hands me her wand. "Transforming."

"Excelente." I hand Lola the light—which burns dangerously low—and then think for a moment.

"Zarela!" Lola yelps as a thin vine wraps around her wrist tight. I spring forward, trying to help her, but several of them curl around my ankles, sliding up under my skirt and coiling around my legs. They press hard, until tears prick my eyes.

"I'm going to ask for dragon gas," I gasp in between huffs of air. Rancio dragons emit fumes that can rot whatever it touches; plants, soil, grass, flowers, and trees are no match for it. If we were to breathe in any of it, it'd burn us from the inside out.

"Surely things aren't that dire," Lola says, looking alarmed, even as more of the plant crawls upward—round and round her chest. She lets out a small cry, even now trying to stay quiet for fear of the guards outside.

"Hold your breath, Lola." I break her wand, quickly whispering the word, and then I inhale deeply, until my lungs burn from the effort. The magic pours from the ends of the wand, releasing a sickly green mist that swirls high and outward. Lola flattens her lips and plugs her nose with her free hand.

I point toward the window. It's our only hope of escape. We take slow, painful steps away from the door, the vines circling around us, squeezing and trapping us within their verdant grasps. The noxious fumes spread, finally drifting down toward the plant, reaching inside to the root.

The fern shudders but doesn't let go.

Lola drops to the ground, landing on her side, near covered in the vicious greenery. I turn toward her, but my feet are tangled in the fern's ropes. I can't feel my toes. The air inside my lungs turns into fire in my chest, wanting to burn a way through.

I look at Lola, at her pale face, her eyes squeezed tight. Somehow she's still holding on to the candle.

Don't die, *please* don't die.

And suddenly I'm angry. I can't lose one more person. I won't. I reach outward, fingers grasping until I yank the wand out of her hands and burn the vines wrapped around her chest. They loosen—and then the rest of the plant starts curling and writhing, the fumes finally working.

I scramble free and help Lola, motioning for her to keep her breath safe inside her chest. The poison is still working, rotting the air between us, slowly killing the fern, its vibrantly green hue turning gray and a dull brown.

Good riddance.

I haul Lola to her feet and shove her toward the window, quickly opening it and helping her onto the ledge. She gasps, dragging in fresh air and then makes the leap toward the branch.

I take one last look at the room—it's a disaster, the desk a mess of parchment rolls and the dying fern covering most of the chamber. There's no time to make things right, and besides, I need air.

Gorgeous, beautiful breath.

I fling myself out the window, drawing in deep gulps of air, and jump onto the branch. The way down the tree is harder, and I'm shaking too hard to go fast. Lola must feel the same because by the time we get to the bottom, she looks quite ill.

I wrap an arm around her waist. "Are you all right?"

"Of course not," she says, her body trembling under my hands. "You should have shoved that disgusting pot out the window."

I let out a startled laugh. "Let's go home and—"

"What are you doing?"

Lola stiffens. Together we slowly turn around to find the guard patrolling the perimeter studying us in cool regard. He's bald and mean-looking, with thick shoulders and an equally thick chest.

"I said, what are you two doing on this property?"

Lola groans and clutches her stomach.

"My friend had a little too much fun tonight. Drank way too much—do you see how green her face is? She really shouldn't drink more than three glasses of wine."

The guard twists his lips in disgust.

"I was just trying to find somewhere quiet," I quickly add, thankful for the noise coming from the street. Music and people shouting and dancing, and generally making merry.

"Get her away—"

Lola moans again and, as if on cue, vomits onto the guard's shoes. I'll have to thank her timing later.

For the rest of my life, I wish to never remember that walk home. By the time we get back to La Giralda, my steps are dragging. I help Lola to her room, take off her shoes, and cover her with a blanket.

"Zarela," she whispers, her voice muffled.

I lean close. "What is it?"

"We almost died."

"I know."

"We should have brought Guillermo. He would have been better prepared."

I smooth her wild curls from off her brow. She never talks about how she really feels when it comes to the mago apprentice. She uses bluster and a loud volume to hide her big secret. "Is that why you like him?"

She nods against the pillow. "He makes me feel safe."

"You should tell him," I say, but her snoring drowns out my words.

I walk to my chamber, exhausted and furious to have wasted the night. I didn't find the proof I'd been looking for, and now the Gremio will know someone has broken in, and it will be that much harder to sneak inside.

Feeling glum, I change into my nightgown, wanting a bath but not wanting to go through the effort of taking one and washing and drying my hair, which takes *forever*. Is there anything worse than drying long hair?

I don't see the note until I'm pulling the covers back. It's a plain sheet, folded in half and resting on my pillow. My name is written in a handwriting I don't recognize.

Dread pools deep in my belly.

I unfold the message, and all the air seems to rush out of the room. My heart slams against my ribs. I don't remember sinking onto the bed. I reread the note, praying the words will somehow change or disappear.

> *Stop pursuing this, Zarela.*
> *Or we'll go after Lola next.*

The words stay the same no matter how many times I read them.

VEINTE

Questions scrape against my mind, sharp and with a serrated edge. Each one more terrifying than the last. I'm clearly being watched, my time outside La Giralda not my own but someone else's to examine and catalogue and stalk. Chills rush up and down my legs. I am equal parts furious and terrified. If the note had only named me, I would have continued pursuing my suspicions.

But it named Lola.

I can't return to the Gremio to search Don Eduardo's desk—it's too dangerous and I won't risk Lola. Whoever *they* are, it's clearly apparent who I care for, and if they know something like that, then there's no telling what else they know: how I spend my day, Papá's illness, how we're sorely lacking money—the list is endless. I'm too vulnerable.

It's enough to make me want to hide underneath my coverlet.

I finish getting ready and make my way to the kitchen. Ofelia hands me a clay plate with a thick slice of tortilla, herb-roasted potatoes, thinly sliced tomatoes, and smoked chorizo. She drizzles a generous amount of olive oil and forces me to sit at the island.

"You look terrible," she says. "You and Lola both do. I sent her back to bed."

Guilt tugs deep in my belly. The smell of food wafts up my nose, and I shove everything away.

The corners of Ofelia's mouth tip downward.

"I have to train," I say as I leave for the arena.

Another hot day in Santivilla, and training is hell on earth. I'm nauseous from the lack of sleep, sweating from the heat and terrified to look over my shoulder. I can barely perform any of the passes, and as Arturo chases me around, I half stumble to escape his advances. Hours pass this way, and several times he studies me, brows stitched tight. But he lets me try again and again until finally he asks, "Are you all right?"

I must look terrible for him to be even remotely concerned. "Of course I am."

Arturo wipes his face by lifting the bottom of his tunic. A stretch of toned, olive skin becomes visible, and I avert my gaze, cheeks burning. I shake my head, reorganizing my thoughts, and focus on what the tamer had been saying. We've been going over the different weapons and tools a Dragonador uses in a fight. The lance, for stage one, the three banderillas for stage two, and the sword in stage three. I know when each weapon ought to be used—but actually wielding them correctly is a whole other matter.

Everything is in a pile by the tamer's feet, and I bend over to pick up the lance. I carry it in my right hand, and with my left, I hold up the capote. Both feel awkward, and I struggle to hold each correctly. "Do you want to practice with the lance again?"

He backs away several feet. "Yes. Now, you're standing in the middle of the ring. The trumpet blasts its tune and the gate opens for the dragon to come out. What do you do?"

"Look for the dragon's weaknesses," I say. "Once I'm done, I watch and see if the dragon will charge or mark a section of the ring as his territory."

"And why is that important?"

"Because a dragon who is defensive is more dangerous than a dragon who is offensive," I say. "It's much easier to attack a dragon going after the cape than try to attack a dragon defending its territory."

"Bien," he says, and the compliment sounds like it's been dragged out of him, almost against his will. "Now that's the first stage. You've observed your opponent and understand what you're up against. What happens now?"

"I use the cape to test the ferocity of the dragon," I say. "If the dragon goes after the cape, then I make my first move, the suerte de capote."

"Do you remember the name of the first pass?"

I nod. "The Veronica. I must pay attention which horn the dragon prefers to hook with."

"Bien," he says again. "Begin."

I try to swing the cape the same way he taught me. But if the cape is heavy with both hands, it's certainly heavy with one. I bite my lip and ignore the sweat slicking my palms.

"Why do you look so angry?"

"I'm concentrating."

"You look like you're going to be sick."

I shoot him a withering glare. "I'm not going to be sick. Stop trying to provoke me or I'll—"

"You'll do what?" he asks in a quiet voice. "Fire me? Send me home? You'll do nothing, that's what. You can't afford to lose me. But fine, I'll refrain from discussing what you do with your chamber pot."

I swear he brings out the worst in me. I have a temper, yes. And my manners can graciously be called abrupt. But this man provokes violence. I eye the lance and consider jabbing him with it. He catches what I'm doing and turns away—but not before I catch sight of a slight smile. One he doesn't want me to see.

This is ridiculous. I need to learn this. "Quit distracting me."

"This is meant to be entertainment," he says contemptuously. "Don't forget, you're supposed to be having a good time."

When I fumble again, the wooden bar of the cape wobbly and out of control, the tamer makes loud disgusted noises at the back of his throat.

"Once again, like this." Arturo takes the cape from me and moves the fabric gracefully, with long curves and loops. "Imagine the dragon following the move of the cape. You'll be dangerously close to its horns, but that's the point. The closer you are, the louder the applause."

That last sentence sounded almost bitter. But Arturo continues with his lesson, demonstrating elegant capework, and as he moves, I do as he says and picture the dragon enraptured by that red flash of fabric. The cape never pauses in front of his body, but even so, it's entirely too close, and I'm amazed by the casual attitude Dragonadores have against personal injury. But he's right. That's the thrill. Audiences judge the talent of a dragon fighter by their honor, and in the way they fight. They rank their daring and skill with wielding the cape and weapons. On their ability to evade death.

"Always remember to ask yourself one very important question," Arturo says as he continues to move. "How far will you go to please the crowd?"

"At this point, I'm only thinking of staying alive," I say. "I'll worry about entertaining the crowd when I've mastered all of these passes."

Arturo thrusts it back into my hands. "Do it again. But better."

With a scowl, I lift the cape and try again.

The sun marches across the sky, resistant of my pleas to go away or sneak behind a thundercloud. The sky remains perfectly blue, the air scented by the hundreds of orange blossom trees planted throughout Santivilla.

I make no improvement.

Despite how much I try. Despite how many times the tamer makes me repeat several passes, they don't make sense. Everything in me wants to avoid death and serious injury. But all the moves against the dragon are meant to provoke, to draw near, to inflame. I'm too stiff, too scared.

"All right, stop," Arturo says after watching me attempt a compli-cated feinting move while holding a banderillero and cape. "Have a seat and let me think for a moment."

"Are you sitting?"

He places his hands on his hips and scowls. "No."

"Then I'm not sitting."

"Do what you want," he says acidly. "I swear you enjoy irritating me. If I were to tell you to drink water right now, you wouldn't out of spite."

"Not true," I say in between panting breaths. "I'm not sitting because it's harder to get off the ground when you're tired. Better to press on, particularly because you've just indicated that we will continue practicing."

He appears bemused by this.

"When I'm dancing," I explain, "I need to learn the whole routine—not learn it, but *know* it, before I let myself sit. Once I do, it means I'm done for the day and I can relax."

"You dance flamenco."

It's not a question.

"I thought you knew that."

His compliment hangs between us. *I think you're a beautiful dancer.*

He nods, a speculative gleam in his dark eyes. "You dance like your mother."

Also not a question.

I look away from Arturo, not wanting to catch the sudden pity that flares up in most people's eyes whenever my mother comes up.

"I've been approaching this lesson entirely wrong."

"What do you mean?"

He sweeps his arms wide. "Because being in a ring with a dragon is like having a very complicated dance partner. They want to lead, but you must be the one to take charge. You must make them feel as if they are in charge, even if they aren't."

"How?"

"By pretending I'm your dance partner," he says. "Let's practice the Veronica pass, and this time, I'll advance as if I'm the dragon. Drop the lance. We'll only practice on your capework."

He lowers his arms and takes a step forward. I pull in a deep breath and lift the cape with my left hand. My arm shakes with the effort, but I push through the pain. Arturo's dark curling hair sweeps across his brow at an angle as he lowers his head and drops his shoulders. He's almost crouching, and I don't care for the way his dark eyes deepen with mischief.

"Remember," he says softly. "You're meant to brush the cape over my head when I draw near—without letting the horns gouge flesh."

"Right," I say, fighting for a brisk tone. "I'm ready."

His lips bend into a small smile. "Oh, really?"

Arturo charges. I lunge out of the way, escaping the broad sweep of his outstretched palms. I let out a smothered cry in between panting. But he smirks, pivots neatly and races toward me, body pitched forward, and feet kicking up sand. I'm not ready for his attack, but somehow my feet propel me out of the way—but he brushes my waist with his palm.

"You're dead," he says, spinning around. "Again."

I bend over, breath coming out in shuddering gasps, and I clutch my left side where a painful stitch roots itself between my ribs. "One minute."

"Don't tell me you're done for the day," he says. "You can do better than this."

I straighten, anger climbing up my throat. He laughs at the murderous expression on my face, goading me to plant my feet and prepare for his next assault. His laughter cuts off, and he bends his knees, levels me with a searing look.

"You're no quitter," he says firmly. "I've never met anyone so stubborn in all my life."

"Take a look in the mirror."

A fleeting grin bends his perfect mouth.

He rushes toward me at a dead run, and this time I use my cape to ensnare his attention, and Arturo gamely behaves the way a dragon might by following the red blaze of fabric. The trouble is the blasted capote. It's too heavy to wave in a wide arc, only to bring it in suddenly over the dragon's head. I try again and again, successfully keeping the tamer close, but not too close. But I linger too long. It's frightfully heavy—and he yells out—

"Impaled!"

We try again and a moment later—

"Death!"

And yet again.

"Bleeding profusely!"

I throw the cape on the ground. "What am I missing?"

"You're not used to sharing the stage," he says. "The animal will behave erratically if you let it. Use the cape to manipulate where it goes next. Don't let me take charge."

I bend forward, huffing air.

"Again? Or have you had enough?"

I pick up the cape and snap up straight. "Of course not."

He studies me for a moment. "Last one."

The sun's rays pound against my flesh, and sweat drips down my face, under the collar of my tunic. I'm covered in sand, and my braid has long since failed to hold in all my hair. It curls wildly around my shoulders. My chest rises and falls in quick succession. Arturo is in the same state as I am, his brawny arms coated in a sheen, smudges of dirt across his brow from impatiently brushing his dark hair off his forehead.

My voice is thin, breathy. "Last one."

Arturo's gray eyes meet mine, glittering in the sunlight like twin coins against the tan of his skin. "You can do this."

There's no time to respond to his words. He charges, and once again, I use the cape to lure him close, flapping the fabric, twisting it and curling it, using the wind to help me spread it wide. Arturo follows the cape, and I dance out of his reach while keeping him near. Every time he's about to touch me, I sidestep or feint out of the way. We're using the entire arena, dancing in and out of each other's spheres. The work is hard, but my heart pounds one joyous beat at a time, carrying my exhaustion with an ease I've never experienced. Everything else fades away. There's only Arturo circling, watching every move, every slide of my hip as I dart out of his reach, carrying the weight of the capote.

And at last, when Arturo rushes past, I lift the cape higher and slow down enough so that it whips over his head. He turns, his face open and clear, hands reaching, but I jump out of the way.

I drop to the ground, cape and all, with a cry of relief. Arturo slowly comes into view above my face, blocking out the last of the sun's rays.

"I think we're done for the day," he says.

"Then go."

But he doesn't leave, and I'm too tired to move an inch, let alone sit up. I may just sleep out here for the next week. Arturo stands above me, staring at me with the most serious expression I've seen from him since we've met. Then he extends his hand. I accept it, and he pulls me up, but he doesn't let go until we're pressed together. There's no give between us. We're both panting, chests crashing against each other. His arms slide around my waist, and I settle under his chin. His heart beats erratically under my cheek.

"I knew you could do it," he says against my hair. His lips slide down, down, down, until they press against the soft skin behind my ear. I shiver and slowly slide my hands up his arm and wrap them around his neck. Arturo pulls away enough to stare into my upturned face.

He's going to kiss me, and I want him to.

I need him to make me forget about the arena, the murderer on the loose, and all the reasons why this is a terrible idea. It feels as if I've traveled miles to stand in this spot, fought monsters and my own doubts, and now that I'm here, in the circle of his arms, I wonder why I fought myself at all.

I stand on my tiptoes, our lips are inches apart. His arms tighten around my waist, fingers splayed against my lower back. But something shifts in his eyes, indecision floating in their depths. Arturo gently removes my hands and steps away. He exhales slowly, and his attention drops to his boots. "There's something I must say."

My jaw locks. His next words won't be a mystery. He's made his disapproval quite clear—despite what I suspect he feels for me.

He opens his mouth, and I'm already flinching.

The sun disappears, and we're cast in a massive shadow.

I blink, glancing upward.

Arturo dives forward, and together we roll away as a blast of fire descends. We scramble onto our knees as the Morcego flies upward, great wings beating wildly. The sand lifts and swirls, pebbles pelt me in the face. And then the monster soars higher, flying toward the beating heart of Santivilla, the city center. Something flutters around its neck, a long banner dyed bloodred and stitched with gold lettering.

The dragon bears the colors of La Giralda.

VEINTIUNO

Arturo yanks me to my feet. "We need to seek shelter."

I stand motionless, his words seeming to take ages to reach me. The world is unfocused, a smudged painting. He grabs my arm, his mouth moving frantically. But I can't understand or hear anything he's saying because my mind can't let go of the fact that it's our escaped dragon flying above Santivilla, readying to kill, to destroy.

Consume.

"We need cover," Arturo says, and this time his words penetrate.

Somewhere in the distance, the bell tower tolls madly and beseechingly. We all know that pattern of sound. It's the specific call that warns the people of Santivilla to stay indoors. It yells: Everyone hide, find cover, *quick*. Arturo lets out a sharp curse and grasps my hand. He tugs me forward, and my feet follow as if by their own accord. He reaches the tunnel entrance first and spins, eyes wide and frantic, searching the sky. It's his expression that brings me back to the moment, jerks me from the guilt pressing hard against my chest. I rush past him, boots slapping the stone.

I have to help them.

I don't know who they are, their faces aren't clear, but in the next half hour there'll be dozens buried under their homes, trapped under overturned carriages. Bloody, broken, and burning. I pump my legs faster, down the long corridor, rush through the prep chamber, and burst into the grand foyer. I barely notice the maids huddling by the front door, heads tipped back, searching the sky.

Citizens of Santivilla have seconds, mere minutes to find a place to hide against the onslaught.

"Keep the doors open," I yell as I race past the length of the room. "Let anyone who needs shelter inside the house."

I burst into the kitchen, where Ofelia is so startled by my presence, she drops a basket of bread. I jump over it and reach the narrow door that leads straight to the stables.

"Zarela!" Ofelia yells.

"Stay here," I toss over my shoulder before dashing out the door. Heavy footsteps thunder after me, but I ignore them as I reach the stable. I don't wait for the stable hand to help me, but race into a stall and leap onto the mare's back—without caution, without saddle. I click my tongue and dig my heels into her side, guiding her out.

Arturo blocks the path. "What the hell are you thinking?"

"Get out of my way."

"You will lose your life." His voice is the snarl of a dragon. "There's nothing you can do. There's nothing anyone can do."

"I have to try." The stable boy rushes in and fits the bit around the mare's mouth, and then hands me the leather reins. "I will run you through if you don't get out of my way."

He locks his jaw, and there's an audible click when his teeth snap. He steps aside, and once again, I dig my heels and the mare lurches forward, neighing. Arturo stands next to the both of us, and then suddenly his hand is on my thigh, fingers digging into me. Heat flares deep in my belly, and I startle at the unaccustomed feeling. A shiver of alarm flares within me. Arturo tilts his head back, chin lifting and cool gray eyes meeting mine. He holds me in place, his palm burning against the cotton of my trousers. Dimly, the bells continue their awful ringing.

If I'm going, I need to go now.

"This is a terrible idea," he says in a hard voice.

"Let me pass," I say fiercely.

Arturo slaps his palms on the mare's rear and jumps, throwing a leg over and settling behind me.

"What are you doing?" I demand.

"Don't ask stupid questions," he snaps.

I don't have time to argue with him. I click my teeth, and we burst out of the stables, racing to the main cobbled avenue. The horse senses my impatience and gallops deep into Santivilla. The streets are empty, but the tolling of the bells threatens to hammer us flat. It's loud and oppressive. My tunic whips in the breeze as we race past shut-up houses and deserted alleys. Arturo bands his arm tight around my waist, chin lifted high, gray eyes roving the darkening sky. Sweat slides from my brow and down my temples.

A massive shadow crosses our path. It swerves, casting everything it touches in darkness.

"There!" Arturo cries out above the slapping of the mare's hooves against the stone. "Heading toward the plaza."

I follow the line of his strong arm, index finger pointing near the bell tower. A streak of dark shadow flying above us, great wings flapping and enormous. The dragon dives, massive jaw unhinging, and a fiery blast shoots from within, scorching several buildings. The sounds of screaming rend the air.

"Oh no." I lean forward, and Arturo tightens his hold, pressing me against the hard plane of his stomach. "Rápido, niña."

The horse canters along the street, making hairpin turns at my urging, the golden-hued walls of the city rising around us like wheat in a sprawling field. We crash into the main plaza, and the heat from the fire warms my cheeks, the taste of ash coats my tongue. I tuck my mouth and nose under the collar of my tunic, eyes watering from the fumes. Several buildings are ablaze, shrouded beneath a thick veil of smoke.

People flood the plaza, gasping for air, fighting to escape the surrounding flames. They clutch wands dipped in potions meant to ward off smoke, get rid of flames, or protect their skin from burns. But no amount of magic can stop the destruction, the terror, the death. My gaze snags on a screaming little girl, tossed around as others brush past, knocking her this way and that. I slide off my mare, my booted feet slapping stone, and race into the crowd. Arturo shouts something after me, but I can't hear him above the roar of the monster flying directly above us.

I reach the girl, tucking her close to my side. She's heavy, her sooty cheeks pressed against mine. Her shrill cries ring loudly in my ears. The sunlight disappears, and I'm drenched in a smothering, black shadow. I tip my head back and recoil at the sight of the beast soaring mere feet above us.

Another eruption escapes out of the dragon, and the blast hits several onlookers at once, incinerating them before my eyes. The girl yells as the wave of fire veers in our direction. Her skinny arms tighten around my neck so tight, I'm left gasping for air. I spin on my heel and pump my legs.

"Estás bien," I pant. "You're all right."

I race away from the crowd, and the slap of heat nearly makes me topple over.

"Pilar!" someone cries out. The girl is wrenched from my arms. A woman a few years older than me holds the girl to her chest, and she shoots me a fleeting, grateful look. Before I can respond, they dart away, clutching each other—

The shadow crosses their path. The flap of wings shoots gusts of wind into my face. I squint against the onslaught of dirt stinging my eyes.

"Espera!" I shout, mouth full of smoke. "Wait!"

My warning comes too late. Ten feet away from me, a long pipe of fire shoots down, engulfing them fully. The dragon drops to the ground, tail whipping from left to right, and it makes contact with a woman. The force of the hit catapults her off her feet and slams her into a nearby stone wall. A man covered in soot races forward with a pitchfork, and the monster snatches his upper body in its maw; the jaw snaps shut, silencing his screams, while the rest of him lands at the dragon's feet. I blink, my jaw opening and closing. I can't make sense of the destruction, the total collapse of a city square.

Someone rushes forward and seizes my hand.

Arturo's sooty face appears, inches from mine. "Let's go!"

We race to one of the corners of the plaza, aiming for the arched overhang surrounding the square, his callused palm rough against mine. But as we seek cover, I notice a familiar face framed in a second-story window, overlooking the town square. Señora Montenegro struggles against the glass, fumbling at the lock. I pull free from Arturo's grasp and run toward her house.

"*Damn* it," he says after me.

He follows, cursing every step of the way. When I get to the front door, I test the gold knocker and it's blazing hot. I scramble down the marble steps and then peer up at her window. She spots me and renews her effort to jerk the window open, her face scrunches from the effort. Without thinking, I rush forward and use the grooves in the walls to hoist myself up, and then balance on the window ledge.

"Here!" Arturo says from below.

I glance over my shoulder as he tosses a dagger with a long, silver handle. It soars over my head and then crashes onto the ground.

Arturo glares at me. "You're supposed to catch it!"

"I'll lose a finger!"

He scoops up the blade and tosses it straight up, handle first.

I grasp the weapon, thankful I caught it at the right spot, and continue my climb up to the second floor. Señora Montenegro slaps the window, frantic, her form obscured by thick swirls of smoke.

When I'm at her level, I use the butt of the dagger to smack the paneled glass. It splinters, and thin fissures spread but the window doesn't give. "Carajo," I snarl, bringing my arm back. With a guttural roar, I hit my target with everything in me, my other hand grasping the ledge to keep from falling.

The pane shatters.

I tear at the larger chunks, casting them over my shoulder. Señora Montenegro leans forward, coughing and gasping for air. Tears streak her handsome, proud face, and her eyes are bloodshot.

"You're going to have to jump," I say, moving over on the ledge to give her enough space to swing her legs out of the burning room.

But she can't stop coughing, deep rattling coughs that make her entire body shake. Plumes of smoke escape in long, snakelike tendrils, drifting upward. My eyes water, burning and itchy. Sweat slicks my palm clutching the wood. My clothing heats from the blaze of the fire.

"Señora Montenegro," I say in between gulping huffs of air. "Salta! Jump!"

She seems to understand me because her fingers clutching the wooden frames let go of their tight hold, and she tips forward, headfirst.

With my free hand, I catch her arm, and the force of her fall yanks my feet away from the wall. I let go of her and she plummets, while I snap my disengaged hand forward to grab the ledge. I look over my shoulder and let out a relieved sigh. Arturo caught her around the waist, her great skirt rustling against the stony ground. He gently lays her on the floor and looks up.

"Tu turno!"

I release my hands, and I crash into Arturo's arms. The rough fabric of his tunic scratches my cheek. He sets me down, and I drop to my knees beside Señora Montenegro.

She blinks up at me. Her lips are dry and cracked, her fine dress smells as if it's been roasting in a hot oven. "You saved me."

I brush her comment aside. "Let me help you up."

Another fit of coughing seizes her.

Arturo bends and helps her sit up. "She's inhaled too much smoke."

"We have to bring her to La Giralda," I say. "And anyone else who needs shelter."

Señora Montenegro laughs, a hoarse chuckle that unsettles me. "No one will come."

Next to me, Arturo stiffens.

"What—what do you mean?" I shake her shoulders when her eyes drift close. "Señora!"

I let out a frustrated cry. She sags against Arturo, and he slowly brings her down, until her back presses firmly against the stone. I lean forward, desperate to hear more.

"He won't be happy until your papá is gone," she murmurs.

"Who?"

"Your father's enemy, of course," she rasps. Her voice is thin, coated in death. I prod her chest, and it rises once, twice and then stills. My lungs trap my breath, waiting for her to come back, to explain what she meant. But she moves no more. I sit quietly, her words echoing in my mind.

Arturo sinks onto his knees.

"She's gone," he whispers. "What do you want to do?"

I drag my gaze away from the body. Destruction covers every inch of the plaza. People huddle together, crying for their loved ones. Scorch marks mar the surrounding buildings, some still spitting red-hot flames from doorways and windows. Too many lie dead on the cobblestones. The dragon is long gone, having eaten its fill and destroyed to its satisfaction.

"We invite the wounded to our arena," I whisper.

But no matter how many times I offer and plead, no one comes to La Giralda. Too many witnessed the dragon bearing our colors, the answer of who to blame all but written across the sky. So many stare at me in horror, in anger and disgust.

I'm not used to seeing hatred up close.

Arturo watches it all in grim silence. My voice is hoarse from repeating apologies no one hears or accepts. I turn away from the devastation, but there's a sudden crack, a loud thud against the ground that startles me. I spin around in time to see the people of Santivilla bring down the statue of my father. It topples over, fracturing into a dozen pieces.

The crowd draws near. Ferocious glares and angry scowls stamp across their faces. They have all the right in the world to hate and blame me. I back away, and then Arturo steps in front of me. His shoulders are straight and tense, both hands carrying slim daggers. The people hesitate, crowding around us, gazes dropping to his weapons. They didn't expect a fight from me, but they'll surely get one from Arturo.

"Not another step," Arturo snarls.

I hold my breath in my lungs, afraid to exhale for fear of drawing notice. Arturo takes a small step backward, and I follow his slow movement until we've put significant distance between us and the mob. Behind them, the main plaza burns, the fire hissing and popping.

"I left your mare secured on the next street over," Arturo says in an undertone. "Walk slowly with me, and don't look behind you."

My knees shake, but I do what he says. Not once do I look over my shoulder, and not once does Arturo lower his weapons, not until we reach Avenida Maria Claudia. I expect him to scowl at me for taking such a foolish risk, to issue some scathing remark that will make me want to sink into the ground.

"Gracias," I murmur. I brace myself, waiting for the onslaught.

"There was nothing you could have done," he says softly. "But you were brave, all the same."

I narrow my gaze, sure I've missed the insult hidden between his words. But his usual scowl is nowhere to be found. Perhaps he can see the shame carved into my face, the guilt I carry on my shoulders. Because instead of looking at me with obvious contempt, he stares at me with a strange kind of intensity that I find impossible to decipher. It isn't contempt or indifference or even impatience, the usual things I see written across the hard line of his mouth.

No, this is something else.

A flush blooms on my cheeks, and I avert my gaze. He moves away, and I follow after him, my heart heavy, footsteps dragging. The Gremio will demand another meeting. Maybe the Dragon Master will insist on dragging my father out of bed in order to mete out punishment. And without proof of his involvement, I have nothing to leverage. I can't accuse him of paying off the Asociación.

I have nothing to defend myself with.

Because I know one thing for certain: The Dragon Master will not let this stand, not for all the gold in Hispalia.

VEINTIDÓS

The summons comes the next morning in a black gilded carriage with golden trim and ornately detailed dragon wings carved into the wooden frame. I know by experience the interior is outfitted in bloodred velvet and can seat four people comfortably. Papá was summoned for various meeting to the Gremio, and I'd walk him right to the carriage door, wanting to admire the elegance.

Today, I want to run from the sight of it.

It is the driver who hands me the thick roll of parchment, tied by a silk ribbon that costs one golden coin. I take the message, so prettily presented and written, and manage a brisk smile at the boy. He's dressed entirely in black, with handsome leather boots that go up to mid-calf. He carries a whip in the exact same color as his shoes.

"That all?" I ask.

They've coached the boy well. His expression is perfectly blank, like a fresh morning without the grind of the day to mar it. "Your father is to come with me as soon as he's read the contents."

"My father is gravely ill and can't travel anywhere."

"In that case, the guild has instructed me to bring you in his stead, as representative of the family."

"Do you mean now?"

His eyes lower for a fraction to what I'm wearing. "When you're presentable."

I bristle. "I have important things to do. Please let them know I'll pay a visit when it works for my schedule. Gracias."

The driver blinks slowly. "I'm to tell you, that if you don't come today, they'll make their decision without your input."

My clothes are a too-tight fist around my rib cage. "Decision? What decision?"

"That I can't say, señorita."

"I see," I say softly. "I'll come with you. I need a few moments."

The driver tips his head forward. "Of course. I'll wait down in the carriage." Then he turns and exits through the great doors that once welcomed the nobility and monarchs of Hispalia, but now only see the rustle of leaves and dirt carried up by gusts of wind.

The summons is heavy in my hands, heavier than the capote. I swallow, and it's painful.

"Do you want me to read it?"

I turn around. Lola sits on the steps of our grand staircase, cradling a cup of coffee, and Arturo—who arrived earlier than usual—leans against the banister, his elbow propped up, and his own cup in the other hand. He sips his coffee and calmly studies me over the rim.

Lola holds out her hand.

I walk forward with my shoulders straight and gently give her the paper. She unrolls it carefully and proceeds to read, shoulders huddled. I stand over her, the midnight ink swirling across my eyes. I'm unable to pick out individual words. I only know they're damning.

At one point during her reading, she scowls.

I can't bring myself to ask her. She finishes reading and rolls the parchment closed. "Pretentious bastards."

Arturo glances between us. "Is there anything she needs to know?"

Lola shakes her head. "She knows the majority of it."

"Then spare her."

I glance at him, surprised. Lola's green eyes brighten, and she taps the missive against her leg.

"Have you two met?" I ask suddenly.

Lola shoots me an amused glance before swiveling on the stair. "I'm Lola Delgado."

The tamer lowers his cup. "Arturo Díaz de Montserrat."

"Oh, I know," she says with a wink in his direction. "I know *all* about you."

A faint sense of alarm flutters through me. "Lola."

She stands, careful not to spill her coffee. "My friend thinks you're the most handsome man she's ever seen."

I have never said such nonsense in my *entire* life. Heat flares in my cheeks, and I shoot Lola a murderous glare.

Arturo's only reaction is a slow blink, and, as if the words merely bounced off him and affected him not at all, he takes another long sip of coffee.

Lola opens her mouth again.

"Stop talking, Lola."

Lola turns to me. "I think it'll help."

"Help?" I ask. "You are certainly *not* helping. I can't think of anything else that would be less helpful."

She merely smiles and turns away from us both. "Come on, let's get you dressed."

I follow up the stairs, careful not to look in Arturo's direction. With every step I take, I feel his languid gaze between my shoulder blades. A warm sensation that nearly buckles my knees. But I don't look over my shoulder.

Lola dresses me in red. It is, according to her, the best color for my olive skin and ebony hair. My power color. It's strapless, with a ruffled neckline and a cinched waist. The bottom half is stitched with bronze hues threaded in orange florals and filigree.

It's a dress designed to fight battles.

There's a soft knock on my door. Lola shoots me a quick glance before opening it. Standing on the other side is Papá.

"You ought to be resting," I scold, but even as the words fly out of my mouth, I notice that his appearance is looking better than it has since the massacre. Color blooms bright in his cheeks, and his gaze is far more alert and clear. He's still too thin, but the shadows don't cling to his skin like they used to.

Papá shuffles to the bed and drops down in a heavy heap. "Eva is coming by this morning. The woman is trying to kill me."

Lola wisely exits the room with a sympathetic look in my direction. Papá is in one of his moods, I can tell. "Have you eaten?"

He scowls at me. But there's no real bite in his expression, not when he's looking at me. His temper is legendary, capable of leveling anyone in the vicinity. Mamá used to smile at his outbursts—while giving him something to eat. She figured out the worst of his behavior could be attributed to him being hungry.

Papá finally sees what I'm wearing. He frowns. "Where are you going?"

I step away and avert my gaze. The less he knows, the better. I don't want to worry him, not when he's clearly on the way to recovery. "I have an errand to run. It shouldn't take too long."

He seems to accept this and nods. "Is the tamer giving you what you need?"

I let out a startled, embarrassed laugh. "What do you mean?"

Papá narrows his gaze. "I'm asking if he's doing his job, Zarela."

"Oh," I say, and for some reason, I still can't quite meet his eyes. The problem is that I don't know how I feel about Arturo myself. He's confounding and infuriating, but then I remember how he went with me into the heart of Santivilla while it burned. How he complimented my dancing and then pulled me into his arms when I finally mastered a pass. The looks he gives me when he thinks I don't notice. I'm sure my confusion is written all over my face, and I don't want Papá to see.

"He's training me well," I say, and I'm incredibly proud of my nonchalant tone.

But Papá notices something in my face, even though I'm desperate to hide it. The blush gathering in my cheeks, the way my fingers have tangled together.

"Is he behaving like a caballero?" he asks, his voice hard.

I frown—there's something in his tone that I don't like. A hint of an argument that I didn't know we were having. The need to defend Arturo rises within me. "Yes. Why wouldn't he?"

Papá straightens his thin robe. "He's . . . a stranger."

I think back to the conversation I'd overheard between them. There's something Papá knows about Arturo, something he's decided to keep from me. "What are you saying?"

He clears his throat and sidesteps the question. "I don't doubt that he'll do his job. As long as that's all there is."

His meaning is quite clear, and don't like it. I gather my things—a small silk bag and one of my mother's painted fans—before I have my expression the way I want it. Perfectly neutral. "He's there when I need him," I say finally. "I have to go."

"Zarela," Papá says with mounting outrage. "He is not for you."

Not that I don't agree with him, because I do, but his tyrannical attitude grates. I can make my own decisions; I'm allowed my own mistakes. "And why not? What is it you don't like about him? Like you said, he's a stranger." I pause for a meaningful beat. "Isn't he?"

"I won't tell you my reasons, Zarela, even if I wish to. But I will tell you this—Arturo is your best chance of staying alive."

"I *know* that."

"Then you know enough—for now." His voice softens. "You're going to have to trust me."

How can I deny him anything? When I thought I was going to lose him, I would have given anything for more conversations, more time with him, another chance to feel his strong arms around me. Papá is out of bed and keeping secrets and asking me to trust him like I once did. Even though the air between us is heavy with things we haven't said, I swoop down and hug him tight. "I really must go," I say and kiss his cheek. "Please get back in bed."

Papá grumbles but leaves the room, and Lola darts back in.

"Do you think he's really getting better?"

"Yes, I do. You know what else? I think he doesn't like Arturo," she murmurs. She rearranges my hair and pinches my cheeks.

"Listening at doors again?"

She shrugs. "Your life is more interesting than mine."

Not even remotely true. I roll my eyes heavenward, and she has the good sense to look sheepish. Lola can talk to anyone, has walked every inch of Santivilla and beyond, and creates the most exquisite art.

At last, Lola deems me ready to face the Dragon Court of the Gremio de Dragonadores. A tiny line forms between her brows as she studies me. The blood has drained from my cheeks, but deep within me, a fire blazes. I will not cower or run from this fight. She reaches for my hand and squeezes. When we reach the grand foyer, she casts her eye around for the tamer. There's a noticeable droop to her bottom lip. He's nowhere in sight.

"You didn't expect him to stay, did you?" I ask almost angrily. "And I can't believe you said what you did. What's *wrong* with you?"

"It was meant to distract you."

"A distraction," I repeat flatly. I have to resume control of this situation or else Lola will run her imaginative mouth again, and I won't survive whatever other dribble she spits out. "I bet it took him seconds to flee the building the moment we went upstairs. I don't need his constant judgment, his animosity. Honestly if it weren't for—"

We both sweep past the main entrance, walking quickly to reach the black carriage when a sudden voice says—

"If it weren't for what?"

I spin around on the marble steps. Arturo leans against the doorframe, one leg bent at the knee, foot flat against the stone wall. The wind tousles his dark hair, and his hands are deep into the pockets of his brown trousers. There's a sardonic curve to his mouth, as if he knew exactly what I'd been about to say, as if he has me all figured out.

I can't keep the shock from my tone, not even if someone paid me in gold. "You're still here?"

He scowls at me and uses his foot to push away from the wall. Then he walks down the marble steps to where the driver waits, and we scramble after him. I flash Arturo a questioning look. He avoids meeting my gaze as he helps me inside, a careful hand steadying me as I step forward and in.

I look past his shoulders to address Lola. "I'll return shortly. If anything happens with Papá—"

"I'll send word," she says quickly. "Try not to think about it right now."

Another figure comes into view, says hello in his polite, low voice—Guillermo, the mago apprentice.

"What's he doing here?" I ask.

"I invited him," Lola says primly.

I'm immediately alarmed. Lola is never prim.

"Why?" I demand. Arturo sees who we're looking at, and his features harden.

"I'm allowed to have secrets," she says coyly.

Secrets and Lola *don't* mix. For one thing, they rarely stay hidden. For another, it usually means she's up to something I'll have to fix later. Like the time she tried to use fabric dye on her hair and ended up with a lovely shade of putrid green.

"You'll be late if you don't hurry," Lola says.

I frown, a protest on my tongue, but she's right. This conversation will have to wait. I look to the driver, who waits patiently by the horses. "I'm ready, let's be off." I settle my back against the velvet cushion and say, "I can't wait to hear about your afternoon, Lola."

She waves, and I suddenly wish I weren't going alone. The driver steps forward and reaches for the carriage handle, but Arturo stops the door from closing with a firm hand and gracefully climbs inside and then sits on the opposite bench from mine. He's so tall and long-limbed, the space seems to shrink. Lola shoots me a bracing smile before turning away and marching up the steps to La Giralda's front double doors, Guillermo at her heels. Arturo scowls while looking out the window, his arms folded across his chest, and his legs stretched out and crossed at the ankles.

I don't know what to say, but I do manage to blurt out the first thing that comes to mind. "Will you move your feet? You're squashing my dress."

Arturo's gaze flickers to mine. "Surely the end of the world."

"Do you need me to drop you off somewhere?"

The corners of Arturo's mouth tighten as he shoots me a black look. Then he uses his fist to hit the roof of the carriage twice.

We jerk forward and away to the Gremio. Santivilla sweeps past, the winding streets full of people starting the day, arms filled with purchases. Vendors cry out the prices for their wares, while carts filled with barrels of dried food rumble past the window. The rich, buttery scent of a creamery floats into the confined space of the carriage, and my mouth waters. My stomach clenches as we approach the main plaza where I know our dragon wrecked homes, destroyed lives. I lace my fingers tightly in my lap.

Arturo eyes my white knuckles. "Are you nervous?"

"Of course," I say. We reach the square, and I can't help looking out into the ruins. Arturo leans forward and snaps the curtains closed, casting the interior of the carriage in shadows. "You don't need to see the destruction."

I swallow back a painful lump. "I'm responsible."

"Dragons attack the city all the time," he says quietly. "The only difference is now there was someone to yell at. They're dangerous creatures and always will be. Don't feel guilty for how dragons behave."

"Easier said than done," I whisper, looking down at my hands.

"Yes, I know."

I lift my gaze. Shadows hide half his face from me, only the silver glint of his eyes are clear, and they stare into mine, somber and haunted.

"Are you speaking from experience?"

"Of course I am."

I wait for him to tell me what happened in his past that'd make his face turn gray, an incident that still grips him in a tight fist. But he says nothing, and I don't press him. If I knew him better, I would. But we're not friends. I don't think. "Why are you coming with me?"

He stays silent, lips flattened into a pale slash.

"Do you have business to attend to at the Gremio?"

"In a manner of speaking," he says slowly.

The carriage makes a sharp turn, and I pitch sideways. Arturo steadies me, grasping my elbow to keep me on my seat. He moves forward, legs encasing mine, his booted feet tucked under the yards of my dress. Heat flares between us, potent and alarming. It's dulling my defenses, twisting my thoughts around until I get lost in them. He has the coldest eyes I've ever seen, frigid mountain caps that warn travelers to stay far away. But here and now, his eyes warm, the color of well-worn silver coins.

"Señorita Zalvidar," he says in a controlled sort of way that makes me think he'd rather be shouting at me. He says nothing else. He doesn't have to. We know exactly what we're fighting, this feeling between us that won't disappear, no matter how much I want it to.

"Why don't you call me by my first name?"

"You haven't permitted me to."

I lean forward another inch. Our knees brush, and the contact sends a warm flutter throughout my body. He doesn't move his leg for one long, measured beat. "Consider yourself permitted." But then he shifts, moving away until we're not touching, and once again his arms fold tight against his chest.

"We don't know each other well enough for that."

I blink, suddenly mortified, and angry, both emotions simmering just under my skin. I mimic his posture and look away, breathing hard. The bastard. He won't even call me by my name? And suddenly I can't take the quiet anymore, can't let him have the last word.

The words rip out of me. "And we never will."

His shoulders tighten. "No?"

"You will always disapprove of my family and who we are, and what we do in our arena. You have the lowest opinion of me, and I don't care to beg for a friendship that's doomed to be one-sided."

"I don't have a low opinion of you," he says softly. "Far from it."

The carriage abruptly stops, and I instinctively clutch the bench to keep myself from sliding. I peer out the curtained-off window, catching sight of the familiar entrance of the Gremio. "We're here."

"So it would seem."

I clench my jaw as I move to open the door, but Arturo's arm flashes and he blocks the exit. I'm half on the seat, half off, and leaning forward, ready to escape the tamer who is starting to take up way too much space in my life.

My eyes widen. In the dimness of the carriage, his silver gaze glitters. He's utterly still, watching me as if I were his prey. "I don't like you," he says at last.

I curl my lip at him. "I don't like you either."

"Bien." He can't quite manage his usual scowl, and instead continues staring, locked on my eyes as if I were hypnotizing him. I haven't moved since he barred the exit. A lock of his hair curls over his forehead, and my fingers itch to brush it aside.

"You're right. I do hate everything your family stands for," he says. His words are meant to hurt me, but they don't. They came out soft and almost insistent, as if he's trying to convince himself of the truth. "And I'm not who you think I am. We're wrong for each other."

He sounds exactly like my father and says it with such finality, I'm inclined to believe him. And yet . . . he hasn't moved away from me, hasn't given me space to even breathe. "Oh, really," I drawl.

He laughs and drags a hand down his face. "You're impossible."

"So are you."

"But you are so much worse."

I think about the effect he has on me. To yell and fight, to charge at him because the desire to hit him nearly overwhelms me. But I remember how he pulls me to safety, how he pushes me to keep up with my training, even when I want to sit down. And then there's the way he sometimes looks at me, as if I were a problem he never wanted to solve but sits down to work out the solution anyway. "I don't know if that's true," I say.

Arturo slowly closes the space between us. My breath catches at the back of my throat. I'm at war with myself. I want to fling myself away. I want to stay exactly where I am. When his face is inches from mine, I force myself to look at him with what I hope is a haughty expression. We stay like that for a long moment, neither of us wanting to give the other ammunition for the next hit.

Then he slants his head, and his lips brush my cheek, trailing slowly down until they reach the corner of my mouth. There they wait. His lips are soft against my skin, and fiery hot. His stubble tickles my jaw.

I don't move. I don't think I'm even breathing.

"What am I doing?" Arturo mutters in an undertone. The question isn't meant for me. He moves away, his eyes shuttering and as inviting as a locked door, and settles onto the other side of the carriage.

The tamer folds his arms. "Go."

I go.

Quickly and without looking back, my cheeks on fire, heart slamming against my ribs. The places where his mouth touched my skin burn. By the time I reach the entrance, I've controlled my inner turmoil and shoved Arturo far from my mind.

I need to focus, force myself to remain calm against what will surely be a trying meeting with Don Eduardo—the man responsible for *everything*.

When I step inside the building, the room hushes. People fill the main entrance area, talking in small groups, puffing their cigars and pipes, and milling around the central bar. But that all stops the moment I'm seen. As one, the crowd turns to face me, contempt steeped in their expressions.

I straighten my shoulders and walk past, heading straight for the front desk. The same boy from before is at the reception table. When he sees me approach, he pulls on a velvet cord. The scent of coffee mingles with the smell of leather and tobacco.

I reach the boy, a stiff smile on my face. "Buenas tardes. I believe you're expecting my arrival?"

"Hola, señorita." His gaze travels down the length of my resplendent red dress. It could have been painted on my body. Gracias, Lola. "Y tu papá? Dónde está Don Zalvidar?"

"My father is ill," I say. Thinking of him, alone and recovering makes me calm my nerves. I can do this. I can stand before these men and women and defend my name and our home.

"He really ought to be here," he says, voice laced with disapproval. "But the Gremio doesn't want to delay."

"Who will I be speaking to?"

"You'll be addressing most of the Gremio members," he says.

The back of my neck tickles. I can feel everyone's icy gazes on me, sharp pinpricks deadly like knives. "Really?"

He nods. "Everyone currently in town."

I turn slowly away from him, my back straight. I lift my chin high, and I stare them all down, every last one of them in their expensive shoes and tailored clothing, the swirl of tobacco smoke hovering over their heads. I pray my expression is frostier than a slab of ice.

Two members dressed in gray show up to escort me. They gesture toward the main marble staircase that leads both up to the offices and meeting rooms, and down into the lower belly of the Gremio de Dragonadores, a place I've never been.

My heart lurches.

Down below is where they keep their cellars. I pause at the top of the stairs. The two escorts are already halfway down, their boot heels clicking loudly against the stone. I half turn away, searching for a familiar face. Perhaps Hector is here. But he's not visible in the lounge area or sequestered in low conversation with some of the guild members.

I turn away and face the stairs once more. Steady my breath.

Then I take my first step and head down into the belly of the beast.

VEINTITRÉS

The two escorts lead me to the bottom floor, an enormous chamber with four leather couches set in hand-crafted oak frames facing one another to form a square, with a woven bronze and black rug resting underneath. Stone archways lead to other rooms blocked off by wooden doors accented by golden pulls.

I'm directed to an entrance that is double wide, with a brass plaque hanging three feet above the frame that reads: SALA DE JUSTICIA. "Through there," one of my escorts says.

If someone were to look deeper inside me, they'd find a coiled knot of fear and shame tangled together and a prey's instinct of wanting to run, run, run away.

"Go in first," says the other escort.

My voice croaks out one word. "Fine."

On the other side of this door, there will be judgment. A veritable roar swallows every one of my thoughts, a collective cry of disappointment. The same exact sound I heard the day the crowd tried to chase me away from the arena with their taunts and booing and demands.

What would my mother do if she faced this door?

It is the saddest thing that I can't turn to her. That she isn't here, guiding me and telling me that everything will work out.

Together my escorts give a great pull, and the doors open with a lurch and squeaking hinges, as if they haven't been used in a very long time. Stone steps lead down into a round sunken room, barely illuminated by a few guttering torches, and surrounded by different levels of seating. As I descend, several realizations hit me at once.

This room is designed exactly like a dragon ring.

It is also completely empty.

In the center of the sunken, circular area, there's a place for me to stand, a round slab of marble, the color of storm clouds. Dragon leather arm-chairs make up the seating of the two levels encircling the bottom floor.

"Stand in the center," one of the escorts barks. I imagine him snapping orders to my recovering father, demanding he face the Dragon Master on his own. I can't prove Don Eduardo's involvement, but think-ing of what he's done to my family, what he's done to Papá, makes my fear lessen. I take my place, and heat spreads to every inch of my body, rising like a fever, leaving my blood simmering.

Somber chatter and loud footsteps drift into the dimly lit chamber. They're coming. They want to hold someone responsible. They want me to burn.

The Gremio members appear at the top of the stairs, and they slowly fill the room, the hum of their conversation booming like thunder in my ears. They are dressed in bloodred robes wrapped around immense frames, collars turned up against their necks, and deep pockets hiding heaven knows what.

My spot is a vulnerable one, with nowhere to hide. I'm exposed and my nerves are raw. I massage my fingers, fighting to hold on to my anger as they take their seats. The Gremio members vary in ages; some are stooped, life's weight having taken its toll, and others move about the room with more zeal. My gaze snags on a familiar figure, tall, with dark wavy hair that brushes the tops of his shoulders. My breath freezes in my chest. I know that brooding mouth, the taut line of his back.

Arturo.

The ground tilts under my feet. My mouth goes dry, tongue coated in dust. What's *he* doing here? He isn't a Dragonador. Is he . . . he *can't* be a member—a *senior* member? Several men and women walk past him, looking for a seat, and as they do, they stop to lay a hand on his arm, voicing exclamations of surprise and delight.

I leave my spot and stalk closer. "Señor Díaz de Montserrat."

Arturo stiffens. Then he slowly, *so slowly*, turns around. Our gazes lock. Anger thrums in my blood, makes my body shake. I have to suffocate the urge to leap over the barrier.

Don Eduardo comes into my line of sight, his feathery white hair gleaming golden from the light of the guttering torches. He moves deliberately toward Arturo. Down the length of the aisle, past the curious onlookers, who switch their attention from the tamer to the Dragon Master. He's dressed in a black robe, with brass buttons and gold stitching that travels from the shoulders down to the hem of his robe. He's a shadow in a sea of red. In his weathered hand, he carries a polished wood cane carved into the shape of a dragon's head. Don Eduardo's expression is remote as he looks between us.

I've been such an idiot. That moment when he almost kissed me, he tried to tell me something. Was this it? It has to be. The great secret Papá and Arturo have been keeping.

"Go stand in place, and we'll begin," Don Eduardo says in his hard, low rasp, roughed up by stone and hard edges.

I shoot a venomous look at Arturo before returning to my spot. Don Eduardo makes himself comfortable in a leather chair decorated in dragon hide and larger than the rest. Loud shuffling disturbs the quiet as the people in attendance follow his lead. The Dragon Master adjusts his robes and then addresses the masses. "We all know why we're here," he begins. "A truly unfortunate business. I summoned Señor Zalvidar, but evidently he's still incredibly ill, and so we must all welcome his representative, Señorita Zarela Zalvidar. I'll remind everyone that the matters discussed in this chamber are to be kept in the strictest confidence. Should word spread of what takes place during this session, all members will be fined ten reales." He gestures to me. "Señorita, are you aware of the extent of damage your dragon caused yesterday?"

I swallow and lick my dry lips. "I don't know the specifics, but I can imagine."

"The death toll rises, but we know there have been at least seventeen deaths," he says gravely, and I flinch. "Sixteen buildings were completely destroyed, and we're still tallying the rest of the neighborhoods to count the losses. La Giralda has been the center of extraordinary scandal and a decision must be made. The city of Santivilla has lost faith in your family's ability to run a dragon ring, and as long as your family remain members of this fine institution, then we risk losing the support and our standing as the most important and powerful Gremio in Hispalia."

"I respect this guild and its long-held traditions," I say. "I am deeply, profoundly sorry for our involvement in the loss of life and devastation to the city. I humbly ask that you let me speak, so that I may share details that have come to light since the day of the tragedy. Will you let me?"

"I think the events speak for themselves," Don Eduardo says.

"Sir," I say, my tone this side of impatient. "My father is a prominent member of this organization, and his voice must be heard. My family has gladly given thousands of helóns to the Gremio over the years. I ask again, will you let me speak as Santiago Zalvidar's representative?"

Don Eduardo leans back against the leather chair, steeples his fingers. "If you're going to launch into a cock-and-bull tale of sabotage, then I regret that I'll have to stop you before you begin."

My jaw drops. "With respect, there have been too many peculiar—"

"Señorita, I cannot allow you to continue," he cuts in firmly. I startle at his words. "It's a ridiculous theory, troubling and incredibly foolish to spout ill-thought assumptions without greater proof than missing locks. It simply will *not* do."

A rustle of noise disturbs the audience, and quiet murmuring erupts from every direction. I search for a friendly face, but I can't find any in the crowd. I refuse to look at Arturo's face for fear of seeing his scowl and disapproval.

I'm going to lose. It hits me like a kick to the teeth. Until now, I didn't realize how much hope I'd been foolishly holding on to. "What can I do to make this right?" I think wildly, as I discard one idea after the next. "I'll hunt down the dragons responsible—"

My words are met with immediate laughter.

"How will you hunt the dragons?" someone from the crowd asks.

I flush, still refusing to look in Arturo's direction. "I'll hire the best hunter in Hispalia."

"And who would want to work for you?" Don Eduardo asks in a scornful tone.

My flush deepens, and I can feel the tamer's hard stare. "There must be *something* I can do."

"You can accept the proper and fitting course of action we must take. What will that be?"

"A vote regarding the formal removal of your family from this Gremio," Don Eduardo says. "And for La Giralda to rightfully become ours as a functioning dragon ring under different authority, according to the terms laid out in the contract your parents signed upon initiation. There are several families who are present today better equipped to helm the fate of La Giralda."

Heat gathers at the back of my throat. Red-hot words waiting to be released. "La Giralda has been in our family for five hundred years. It's our home; it belongs to the Zalvidar name and their descendants."

"We face enormous pressure from the citizens in Santivilla. Already, several other dragon rings have seen a dip in attendance."

My breath comes out in great huffs. I can't stop shaking. "I know that we're partly to blame—we ought to have had better security. I ought to have done more; it never occurred to me that someone might try to—" My voice cracks. "Everyone knows you can't stand my father. You're doing this to get rid of him."

The murmuring in the chamber hushes. I've thrown open the doors to let the light in. Don Eduardo's secret can't hide in the dark anymore.

"How I feel about your father is irrelevant to this conversation."

"I think it is," I say quietly. "If you don't want him to succeed you."

"That is the outside of enough," the Dragon Master snarls. "We vote now."

"Por favor. What can I do?"

"There is nothing."

"No," I say. "I can't accept—"

Don Eduardo stands, and his chair makes a resounding screech against the ground. "Let us vote. All in favor of the permanent removal of the Zalvidar family and all subsequent heirs from our Gremio, raise your hand."

An immense weight on my chest makes it hard to breathe. Hard to think. I fight to remember the unyielding line of my spine, to remember that I have a voice, just as important and loud as the Dragon Master. If I can't remember that, then I have failed my ancestors, failed my descendants.

I force myself to stare at my feet, so I don't have to witness the people turning their backs against my family—against my father—when the chamber doors open with a loud bang. My face jerks up in surprise. And there, standing at the entrance, is a face I've known all my life. Weathered and thin but so dear. He takes a wobbly step, and the light casts flickering shadows across his gaunt figure.

My father has come. I crumble to the floor.

He stands perfectly straight, wearing his best suit and leather shoes, polished to a sheen. His beloved capote sits around his shoulders, red and furious in the guttering light. No one speaks. Even Don Eduardo sits back down. Papá makes his way down to meet me. Fat tears drip down my face, and I can't move, not even to wipe them away. I never meant for any of them to see me cry. Papá uses a gentle finger to coax my chin upward.

"Querida," he says softly. He uses his thumb to wipe my cheeks. His features are stark, too angular, too pronounced, and his clothes are loose and immense. But all the same, he's handsome and proud and, in this moment, truly alive in a way I haven't seen in months. Some of his old strength holds him upright, keeps his chin lifted high. Papá places a firm arm around my shoulders, and we face the Dragon Master to-gether, side by side.

"Señor Zalvidar," Don Eduardo says. "My old *friend.*"

The rotten liar. Papá must feel the sudden tension stiffening the lines of my back because he tightens his hold.

"Forgive the interruption. Before the vote is cast, I'd like to say a few words if this great assembly will permit it," Papá says.

The Dragon Master doesn't speak for a long moment. With me, he was stern and inflexible—hard and dead set against me. But Don Edu-ardo isn't looking at me. "State your piece."

Papá's voice rises, a deep timbre that warms my soul, fills every hidden corner of my heart. "Before you decide the fate of my family, I ask that you remember the man that I am. Some of you may know me as a friend, as a colleague, as a lover of our tradition in the ring. For those of you who call me amigo, I ask that you remember what I live for. Above all else, I am a protector of my family and of my name, and I would never do any-thing to risk either. My daughter believes there has been foul play under our roof. I ask that you consider the mistake you might make in voting against me today, should she be proven right. You will have destroyed my legacy. I ask, no"—my father's knees start to bend—"I beg that you think very carefully. If you have any doubt, please do not vote to ruin me."

My father's knees hit the ground, his hand wrapped around my waist. I wait a long moment, at war with myself. Pride is a relentless taskmas-ter, and I've been enslaved to it for most of my life. With a shuddering breath, I drop to my knees.

The room is quiet for several heartbeats.

"Santiago," Don Eduardo says. "Whatever happens in the next mo-ment, I want you to know that I conducted this meeting fairly, despite what your daughter might think. We have our differences, but I assure you that I've set them aside during my deliberations. Perhaps there was something nefarious at work in your home, but it is your name on the door, and someone must be held responsible. The people demand it, and I will vote accordingly and encourage our members to do the same."

Papá glances at me, and a sad smile twists his mouth. He squeezes my shoulder, and I understand what his gesture is meant to convey. He's preparing me for the inevitable. The Dragon Master casts the vote. Like before, I force myself to look at the ground. My heart can't take looking at all those raised hands.

After a moment, Don Eduardo clears his throat. We both come to our feet. My heart is a wild thing, an animal wanting to survive the next second.

"By almost unanimous vote," he says softly, "this Gremio will permanently remove the Zalvidar family from its books and transfer La Giralda from their hands to ours. We'll allow you a period of time to pack up your belongings and settle into a new location."

It takes everything in me to remain upright, to hold on to the shreds of my dignity.

"Will we be able to appeal?" Papá asks, voice dry.

"On what grounds?" Don Eduardo demands.

"We don't have proof—but if one of the charges against me is my inability to run a dragon fight safely, allow me to prove to this board, and Santivilla, otherwise. If patrons once again can trust La Giralda, it will bode well for the other arenas. Give us this chance, and if we succeed—promise you'll host another vote to allow reinstatement of my membership and for La Giralda to remain ours."

"That is out of the question," Don Eduardo snaps. "Another fight at La Giralda—"

I jump to my feet. "But think of the turnout—the *last* event at La Giralda. People will come. Out of nostalgia, out of curiosity." My voice cracks. "Out of love for my mother."

That silences him. A pregnant pause follows, the utter stillness of everyone holding their breath, waiting. Don Eduardo may not like my father, he may barely tolerate me, but he indulged Mamá. She could charm anyone, coax a smile from even a dragon.

"And who will battle in the arena?" Don Eduardo asks finally.

Time seems to slow, until I can only hear my own heartbeat rattling against my ribs. I can tell them all the truth—that I will be the Dragonador in the ring. Except I know, I *know*, deep down in my bones, that I won't be received or accepted by any of them. I can't risk telling them the truth.

I want my chance, and for that to happen, I need to lie.

Arturo is not going to be happy about this.

Slowly, I look toward him. He's gazing down at me, brows pulled in tight, lips shaped into a hard line, preventing him from shouting a curse at me. He knows whose name I'm going to say. But my will is the cold hard face of a mountain, enduring the worst of weather and time.

My voice is as clear as Santivilla's singing bells. "Arturo Díaz de Montserrat."

A ripple of noise courses through the aisles. For some reason, this information surprises the Gremio members.

"My *nephew* will be fighting in your arena?" Don Eduardo asks, brows climbing his forehead.

I blink, stunned.

Once again, I'm robbed of speech. His nephew? I slowly crane my neck to look at the tamer. He sits stock still, arms draped over the armrests of the leather chair, mouth set in a pronounced scowl. The dim lighting in this chamber casts deep hollows under his cheekbones, and I'm struck by the similarity to Don Eduardo's face. Identical hollows, identical shadows. Arturo is related to the Dragon Master. The ramifications nearly level me to the ground.

Don Eduardo is responsible for my fate . . . and Arturo has been frequenting La Giralda, has been down in our dungeons, and has a *key* to the damn cells.

He's seen my bedroom.

He could have been spying on us the entire time—and I've been too busy, too distracted by him to see the signs. And now I've just handed Arturo the means to destroy me. He can renounce my words, out me in front of all these people, and we'd be forever turned away from the Gremio.

I gave him a sword to use against me in this fight.

Now all he has to do is run me through and watch me bleed.

"Is this true?" the Dragon Master demands. "Will you be a Drago-nador once more?"

I'm not so much of a coward that I won't meet the eyes of the person who holds my fate in his hands. His anger is a tangible, terrifying thing. Fists clenched in his lap, the fury leaping off him as if there were flames licking his edges. He could burn me with one breath.

"Yes," Arturo says in a snarl. "It's true."

The words sound like they've been dragged out of him. I don't be-lieve them at first. Not until they sink into my bones. He's not going to ruin me. I meet his eyes, and he's still *so* angry, but there's a look on his face that steals my breath. He's on my side. Comrades fighting in the same war. I don't know why; I possibly don't even care. It only matters that he showed up.

The Dragon Master clears his throat, and the noise drags my atten-tion away from Arturo. I expect him to be annoyed by the apparent support of his nephew to my cause, but my assumption is dead wrong. A silent communication zips between the two men, impossible to in-terpret. It ought to make me uneasy, but I'm still riding a euphoric current, carrying me to exactly where I want to go.

"All in favor of allowing the Zalvidar familia to host one more dragon fight at La Giralda?" Don Eduardo asks.

Many hands fly into the air. Some slow, some fast. Arturo raises his hand, my comrade in battle. My breath catches at the back of my throat.

Majority wins.

The Dragon Master pushes back his great leather chair, and the sound crashes around the room. "This session is over."

I face Papá, my eyes filling with tears. His expression matches mine, and he grips my hands tight against his chest.

This is it.

The last chance to save our home.

VEINTICUATRO

Papá and I sit at the kitchen island, sipping hot coffee and enjoying toasted bread slathered in smoked olive oil. It's the next morning, and I can hardly believe that my father is upright, color on his cheeks, his dark eyes bright and merry and hopeful. He's getting better, hour by hour, minute by minute. He reaches for my hand and I clasp his tight, relieved to feel the strength in his grip.

Ofelia putters around us, filling our cups and plates. When she thinks I'm not looking, she mops at the corner of eyes with her sleeve. Loud banging at the kitchen door startles me, and I almost drop my drink.

"Why is this door locked?" Lola asks. She bangs louder. "Hola?"

I jump to my feet, flushing. We usually keep the side door open, but I've been locking up La Giralda tight every night. I let her in and raise my brows at the sight of her. She's gasping for breath, her hair a wild disarray.

"Nice of you to join us," Ofelia says testily. "There are beds to be made, dishes to wash."

Lola clutches her side, a deep flush blooming in her cheeks. "Sorry I'm late."

"My God, Lola. Did you run here?" I ask. "Was something chasing you?"

"Be quiet and listen to me," she huffs. "The news is all over town."

"What news?" Papá asks. "Lola, dear excitable child, have a seat before you fall down."

"Have breakfast," I say, cutting her off before she can speak. I push the plate of olives and thick slices of grapefruit toward her. Fortunately, produce from the market is still relatively inexpensive. We're on a steady diet of bread, tomatoes, olive oil and olives, fresh greens, and whatever fruit is in season, which currently means a lot of citrus can be found in La Giralda.

Ofelia stands and refills our cups with coffee. "You're spoiling the girl," she mutters under her breath.

Lola brushes the comment aside. "A dragon has been left outside the front door of the Dragonador headquarters."

I slowly stand to my feet. "Which one?"

Her eyes flash with impatience. "Yours—the Morcego. It wears the ribbons of La Giralda."

I place my hands on the table, the grooves caressing my palms. "Dead or alive?"

Lola cackles loudly and slaps the island. "Alive, of course. You know he doesn't believe in killing them."

My mouth barely shapes the word. "*Quien?*"

Lola leans forward, eyes gleaming brightly in the morning light. "Arturo."

I have to forcibly close my mouth. We all stare at her as if she's just announced the Dragon Master wants to host his next birthday fiesta on the moon. Perhaps I haven't had enough coffee this morning. Because it's impossible Arturo would do me this favor. Yesterday, he'd been furious with my deception.

"He couldn't have."

Lola winks at me. "I'm sure he did."

I finally notice that she's wearing her bed clothes, as if she hasn't seen the inside of her room all through the night. "Have you slept?"

"Not a wink," she says cheerfully, helping herself to a plate of food. "Ofelia, did you make any tomato jam?"

She rolls her eyes in response.

"In that pot over there," Papá says, pointing to one of the shelves.

"Are you saying," I begin carefully, "that Arturo left the Gremio yesterday and went straight to hunt one of our escaped dragons? And that he was successful—*in less than a day?*"

She plops down onto the empty stool next to me. "Someone is infatuated." If she could have sung the words, I really think she would have. The silly idiot. But then for one breathless moment, my mind focuses on that moment in the carriage. His lips against my skin. The way it made me feel. Confused. Wanting.

The way he backed my outrageous lie in front of the entire Dragon Court.

And yet he'd kept his membership to the Gremio a secret. He never told me the Dragon Master is his uncle. All this time, I thought he was a disillusioned Dragonador, someone who'd left the profession in disappointment. But it had been more than that—he has familial ties to the most powerful man in Santivilla. For all Arturo's talk about wanting nothing to do with dragonfighting or presumably the Gremio, he still showed up yesterday for the meeting in order to vote.

I don't know what any of it means.

He clearly has secrets, and I may never fully understand why he chose to help me, but in a hidden corner of my heart, the one I don't share with anyone, I hope he did it for me. The thought feels ridiculous, a wish made of make-believe.

"Do you still think it's a good idea to train with the tamer?" Papá studies me shrewdly, as if seeing the fairy tale spinning in my mind.

When I'm sure I can respond the way I want—self-possessed, without the slightest betrayal of the confusion I feel, I tell my father the closest thing to the truth. "I'm angry with him. I don't trust him. But I'll continue my training."

Papá nods.

He opens his arms and I walk straight into them.

Both of his hands wrap tightly around my shoulders. He smells like coffee beans and his tobacco pipe. "I need you to keep getting better, that's the most important thing."

"I don't like everyone fussing," he says with some of his old fire, and it warms my heart.

"Pity," I say with a small smile. "Prepare yourself for more of it." I look at my best friend. "Lola, will you take him upstairs?"

Lola wraps her arms around Papá's waist—he lets out an outraged protest—and together they shuffle toward the doorway, huddled together. Papá shifts and becomes smaller, and I hammer my grin flat. All of his talk of not wanting a fuss is just bluster. He loves the attention, loves to feel cared for and nurtured. Lola looks over her shoulder, trying to press her lips together to keep herself from laughing.

The bell tolls and I remember the day ahead, and as wonderful it is to see Papá acting like his old self, I still have to face the dragon tamer.

His questions. His fury.

I wait for Arturo in the middle of the arena, sitting on the sandy floor with my knees close to my chest, in my training outfit. His furious face leaps in my mind. I brace myself for the fight I know is coming.

I stiffen at the sound of someone approaching. My gaze remains straight ahead, away from the entrance. Arturo's scuffed-up leather boots and tan trousers come into view. He squats down so we're at eye level. He's grim, mouth thin, the long lines of his body steeped in exhaustion. The capote is in his hands. A small part of me thaws. But then I remember seeing his face yesterday at the Gremio. The anger and keen sense of betrayal return, overpowering any soft feelings I have for him. They're at war with the memory of him voting for me, at war with the possibility of him hunting down our missing Morcego.

My voice is flat. "The Dragon Master is your uncle."

"That's right," he says neutrally—but he's not fooling me. Anger burns bright behind that impenetrable wall he's built around himself, and a treacherous moat besides. It's probably filled with venomous snakes.

"Why didn't you tell me?"

Arturo arches a dark brow and asks scornfully, "Are none of my secrets safe?"

He's completely unapologetic, and I hiss fire, my vision exploding into a vibrant red. The color of my capote, of war, of blood. "How *dare* you? I'm owed better than that."

"Your fury is directed at the wrong person," Arturo says coldly. "I had *nothing* to do with my uncle's decision to mete out punishment for what happened in La Giralda."

Arturo thinks I'm mad for the wrong reason. He doesn't know that I've found the person responsible for the massacre at La Giralda—his uncle. It's on the tip of my tongue to tell him, but I keep the words buried. I don't trust him enough for that.

"And what about *you*?" he asks, deceptively calm, and goose bumps flare up and down my arms. "What about what you've done?" he repeats, but louder this time, and I wonder if I ought to be on my feet for this conversation. "I'd like to know why the *hell*—" His voice raises to a distinct roar, and I lift my brows warningly, and his lips flatten mulishly. When he speaks again, his tone is moderated, but strained, as if the effort costs him. "I have told you that I will never fight again. *Not ever.* What were you thinking?"

I'm not giving him an inch. It serves him right. "Have you been reporting to your uncle?"

He appears stunned. "Reporting to my—*no*. Tío Eduardo has paid for my membership since I was thirteen. He continues to pay the yearly fee in the hopes that I'll change my mind and take his place as a Dragonador once more. Which I won't," he adds, glaring at me.

He's answered my question, but I'm not satisfied. I still don't know if I can trust him. But before I can press further, he drops to one knee on the sand, his scowl returning, sharp enough to cut flesh. "How could you do that to me? You know how I feel about the profession!"

"Of course I do!" I shout angrily. "And I would never make you fight a dragon in the arena."

"Oh, really?" he asks in a scathing tone. "Yesterday it sounded like that's exactly what I'll be doing."

"I was lying."

His frown softens, almost disappears, except for the faint line of skepticism crossing his brow. "What?"

"It's still going to be me fighting in the arena. I only said your name to secure my last chance."

"And when they see it's you in the ring? What then?"

I bite my lip and shrug. "Maybe they'll be impressed by my daring. That's what you're always telling me, isn't it? Being a Dragonador isn't actually about killing the dragon. It's a living and breathing work of art, a performance showcasing the fighter's bravery and honor."

Arturo frowns. "It's risky."

"It's the only move I left." I narrow my gaze at him. "Why didn't you out me in front of your uncle when you had the chance? You could have told him that I was lying, that you didn't know what I was talking about."

"It doesn't matter." He flushes and then quickly changes the subject. "Are we going to train or not? I don't want to waste any more time."

I stare at him. Has he learned nothing about me? "You know what my answer will be."

He holds out a hand to help me up. "Then get off your ass."

Arturo yanks me to my feet, and I tip forward, losing the battle for balance. He clasps both hands around my arms to steady me—and to keep me from coming closer.

"¿Por qué?" I whisper.

His face is impenetrable. Still as stone. A veritable fortress. "It's time to work."

I take a step forward, until we're a breath apart. He holds his ground, like I knew he would. "Did you hunt down our missing dragon and deliver it to the Gremio?"

All I get is a slow, measured blink. Nothing else. He turns his face away, but I'm not done pushing him. "I need to know the truth."

Arturo unfurls the capote and holds it between us like a barrier. "What does it matter? A dangerous dragon is off the streets—"

"Was it you?"

His lips twitch. "I hunt dragons. It's what I do—"

I take a hold of the capote. "It *was* you. But why—they'll kill it."

"I know."

He'd hunted down the dragon anyway. I let go of the cape and back away from the tamer, my jaw dropping. "But *why?*"

"I told you," he says in that flat tone I've come to learn is his friendliest. "I'm a dragon hunter. Nothing more. That's all I am to you." And for a moment, his face isn't as guarded, and I realize he's trying to tell me something about yesterday. About the moment in the carriage.

About the kiss.

He's saying it didn't mean anything. The finding of the dragon, what happened between us—none of it connects, and especially not in the way Lola suspects. I want to laugh at myself, or maybe cry—for wasting even a moment of my life thinking about him, for being confused by him.

He's not the only one with a job to do.

"Yes," I say briskly. "You did tell me."

He nods. Short and curt, and he's withdrawn from me again, in the space it takes to tip his chin. "Good, because tomorrow you'll face the dragon. You'll be fighting in the arena four days from now," he says quietly. "It's high time you face the monster you're meant to kill."

"Am I ready?"

His lips flatten. "You'll have to be." Then he goes and grabs the lance from within the chest where all the weapons are stored. He drops the cape on top of the lid and then he tosses the lance to me, and I catch it with one hand. The tamer quirks a brow. "Let's see if you can stab me with it."

I hold up the lance as he comes at me in a run.

VEINTICINCO

Three days from the show. I ought to be practicing this morning, but instead of a lance, I hold a bucket of paint. I dunk the brush back into the pail and stretch my arms high over my head, slightly dizzy. Probably from lack of sleep. Or too much coffee and not enough to eat. Lola, on the other hand, finishes her section with a flourish and her brush joins mine.

Together we take a step back to admire our work. La Giralda is an immense building made of brick and golden stone with blue-tinted glass windows shaped into delicate arches. Near the main entrance is a plain patch of wall, with no ornament, but Lola convinced me to let her paint a mural of our dragons fighting in the arena. She also added the date and time of the last show in large lettering painted a bold red.

It's almost finished, the bright colors a pleasing contrast against the solid hue of the wall, the striking depiction of the Morcegos with their short, bat-like wings and black scales that gleam in the sunlight. The dawn draws near, a hazy purple drenches the morning, with touches of golden light illuminating the still-quiet street. The only sounds I can hear are the soft rumblings of wooden carts and vendors setting up near the main plaza. Work on La Giralda is nearly finished. All that's missing are the white sands from the coast. Ofelia said the carts will arrive tomorrow morning.

Lola swings her arm around my shoulders and squints up at the mural. "What do you think?"

I follow her line of sight, and my gaze lands on the painting she did of my likeness, dressed in a beautiful red dress, the hem lined in ruffles and lace. Lola added a white jacket, similar to the traje de luces Dragonadores wear in the arena, with vibrant colors: the fiercest red, the purest gold, along with shades of lavender and soft pink. My hair is loose and wild, adorned by an equally arresting headband that glimmers and shines. She's somehow rendered me to look stronger than I feel. Capable and brave. I am a dancer and a fighter.

"Is this how you see me?"

She glances at me in wry amusement. "Zarela, this is you."

I smile, and together we gaze up at the immense mural. A pulse of delicate hope thrums in my veins. Now everyone who walks past La Giralda will know about the show. They'll be expecting Arturo Díaz de Montserrat.

But it will be me. Not as my mother, the talented flamenco dancer. Not as my father, the brave Dragonador. A blend of the two people I love the most. I hope I can make them proud. Because if the crowd tries to run me off the stage, I'm not sure if I'll ever be able to perform again.

"I like the addition of the jacket," I whisper. "I can't wait to see it in person."

"Oh, I know," she says with a wink in my direction.

I laugh and untangle myself from her. Seeing myself in a flamenco dress has flooded my body with an acute yearning to stomp my feet, twist my hands high up into the air.

"Where are you going?" Lola glances up to the sky. "Is it time to train already?"

"Almost," I say. I can't remember the last time I danced. There's a hollow ache in my chest that grows wider and deeper, and if I don't put on my velvet flamenco shoes soon, I'm afraid I never will. "I'm going to dance before Arturo gets here."

She nods approvingly. "But what about the music?"

"I can hear the melody in my head," I say with a smile, and then I leave her to finish the painting while I go in search of my dancing shoes. I find them under my bed, covered in sticky sand, unworn since that terrible day in the arena. On a whim, I throw on a simple three-layered ruffled skirt in a blue that hides the stains, one of the few I own to practice in. Then I make my way out to the ring. The sun's glare makes me squint, its rays a hot slap against my exposed skin.

I stand in the middle of the arena and shut my eyes, willing myself to quiet so I can hear the melody I carry in a corner of my mind. Slowly, it comes to me, one note at a time. The sultry sound of the guitar, each persuasive thrum making my blood come alive. I twirl my wrists high over my head. My back automatically arches, lengthening my spine. The beat in my head roars louder and louder. There's no wooden platform under my feet, but I make do, stomping the balls of my feet against the hot sand.

"Uno, dos, tres," I number the beats under my breath. "Siete, ocho, nueve, diez."

I practice balancing on my tiptoes in order to complete continuous spins, going around and around but never once getting dizzy, my arms two perfect curves while I whirl. Taking up the corner of my skirt, I swish the fabric to the left and right, my feet tapping and shuffling, the lines of my body curving. Sweat beads at my hairline, drips down the back of my neck. Dios, I've missed this, can't believe I haven't made time to dance. I feel so, so alive.

The sun continues its march along some invisible path in the sky, but I hardly notice.

The music in my head becomes all too real. Catching me in its irresistible net.

The notes are loud, louder than I think possible, until I glance around and catch sight of a spectator, sitting high up in the stone seating encircling the arena.

Arturo strums my father's guitar, and he plays the same way he lives, confident and unapologetic. Our eyes meet for one hot, breathless moment, and then I twirl, sinking into his song. The instrument is an extension of who he is, the notes bold and angry and obliterating. I throw one hand in the air, the other slaps my thigh as I stamp forward and back, my heels battering the packed sand.

Arturo stands, his fingers don't stop their playing, and he makes his way down to where I'm dancing. Arturo makes the guitar roar, and my body answers the battle cry. And then he slows the melody, coaxing me into a languid last spin. I end with my arms curved downward, one foot in front of the other.

His stare is ruthless, hostile. As if I were a threat to his well-being. I'm inordinately pleased by this.

He hauls himself over the railing, the guitar still clutched in one hand, and then he stalks over as I steady my breath.

"You dance as beautiful as ever," he says when he reaches me.

"Is that an accusation?"

"What?" he asks, exasperated.

"Well, you sounded angry. It's hard to tell when you're giving me a compliment." I grin at him, and he looks away, flushing, lips stretched into a grimace.

A short pause. "It was a compliment," he says in a curt tone.

"Gracias. You play very well," I say sincerely. He blinks in surprise, and then he ducks his chin, and I'm amused by his sudden shyness. "Who taught you?"

Arturo's expression shutters, slams the door so loudly, I'm surprised my ears aren't ringing. "My father."

I watch him closely. "What happened to your parents?"

"They died of the fever a few years back."

The sickness had spread like wildfire, decimating the population like a wave battering the seashore. Scores of people perished, and for a long time you couldn't walk to the plaza without seeing a funeral procession. "Lo siento."

"I've made my peace with it."

"Doesn't make it less sad," I say quietly. "Thank you for the music. It's been too long since I've danced."

"Lola asked me if I could play and then handed me the instrument. Your father's, I presume?"

I nod.

Arturo's expression turns grim. "I'm bringing up the dragon today."

"I know." I pluck one of the strings, my mouth dry.

"Let's warm up by doing a few passes," he says. "And then I'll go down below. Will you be able to practice in that skirt?"

My stomach clenches, but I nod.

Arturo peers at me, brow furrowing, as if sensing my disquiet. He makes a small move toward me, raising his arm, index finger stretched and close to my cheek. I hold my breath, waiting for the soft touch. But he drops his hand, makes a noise of impatience—not at me, at himself—and then he walks off, propping the guitar against the wall. Then he turns toward me, raising a single dark brow. "Ready?"

We face each other, spaced a few feet apart, panting for breath. Arturo had me run through each stage, practicing drills and passes. Every time, he moved like a dragon might, sudden and wild and combative, in short bursts of relentless energy. Every time, I was able to dance out of danger, smiling and stabbing the lance in his direction when he got close. I've started adding spins whenever I evade him, tight circles across the arena as he charges. When we're done, he looks over at me and nods.

"Does that mean I'm ready?"

He flicks sand off his leather boots. "Yes. Hand me your capote."

A flutter of alarm passes through me. My toes curl in my shoes. "Do you need help dragging the beast out here?"

He shoots me a look of such withering scorn, it makes my toes curl. As he moves away and toward the tunnel entrance, his free hand reaches for the guitar propped against the wall, his fingers brush the strings before disappearing into the shadows. I pick up the hem of my skirt and shake out the creases and sand. I settle into practicing more spins and passes, imagining a feral beast before me, and then a short while later Arturo comes out again, the thick chain wrapped up his arm, while carrying the cape in the other. The Morcego snaps in the direction of the red fabric, utterly enraptured.

Arturo leads the monster out into the arena, dodging its maw, and the red fabric flaps with precise flicks of his wrist. He's calm and unafraid, shoulders straight, spine made of iron. He hooks the chain to an iron ring attached to a low platform made of stone.

"I fed her water so we don't have to worry about her blast," he says once it's secure.

"How do you know it's female?"

"Males have longer and thicker tails," he replies as he hands me the capote.

The dragon jerks forward toward the tamer, jaws snapping toward the bold flash of color. Its black scales shine dully under the ferocious sun.

Arturo backs away, attention trained on the beast. "I've kept the chain loose. You can begin now."

Fear nips up my spine. The echo of my heartbeat roars in my ears. I hold up the cape with both hands, and I wave it in a smooth arc away from my body. It resembles a triumphant flag fluttering from a castle tower. I move the way Arturo taught me, my steps short and graceful. The capote does its work, and the dragon stops charging at the tamer and then swerves to face me.

The Morcego dragon. Black and beautiful, powerful and dangerous. Its scales are the toughest shield, its lambent gaze hypnotizing and alluring all at once. I swallow and hold the cape higher. Move it forward in quick bursts. The dragon roars and then charges, kicking up sand. When the beast is a foot away, I move, darting sideways, one foot over the other, the cape flapping at my side. Arturo's rules flash in my mind.

Always keep a foot between you.

Never hold the cape in front of you.

Step one is the first pass. The Veronica.

The dragon follows the movement of the cape, jerking its head wildly, trying to pierce the fabric with its great horns. Every swipe is closer and closer to my body. I whip around in a tight circle, and as I do, I brush the cape over the head of the dragon. Arturo lets out an exultant yell, the dragon roars in fury, and the blast of air whips at my hair.

I don't stop moving. I keep turning and darting away, close and then several steps away.

"Watch out!" Arturo bellows.

I don't see the lance lying on the ground until it's too late. I trip over the thin blade, and the cape flutters above me and then drops, hitting me square on the chest, puffs of sand smacking me in the face. I cough at the impact, dimly hearing Arturo yelling—and then the beast stands above me. Saliva drips onto my face, onto the cape. It smells foul, like dank water hidden in a cupboard for months. The dragon lets out another feral roar. My heart slams against my ribs. I shove the cape off me just as its great jaws lurch close—I let out a guttural scream.

A melody pierces the air, drifts softly nearer. The music reaches us both, human and beast, and we freeze, mystified. The dragon huffs above me. I'm between its thick legs. I glance at the tamer, but his attention is ensnared by the Morcego. He plays the guitar, and the melody scores the air, disturbs the sudden quiet.

"Easy now," Arturo says over his playing. Tension laces his voice, a line stretched taut, seconds from snapping, "I've discovered that noise distracts them. Move slowly."

The notes drift through my mind, hazy and potent. I crawl out from underneath the dragon, muscles straining, inch by inch. The dragon watches the tamer, but at my movement, it veers its giant head in my direction. Puffs of air escape its blade-thin nostrils. Each huff whips my hair, turns my stomach. It is foul, the stench of something rotting from within.

But the monster does not roar. It does not sink its half-a-foot-long teeth into my skin.

I stand slowly, a mere foot away. Sweat slides down the side of my face. My body shakes with the temptation to flee. The dragon waits for my move. My gaze flickers to the lance. It's still underneath the belly of the beast. Should I reach for it? I take a step forward, and the creature growls. The hairs on my arm stand on end.

"Don't move," Arturo says as his music fills the arena.

Insistent. Loud. Distracting.

The dragon should turn away from me. But it doesn't. We're locked together in a game, and I don't know how to win. How to survive. Its teeth gleam in the sunlight. I take a small step back, and the dragon steps forward, matching my move. Heat gathers in my palms.

The melody of the song swirls in my head. I can't account for what happens next. I'm terrified, desperate to get away, but the music is relentless, and somehow, as if by their own accord, my hips sway to the rhythm of the notes pressing into my skin.

The Morcego watches.

And it, too, begins to sway.

The music falters. And the beast lets out an outraged hiss. Arturo recovers and starts anew. I sway again, moving backward and forward, letting my body ride the music as if it's a cresting wave.

The dragon does what I do.

It's incredible and terrifying and marvelous.

Arturo plays a familiar song. I wait for the beat, and then I stamp my feet against the sand. The routine lays out before me. I lift my arms high over my head, curling my wrists, twisting my fingers. My ruffled skirt twirls around my ankles.

The dragon follows my moves, swaying and stomping along with me. It moves around me in a tight circle, thumping its tail, lifting on its hind legs only to slam down onto the ground when I do. Then the tail starts curling like my wrists, twisting over and under. I let out a gasp, but I don't dare stop.

We're dancing together.

Human and dragon.

Prey and predator.

We use every inch of the arena, Arturo close by, creating art in his hands. When my arms start shaking and my thighs start to burn, I meet his gaze and widen my eyes. He nods and steps in front of me, playing louder and more passionately, ensnaring the Morcego's attention. I slip away, moving farther from the pair, panting for breath, waiting for my heart to stop racing.

I look at my shaking hands, my sand-splattered skirt, my dirty shoes and think: *I just danced with a dragon.*

Arturo leads the dragon to the tunnel, and as one, they disappear into its depths, the music fading until I can't hear it anymore. I shuffle to the wall, and I lean against it, appreciating the solid feel of it against my back, holding me upright.

The beast shouldn't have responded that way. Dragons are feral, dangerous, and bloodthirsty creatures. A wolf prowling on land. Vultures in the air. But it danced with me while under the spell of the music. It moved with me as gracefully as any dance partner might.

Why? How?

Arturo materializes at the entrance of the tunnel. He crosses the arena with long strides until he's standing in front of me. We're dumbfounded, blown away. Unable to tear our eyes from each other. Something shifts within me, and I sense a change in him too. His gaze is less hostile. Unguarded.

A young man delighting in the impossible.

He whispers my name for the first time. "Zarela."

VEINTISÉIS

The word brushes against my skin, and I shiver. He pulls me into his arms, hugs me tight. His chest rises and falls against mine. "Are you all right?" he whispers near my ear.

I nod as I wrap my arms around his waist. We stay locked together for minutes, hours, the rest of the day. Time moves without my knowing. My senses are on high alert—the feel of his tunic pressed close to my cheek, the sun beating down over our heads, the way he's holding me, as if he never wants to let me go.

But a moment later, he does.

I lick my lips. "Are you ever going to kiss me, Arturo?"

A ghost of a smile bends his mouth. "Trust you to not be coy."

I shrug. "I've never been."

Arturo tucks a wayward strand of hair behind me ear. "It suits you."

He doesn't answer my question, or kiss me. He steps away from me, a flash of regret crossing his face. "Are you sure you're all right? Any mortal would have lost their mind."

I tilt my head. "Mortal?"

He shrugs, mimicking my earlier gesture.

When he doesn't explain further, I pick up the thread of conversation. "That was terrifying." I remember the dragon's foul breath brushing against my face, the scent of it, all smoke and fire and death. Its two giant legs on either side of my head. "I thought I was done for. If you hadn't been there . . ."

He grimaces.

"What made you think to play the guitar?"

He's silent, considering. "Sometimes, I play at night out in the field where the pens are. I've noticed that it calms them, makes them less restless and hostile. I think they enjoy the sound. I thought about attacking it, but worried it might step all over you in the process. The guitar was in reach."

"You saved my life," I say.

He shrugs my comment away. "What made you think to dance?"

"I don't know," I admit. "It felt right."

"You have great instincts."

"Careful," I tease. "That sounded like a compliment."

"It was," he says coolly. There's a trace of smile bending his perfect mouth. It enchants me to see something that soft on his hard face, with the square lines of his jaw and angled cheekbones, the straight brows perpetually pulled into a frown. I shake my head, trying to force myself to focus on the words said out in the open and not the words we won't say to each other for some reason.

"Have you ever seen a dragon behave that way?" I whisper, as if the moment is too precious to share with anyone but him, not even the soft breeze that gently stirs the sand under our feet.

He shakes his head. "I've been observing them for years. Dragons are proud, secretive creatures. They don't perform for outsiders, least of all for humans. But then, I've never tried to dance with one either—"

"Zarela!" We both turn at the sight of Lola hovering by the entrance. She runs to meet us, her braid swaying widely. With a start, I notice the sun is close to the horizon, it might be just past the sixth bell. Twilight turns the sky to a bruised purple.

"What is it?" I ask her.

"You made me run all the way to you," she huffs. "How dare you."

"Lola," I say as fear cuts into me, realizing something might be wrong. "Is it Papá—"

She bends over, panting for air. "Not your father. There's a mob, and they've organized a march outside La Giralda."

"*¿Qué?*"

She points toward the main entrance. "There are hundreds of them."

The three of us quickly race out of the arena and to the grand foyer. Ofelia and two of the maids stand with her, mouths agape as they stare out the window. I dart to their side and gasp. Hundreds and hundreds of marchers fill the avenue, their clothes and skin stained the color of blood. They hold up signs demanding our ruin, shouting for La Giralda's end. And standing on a crudely built wooden platform is Martina Sanchez, waving her banner of protest.

The crowd looks like a long snake encircling the building, readying to consume it.

"I don't understand," Lola says. "What are they yelling?"

I fume. "'Cierra tus puertas.'"

Close your doors.

"They don't want La Giralda to host the fight," Arturo says from somewhere behind me. "The painting on the outside wall wasn't exactly subtle."

"What can be done?" Ofelia whispers.

I press my forehead against the cool glass. Willing an answer to present itself. But I have nothing left. I've given so much of myself to the arena.

"Do you think it's caught on with the rest of the city?" Lola demands. "Maybe the marchers have kept to this area?"

Arturo points to several onlookers, carrying bundles of paper and sketch pads. "There're the chroniclers." He points to a few more people who avidly watch the events, dressed in blue and gold tunics and plumed hats. "And the town criers have arrived."

"Which means the news will spread to every corner of Santivilla," Lola says. "This is my fault. I've been painting flyers detailing information about the dragon fight. Guillermo enchanted them to appear in public places."

"This is not your fault," I say angrily. Señora Montenegro told me herself—Don Eduardo will do anything to turn public opinion against me. I don't know how, but he's had plenty of time to figure out how to poison our upcoming event, spread falsehoods. For all I know, he could have paid Martina to show up tonight with her masses.

"Look." Lola gestures to the window. Night creeps forward, blanketing Santivilla in inky shadows, and the marchers have lit hundreds of torches and candles, votives and matches, and together they continue circling La Giralda, until it's enveloped in a ring of fire.

"This can't be happening," I say. "Who's going to buy tickets now? This has to stop."

I push away from the window, the sounds of Lola and Ofelia protesting in my wake. Someone says, "I'll handle the little fool," and Arturo's footsteps roar in my ears. I'm halfway down the marble steps, blood boiling, near shaking with fury and outrage—how dare they—how *dare* they—this is our lives, our home.

I won't let them take it away from me.

Strong hands grab my arms and spin me around on the marble step. "Zarela, think for a minute."

"I'm done thinking. I *need* to do something."

He holds up his hands. "Take a breath."

As if I have time. Any minute they might come inside. I scoff and race the rest of the way down. I'm almost to the street when I'm lifted off my feet and upside down as if I were a sack of potatoes. Arturo has a firm hand on the back of my thighs, and I'm lying over his shoulder with a spectacular view of the ground.

"What the hell are you doing?" I yell.

He ignores me.

I thump his back, but he only moves quicker, his shoes thudding against the stone, and we enter the preparation room.

"Put me down," I snarl.

He flips me around and gently places me on my feet. I scramble away, seething. There's a candlestick on one of the end tables, and I launch it at his head. He catches it neatly with one hand and calmly sets it aside as if I didn't just try to murder him with it.

I try to walk around him, but he moves quickly to stand in front of me. I move to the left, and he does it again. He's incorrigible! I thread my fingers through my hair and pull at the ends.

Arturo moves to stand in front of the door. Blocking the exit. Why is he always blocking exits?

"Let me through."

"No."

"Who do you think you are?"

"Remember your father."

My anger deflates. I inhale deeply, feeling my lungs stretch and fill, and I push everything out, all my rage, the fear, how out of control I feel. But it doesn't help. I remember the sight of the burning torches encircling my home. The shouting, the banners with their hateful messages.

"I know your uncle is responsible." I pace the length of the room. Arturo leans against the door, ankles crossed, and follows me with his gray eyes. Up and down, up and down.

"For what, exactly?"

"Everything!" I explode. This room feels too small. It can't hold my anger. "I can't prove it."

"Calm down."

I throw him a murderous look. "Do you deny it?"

His gaze narrows. "Is there an accusation in there somewhere?"

"He's *your* uncle."

"So? We're not close." He adds dryly, "Turning your back on the family trade will ensure that."

His family history doesn't interest me. Not when there are hundreds of people dragging my name. "I don't have time for this," I snap, striding forward.

"You go out there and you will lose your life." His brow darkens. "Why are you always putting yourself in danger?"

"What do you mean *why*? My home is under attack. What would you do?"

He has no answer for this because he knows I'm right. There are some things that are worth your life. I take a step closer and poke his chest. "Why do you care?"

He clamps his mouth shut and stares at me coldly.

I've waited a long time to hear what he thinks about me. If he barely tolerates me, if he's just humoring me, playing with fire when he knows he can't be burnt. I lean forward until my mouth is an inch from his. My whisper comes up my throat, deep from my belly. "You care about me. Admit it."

Arturo's gaze drops to my lips, and his fists clench, knuckles bone white. I'm very interested in the battle he's visibly having with himself. "Sometimes, I really can't stand you," he mutters.

But the way he's looking at me, the heat in his dark eyes, the way he's holding himself back, tells me differently.

Outside, the yelling grows louder. Distracting. I try to back away, but then Arturo reaches out and grabs both of my elbows, brings me forward until I'm a hairsbreadth away from him. So close that I can see every rough stubble on his cheeks.

"Can't you understand?" I whisper. "I have to do something."

"You *are*," he insists. I try to protest, but he shakes me. "You've been training, worrying about the repairs, managing an entire household," he says. "Do you ever get tired? Because I feel tired just looking at you."

"I'm fine."

"You're exhausted. You have bags under your eyes. You look terrible."

I glare at him. "That's rude."

"You know what I meant." He pulls me even closer, now the toes of our boots touch.

"Be careful, you almost sound concerned for my welfare."

His voice is flat even as his thumbs draw light circles on my skin. The gesture soothes me, and I sink into the feeling, putting it on as if it were the softest blanket. "I'm not."

"Are we becoming friends?" I ask, bemused.

A scowl rips through his features. "Just stay off the streets. Promise me."

"You mean forever? That's hardly practical."

Both his hands move upward and toward me as if he wants to shake me. "Damn you, Zarela."

But then he places his hands on my shoulders and tugs me forward. Our foreheads press against each other, and we breathe the same air. His thumbs draw small circles, and the movement makes me feel boneless and soothed. Our lips are so, so close. One inhale, one step forward, and I'd feel his mouth against mine. But the words we won't say stand between us, and I don't dare draw closer.

He wants me, I know it, but he won't let himself surrender.

Arturo brushes his lips against my temple, against my hair and then whispers, "Please stay here."

He straightens away and with one last piercing look, he leaves the room.

I look toward the window where the world outside burns. There's nothing I can do about Martina and her mob. Reluctantly, I admit defeat because tomorrow the real battle begins.

Tomorrow I practice fighting the dragon for real.

VEINTISIETE

When Ofelia knocks on the door of my bedroom the next morning, I already know it's going to be bad news. It's the slow, soft knock, as if she doesn't really want to disturb me, hoping that I perhaps won't answer.

But I do.

Better to face these sorts of things head-on. I brace myself for what she might say, prepare myself to add something else that I'll need to fix to the long running list in my head. Have the dragons become ill? Have we run out of money to buy food?

I open the door and wish I hadn't, because it isn't Ofelia.

"What are you doing out of bed?"

Papá straightens to his full height, his silk robe wrapped around him tight. I'd said the words without really noting his appearance. Relief spreads thick, a delightful warm feeling settling deep in my belly. He's looking sharper, better.

"I have energy enough for this, hijita," he says.

My relief and good feeling disappear in an instant. The corners of his mouth are more pronounced than usual. Never a good sign. "For what?"

"Querida," he says softly. "I need you to come with me."

I clutch the door. "What is it, Papá?"

He hesitates. "Get dressed in your training ensemble then come down. I'll make your coffee. Then I'll show you."

"Show me?"

He doesn't answer, but turns away to shuffle down the long corridor, his footsteps softly padding away. I watch him walk, his slight frame barely wider than my own. A sharp gust of wind could blow him right out of my life. But he seems stronger, and I make a note to speak with Ofelia to start feeding him heartier fare.

I close the door and pull on a worn tunic and matching skirt, stuff my feet in shoes caked with sand, then rush out of my room to meet my father, my heart hammering hard against my ribs. What could he have to show me?

But it isn't just Papá waiting for me at the foot of the grand stairs; Lola with watery eyes, Papá, tall and grim, Ofelia, tottering nervously, holding a coffee cup. I take it from her with shaking hands.

"Have several sips of that," Lola says.

My dread mounts. Building a wall around me, closing in, brick by insurmountable brick. "Seriously? What the hell is going on?"

But I do what she says and drink several gulps. The liquid warms me instantly. I hand the mug back to Ofelia, and they lead me out the front doors of La Giralda. The sun shines bright, scorching and fierce, and I squint, my eyes unadjusted to the glare. The first step outdoors is met with a sudden stench that makes my stomach heave.

My eyes finally adjust to the sunlight.

There's mierda everywhere.

In piles, smeared on the marble steps. I plug my nose and walk down to the street, trying to avoid making contact with any of it. Dirty piles of pamphlets are strewn everywhere, some are old newspapers, others are advertisements for the coming show. Lola's hard work, destroyed. People dumped their trash right in front of the arena. I keep walking, blinking rapidly as if to dispel what my eyes are seeing. I'm so intent on where I place my feet, I almost miss seeing the real travesty.

The exterior of La Giralda's beautiful brick walls have been splashed with red paint. The mural we worked on has been destroyed. A smattering of insults covers the walls. *Murderer. Dragon lady. Puta.* They even smashed some of the stained blue windows.

Lola silently cries, angrily wiping at her tears with the back of her hand. Ofelia has already gone and grabbed a bucket, and she sits on the steps and begins to furiously scrub. Papá takes a spare cloth from her and does the same. I can read his heartbreak in the curved line of his back. This building was the crown jewel of Santivilla. Home of our respectable name, our legacy.

It's now a place where people desecrate its steps.

I see red. If I could breathe fire, I swear I would. I want to scream, to confront the people responsible. I curl my hands into tight fists. Scalding tears gather in my eyes, and I press the sleeve of my tunic to my face to prevent them from falling. Anger always makes me cry. It's infuriating, as if my body doesn't know what to do with that emotion but shed it through pitiful tears. My chest heaves with the effort to control my fury, my hurt.

Lola comes to stand next to me.

"Your tamer is here," she whispers, jerking her chin in the direction of the street.

Sure enough, he sits on his copper horse, his eyes flickering from one thing to another. When his gaze lands on the offensive words on the wall, he takes a quick and furious inhale. He breathes hard through his nostrils, and his fingers clutch the reins tighter until his knuckles turn white. He looks to me, serious and grim and quietly seething.

I walk over to Papá and help him stand. My hope is to comfort him, but the words don't come. His shoulders slump, his proud chin lowered. "Why have the people of Santivilla done this?"

"It wasn't them," I say. "It was the Asociación."

And privately, I think: *and the Dragon Master.*

This demands a response. I must retaliate. I can't let this slide.

Ofelia brings out several more buckets, bars of soap, rags. Lola immediately grabs one of each. I tell my father to rest, but his dark eyes flash murderously. "I can scrub," he says fiercely, and he immediately starts cleaning the top step.

I'm so proud of him, my heart may tear again from it.

I reach for a pail, but a bronzed hand crosses my vision and snatches the handle from right under my nose. I slowly look up, my hand outstretched. I expect him to hand it back to me, but he doesn't.

"I can't possibly train today," I explain. "Not until this is all cleaned."

Arturo ignores me and grabs the soap and rag, and then makes his way to the bottom marble step where he kneels and scrubs the marble with short, even strokes, dark hair curling over his forehead.

Papá watches Arturo clean up piles of crap. "We don't need your assistance for this."

Arturo stops scrubbing and, without looking up, says, "Yes, you do, señor."

It will take *all* of us to make this right. "Accept the help, Papá."

For some reason, this only makes my father frown. But he doesn't argue it further. We work all day, well into the early evening, when the sky deepens into the color of a bruise, spreading from one end of the horizon to the other. A handful of people sneer at us from across the street, and it takes all of my will to ignore their jeering, the insults and yelling. They laugh at us cleaning up the mess, laugh as I scrub and my fingers wrinkle and cramp. Each harsh laugh grates against my skin, louder than an exclamation point, than the call of Santivilla's bells.

I hold on to my anger, keep it close because if I don't, I'm terrified I'll cry in front of the very people who wish to tear me down. I almost falter, I almost give in to my rage, but Arturo steps into my line of vision and glares at me.

His eyes tell me to hold it together. "Don't you dare break down and give Martina and the rest of them the satisfaction."

"Do you know that awful woman?"

He lifts a shoulder. "Barely. She tried to recruit me when I walked away from the Gremio and my profession, but I made it clear I don't like her approach, even if I agree with her politics."

"How can you—"

"I can't stand her methods, but we want the same thing." He scowls at me when I try to protest again. "I told her I'd *never* join the Asociación.

There has to be a better way to win the argument." He gestures to the mess surrounding us. "What they did here was despicable."

I think about the day of the massacre, the deaths, the destruction. "Do you think they're dangerous?"

He mulls it over while wringing a cloth. "No, I don't. Shortsighted? Absolutely. But evil?" He shakes his head. "Martina wants to make a point, not war."

But this *is* war. Me against her and the Asociación and Don Eduardo.

By the time the sixth bell tolls, my back is sore from bending over, my fingers cramped from scrubbing. I wipe the sweat off my face with my tunic sleeve. My hair hangs in frizzy coils, and my skirt has watery brown stains on it. I've never gagged this much, from the smell, from the sight.

"We ought to take a break," Lola says. "I want to look at something else that doesn't remind me of the inside of a chamber pot."

"I think we need drinks," Ofelia says, getting to her feet. "All of you in the kitchen right now. I know there is some of the good wine left."

"I love it when she's bossy about alcohol," Lola says, trailing after her. She takes my father's arm and helps him inside. He moves stiffly, and guilt pecks at me like a hungry vulture. I ought to have insisted he rest. Just because he's recovering doesn't mean he can push himself too hard.

"You missed a spot." Arturo drops his bucket by my hands where I'm busily wiping the last miserable marble step. I swipe at the place he indicated. Then he points at another stretch of marble. "Here's another place that needs your attention."

"I had no idea you were so helpful," I mutter. He tucks his chin and tries to hide his smirk from me, but I catch it. I throw my rag at him, but he easily ducks out of the way.

"That's dirty," he says in mock consternation. "Literally covered in excrement, and you were aiming for my face."

"Gracias. For today." I sit back on my haunches, and he waves off my gratitude. "You didn't have to help," I say.

He sinks his hands deep into the pockets of his trousers. "Debatable."

"Zarela!" Ofelia roars from within the building. "Do you want wine or don't you? Need I remind you that Lola is in this room and she will drink every last—"

I can hear Lola's muffled, outraged interruption even from out here.

"Coming!" I glance back at Arturo. The next words that come out of my mouth surprise us both. "Would you like to stay? I'm sure Ofelia is setting the table. It's the least we can do."

He quirks an eyebrow. "You've paid me for my time."

I stand and then wring my tunic of the soapy water I kept spilling on myself. So he doesn't want wine or food, and the only reason he stayed to help was because he viewed it as a working day. What a perfectly sensible way of looking at the situation. Logical even. It stays at the back of my throat, a hard lump. "You're right. I did. Have a safe journey back to the ranch."

"I enjoy the ride through the desert." He pauses, and I get the sense that he doesn't want to move from this spot. That he'd rather stay and talk than ride away on his red horse.

I collect the buckets, stuff the rags inside them, and round up the bars of soap. "Despite the threat of dragons?"

"Despite that. It makes me feel alive."

A peculiar way to embrace life, taking a chance with a monster. Why won't he go? He rejected my offer. "See you tomorrow, then," I say coolly, turning away with my cleaning supplies.

"Wait. Zarela, wait," he orders, and then softly adds a *por favor*.

I pause with an impatient noise. "What *is* it, Arturo? I invited you for dinner, you said no—"

"Not what I said," he snaps. "I'm still deciding."

"It's only wine." I arch a brow. "Just dinner."

"Oh, I think it's way more than that, Zarela." He adds quietly, "Don't you?"

Warmth blossoms on my cheeks. "You make it *so* difficult."

A contained smile softens his mouth, so faint, I can barely see the curve. "I know I do."

"Well, quit it," I say angrily. "And stay here and sit down to dinner with us."

He tucks his hands deep into his pockets and regards me steadily, considering. I roll my eyes and march up the steps and will myself not to look back. I make a quick detour so I can change into a clean tunic and skirt. There's nothing I can do about my hair, but I tie it in a knot at the crown of my head. When I reach the kitchen, my family sits around the little wooden island, spooning gazpacho into their mouths and drinking wine. Lots of it. Lola refills her glass, and when she sees me, she hands me a goblet, the wine reaching the rim. Ofelia hands me a clay bowl, and I drizzle more olive oil, add more of the toppings: diced cucumber and tomato, thick squares of toasted bread.

I take several long sips of wine, and I enjoy the taste, the way the alcohol shoots straight to my mind, dulling my frustration, the hurt that lingers from what the Asociación did.

Arturo's rejection.

The only sounds come from the spoons scraping the bowls. And then there's no noise at all. A sudden quiet that makes me look up from my food. I shoot my father a questioning look, but his attention is on something over and past my shoulder. I slowly turn.

Arturo stands at the doorway, hands still shoved deep into his pockets. He seems uncomfortable with all the attention, and as we continue to stare at him, his scowl becomes more pronounced, and a deep flush punctuates his cheeks, so bright a red it might have been painted on his skin. He's utterly mortified. I'm afraid to open my mouth, afraid to breathe. It's incredibly warm in this room, why didn't I notice earlier?

It's Lola who saves us both. "We have more than enough wine, don't we?"

Ofelia comes to her senses and drags him into the room and then hands him his own bowl. I pick up the bottle of olive oil and drizzle a hefty amount over the chilled soup. "It's delicious this way," I tell him. Then I add smoked chorizo and the rest of the accompanying vegetables, and he has to pull the bowl away from me because it's nearly overflowing.

We have warm bread on the table, black and green olives, of course, and from somewhere Lola finds yet another bottle of wine. The tamer polishes off a glass, and she immediately refills it to the brim. I'm not used to seeing him this way. He's usually aloof and guarded and extremely prickly. But he stayed behind, drinks the wine and finishes his cold soup. I try not to stare as he fills his plate with more olives and bread.

What changed his mind?

Arturo eats beside me on the only remaining stool, and occasionally, his elbow brushes against my arm as he polishes off the last of the food. I shift in my seat to give him room. But it happens again. Bemused, I glance in his direction.

He's staring at me.

His lips are soft, not bent into their usual smirk. My stomach swoops, as if I've fallen from a great height. He brings the cup of wine to his lips and continues gazing at me over the rim of the glass. When he lowers his arm, I take the wine and set it far from him on the kitchen island. He's had more than enough.

Because I cannot possibly handle a softer Arturo Díaz de Montserrat.

"In case you say or do anything you might regret," I mutter under my breath so no one else but him can hear my words. I expect him to sneer, to say something caustic like how no amount of wine will change his low opinion of me, or at the very least, I anticipate the return of his scowl. But he does none of those things.

He quietly laughs.

It's enough to give me *hope*—which I don't want to feel because it terrifies me. It's a little like what happens when I watch my father enter the ring: I'm robbed of breath, wondering if this is the last time I'll see Papá alive, and then he survives the fight and blessed air storms back inside, and the relief is so palpable, it might knock me off my feet.

That's what hope feels like to me. The sweetest air you've ever breathed after enduring the worst fear of your life.

It's painful.

Maybe it's the alcohol, and the way its cloying sweetness pokes holes in my defenses. Maybe it's because we've cleaned mierda for hours, and it's been a terrible day. But in the space of a few heartbeats, my guard drops, and I smile at the sound of his laughter. I haven't heard it before, and my life seems better because Arturo isn't looking at me as if I were his enemy. He's not even looking at me as if I were his friend, but something more.

And my hope stubbornly remains.

The moment is ruined by my father.

"Zarela," he says in a warning tone.

I look over, my grin vanishing. Papá grips his goblet of wine tightly and frowns at Arturo. "It's time you went home."

Arturo sets his bowl on the island carefully, only a soft sound when the clay meets wood. He throws back the rest of his wine. "Gracias para la comida."

And then he's gone. Gone before I can understand how we went from all of us having a meal together, Arturo drinking wine and laughing, to this oppressive silence filled with my father's disapproval.

"Why do you hate him?" I ask Papá.

"He's not for you."

Questions threaten to burst from my lips, but I keep them down. Anguish carves itself onto Papá's face, digging deeper grooves, forming new lines on his already-weathered skin. I can't ignore it. Whatever Arturo did, or said, left a mark on my father. I remember how Papá asked me to trust him. I don't know if I want to anymore. Not about this. The trouble is Arturo has a left a mark on me too. I didn't ask for it, I wasn't looking, but here we are. Half of me wants to pursue whatever messy thing exists between us. The other half doesn't want to see another line on my father's face because of me.

Papá changes the subject. "Have we sold a lot of tickets for the show?"

I have to disappoint my father again. "Very few."

His shoulders slump. "Zarela . . ."

"People buy them on the day of the event all the time, Papá," I say quickly.

"What happens if the mob returns today and does more damage?" he counters.

"We'll deal with it should that happen."

He shakes his head. "Zarela, it's over."

The world seems to tilt, and I struggle to remain upright, my hands fly out to catch the edge of the kitchen island. "It's not," I say. "How can you think that? We can't give up. We had a tough day—a setback—but that doesn't mean it's over."

Papá folds his arm across his chest. "We can't have another day like this, hija. Ofelia has other responsibilities. Lola has been here day and night. And I'm"—he coughs, embarrassed—"a little tired."

Guilt pricks me. Dagger-sharp. "But—"

"Zarela," he says firmly, "it's time we find a new place to stay. Perhaps an apartment to rent. We have to pack."

"The show is two days away. Who cares if Santivilla doesn't come? The Dragon Master himself is attending, that's all that matters."

"And let's say everything goes the way you want it to, and the Gremio reinstates us as members. What then, hija? It will cost money to maintain La Giralda, and if we don't have people, then we don't have an income." He sighs, and the sound is like the most horrible kind of rattle, as if his breath were trapped in an iron cage. "I need you to think of your future."

No. I know what he's going to say before the words poison the air. But I'm not ready for them, all the same.

"You might consider marriage," Papá says quietly.

Lola shoots me a sympathetic glance. I squeeze my eyes tight, willing myself to keep breathing. Everything is on fire, everything I touch turns to ash.

"I can't believe what I'm hearing," I say. "You can't let them win." I finish my drink and then hand the empty cup to Ofelia. I need air. A place to think. "I'm going out."

"Where?" Papá asks sharply.

"*Out*," I say as I storm from the kitchen, out the little side door and to the stables, moving quickly because my eyes are prickling, and I can't let any of them see me cry. My body shakes with frustration, with anger. This is how I know the tears are coming. I can't stop seeing red.

Has everything I've done been for nothing?

I reach the stables, startling our driver, who has the latest journal on his lap, reading by candlelight. He looks up, guilty, and attempts to hide the paper from me. But I hold out my hand, and he gives it to me before scurrying away. The smell of hay tickles my nose, but I ignore it and flip to the front page.

It's an illustration of La Giralda, surrounded by the mob, and the title reads, "Fallen from Grace." I crumble the sheets and hurl it as far away from me as I can.

We're doomed. Even if I win back our home, it won't matter. No one will buy tickets. The tears come, cold against my hot skin.

Footsteps draw near.

I stiffen and slowly turn, expecting to see Lola, and for once I'm ready to tell her that I want a night exploring Santivilla, that I want to dance on tables and have the kind of fun I haven't had in a long, long time. But it's Arturo. He takes one look at my face and then shoots a swift look at his horse. Clearly deliberating whether to go, probably alarmed to encounter a crying female.

He walks to his horse and climbs onto the saddle in a swift, graceful move so much like my father, it makes my head spin. He clicks his tongue, and when rider and horse are next to me, he glances at me, his expression unreadable.

He's going to leave. I'm a mess, fallen from grace. But he holds out his hand to me. I stare at it, unsure of what I'm seeing. My vision blurs with ridiculous tears, and I angrily wipe my eyes. His hand is still there.

Slowly, I tilt my head back to meet his gaze.

"Ven conmigo," he says.

Come with me.

I slip my hand in his, and he pulls me up, but this time, I'm sitting in front of him, and together we ride out of the stables and into the cool night.

VEINTIOCHO

The terrain out here feels alive and dangerous. We ride outside of the outer city wall, passing under the arched gate to unprotected sparse land breathing quietly beneath a million stars. The memory of what happened the last time I stood outside of Santivilla rushes back, and I stiffen. I'd survived that dragon attack because of Arturo. Without really wanting to, I glance up, dreading what I might find flying above our heads.

Arturo's arm snakes around my waist, and he squeezes me gently, as if understanding my sudden terror. "Dragons have terrible vision. Especially at night," he whispers, and his breath kisses the back of my neck. It smells of sweet wine and something else, something I'm too afraid to name. He tightens his hold when the horse gallops faster over a stretch of dirt path, lined by grass that resembles the tails of a wild rabbit, bushy and feathery.

We're silent for the entire ride, and for some unaccountable reason, the quiet doesn't feel caustic. I'm not worried about what he might say or his tone. I'm not worried that he'll pull away and shut me out. Tonight feels much different than the miserable ride we had traveling into the city with the dragons. Neither of us want to ruin the moment of peace, tenuous as it is. His body presses against the back of mine, lean and strong, with a warmth that guards against the chill. The path splits into a wide crossroad. Straight on will bring us to his ranch. To the left another city and to the right, a small coastal village.

I expect us to move forward, continuing onward to the ranch, but instead, Arturo takes us off the path, between the road to his home and the sea. The horse doesn't startle or protest heading into a thicket of aleppo and stone pine trees. The leaves overhead block the sight of the moon and its many glittering companions. The darkness looms, thick and sinister, and I tuck myself closer to Arturo. He doesn't let go of me. An owl hoots, and the sound of rustling leaves and branches snapping disturbs the still quiet of the cool night. Goose bumps flare up and down my arms.

Arturo flicks the reins, expertly guiding us around trees and rocks and supporting roots tangling into the dirt. We reach a clearing, its only notable landmark a large cavern surrounded by a grouping of trees and jagged rocks. Arturo hops off his horse and then reaches up to help me dismount. I slide off the saddle and land lightly on the soft ground, tangled with leaves and roots, his hands hot against my lower rib cage.

He places an index finger against his lips. "Quietly," he says in a hushed tone.

"What are we doing here?" I ask, matching his tone. But Arturo walks away from me, moving silently toward the cavern entrance. I follow behind him, filled with questions. About him and me, about this night and what he wants to show me. The fortress he's carefully constructed around himself has vanished, and I haven't seen him scowl in hours.

I instinctively understand that this place means something to him. The surrounding area provides perfect cover for us, tucked underneath oak and pine trees. Arturo stops at the foot of the cave, and when I try to stand next to him, he firmly, but gently, maneuvers me behind his back.

We're silent, facing the yawning entrance with its hidden depths and long-forgotten secrets. No sound or smell or even light comes forth. The dark tunnel, immense in height and width, open like the jaw of a predator. Arturo lets out a soft whistle, one high note and two low. Then he walks forward, reaching behind me, his hand outstretched. I take hold, and together we walk inside. The expansive space is damp and faintly smelling of stale river water. The walls are craggy, with fissures spreading in every direction, grooves that make pretty patterns against the rock.

I ought to be more nervous than I am, but Arturo's calm assurance settles my nerves. He's been here before, many times; I'm sure of it in the same way I recognize the right beat to begin dancing. We've taken fifteen steps inside when Arturo bends forward and picks up a canvas sack propped against the wall.

He drops my hand and reaches inside, pulling out a wooden torch. I wrinkle my nose. Oil drenches the end of the cloth. He strikes a match and lights the torch.

Arturo takes my hand. "Don't scream."

Then he turns us around. A shape materializes in the dark, massive, maybe ten times my size. My palm jerks in his, but he holds on to me, squeezing my fingers. The beast draws near, looking down from high above our heads. It has a long neck and an even bigger head. My breath comes out in frantic huffs, and I instinctively try to pull free from Arturo but he holds on.

"No sudden movements," Arturo says in an undertone. "Trust me."

I swallow, and it's painful from holding in my screech of terror. Its wings unfurl, and the musky scent hits my face. Green eyes with pupils shaped into slits regard me coldly. The scales appear to be a dark hue tinted golden by the light of the fire.

Dragon.

I face a monster without any weapons. I try to pull away, but Arturo still won't let me move. I open my mouth, a scream climbing up my throat. Arturo covers my lips with his rough palm, smothering the sound.

"Sssh," he whispers. "Relax. I promise Roja won't hurt you."

My feet itch to run, to scramble away. But I'm rooted to the uneven floor. "You and I are going to have words later," I hiss against his hand. "Several of them."

"Looking forward to it."

The dragon leans closer to Arturo and sniffs. Sweat slicks my palms, and I let out a whimper. The nostril slits are about as long as my forearm. Arturo turns us around, and we walk away from the dragon and toward the cavern entrance. I try to speed up, but again he keeps me firmly at his side.

"Do not run."

I exhale sharply. "I'm going to kill you for this."

He chuckles. The bastard.

When we're out of the cave, I inhale deeply, tasting the cool breeze rustling the bushy desert plants. Arturo finally lets me go, and I turn to face the monster slowly coming out into the night, one booming step at a time. Its long tail scratches the rock, moving like a snake. My heart slams against my ribs, thundering wildly.

Arturo leaves my side and clicks his tongue, drawing the attention of the beast. The dragon wraps its body around Arturo, like a predator before suffocating its prey. I want to yell out a warning, but Arturo anticipates this and shoots me a pointed look. He reaches out and brushes the side of the monster's head, its scales shining in the dark.

"It's red," I say dumbly. Beautiful, glossy, bloody red from tail to snout. It unfurls its four-spined wings, and I'm reminded of one of my mother's beautifully painted fans. "This is . . . this is an Escarlata."

"Astute of you," Arturo says, and some of his usual impatience weaves back into his voice. The dragon is very familiar with the tamer. While not exactly friendly, it lets itself be touched. The feral quality all dragons have is still there. The sharp teeth and claws—both six inches long—are good reminders that in any moment, it can kill with one bite.

"Say hola to Roja," he says at last. "I found her egg abandoned in that old cave a year ago. I was there for her hatching, and I think she's quite taken with me."

The dragon doesn't look nearly as interested in him as he is with it. And not just any dragon—a damn red one. The rarest and most dangerous monster lording over us in the sky.

"I've seen one before," I say in a hushed whisper. "Just once."

This is the breed that killed my mother.

Arturo carefully strokes the side of Roja's neck with a single index finger. "The magos hunted them down centuries ago. Evidently their scales have powerful magical properties the Gremio de Magia would readily kill for."

"Will you please step away from the monster?" I swallow hard. "I'm having trouble breathing."

He smiles, but it's not for me. His adoring eyes are fastened on the dragon. If I hadn't been watching closely, I would have missed it.

"Isn't it dangerous?"

Roja eyes Arturo as he switches to using both palms to caress her scaly neck. The dragon watches him move, every breath, every gesture. I get the impression that it's still learning Arturo, wondering if he's trustworthy, if it ought to be this close to him. I can certainly relate.

"I believe she tolerates me," Arturo says finally. "There have been months when she'll disappear. Just when I think she's gone forever, she returns to this cave. She's getting ready to leave for a spell."

I take a step closer, marveling at how he's touching the creature freely without any fear or hesitation. The dragon doesn't purr or growl or show any signs of pleasure or displeasure, and I realize Arturo is entirely right. The dragon behaves like an aloof cat.

"Why do you think it's—*she's*—leaving?"

Arturo gives me an approving smile. "Because she doesn't stay for longer than a week. It's already been eight days since her last disappearance. When I said that I've been traveling back to the ranch, I was lying. Any free moment I have, I'm here."

"Does she ever fly over Santivilla?" I'm unable to ask what I really want to—if she's turned her blast to our city. If she's killed and destroyed lives, homes.

But I don't need to clarify. As usual, Arturo knew what I meant. "I've never seen her attack the city."

"What do you two do together?"

"I can show you," he says, his voice just this side of mischievous. "If you're brave enough."

"Are you trying to manipulate me?" I ask. "That's cute. I don't do anything I don't want to do, so you may as well just tell me."

He laughs, and right then, I vow to myself that I'll do whatever I need to do in order to hear that sound again. Unguarded, slightly drunk Arturo might be my favorite thing. He turns around and climbs onto the back of the dragon.

Climbs onto the back.

As if it were a harmless tree. I gape at the pair of them. The creature flaps its clawed wings, and Arturo slips leather reins around her neck.

"Zarela," he says in a coaxing voice. "Tell me you don't want to fly."

The dragon studies me, and I swear if I didn't know better, I'd name the expression on her face as prickly impatience. I look away, considering. These creatures have brought on years of misery. My mother *died*. Gone in a sudden, treacherous blaze. What would she say if she could see me now? She might be betrayed, or she might insist I not let fear keep me from doing the impossible.

I don't want to be afraid anymore. I want to rip the fear out of me, like a harmful weed threatening to overtake a garden, preventing growth.

Arturo waits patiently—for once. I wonder if I'll ever have this chance again. To soar high into the heavens and catch sight of a view not meant for human eyes.

Do I dare?

I take a step forward, and Arturo grins.

"I'll do it," I say. "But answer this first."

His smile dims. When his chin dips once, I take another step.

"Will you regret bringing me here tomorrow?"

Surprise flickers across his face. "Probably. But do it anyway."

Fair enough. I walk the rest of the way, legs shaking, terror clawing up my throat. But I am a Zalvidar, and I want to be worthy of the name. I stand close enough to the dragon to catch every glimmer in her tomato-red scales. The beast's chest expands and contracts in a steady rhythm, her breathing heavy and sure. Arturo holds out his hand and helps me climb up the dragon; I prop my foot against its front leg, bent at an angle.

Arturo positions me in front of him. The reins are in each of his hands, and he snuggles close. My heart races, and the storm in my chest thunders.

"Relax," he whispers. "And hold on to those horns." He gestures to two spikes protruding from the dragon's scaly mane. The horns bracket her great jaw, and I try not to think of the fire she holds deep in her belly. I take hold of them, surprised to discover they're smooth, if a little gritty, and almost the same shade of whipped cream.

The dragon lurches, and I let out a startled gasp. She races ahead, wings flapping, and I squeeze my legs against her sides, feeling the way her strong muscles move. The wind whips at my face, at my hair, makes my eyes water. She heads up the hill, darting between thick tree trunks, until a cliff becomes visible.

"Hold on!" Arturo says over the roar of the dragon's footsteps on the ground and the strong gust of air bellowing in our ears. "Try not to scream!"

Ten feet from the edge.

Five.

Two.

Her large wings stretch wide, and she propels herself off the edge, falling down, down, down to the ravine below. My stomach lurches and I almost yell, but I keep my jaw clenched. The dragon continues her descent, and it feels like I'm falling. I'm half a foot off her back, and it's only Arturo's arm that anchors me. Roja turns her nose skyward, and her wings ferociously flap. We bob upward, and Arturo's laughter cuts through my thoughts.

His joy is infectious, and a grudging smile crosses my face, even as I keep my stomach tightly clenched. The trees below become smaller and smaller, until they're tiny dots against the landscape. We glide through the clouds—*the clouds*—and the beauty of the moment steals my fear away. Stars glimmer and look close enough to touch, to wear like jewels around my neck. The dragon's body moves and widens with every deep inhale. The barrel of her chest is strong. I feel weightless, safe. She will not break apart in the air; she's not flimsy.

She's a legend. The villain of fairy tales.

Arturo taps me on the shoulder and points to something below on our right.

Santivilla. Outlined against the night by hundreds of glittering torch-lights. Roja dips closer and the bells begin to ring—I let out a gasp. But the sound carries high, and I recognize the warning of a dragon flying over, and not attacking, the city.

Roja takes us away from the tolling bells.

It's frigid among the dewy clouds, and I'm shivering so hard my teeth clap against one another. Even Arturo lets out a long hiss when a particularly cold blast whips around us. But I don't care. I want to stay up here forever. I want to stay up here with this dragon, gleaming under the moonlight, and with Arturo pressed tight against me, attempting to keep me warm.

Roja takes us back to the hill, uses the flat stretch of land near the cliff as her landing strip. She drops onto the ground at a run, and I'm jostled upward. She races through the trees and at last stops in front of the cave. Arturo slides off first and then holds out both hands to help me down. My body drags down the front of his, one slow inch at a time. His hands stay longer around my waist than they need to. A lingering beat I feel all the way down to my toes. I can't wrench my gaze from his, and a faint blush warms my cheeks.

We step away from the dragon as she shakes her body, the way a dog might when ridding itself of water. And then she ambles down the cliff, without another look in our direction, entirely regal, her tail like the long train of a dress.

"That was—" Arturo begins.

I spin him toward me, my lips crash against his, and he lets out a star-tled exclamation against my mouth. I taste the outrage on his tongue.

But then he sinks into the kiss, and whatever feelings he keeps hidden from me bubble to the surface and it burns us both. There's nothing shy about the way our mouths move, about the way his hands slide down my body. His tongue sweeps into my mouth and he tastes me, and warmth spreads to every hidden corner inside me. His fingers dig deep into my back and we press closer. I wrap my arms around his neck, thread my fingers through his thick hair. His lips are hot against mine. He's all of the warm and sultry flavors of Santivilla. I hold smoke and fire and sweet wine in my mouth. We catch on fire under a million stars. Together we burn.

I've been kissed by boys before from respectable families, and every time it was just . . . nice. Nice in the way plain bread and butter is nice. This is different, this is the best meal of my life after not eating for days and days.

And then he shoves me back, panting.

His gray eyes glitter in the moonlight, his mouth parts. "*No.*"

I blink, still in a haze, still feeling his mouth against my own—and then I realize what he said, and it sinks in fully, until the word lands with an inelegant thud between us.

He's rejecting me. After everything.

Anger, hurt, mortification. I feel everything at once, in every corner of my body, filling me up as if I were bowl or a cup. I'm not big enough to contain the sudden swell, and I turn away, my breath ragged from his shattering kisses. "Take me home," I say hoarsely. "Take me home before I scream."

"Zarela," he whispers. "*I can't.*"

The awful thing is I understand what he means. The Gremio stands between us, the specter of his uncle. "You can't," I spit out. "Well, neither can I, but I want you all the same."

He drags in a shuddering breath, and I wait for him to make his decision, to choose *me* over his dragons, his uncle, the Gremio. But he says nothing, and I'm done. It hurts too much to stand in front of him, feeling the way I do and not being picked.

"Take me home."

"Not like this." He's half pleading, half nervous. "I don't mean to hurt you, and I don't want you to go. Will you stay?"

I finally face him. He's strung out and fidgeting, hands clenching and unclenching. Probably furious with himself for asking the question at all.

"*Why?*" I demand and he flinches. "Tell me why I should."

"Because it isn't about my not wanting you," he shouts. "I do, damn it. *I do.* So stay and talk to me, because if I can't have more, then let me have less." He takes in a deep breath. "If you can stand to have less, talk to me as a friend might, and *please* stay."

Not for the first time, I wonder what's keeping him from me. I wonder why he won't let himself have someone he clearly wants. His eyes shine like silver coins, cold and shimmering. They're almost menacing, deep wells hiding terrible secrets.

Arturo holds out his hand and waits.

I let him lead me into the cave.

VEINTINUEVE

Arturo has been living in this cave.

I'm careful not to step on any of his possessions: discarded clothing and shoes, pewter cups and knives, piles of parchment covered in scribblings and drawings. He pulls out a blanket folded inside his canvas bag, shaking it so that any dirt flies off and lays it flat. He toes his pack so it sits on one of the corners. The torch is jammed into a deep crevice, and it casts sinister shapes on the opposite wall.

"Tienes hambre?" he asks, settling onto the ground. He rummages through the sack and pulls out two red apples, offering me one. My nose picks up the scent of cheese and bread. There's a clay jug at his elbow—perhaps filled with wine?

It wouldn't be wise to continue drinking. I may not be able to leave this cave in the morning without him, and he's made it clear where the line is drawn.

"Zarela?" Arturo asks again. His hair is charmingly rumpled from my hands.

I shake my head. "Not hungry."

He tosses the fruit back into his bag and props himself against the craggy wall, then he stares up at me and bites his lip, silently considering me as if he doesn't quite know what to do with me now that I'm here in his private space.

I hesitate. I should go home. Papá might worry where I've gone. Lola will calm him down, make some excuse for my behavior. But this situation is different than when I'd disappeared to the ranch for a couple of days. My father was barely conscious, and when he was awake, he understood I was away on business for La Giralda.

Perfectly respectable.

I stand rooted to the spot, knowing that if I stay, I'll learn so much more about the elusive, grumpy tamer, and the certainty of it thrills me.

And besides.

He said *please*.

The cold press of the walls creates an intimacy between us that makes me nervous. We've never been alone like this, miles from people. The enormity of the situation makes me fidget, and I bend down to scoop up his stacks of parchment. I raise my brows at him, silently asking for permission.

His jaw locks, visibly weighing whether to let me see so much. After a long beat, he inclines his head, and a dark curl sweeps down onto his creased brow. The paper contains dozens of sketches of dragons, different breeds, all drawn meticulously and labeled in his distinct lettering that isn't cursive, but isn't messy either. Technical terms I've never heard or read before leap off the page: *wing span, brain cage, horn cove, knee joints*. It's fascinating, and before now, I hadn't realized how much he'd been studying them.

"These are incredible."

A deep flush blooms, twin spots of red on his cheeks. His voice is a low mutter, and I have to step forward in order to hear it. "Gracias."

I flip the parchment, and the next drawing steals my breath, a thief I didn't see coming. My hands shake as I hold up the paper to the guttering light. It's a drawing of me dancing with the dragon. He's sketched the lines of my body in a firm hand, and altogether I look strong and brave. Beautiful. I lift my eyes and meet his gaze. He holds my stare steadily, and now it's my turn to blush. He knows my face by memory, the curve of my hips, the wild squiggle of my hair.

"You drew me," I say dumbly.

"Yes."

No one has ever captured my likeness like this. Usually I look so stiff and formal, but this is a version of myself I'll treasure forever.

"Do you have any regrets coming with me tonight?" Arturo asks softly.

His expression is unreadable, tone mild and unassuming. Only the subtle tightening of his shoulders reveals how nervous he is. I pile his art neatly and then drop onto the blanket, and without overthinking it, I slide close to him, until our bodies press together. If we were to turn our heads toward each other, our lips would touch. I want to kiss him again.

That's a lie.

I want so much *more* than that.

Because of the way we're sitting, we both end up looking straight ahead, or down to our hands resting on our laps, or our booted feet that aren't touching. I don't attempt to move my head and neither does he.

"Questions," I clarify. "I have a few."

"Of course you do."

There are so many burning on my tongue, but I pick the safest one. "How old are you?"

"Twenty. You?"

"Eighteen." Now for a harder question. "Will you tell me about your uncle?"

His fingers flex. "When my parents died, I was sent to live with him. My other aunts and uncles thought it best, given my talents in the arena. He's passionate about the family legacy, and he believed I'd achieve great things in our name."

"What happened?"

A muscle in his jaw ticks. "I fought many dragons and survived. Did well in school. But there was an . . . incident. I'd failed, rather spectacularly, and it showed me just how vile and dangerous the practice of dragonfighting is. Dragonadores die every year in droves, and yet the city funds the tradition, the training schools. I gave it up, but he didn't really believe I'd stay away."

"So he continues to pay for your membership, hoping you'll assume the space he's saving for you."

He nods. "Whenever I catch a new dragon, it must be registered. That means a trip to the Gremio. I hate being in that building. But he insists on seeing me every time."

"And you're required to vote on sensitive matters?"

He shakes his head. "That was an anomaly."

I snap my head in his direction to find him leveling me with a look. "Por qué?"

He smiles wryly. "I can't seem to make level-headed decisions when it comes to you."

Oh. His honesty is disarming; every word spreads warmth down to my toes. It makes me brave enough to ask for more. "Tell me something no one knows about you."

Arturo winces. "I'm not good at this."

"Try anyway."

He tilts his head back so it rests against the wall. He's not looking at me, but up at the rocky ceiling. "I'm afraid of heights."

"What?" I ask in amusement. "But you—"

His lips twist. "I discovered it while in the air."

The image of Arturo—capable and efficient and aloof Arturo—realizing the moment he'd rather *not* be miles above the ground makes me laugh until tears slide down my cheeks. I can picture the horror on his face, the *oh shit* moment as Roja took him higher and higher.

"It's not *that* funny."

"It is absolutely that funny."

He rolls his eyes heavenward.

"More," I demand. "Tell me something else."

"I have dreams, goals I want to meet in my life. There are so many, I worry I won't get to them all." He licks his lips. "I want to write a book about dragons, filled with my notes and observations and drawings. I want to run my own ranch. A safe place dragons can roam, a place where they can raise their young. A refuge."

"Won't that be dangerous for you? For the people looking after the land?"

He shifts his head to look at me. "Doesn't mean it shouldn't be done. Imagine living in a world without dragons because we've hunted every last one. Future generations will look back at us and wonder how we could have squandered living among legends."

"But you hunt them now."

"I know," he says in an anguished voice. "Because I gave up my profession, I can't own a business or work for anyone who isn't a member of the Gremio. I thought about leaving Hispalia without a real to my name, but that's when Ignacio gave me a job. Asked me to stay for two years. If I did, I'd own the ranch and the surrounding land. I signed the papers and it was done."

"A hard decision."

"I still don't know if I'm doing the right thing."

"How much more do you have left in your contract?"

"One more year."

Slowly, I lift my hand to smooth the hair curling above his brow. Incredibly, he lets me. "I asked you questions. Now it's your turn."

"Nice of you." The note of amusement in his voice makes my lips twitch. He's funny when he's not scowling. "Why did you get on the dragon?"

I stumble to try to find the best words. It's a test of sorts. And while I know the right answer, the answer he wants to hear, it's not the reason why I climbed onto the dragon's back.

"I'm afraid of them," I say. "I didn't use to be. Before my mother died, I only thought of dragons as part of Papá's job. I never feared for him when he fought a dragon, not really."

He swallows hard. "And then?"

I close my eyes, picturing that awful day near the citrus groves. Mamá had just finished her routine, and together we'd gone back to the dressing room in order for her to change. I was going to fix her hair. She looked beautiful, she always looked beautiful. I'd been rearranging her hair when the screaming started.

Arturo takes my hand. With a start, I realize I'd been talking out loud. His thumb draws light circles against the inside of my wrist.

"She told me to stay in the room, and then she ran out, wanting to find Papá." The words knot in my throat. I'm only able to untangle a few. "I followed her."

A little line forms between Arturo's dark brows. He waits for me to continue, and the memory comes out slow and haltingly.

"Zarela," Arturo says in an anguished whisper. "I am so very sorry."

"It's not your fault."

His hand tightens around mine, angry shadows dancing across his face.

"Do you want to know what surprises me the most?" I whisper. "After it happened, I found that I could still get out of bed. The pain of losing someone you love doesn't *actually* kill you, even though it feels like it should. I could still talk and eat, and at some point, find something to smile about. I miss her every day, but I also forget to think about her for hours. How does that happen? *Why* does that happen?"

My pain isn't satisfied being buried deep. It rises up, thickens my throat. I cover my face with my hands. I never show this much, sometimes not even with Lola. I have people fooled, letting them think that I've been transparent, but I hold a part of myself back every time. I'm only as honest as I want to be.

Arturo moves against me, shuffling closer, and then drapes a strong, reassuring arm across my shoulder. His fingers caress the sharp blade of my back. I turn my face toward his chest, press my cheek against the warm skin of his neck. His pulse jumps.

"I rode on the dragon's back because I'm sick of them owning a part of me," I whisper.

"It was a brave thing to do," he says gruffly. His other hand lifts and settles in my hair, smoothing the strands away from my face. I breathe his scent in, the lush pine and hint of smoke. So much like Santivilla.

I want to get closer.

"If you wondered how it began for me, you have your answer," Arturo murmurs against my temple.

I pull away so I can peer into his face. He flushes, mortified. My heart kicks up a notch. "How what began?"

He glares at me. "Me and you."

"My stubbornness is attractive?"

"Your determination," he says. "I thought for sure you would have left after the first night. Muddy, wet, but sleeping outside my door against a tree, demanding to be trained. I never had a chance. You are *ruinous*."

His words are a balm to the ache weighing me down. I'm overwhelmed by them—unable to breathe properly. "I'm not the only one to blame here."

"And what have I done?" Arturo asks, outraged.

I lean close, the words in my throat burning hot, wanting release. "What have you done to me?" I repeat, incredulous. "You took me *flying*."

He smiles sheepishly.

My eyes drop to his mouth.

His lips twist, silver eyes losing their shine. "I can't kiss you again, Zarela."

I reach for the lock of hair falling haphazardly across his brow. I push the dark lock back, my fingers lightly brushing against his warm skin, and he makes a low sound of pleasure. When I lean forward, his hands swing up and trap my wrists.

"Let me take you back." Arturo stares at me with a kind of panic in his eyes. Amusement flares within me. There's something incredibly alluring about making a man like Arturo squirm.

I look out of the cavern entrance, barely making out the surrounding trees and hills. No sense in heading out in the middle of the night.

"We'll go in the morning," I say casually.

"That's a terrible idea," he says angrily. "We'll go now."

If tonight is the only night I'll have alone with Arturo Díaz de Montserrat, then I certainly am not going to waste it. I roll forward onto my hands and knees and crawl toward him. His brows raise to his hairline. But he remains still. His face clears to make room for a haughty expression, disdain carved into every line and curve. Then his lip curls, as if he doesn't quite believe I have the nerve. But this only drives me forward, my hair falling at an angle across my face, messy braid over my shoulder. When I reach him, I push his hands out of the way and crawl onto his lap.

He regards me with a mixture of alarm and horror. "What did I just say? Let me take you home like a proper caballero would."

"Calling yourself a gentleman is quite generous."

"Zarela," he groans. "Haven't you been listening? We can't do this."

"Remind me why again."

"There's something I know that will hurt you."

I stiffen. "What is it?"

He meets my eyes. "I can't tell you because I want to keep you safe."

I poke him in the chest. "How can it both hurt me and keep me safe? You're not making any sense."

"I know," he says sadly.

I stare at him, considering. "Can I trust you?"

"With your life? Absolutely," he says fiercely.

"What's more important than that?" I lean forward. "I don't care about the rest."

He opens his mouth to protest, but I stop his words with my hand.

I know enough, and then I replace my hand with my mouth. One light kiss, and he groans.

I don't know where I have the nerve to do this to him. But I grin, and it's mean and sharp. His face pales. Now he knows he's in trouble.

We both are.

"I want you to kiss me without thinking about anything or anyone else." I drop my voice to a husky whisper. "I want you to kiss me like you've been thinking about it since the day you tried to run me out of the ranch. I stayed then, and I'm staying tonight."

His chest trembles beneath my hands, but he can't take his eyes off me, can't help reaching for me. We're both fighters, and we will go to war for the things we want, even when the world says we can't have them. Slowly he leans forward and places a soft kiss where my neck and shoulder meet.

I shiver. "Yes or no, Arturo?"

"I want you more than *anything*." His jaw clenches as I press my lips to the corner of his mouth. "You are the worst."

I arch a brow and wait.

Then he yanks me forward in the dark, and he brings my lips against his for a desperately hot kiss that rattles my bones. I let out a noise of triumph, and he laughs into my mouth. My fingers curl into the rough cotton of his tunic. He holds himself rigidly, but I move my legs on either side of his waist until I'm straddling him. Then he growls, wrapping his arms tight around me. He kisses me like he's teaching me a lesson. If I draw near a flame, I will burn. His gray eyes heat, burning like twin fires in the dim cave. The long line of him presses against me.

My eyes fly to his.

I want him to be the first. A terrifying thought that streaks through my mind, startling me. Delicious warmth pools in my belly, and I gasp when his hips rise, then cry out again as he drags me up and down against himself, finding the exact spot that steals my breath. His fingers dig into my hips.

"Arturo," I say, breathless.

"Damn it," he says weakly.

He moves me faster. Pressure builds, an immense wave that crashes over and over again, until I'm swept away, and the only thing I can focus on is his hot mouth against my neck. His hand slides up my waist, gliding over my tunic, and his palm cups my breast, his thumb gliding across my nipple. That wave rises again, and I'm pulled under, scrambling for air. He moves against me again and again, pressing tight between my legs, hard and fast until I'm gasping into his mouth. And the wave inside my body floods my every thought, rides my heartbeat until every inch of my skin tingles, and the strong current makes my knees shake.

He wraps his arms around me, and we stop, the last thing I want. I want him to feel what I did, that same demented wave that swept me away. I make a sound of protest against his tangled hair. I lean back and catch his faint, smug smile. The gentle set to his mouth robs me of breath. No more harsh lines bracketing his lips or running across his forehead. He smooths back my hair and presses a soft kiss under my ear. I rock against him, but he grips my hips and keeps me still.

"Zarela, I want it all," Arturo whispers hoarsely. "But I can't go further tonight."

This is about his secret. He's unable to meet my eyes.

"Why does my father dislike you?"

He lifts me off his lap and settles me close to his side. The blanket is tangled around our legs, and my fingers itch to straighten out the fabric. I need something to do while Arturo sits next to me, silent and grave, hands clasped tightly in his lap.

"He has good reason," he says finally.

"So I've been repeatedly told," I say angrily. "But I'd like to know what it is."

"I promise to tell you after the fight." He meets my gaze, and I'm surprised by the weary resignation lurking in the depths of his eyes.

And then I understand what he's been trying to tell me. He's worried I won't continue training with him, should I know the truth. He's worried about my safety in the arena and whatever secret he's hiding will put me at risk should I find out beforehand.

"Just confirming—you're not trying to ruin us?"

Arturo shakes his head. "No. I had nothing to do with the massacre at La Giralda, nothing to do with my uncle and his plans—whatever they might be."

The instant Arturo mentions Don Eduardo, I remember the note I found in his desk. What had it said? *Do not give up on him.*

"Zarela, what is it?" Arturo whispers.

"Do you know anyone named Hortensia?" I ask, my tone careful.

He stills. "Hortensia was my mother's name. She died from a sickness two years ago."

All this time, I'd had a clue about Don Eduardo being Arturo's uncle and I hadn't known. And now that I do, it doesn't bother me as much as it did. I believe him when he said he'd had nothing to do with the massacre.

I take his hand. "We'll figure this out together."

A hoarse laugh rattles in his throat. "I hope you remember that."

TREINTA

It's the dragon who wakes me. Roja crawls into the cave, her heavy tail scraping against the ground. All my senses flare to life. The cavern warms instantly, chasing away the cold clutches of the night. My heart races, beating hard against my ribs. I never thought I'd be attempting to sleep next to a dragon. I never thought I'd fly with one either.

It makes me wonder what else might be possible.

Arturo mumbles and then settles down, his hand reaching into his hair, and I'm struck by how boyish he looks. He's older than me, but in this moment he looks young, the scowl missing from his face. The dragon peers at me as she walks past, lambent gaze meeting mine. I shudder, and she exhales loudly, and the blast of air teases my hair.

Roja curls into herself, eyelids drooping. Every now and again, her tail twitches unconsciously. Great puffs of air disturb the deep quiet of the damp cave. Her claws scratch at the stone floor, and I have to plug my ears against the screeching noises that follow.

Arturo sleeps through it all.

We lie on our backs, side by side, tangled in the blanket. My cheek is pressed against the rough cotton of his tunic sleeve. His steady breathing fills the cavern, joining the dragon's inhales and exhales. It's time to get up, time for me to go home, and yet I don't want to move away from his warmth. The guttering torch casts long shadows against the jagged walls of the cave, and my gaze snags on the guitar. If he played while I danced, would Roja join me?

An idea niggles at the back of my mind. Creeps closer in the dark, presses a soft whisper against my ear. I'm on the cusp of something. An elusive compromise just waiting to be discovered.

The answer comes before daybreak.

I sit up, clinging to the thought, thinking it through to every possible end. Poking holes at it, assessing the risk, coming to a decision. Roja wakes and thumps her tail, yawning hugely, teeth gleaming in the shimmering light pouring into the cave. Arturo stirs next to me. He rubs his eyes and then blinks up at me.

"We fell asleep," he says in a marveling tone. With a gasp, he hurls himself to his feet. "Dios! Zarela, we fell asleep."

"Indeed," I say. "Buenos días."

He stares down at me, exasperation dawning. "Why aren't you more concerned? Your father—"

"I've had an idea."

"Is this really the time?"

"Yes," I say firmly.

He rolls his eyes, but waves his hand for me to continue.

I shoot a quick look at Roja, who lifts her head, as if fully aware that my plan involves dragons.

"Well? What is it?"

I inhale and slowly exhale, bracing myself for his response. "I don't want to fight in the arena. I don't want to kill the Morcego. I want you to play the guitar while I dance with him."

He's quiet for a long time, studying my face, and then he holds out his hands. I grasp them, and he pulls me to my feet in one fluid motion.

Arturo grins, right before kissing me.

Papá waits for us on the main staircase in the foyer. He leans against the rail, cheeks flushed, brow thundering. The house is quiet, too still for what ought to be a usual day for dragonfighting. I've worried him and owe him an explanation.

"Where have you been?" he asks coldly, his words are directed toward me, but he stares at Arturo.

Arturo clears his throat. "Señor Santiago—"

"Papá, I thought about our situation all night," I say, cutting him off. "And I've come up with a solution."

"Where were you?"

"We came up with a show," I say shortly.

"*You* did," Arturo says, and in his quick sidelong glance, I read the subtle note of pride in his gaze. The discovery warms my heart. "I know you're mad, but please listen to your daughter. Her idea means she won't have to fight in the ring."

Papá's anger deflates. "What are you talking about?"

I walk up the stairs and hold out my hand. "Let us show you."

Together we make our way to the arena, collecting Lola and Ofelia on the way. Papá settles onto the first row, while Ofelia rushes to retrieve Papá's guitar. Arturo disappears into the tunnel with the capote.

"Something has happened," Lola says under her breath. We are standing in the middle of the ring, and there's no need for the whispering, but I think she likes the sense of secrecy.

Of course I know what's she's asking, but I feign innocence. "What are you talking about?"

She places her hand on her hip in mock consternation. "Zarela Zalvidar."

I merely smile.

"If you don't tell me, I won't give you your new traje de luces."

I gasp. "Is it finished?"

"Almost." She bites her lip. "We're trying something new. I think you'll approve, but you have funny opinions sometimes, and even *worse* taste, and I never know—"

"We're?" I narrow my gaze at her. "Who are you working with?"

She blushes and I gasp.

"You're working on my dress with Guillermo?"

Her blush deepens, and I know I have her.

"Well, it's supposed to be a surprise."

Footsteps draw closer, and we both turn to see Arturo lead the dragon out from within the tunnel and onto the newly imported white sand. He hooks the chain onto the iron ring and then shoots me a wink. Lola lets out a triumphant noise, and I shoo her away before she can say something outrageous. Ofelia returns with the musical instrument and hands it over to Arturo, a bemused expression on her face.

The Morcego is furious, teeth snapping and tail whipping in our general direction. I step closer to the dragon. This is the one I danced with. The one that will play an integral part of my new performance. The crowd will be expecting a slaughter.

Not a dance between a dragon and its prey.

My stomach twists. In order for this to work, I have to do something extraordinary. I must face the dragon with nothing but my cape. "Unchain him and have your guitar ready."

Not even Papá or Mamá have done something like this.

Arturo slips his key into the lock, and there's a loud scraping sound when iron meets iron. The beast immediately recognizes the shift in how the chains become looser.

He senses his freedom is near.

Arturo immediately begins playing a soft, soothing melody. The dragon quiets and tilts its head and keeps its serpentine eyes focused on the tamer.

I snap the capote, the red fabric flapping, welcoming the monster into a new kind of battle.

"When I tell you," I say as the dragon's attention becomes ensnared with the bloodred cape, "play something lively."

Arturo's brow puckers, but he nods. I lift the capote and push it forward, and then quickly back. The dragon growls and rushes at me.

"¡Ahora!" I say as I spin away, the beast rushing past, horns slanted toward my body. The notes swirl around us as I lift my cape again. My feet stamp against the tightly packed sand, hips twisting in tune with the music. I try not to see the dragon as a monster, as a predator.

I look at the Morcego as my dance partner.

I use the cape the way I'd use my painted fan. A prop for my stomping and twirling fingers. The cape is much too heavy to hold with one hand, so I use my feet to create a new kind of routine.

Arturo's song is lovely and sweet, but with the addition of my stomping, soft as it is from all the sand, the music turns into something vibrant. A blend of sounds that makes my breath push out faster. The dragon watches me dance, twirling the cape, swaying my hips, moving around the arena. I look back at him routinely, urging him to dance with me.

Then at last, he does. At first, the Morcego merely circles me, curious but cautious. I continue moving, creating beats, hearing the notes bleed into my skin. The next time I twirl, I'm right next to the dragon. He bends forward with his long neck and plucks the cape out of my hands and shakes it back and forth, in a wide sweep.

Not unlike what I was doing.

I clap my hands, my feet thudding against the packed earth, and I move away, wrists bending and curling. He follows me, carrying the capote between his large teeth.

We move around each other. Sweat drips down my back, but I ignore the heat, the scorching sun or the way my hair sticks to the back of my neck. The dragon and I dance and dance and dance. Arturo's playing softens into a whisper. The music stops, and the world is silent once more. I ought to move away from the dragon, but it's still holding my capote, still watching me, waiting to see what will happen next.

I dip down into a curtsey. He spits out the cape and heads for the tunnel, seeking shade and respite from the heat. The creature knows there's water in his cage too. Arturo rushes after the dragon, sending me a bemused look as he runs past.

My breath comes out in panting gasps. I won't have to fight the dragon. The Morcego danced with me, moved with me. This is how I'll win back La Giralda—by offering something no one has ever seen.

I let out a shaky laugh and then face my father.

Tears carve tracks down to his chin. He brings his fingers to his lips and lets out a sharp whistle, and then he claps, and Ofelia and Lola join him, laughing and cheering.

I can do anything.

"I'll be right back," I call to them, and then dash into the tunnel. I'm halfway to the dungeon when I hear Arturo's approach.

"What did you think?" I ask him.

He takes quick steps and wraps his arms around my waist and hoists me high above his head. The smile on his face, the unguarded joy in his eyes makes my body tremble. He slowly lowers me, until just the tips of my boots touch the stone floor.

"It was fine," he says, then he lowers his head and kisses me. His mouth slants over mine, soft lips tasting me. I tuck my arms around his neck, and his fingers splay against my back, holding me up and close to him. Slowly I wrap my legs around his waist. He bounces me higher, until I'm cradling his upturned head in my hands, catching every sigh, every breath that escapes his mouth. I press my lips to his closed eyelids, his cheeks, his nose.

I lift my head, until my mouth is hovering a mere inch from his. He opens his eyes, drowsily, as if drunk from my skin, the close space of the corridor heating our bodies, the hard stone underneath our feet, and the warm breeze that curls around us in a soft embrace.

"You've ruined me for anyone else," he whispers.

"Good," I say, unable to stop my smirk.

He pinches the back of my thigh, and I squeal.

Someone clears their throat. We pull apart, and a ripple of timid laughter escapes me.

Papá, Lola, and Ofelia stare at us in various degrees of astonishment, outrage, and bemusement from the tunnel entrance. The three of them are outlined in sunlight, and I have to squint in order to clearly see their faces.

Arturo takes my hand, his attention on Papá. There's a charged moment between them, the air tense.

"Have you told her?" Papá asks in quietly menacing voice.

Arturo's fingers tighten against mine. "No, but I will. After her performance."

"Then you shouldn't be holding her hand." Papá reaches out to take hold of a craggy groove in the wall. His breathing is labored, as if he's in shock.

"Papá," I say in hard voice. "I'm not a child."

He shuts his eyes and nods. "I know. And you'll make your choice when you know the truth."

A flare of panic detonates, deep in my belly. If there were a village living inside me, nothing would have remained. Not one house. Footsteps draw near, and I make out the shape of Tió Hector coming toward us, at first curious, but when he sees Arturo, he jerks back as if he's been kicked in the stomach.

"Tió?" I call out, uncertain.

"What is this?" Hector asks in a low growl when he reaches us. He steps around Papá, Lola, and Ofelia. His gaze drops to our clasped hands, and his shoulders tighten. Twin red spots appear on his cheeks.

His words are an angry snarl. "Step away from her."

"Tió?" I ask again. I've never seen him this angry. He's never used that tone of voice around me.

But Hector lifts a finger toward Arturo. "Take your hand off her."

Arturo releases it without argument. I throw him a look. "Wait a minute—"

"Hector, I'll handle this," Papá says.

Lola and Ofelia back away, eyes widening in alarm.

"Have you lost your mind?" Hector says to my father, each word growing louder. "You must have, to allow this atrocity."

Papá's brows snap together. "Hector, Arturo is training Zarela—they've merely gotten carried away."

"Training? *Training?* You mean—" Hector sputters, his gaze shooting to my sandy outfit. Realization dawns, and his lips twist in horror. "No. Santiago, you wouldn't let her."

I lift my chin. "It's true. I'm going to fight in the arena."

Hector pales, becoming utterly still. "And this reprobate is teaching you how to become a Dragonador."

Arturo says nothing. My blood reaches a boiling point. "I don't understand how any of this is your concern."

Hector's lips turn white. "Not my *concern*? Don't you understand who he is?"

I roll my eyes. "I do, actually."

"He's not talking about my uncle," Arturo says quietly. "He's talking about the day your mother died."

His words reverberate inside the tunnel. Crashing against me like heavy rocks. My hand slips from his. "Explain what you mean. Right now."

"Zarela," he says in a low, flat tone. "I was the Dragonador who failed to kill the dragon in the arena. Your mother is dead because of me."

A sharp pain stabs my belly. No one breathes, no one moves. And then Lola is next to me, offering her support without words. The only reason I'm still standing is because of her. Hector and Papá yell furious words, awful things that can't be unsaid.

"This is so like you," Tío Hector snaps. "You don't care about who you put in danger as long as it doesn't disturb your career, your plans, your image."

"I *love* my family," Papá says, in between huffs.

"Then you ought to protect them," Tío Hector says coldly.

"Who made La Giralda what it is to—"

Arturo steps closer, and his voice is low and urgent, blocking out the rest of their argument. "Zarela, listen to me. That was the last time I ever stepped foot in the arena, the last time I ever performed as a Dragonador," he says.

I bend forward, hands wrapped around myself as if to protect myself from his damning words. Lola clutches my arm, keeps me from keeling over. I barely notice. For a long time, I played a game of what if: What if my mother never performed that day? What if she'd stayed with me, instead of rushing out of the dressing room to find my father?

What if the Dragonador had done his damn job?

"Zarela. Look at me."

But I can't. I don't think I'll ever be able to again. There were so many times he could have told me the truth. "How could you not tell me?"

He's quiet. And then, "The dragon survived because I hesitated in delivering the killing blow. It was only a second, but the damage was done. I couldn't regain the ground I had lost, no matter how hard I fought to reclaim the upper hand. After what happened . . . I was sickened by all of it. What I'd done. All the senseless killing."

"How could you not tell me?"

"If I did, you wouldn't have let me train you anymore. Your life mattered more to me than telling you the truth. I'd make the same decision again."

I don't know why I asked the question when I'm in no way ready to hear the answer. I'm not remotely satisfied by his words. Not by miles. My mother is gone because of his ideals. He hesitated because he didn't *want* to kill that dragon.

And it cost me everything.

"I am so sorry, Zarela," Arturo says in an agonized whisper. "Lo siento."

"You should be," Hector snarls.

"Please leave," I whisper.

Arturo dips his chin. Then he goes without another word.

When I turn away from the sight of him leaving, Papá is on the ground.

TREINTA Y UNO

I sit beside Papá who lies tucked under several thick quilts, shivering. He peers at me through bloodshot eyes. I clutch his hand, finding it clammy and cold. He opens his mouth to speak, but the words are paper thin, nearly transparent. I shift forward, bringing my head near his. Dios, I hate seeing him like this. After Arturo left, we all helped Papá to his bed, and then I went to fetch the healer. Her diagnosis wasn't reassuring: he's relapsed, doing too much, too soon. It's my fault for not telling him to slow down.

"Did Hector leave?" Papá asks.

I nod. "He stayed for an hour, looking after you. Refused to speak to me. I've never seen him so angry."

"I couldn't tell you. I'm sorry."

"Yes, you could have," I say. "I can decide for myself who to love, who to be mad at." I take a deep breath. "Who to forgive."

Papá licks his dry, cracked lips. "I was trying to protect you. If he'd done his job, your mother would still be alive." He looks away. "But then I remember there were times I was unable to kill a dragon in the arena. It only happened twice, when I was first starting out. I was probably his age."

Hurt wraps around my heart and squeezes. "You hate him."

Papá shuts his eyes. "I do. He was a part of Eulalia's death. There's no escaping that. Is he to blame? No, I can't fault him for being human. But he didn't kill the dragon, and so I can't look at him without remembering who I lost." He coughs, a rattling cough that makes his entire body shake. "But that's *my* problem. I can live with that if he's who you want. I only wanted you to know the whole of it before you decide." He watches me carefully. "What will you do?"

"I don't know, Papá."

"Just because I can't forgive him, doesn't mean that you can't. Perhaps you should." He sighs, a long exhale dragged out of him. "It wasn't his fault."

I waffle between hurt and anger. Hurt that Arturo hadn't told me, and anger because I realized how badly I wanted to make sense of her death. Arturo's part in the tragedy wasn't the answer I wanted. But I may never fully understand why she died. Blaming Arturo won't make me feel better. That dragon acted in accordance with its nature. It was brought to the arena against its will and fought to survive.

But he still should have told me.

"Continue with the show," Papá says. "You must. It's too good not to be seen."

"I don't have a guitar player anymore."

Papá gives me a knowing smile. "The tamer will be back. And if he doesn't, Hector will play for you."

"No, he won't. You heard him. He doesn't want me anywhere near a dragon."

"Bring Hector to me in the morning," Papá says. "I'll make him see reason."

I lean forward and press my forehead to his chest, a great sob heaving out of me from the depths of my pain. "You will recover."

"Of course I will." He tangles his fingers in my hair. "Zarela, I have never seen you look so much like yourself than when I saw you dancing with that dragon. In love with flamenco again. I'm proud of the woman you are. I know I probably don't say that enough."

"Papá," I say, my voice cracking. He holds me for a long moment until I hear the even sound of his breath, feel the steady rise and fall of his chest.

I don't know how I manage to walk to my room, exhaustion stealing the small moments between dressing for bed and lighting candles. I slump onto the bed, eyelids drooping, heart heavy, when an insistent scraping noise disturbs my attempt to sleep, like something scratching against rough stone. The sound of someone cursing makes me instantly alert, up on my feet, and marching toward the balcony.

I throw the doors open, furious, wanting a fight, and stalk up to the railing and look down onto the street, sure I'll see someone waving a banner, maybe Martina herself.

But it's not a member of the Asociación.

Arturo clings to a ledge, the toes of his boots perched on a single brick protruding from the wall. He tilts his head back, lifts his chin. The darkness softens his face, the sharp angles of his cheekbones, his sullen mouth. There's enough candlelight coming from my bedroom to illuminate the hazy outline of his body pressed close to the wall.

"Hola," he says stiffly, trying to sound dignified but failing. "I came to deliver a letter."

I raise a brow.

"You couldn't have left the missive at the front door?"

"I wasn't sure if anyone would have passed on my note. I was planning on sliding it under the balcony door." He watches me closely, and he quickly adds, "I can go if you wish."

I study him for a long moment, considering. "Get inside."

I turn away and stalk back into my room, fold my arms tight across my chest. He makes quick work climbing the rest of the way, throwing one leg over the railing and then the other. I stand in the middle of the chamber while he quietly takes a single step inside. He's dressed in that way of his that reminds me of a fortress: dark linen tunic, equally dark trousers, scuffed boots, hair tousled, and his mouth bent into a grimace.

He reaches behind him to untuck a roll of parchment he's stored in the waistband of his trousers. The note hovers between us, tucked in between his fingers. I take it and toss it onto the bed. "Say it to my face."

Arturo nods, as if he expected this. He remains quiet and grim for so long, it gives me time to sort out my own feelings. I'm happy to see him. Happy he came after I sent him away, relieved he wanted to deliver a message to me badly enough, he climbed a wall. But what if my feelings for him are clouding my judgment?

Papá's words roar loud in my head, in my heart: *It wasn't his fault.*

"You don't want to see me," he says at last. "I know that. But I'm here to say one thing, and one thing only: lo siento. I'm to blame for every-thing. Zarela, I'm sorry—more than I know how to say."

He doesn't pull his eyes from mine. They're red-rimmed and blood-shot, as if he hasn't slept in days. Exhaustion tugs his chin toward the ground, carves deep grooves at the corners of his mouth, across his brow. I want to smooth each line away with a careful finger. His shoulders are tense, and he hasn't moved from the balcony, as if any moment, I'll demand he leave my sight. I don't blame him. I've done it to him before.

But I'm not going to do that.

I take a step forward, and then another. Arturo stiffens, inhales sharply. I come to stand in front of him, and I slowly grip his elbows. At my touch he exhales, and his warm breath blows across my cheeks. He's rigid under my hands. Afraid to soften, afraid to hope.

"Lo siento," he says again, his voice a hoarse whisper.

"A dragon murdered my mother."

His chin jerks up, mouth parts. "If I hadn't hesitated—"

I slap my hand against his mouth. "Be quiet."

His gaze narrows, and I can read his annoyance, his exasperation. I'm relieved to see his prickly demeanor return. He's ready to fight me. He doesn't believe he deserves any grace, any forgiveness. Maybe he'll punish himself forever.

Ridiculous.

"It wasn't your fault." He melts beneath my touch, and my heart soars to see his relief, the glassy sheen in his gray eyes. "I have a question for you, Arturo. Will you answer me honestly?"

He nods, and though I'm covering the lower half of his face, his ex-pression tells me he will deny me nothing.

"Why did you hunt the dragon?"

I remove my palm.

"I did it for you," he says, his voice hoarse.

"Why?" I tug him forward while I back up toward the bed, one step at a time. Arturo's gaze flicks beyond my shoulder, and when he sees our destination, he immediately stops moving. "Zarela."

He's warning me.

I am in control, and I want the truth. "Answer me."

"Because I love you," he says at a near shout, and I smile, which makes him scowl, embarrassed and vulnerable. I tug him again and he resists. I let out a noise of protest. I'm done with people making decisions for me. Done with people protecting my feelings. Arturo taught me how to survive the arena. Came with me while the city burned. Showed up to help clean the front steps of my home. Took me flying. Believed in me.

He trusts me. Loves me.

With him, I feel safe. With him, I feel heard.

He is who I want. I take another deliberate step back. I tell him my secret. I speak it clearly, my chin held up high, my eyes not leaving his. "Te amo, Arturo."

"Is that right?" he asks softly.

My voice is steady. "It is."

His expression turns wolfish. My heart jumps and warmth pools deep in my belly. In a million years, I never would have thought I could feel so much for one person. Arturo slowly advances until my knees hit the back of the bed. Together we crawl backward with him hovering above me, his attention on my black hair spilling across the pillow, on my mouth, the slide of my robe parting down the middle.

Arturo leans down and brushes his lips against mine. "Are you sure, Zarela?"

Nervous anticipation builds under my skin. "Yes."

He hesitates. "Have you done this before?"

A blush steals across my face. I shake my head.

"The first time might hurt," he says, whisper-soft. "Is this what you really want?"

I nod, knowing he'll be gentle, but worry bubbles to the surface. I have no idea what I'm doing. My attention lands on the broad line of his shoulders. Slowly, I tug his tunic up his back, and he pulls his arms through the sleeves, tosses the shirt to the side. I curl a lock of his thick hair behind his ear and his eyes gleam in the candlelight.

"I don't know what to do next," I admit in a hush.

He gazes at me tenderly, and this time when he kisses me, I feel it everywhere. He tastes me, nibbles my bottom lip, lips slanting over mine until I can no longer think straight. All I know is how badly I want to be close to him, closer than I've ever been with anyone else. I've waited for him for so long, and it makes me greedy for his touch, the feel of his arms around him. Shielding me from everything else. He drags his tongue down the length of my throat and I gasp. My hands shake as I tug the robe off my shoulders, and Arturo helps me gather the silk and flings it off the bed. The sheer linen of my shift hides nothing from his hungry gaze. He slips a warm hand under the strap and slides it down my arm. I pull at the bottom hem and yank it over my legs, my waist, my head. No one has ever seen me this undone, this bare. What if he doesn't like the shape of my hips? What if—

"You're so beautiful," he murmurs, and then his callused hands glide up my legs, curve around my waist. I kiss the scars running up his arms. Burn marks from years of handling dragons. We are the same, carrying the marks of a blaze that wrecked our lives. In a daze, I stare up at the ceiling as he explores every inch of my body, touching me everywhere. My breath comes out in quick huffs. A part of me can't believe this is happening. Another part knows this was inevitable. We were always going to end up here. Together.

I urge him closer, and he grinds himself against me. I remember that perfect moment in the cave, the way he made me feel, and I yearn for that same release. He understands what I want because he smiles against my neck and doesn't slow his pace. Pressure builds and builds, and then reaches the summit. I close my eyes and leap off the cliff, trusting that he'll be there to catch me. He kisses me deeply while I pull off the rest of his clothing, desperate to get closer. I tuck my hands in his hair as he moves over me, his breath ragged. Arturo lifts his head, pierces me with a look, one more question. "Are you sure? We don't have to—"

I wrap my legs around his hips and a nervous exhale escapes me, even though my heart is steady. "Yes."

Arturo slowly dips inside me, and it hurts. I let out a small gasp. He immediately stills, his breath ragged above me as he apologizes over and over, his soft voice working like a balm. The pain becomes less, transforms into a healing we both desperately need. Then there's only our mingled breath dancing in the dim room as we move together. What happened in our past remains there, where it belongs. There's no room for secrets or regret or guilt.

Afterward, he tucks me close to his side, his chest rising and falling under my cheek. We stay that way until sleep comes for us both.

I'm slow to wake; my body feels groggy and a bit sore. I crack an eye open, surprised to see it's still dark outside. A heavy hand curls around my waist, pressing me close to Arturo's bare chest.

"Buenos días," Arturo murmurs. He kisses the back of my neck and goose bumps flare up and down my arms.

I turn to face him and smile at the sight of the sleepy dragon tamer, hair disheveled, pillow creases marring one side of his face.

"You need a haircut."

His smile is slow. "Do I?"

I nod and he leans forward but I turn my head. "I'd kiss you, but I need to chew on mint leaves first."

This draws a startled chuckle from him. "Where are they?"

"Behind you on that little table next to the bed."

He half turns and plucks a handful from a ceramic bowl and then divides it between us. He swoops down to kiss me the minute I finish, and I laugh against his mouth.

"When can I see you again?" I ask.

"Zarela," Arturo says in mock consternation. "Today is our last training day."

I groan and he rolls on top of me.

"You have to leave," I say between kisses.

"Lola?" He draws a line with the tip of his nose from behind my ear and down to my collarbone.

It takes me a minute to answer. What he's doing to my neck robs me of breath. "Lola, Ofelia, my father."

Papá. My breath freezes in my chest. I can't believe I fell asleep. What if he needed me during the night? I have to go. Right this minute. "Arturo," I say in an anguished whisper.

He immediately lifts his head, searches my eyes, and I don't even attempt to hide my panic, my fear. He rolls away and gently pulls me out from under the soft bedding. He grabs my nightgown and I lift my hands. He slides the garment over me. I pull on my robe, and he draws the ends together tight, making a secure knot with the silk belt. He kisses me one more time. "Go to him."

This is why I'm in love with him.

I walk to the door, spare a second to look over my shoulder. Arturo has dragged on his pants, hands on his hips as he searches for his tunic. He sees me staring, and his lips soften into a small smile. This is the dragon tamer defenseless, all soft edges and vulnerable eyes, the wall between us shattered.

"I'll see you soon, mi amor. Go."

I run in a mad rush, racing down the corridor, my heart in my throat. Guilt pricks my heart, sharp needlelike stabs I feel behind my breastbone. La Giralda can't have another vacant seat at the table, a bedroom emptied. Ofelia has the same idea because she's climbing up the grand staircase, two at a time. She carries a tray with a bowl filled with broth and a pitcher of cool water. We reach Papá's door, and I quickly duck inside, Ofelia at my heels.

"Buenos días," Papá says with a wan smile. Sunlight pours into the expansive chamber, the velvet curtains around his bed lay wide open. He's propped against three pillows, idly reading the morning paper.

"Papá—look at you!" I say, my voice cracking.

He grimaces. "I won't look in a mirror until someone trims my beard."

Ofelia and I laugh, and I draw close to his side, kiss his cheek. Relief, delight, and joy play a merry tune in my mind, the melody making me want to dance, to shout from the rooftops. Papá turned a corner and will recover once again. Ofelia can't hide the tears brimming in her eyes as she sets the tray on the end table by the linen-covered bed.

Papá eyes the bowl in distaste. "You're trying to kill me with all this broth, woman."

Ofelia's face turns stern, and I laugh and then swoop to kiss Papá's cheek once more. "I'm off to bring Hector to you."

He nods. "Bien. I need to make things right between us."

"Promise to do what Ofelia says?"

Papá scowls and Ofelia lets out a triumphant noise. I leave them to their argument with a smile on my face. He's going to recover.

It's a beautiful day in Santivilla, not a cloud visible in any direction. Carriages and vendors crowd the wide tree-lined avenues, people stroll in the public parks under a canopy of thick branches. I'm thankful I can easily weave through the throng of shoppers and passersby. Someone plays the guitar one block over, and the sound carries up and down the length of the cobbled paths. I urge my horse faster, not caring for the many stares I get for my uncovered head, and my unladylike riding.

I reach Hector's home and leave my mare with the attendant before rushing up the polished marble steps. His butler answers, and when he sees the state I'm in, he ushers me inside quickly. I'd left in such a rush, dressed in my sandy training outfit, eager to complete this errand so I could return to the arena to train.

"He's having his morning meal, señorita," he says, already turning away. "Would you like to wait?"

I shake my head, not wanting to waste time. "I'll go to him."

The butler walks with me across the grand foyer, our footsteps echoing in the expansive hall. He opens the door to the dining room for me. Hector sits at the head of the table, reading the paper and sipping on coffee. The butler leaves me with a polite nod, and I venture inside, my attention dropping to his knuckles turning white.

He's *furious*.

"Tío, I know you're angry with me," I say. "Papá wants to see you. I don't like to see this rift between you."

"And what about what's broken between us?"

Shame burns like acid in my gut. "Tío—"

His brows lower as he considers me. "You lied to me, Zarela."

His tone is laced with strong notes of disapproval and disappointment. "Tío, I did, but it was because I didn't want you to worry or talk me out of my decision." My voice becomes stern. "And it is *my* decision."

"You're right," he says finally, eyes burning into mine. "I would never have approved, and neither should your father have. It's entirely selfish for him to risk your life in order to save his reputation."

Anger rises, and my chest feels as if it contains boiling water. "Papá didn't know my plans until it was too late to change them. Don't blame him—"

"But I do," he says. "Your life is more important than his name."

There's no way I can ask him to come with me. Not when he's acting like this. My father needs peace.

"I think it's best we continue this another time," I say stiffly. "When you're calmer, stop by La Giralda to see Papá. He wants to mend things," I add, hoping that might be enough to soften him. "He woke up feeling much better."

He stares at me for a long beat and then concedes a nod. "I'm glad to hear it."

"I knew you'd be pleased. Won't you come with me after you're done eating?"

"All right, Zarela. You will have your way." He shoots me a disgruntled, wary smile. "As you always do."

"Thank you, Tío." I beam at him. Really, it's more than I deserve.

Hector stands and pulls out one of the dining chairs. "You may as well join me. Knowing you, it's been hours since you've last eaten."

I haven't eaten anything since the day before, and at the mention of food, my stomach growls. "Yes, all right. Gracias."

"I'll be right back. I need to let them know to bring out an extra plate. Do you want coffee?"

"Always."

He shakes his head ruefully, then disappears through the adjoining door. I lean forward and place my elbows on the table, resting my forehead on my palms. Exhaustion seeps into my bones. I'd gotten maybe four hours of sleep. The sweet time with Arturo feels like it happened forever ago. I let out an enormous yawn.

"I see café was the right choice," Hector says, his butler at his heels, carrying a silver tray with a glass of wine and a smaller cup. The nutty aroma fills my nose, makes me sit upright.

"Perfecto," I say gratefully.

The butler sets the drink in front of me, along with a little bowl filled with sugar. I drink it black. The hot liquid slides down my throat, instantly warming me. I continue to sip as Hector's food is brought out on silver trays. Thin slices of prosciutto and cantaloupe, wedges of hard cheese, bundles of grapes, and a handful of green olives.

He fills a plate for me and then one for himself. "I insist you eat, Zarela."

Half my food disappears before I know it, and Hector shoots me an approving smile. "Do you want more?"

I shake my head. Now that I've eaten, I'm impatient to return. "We ought to go."

He smiles, but it looks wrong, like wearing shoes that don't match. "I'm not coming with you," he says slow and kind.

I blink, confusion rising. "Y por qué no?"

Hector watches me nurse the coffee between my hands. His next words are soft. "You've always been precious to me, Zarela."

His words aren't what I expect to hear. "I know, Tío."

"Everything I've done, I've done for you."

I stiffen and tension zips up my spine. He's gearing up to talk me out of performing tonight. He doesn't want to make things right with Papá. I've been wasting my time here. I push the chair back and stand. The motion makes my head spin. "Uncle, I don't have time for a lecture. I have to train and Papá needs me."

I press my palms against the table in order to steady myself. I'm weirdly light-headed.

"Sit down, Zarela, before you fall over."

He's not making any sense. "Why would I fall over?"

Hector winces, in a gesture that seems to say that he's terribly sorry for inconveniencing me. "Because I've drugged your coffee."

Blackness sweeps forward on my garbled moan. I slump forward.

When I wake, I'm not alone. I blink away the crowding darkness, the unsettling realization that I'm by myself and vulnerable. My hands can't move. I glance down and understand why: I'm bound to a leather chair, in a beautiful room with the finest furnishings I've ever seen. Hector sits across from me, in an identical leather chair, with only a small round table separating us. A plate filled with bocadillos, sandwiches filled with jamón and queso, is within easy reach. Churros coated in cinnamon sugar are piled high on another plate, a small bowl filled with dark chocolate for dipping next to it. An expensive bottle of wine with two goblets sits next to it. A quick glance to the window tells me we're still hours before sunset. I haven't been out for too long.

"You're awake. How do you feel?"

"Cut off the ropes," I say in a furious whisper.

He takes one churro and dips it into the chocolate, then leans forward and coaxingly offers it to me. "Your favorite. Why don't you have a bite?"

"Get that out of my face and set me free," I seethe.

Hector drops the food back onto the plate and then leans back against his chair, silently studying me. I yank against the binding, but it's thick and unyielding. My skin burns from its touch, stinging and raw.

"You'll hurt yourself."

"I don't care," I say through gritted teeth as I continue to thrash. "Hector. Please. I have to go back."

"You'll fight in the arena if I let you go." Hector opens the bottle and pours himself a glass. The red liquid fills to the brim. "Your father won't survive the day, Zarela. Prepare yourself for that eventuality."

"You're wrong. He's recovering. I saw him myself this morning—"

"And I just sent a tonic with a note of apology," Hector says. "I'm sorry to tell you that I added poison to the herbal remedy. Ofelia is so efficient, she'll make sure he takes it."

"No," I say, my voice hoarse, as if I've been screaming for hours. "No. Por favor."

He raises the glass to his lips and takes a deep sip. "It was me who set the dragons free. Me who murdered Benito with the encanto."

I gape at him. "*What?*"

"Dragon smoke is a silent killer."

His words don't make sense. It was Don Eduardo working with the Asociación. "No, it can't have been."

Hector says nothing.

The silence weighs heavy between us, and his words fully register— all the ramifications: the removal of our family from the Gremio, the potential loss of our home, my mother's precious dresses. But more importantly—my father's life.

"I went to you for help," I say quietly. "And you lied to me, told me the Dragon Master was behind all this." Something clicks in my mind. A sudden understanding on what Señora Montenegro had meant when she lay dying in my arms.

"She was talking about *you*," I say, horrified.

He startles. "What?"

"After the dragon attack in the plaza, I tried to save Señora Montenegro, but she was too injured. Before she died, she said, '*He won't be happy until your papá is gone.*' At the time I thought she was talking about Don Eduardo, but she was talking about you."

Hector rolls his eyes heavenward. "One of my foolish mistresses."

"Why? *Why* would you do this?" I demand again.

His eyes blaze fire. "Eulalia."

Her name burns the air, scorches my hearing, inflames my mind. The possessive way he says her name scrapes against my skin.

"Santiago took her away from me." He takes a long gulp of wine. "She was mine first, did you know? Our families wanted us together. To fall in love and become the toast of Valentia. We were going to build ships, hire navigators, explore the sea together. My sister dreamed of the day when we'd have children. Your mother and I had an *understanding*. When I made enough money, she said she'd marry me." He grips the stem of the goblet, knuckles white. "You could have been my daughter. If she hadn't met Santiago and run away to Santivilla, you could have been the child I wanted."

My heart freezes. Veins fill with icy blood that sends a shiver down the length of my spine.

"She broke our betrothal, and I had to come to terms with that. But I couldn't stay away, and so I paid an enormous sum to switch Gremios and learned to fight dragons, when I would have preferred to be on the water. I thought maybe if I became someone she wanted, Eulalia would come back to me. But she didn't." He continues in a low voice. "Then you were born, and I loved you the first moment I held you. I learned to live with the pain and helped your father with his appalling finances and gambling debts and whatever else." A bitter wistfulness pinches his lips into a flat line. "Perhaps I ought to have let him destroy himself. But it wasn't good for you or Eulalia, and she made it clear that she'd never move back to Valentia, even without Santiago. I couldn't risk her marrying someone else who might disapprove of our friendship, and besides, your father promised me he'd keep her safe."

Another long sip.

"Do you remember the month that she died?"

I flinch. As if I didn't carry her death everywhere I went. Didn't live or breathe it every moment.

"An Escarlata dragon had been spotted outside of Santivilla. Violent and frequently attacking travelers inside carriages, on horseback, walking. And then it was captured, and everyone wanted Arturo to slay the beast. He was the rising star of Hispalia at the time. Your mother wanted to perform as the opening act before he took the stage." He shoots me a sad, wry smile. "She did what pleased her, your mother. I tried to talk her out of it. But she wouldn't listen. I turned to your father. But he supported her, supported her every whim. He's weak—I'll never understand what she saw in him. And then Santiago took both of you—the people I loved most in the world—outside the city walls. It was his fault your mother died. Don't you understand? I could have lost you too. That's when I realized what I had to do. It took me months and months to figure out how to make you legally mine. I was going to be the only one you loved who remained at your side."

"How can I possibly love you after this?" I ask quietly.

"I never planned or wanted you to find any of this out," Hector says sadly. "Your father was injured during the massacre—a lucky accident, which saved me the trouble of having to kill him myself at the time. But when I found out it was going to be *you* in the arena fighting tonight, I had to move quickly to save you from your own reckless behavior." He hesitates. "In time, I hope you'll be able to understand why I've done what I had to do. Santiago is not fit to be your father. I am."

"Listen to me carefully," I say through my teeth. "You are not my father, no matter what your disillusions tell you."

Bile rises up my throat. I'm having a hard time comprehending how I could have misunderstood him so badly. All these years, he's harbored hatred in his heart. All he needed was a reason to release it.

"Do you know what will happen if you lose both your parents?" he asks quietly.

I swallow. It's painful. As if there were a dagger at the back of my throat.

"I become your guardian. Everything you own belongs to me. The laws of the land give me absolute control."

I shake my head, desperate. I don't want to hear any more.

"You will be looked after. Cherished. No more needless risks." His eyes flash. "No more dragonfighting."

"These are not your choices to make."

"Had you been my daughter, they would be." He softens. "I know why you've been training. But no more, Zarela. With me, the only thing you'll have to worry about is what dress you'll be wearing for the day. What to serve for lunch. No more friendships with questionable influences."

He gives me a pointed look and understanding dawns. "It was you." I thrash against the rope again. "It was *you* who wrote that note threatening Lola."

"You'll be mistress of my home until you marry a man I approve of," he continues as if I hadn't spoken.

The blood drains from my face. I feel it pool to the bottom of my feet. "No."

"This is happening whether you're ready for it or not. Eulalia can rest in peace knowing her only daughter is being looked after in the way she ought to be taken care of."

"And you don't think I'll go to the Gremio with this?" I snarl.

He calmly nods, accepting the question because he'd been anticipating it. "You have no say or rights within the Gremio. Santiago is a disgrace, and after he dies, you will be in my care. No one will question this, no one will believe the hysterics of a grieving girl. You have no voice in this argument. Don't you understand, Zarela? Your parents named me your guardian."

Panic claws at my edges.

He drains the last of his wine and then stands. Slowly, he comes around the table and looks down at my upturned face with a tenderness in his eyes that makes my skin crawl. He cups my cheek, and I jerk away, fighting tears.

"Did you know that it was me who gave Eulalia your name? Zarela. I've always loved it. My mother and grandmother shared the name. You see, hija? You were always meant to be mine."

Hector leaves the room, taking my whole world with him.

TREINTA Y DOS

After Hector leaves, a maid carrying a pot of coffee ventures into the room. A guard accompanies her. "Buenas tardes, señorita."

I stare at them both in impotent fury.

The guard shuts the door behind him with a measured click. He places his hands on his hips. "I'm here to untie you so that you may eat, but only if you don't hurt me or Carla. Understand?"

My pulse jumps in my throat. This is an opportunity, a real chance at escape. I'm a match waiting to be struck, waiting for the flame. I keep my face neutral so as not to betray the fire burning from within.

"Señorita, entiendes?"

I nod, confirming that I do, in fact, understand. I understand that you're vile and you work for a monster. The guard smiles. He's closer to Hector's age, barrel-chested and with light brown hair, graying strands woven throughout. He steps carefully toward me, as if any moment I might escape my bonds and lunge for his throat.

Which is exactly what I want to do.

He pulls out a dagger and hacks at the rope binding my wrists. The slivers fall onto the floor. The maid—Carla—comes forward and pours the coffee. The chicory smell perfumes the air, and I drag it in, filling my lungs. The guard steps away from me.

My gaze drops to the tray holding the plate of bocadillos. The sandwiches are filled with tuna and pickled red pepper, hard boiled eggs and grilled onions. They're my favorite, but they do the opposite of what I'm sure Hector intended. Instead of endearing me to him, they make me recoil in disgust. Does he think serving my favorite food will make me less mad? I reach for the coffee and take a tentative sip, and of course it's delicious. But I twist my lips and make a face of disgust.

"Tienes azúcar?"

Carla takes stock of the contents on the table. "I meant to add it onto the tray. Let me go down and bring the sugar."

She crosses the room and opens the door.

I jump to my feet and throw the scalding hot coffee in my guard's face. He doubles over, bellowing. Then I slam the tray down on the back of his head. Carla lets out a shriek when I shove her aside, racing for the door. My steps stall as I take in my surroundings: a long corridor with wooden floors and a bannister up ahead. I'm on the second or third floor. My feet propel me down the stairs, pounding against the marble.

I can't believe this is happening.

Running for my life in Tío Hector's house.

From above, the guard lets out a loud warning. My heart slams against my ribs. The navy-and-white checkered floor comes into view. I'm almost to the bottom floor. Almost to the front door. But a lone figure waits for me at the foot of the steps, arms folded across his chest. I don't slow down. I'll level him to the polished floor if I have to—I won't back down.

Five steps to go.

Three.

He reaches for me, but I use my shoulder to barrel past. He grabs my arm, and I slam my elbow to shove him off. He grunts, tottering away from me. I race to the foyer, legs pumping. The entrance is in sight.

A line of six guards blocks the exits.

I scream in frustration, stopping so abruptly that I slide forward, and I have to windmill my arms to keep myself from falling. I whirl around, desperate for another way out of this infernal house. But the guard from upstairs approaches, clothes damp, smelling of coffee, rubbing the back of his head. His skin is blotchy and red. Hector follows at his heels, clutching his side.

They encircle me, foreboding and grim and quietly menacing.

Hector takes a careful step forward, and I snarl at him. "Murderer!"

Anger pulses in my blood. I want to yell and kick and thrash until I'm free from this horrifying mess. But I'm alone and trapped.

"If my father dies," I say, my tone as sharp as the point of a knife, "you are all responsible."

"When," Hector corrects gently. "*When* he dies."

I don't understand the sympathetic, warm glow in his eyes. He's a monster.

I curl my hands into fists. "I hate you. I will always hate you. There will never be a time that I won't try to leave you. I will tell the world of what you've done at every opportunity. Do you hear me? I will not yield."

His expression turns sad, the corners of his lips drooping. "Then for your whole life, until I'm gone, I will have you to myself. We'll retire to my country estate, far from Santivilla."

I choke on my rage. "I'll kill you. I swear it."

Hector nods to the guards, and they close in. Then he raises his brow. A silent question.

Will I put up a fight?

I'm tempted. But he might drug me again, and I need to stay awake and alert. As they lead me away, Hector reaches for my arm, but I swerve away from him, pulling my hand close to my chest.

"I do admire your spirit, hija."

They drag me up the stairs, tie me back to the leather chair. The afternoon light seeps into the stuffy room, heating the space as if it were a furnace. My stomach rumbles, but Carla took away all the food and plates with a reproachful look in my direction.

I try not to sink into despair.

But the facts do nothing to ease my panic. Only Ofelia and my father knew I was coming to La Doña. Neither will think to look for me. Papá might not even be conscious.

A shuddering sob climbs up my throat.

Arturo will have noticed my absence for the last training session, but will he worry? I give in to my tears, let them reign. I hate crying, hate the way it makes my head pound and my eyelids swell. I clench my fists against the armrests and yank on the rope. The rough material scratches and bites into my skin. There's no give.

Papá needs me.

And I'm here, trapped in the gaudiest room I've ever seen with a man I trusted. I can't help Papá. An anguished scream rips out of me. The noise fills the room, rings in my ears, rides the blood coursing in my veins. I scream and scream and scream. Loud and long and relentless. The sound carries all of my rage and hurt, and promise of retribution.

My voice gives out. I hang my head, breathing hard.

The guard bursts into the room. The same one from earlier, now bearing red welts on his face. I'm not the least bit sorry. He takes a step into the room, raises his fist, and shakes it at me.

"Keep your mouth shut, or I'll do it for you. Do you understand?"

I lift my chin, but stay silent. I don't want him to gag me. He leaves, slamming the door. The sound reverberates in the chamber, and I'm alone again. I don't know what time it is. I look over to the window, the curtains pulled back revealing the rich blue of a perfect afternoon sky.

Only a few hours left before I'm supposed to walk into the arena.

I rock back and forth on the chair and use the momentum to hop. I let out a happy cry when it works, even though I've only moved about an inch. But it's something. I repeat the motion, aiming for the window. Someone might be able to see my face. It might be futile, but I can't sit around doing nothing. Again, I rock back and forth, and hop once, twice, three times. By the time I make it to the window, I'm sweating profusely, and my wrists blaze from the friction with the rope. I line myself up against the frame, maneuvering the chair parallel to the wall.

La Doña sits on a busy street, on a corner lot surrounded by immense oak trees. The window has a view of a side street and faces another brick building. Unfortunately, all of those windows are closed, the curtains drawn. People walk on the main avenue, hurrying along and seeing to their business. No one strolls down the smaller side path. It's enough to make me want to scream again.

But my voice has gone hoarse.

I press my temple against the warm glass. I watch the pedestrians for a few more moments, discarding one idea after another. My thoughts revolve around what I'll do to Hector when my hands are free again. That's when I see a familiar man slowly walking across the street. He peers down the smaller cobbled path running under my window, slowing until he comes to a stop at the middle of the road. Another figure joins him, slighter frame, wearing a bright red dress that came *straight* out of my wardrobe.

Arturo and Lola.

My heart leaps to my throat. I open my mouth to yell—and stop myself in time. Another outburst from me and the guard will return, and this time he'll bring something to stuff into my mouth. But can I grab their attention? My wrists are bound; I can't wave or scream. The window is closed—would the noise even carry three stories down?

Arturo and Lola continue walking, passing the side street and disappearing from view. Tears of frustration prick my eyes.

They're gone.

More time passes, and with each minute, panic claws to the surface, making my heart race. I haven't moved from my spot against the window. The sky turns a deep dusky gray. The Dragon Court will be making its way to La Giralda, a long line of gilded carriages snaking through the city.

They will all see me fail.

I peer at the main street. Several people travel by carriage down the bumpy path, and a few by horseback. It's a wealthy area, and people are dressed in their finest attire: velvet jackets, vibrant silk, ruffled hemlines. Hardly anyone looks up at the third story windows. If they did, they might have seen my face, might have recognized me. But then what? I can't write a message, and though I can move my lips and try to communicate my plight, who would understand?

My body numbs and becomes listless, my butt sore from sitting for hours. A closer inspection of my wrists reveals raw and inflamed skin. I tilt my head back, trying to stretch my tight neck muscles.

Something thuds against the wall.

With a gasp, I press myself close to the glass. A small pebble smacks it. Coming from . . . I search for the source. And then I see him. Hidden behind a tall topiary. He's in the shadow of the plant, next to an iron gate.

Arturo.

We meet eyes.

Relief feels like the loosening of a tight fist around my heart. He stares at me steadily, his upturned face barely clear from the distance, but it's him. He's cut his hair. I jerk in the chair, pulling on the ropes, hopping in place, hoping he'll understand that I can't move, I can't meet him down where he is.

Even from up here, I sense his scowl.

Arturo lifts his hand, a kind of wave that makes my heart melt. It's a promise. He means to free me. I nod, one, twice, a dozen times. Then he's gone, vanishing into the crowd. I press my temple once more to the glass.

Soon.

There isn't a clock in this room, no way to know how much time has passed, but in the meantime, I prepare myself for whatever Arturo has planned. I ought to return the chair to its original location, and once again, I hop across the room, settling next to the table. My wrists burn from the effort. I swallow, and it's painful. I'm thirsty, hungry, wounded.

The door opens, and Hector strides in, looking harassed. He points in my direction.

"Untie her, por favor, and load her into the carriage."

I lock my jaw. Here we go.

Two guards march inside. At first, I think they're going to cart me around, bound to this infernal chair, but one of the men pulls out a long serrated knife from its sheath attached to his leather belt. He hacks at the rope and the pieces fall in unraveled scraps to the wooden floor.

Hector lifts one of my wrists, rubbed raw from the rope. "I'll have my physician tend to this when you arrive at my estate."

I pull free with a mutinous glare. "Your physician won't touch me."

"The wounds will scar," he says coaxingly.

"I don't care." I jump to my feet, backing away from the two guards and Hector. "I'm not going to your estate."

Hector's smile is pained. "Don't make this difficult for my men. If you cooperate, they won't bind your wrists together."

I glance down at them, shuddering. The last thing I want is for more rope on the wounds, so I nod. The guards draw closer and usher me out the door.

Hector trails behind us. "I'm sorry I don't have anything for you to wear. I'll visit the seamstress and order an entire new wardrobe for you."

I barely hear his words. My mind races with one idea after another, scrambling for ways to stall. Will Arturo get here in time? I miss a step on the stairs, and Hector reaches for me, preventing my fall. The heat of his fingers on my sleeve makes my skin crawl. The rest of the way down, he keeps his hand on me, not trusting me to remain upright. When we reach the bottom, he offers me his arm and smiles at me. I wish I would have noticed how that expression is all teeth.

I shoot him a withering look.

Several guards join us, and they press in, surrounding me as if they're a tower of muscle and steel. I can barely see what's in front of me. Instead of the front door, they lead me to the back of the building where I know there to be a courtyard and fenced-in garden, kept nearly hidden by immense trees.

Dread seeps into my bones. There's no sign of Arturo. He's not going to make it in time; he won't know where Hector plans to send me.

I need to stall because the minute I step foot in that carriage, I'm lost. They'll never find me. Hector has three estates scattered around Hispalia. The iron gate looms ahead. We're close to the stables. Close to the carriage that will cart me off away from my family and friends. Away from Papá. I can't let that happen.

I won't.

With a strength I barely knew I have, I shove the guard on my left. He stumbles, and I break away from the circle. My feet pound the pebbled path, arms swinging wide. I let out a scream when someone grabs my waist. A gloved hand claps over my mouth, and another drags me backward until I'm pressed tight against a tall frame. I kick, aiming for his groin, but another guard grabs both my feet and lifts me up. I squirm and try to bite the man's wrist, but his fingers dig into my cheeks, press against my mouth so hard, I know I'll have bruises.

Hector barks orders to stuff me inside. I bend and tug and jerk my body in every direction, but I'm held too tight. I can't break free. My mind fights the panic coursing through my body, tries to think logically. But my vision blurs as the guard's glove slips higher and covers both my mouth and nose.

I can't get enough air.

Can't breathe.

I struggle harder, my heart pounding against my ribs, one painful thump at a time. He's going to kill me if he doesn't move his hand. The more I struggle, the tighter his hold becomes. Everything becomes blurry.

My eyes shut.

"You fool!" Hector snarls. "Put her down."

I blink. One, two, three times. My vision remains foggy, as if I were looking through a window marred by thick raindrops. The ground is hard beneath my cheek, my bent knees. I drag in air and cough from the effort.

Hector kneels beside me, and he reaches for me with gentle hands and cradles my head in his palms.

"If you didn't struggle, this would not have happened," he whispers. "I'm going to have to gag you, Zarela, for the duration of the ride."

"No," I say, my voice hoarse from screaming. "Why can't you leave me alone?"

"You're everything to me. We're going to have a good life together, you and I."

Someone hands him a long silk cloth, the shade a deep blood red. I feebly shove his hands away, but he wraps the silk around my head, parting my lips, and knotting it tight. They bind my hands behind my back, and when one of the guards motions to my ankles, Hector nods.

My eyesight returns to its normal clarity. Two men lift me, one holding my legs, the other my underarms, and they carry me through the iron gate. The stables loom ahead, the wood painted the color of an impending thunderstorm, gray and ominous. Hector points to one of the carriages and then snaps his fingers.

It's brought forward a moment later, and he opens the door. "Put her in. Gently."

I come alive again, writhing like a worm. The two guards place me inside, positioning me longways on one of the velvet benches, a deep purple, the color of bruises.

Hector leans against the doorframe. "You're heading to one of my estates in the north. It's maintained well, but I've written a letter to allow you some liberties. You'll have access to the garden, and perhaps one day, the horses. I'll join you as soon as I put to right my affairs in Santivilla. It won't be long, perhaps a week." He clears his throat, glancing away from the fury in my gaze. "In time, I hope you'll realize this is what your mother would have wanted. She would have never allowed you to fight in the arena. I vow to you that you will never want for anything."

I wish I were a dragon, because in this moment I could breathe fire. Spew flames until nothing remained of Hector Valdiz.

Hector straightens, and without another look in my direction, he shuts the door with a measured click. He pounds the roof twice and the carriage lurches forward.

I'm out of time.

TREINTA Y TRES

The carriage rocks to and fro, ambling out of the city and toward Northern Hispalia. A long journey that will take days. I force myself to breathe deeply and slowly. To shove my panic as far from my mind as I can. Because worrying is working against me. Makes me dizzy and scared. I need to focus. Come up with another plan.

I study the interior. It seats four people comfortably. Under the velvet cushions are drawers that might contain something useful. I'm lying on my hands, and I test the bonds. There's no give, and every tug makes my eyes water. My wrists burn fiery hot.

Thick drapes in the same purple as the seating cover the windows. My first quandary. If I can move the curtain, perhaps someone will be able to see my face. I sit up and scoot to the window, shimmying along as if I were a snake. The carriage bounces, and I tumble off the seat. My hip bone smacks against the floor. Shooting pains flare up and down my body.

Benches block the narrow space and there's not enough room to wiggle around, let alone sit up since I'm lying on my side. I take a deep, fortifying breath through my nose and force myself to squeeze onto my back, bending my legs so my feet are flat on the ground. At last I'm able to sit up, and I use the knobs of one of the drawers under the bench to help leverage me off the ground. It's awkward, but I somehow manage to resume sitting on the bench.

With my feet securely planted on the floor, I lean forward and use my chin to move the curtain. It's heavy and the fabric keeps bouncing and flapping in my face. I press my chin hard against the velvet, until it hits the glass, and slowly inch it to the side. The cobbled streets make my chin and the window smack against each other, and if I lose one of my teeth, I won't be the least bit surprised.

At last I'm able to see through a sliver of glass. We're still in Santivilla, but not far from one of the perimeter gates. The sky slowly turns into a deeper blue, sinking into night's cool embrace. We're on a narrow street, and it's completely deserted. Hector is smart enough to have instructed the driver to take the paths that don't run anywhere near main thoroughfares.

Damn it.

The carriage swerves onto a smaller street that opens to the arched exit. It's a looming tower, with iron teeth and guards fortified with arrows. Hispalia is known for their bowmen and steel. As we draw closer to the gate, my hope rises to dizzying heights.

One of the Santivilla guards might see me.

The carriage swings under the arched iron gate and comes to a stop. A lone sentry comes to question the driver. The voices are low murmurings, and I strain to hear. They continue their discussion and the carriage lurches forward.

No. No, no.

He has to see me. I press my face to the glass, widening the curtain, and as we move forward, the sentry's gaze lands on mine. I widen my eyes and groan loudly. The city guard takes a step forward, blinking wildly.

"Espera—" he says.

One of Hector's guards brushes past my window, and he jabs at the sentry's side, hard. The man slumps to the ground, head lolled to the side. He looks drunk or asleep or both. Hector's man faces my window and glares at me. He yanks the door open and pulls the velvet curtain shut.

"Stay out of sight," he growls.

The carriage resumes its brisk pace, the ride bumpier on the pebbled, desert path. I immediately slide the curtain so I can see outside, hoping for a glimpse of another traveler. My stomach plummets to my toes. There's no one in sight. We curve around a thick patch of trees and cross over a hill, and by the time the road straightens again, Santivilla is miles behind me.

And then, as if I'd conjured a person from thin air, from out of hope and desperation, a lone figure appears atop a hill. I blink and then blink again. The desert can sometimes trick people. But no, there's someone dashing toward the carriage, scrambling down rocks, side-stepping cactuses. It's a woman, her curly hair flying behind her.

"¡Ayuda!" she screams.

That voice. I forget to breathe. The air traps itself in my lungs.

Lola, Lola, Lola, Lola.

Running as if a dragon were behind her—I've never seen her move so fast—and rushing toward the guards on their imperious horses. The carriage stops, and I jerk forward, but thankfully my braced feet prevent me from sprawling to the ground again.

The guards jump off their horses and draw their weapons, stepping in front of the carriage door. I count eight of them. Their collective bulk shields me from any potential threat. I can still make out my friend as she races down the hill, screaming. Lola is a beautiful maid, with her luminous eyes and full lips, wild hair down to her waist, and lush figure. It's no surprise to me that the guards immediately lower their weapons. One of the men goes so far as to dart forward, as if to catch her in his arms. She reaches him, inconsolable, babbling about an attack on her home beyond the hill. Will they come? She sways on her feet and another guard reaches her, steadying her.

"Dónde vives?" another one demands. "Where is your home?"

She points to where she came from, hand shaking. Not once does she glance in my direction. Impatience sizzles in my bloodstream.

"Go. You three. The rest wait here with me," one of the captors says, the same one who murdered the unsuspecting sentry. Then he focuses on Lola and says in a hard voice, "You better not be planning any mischief."

Her eyes widen. "Señor, I would *never*."

Even I believe her sincerity, and I *know* better. He jerks his chin toward the hill. "Show my men the way to your home."

She rushes away and three guards follow closely, bolting up the incline. I press my face against the glass, unable to look away from the sight of my best friend running away from me.

What on earth is she planning? The group disappears after they crest the hill.

Seconds past, then minutes.

The bloodcurdling screams take us all by surprise. A chorus of terror, voices converging together at once, making the hair on my arm stand on end. The captain yells out an order. Three more guards charge up the hill, yelling a battle cry, their swords raised high over their heads. An orange glow streaks through the sky. It's hazy, but bright, as if someone had lit a thousand candles on the other side of that hill.

"I don't like this," the captain mutters to the last remaining guard standing outside the carriage door. "Something isn't right."

The other guard notches an arrow. "Strange the dragon hasn't flown."

"No, it's the girl. There was something off about her."

"Look!" the bowman cries. A scarlet shape shoots high up into the sky, enormous wings flapping furiously.

The red dragon.

Roja.

The captain and his man shoot their arrows, missing spectacularly. Roja flies closer, her great wings cracking like thunder. The horses are wild with terror, neighing and running off. A familiar rider expertly maneuvers the dragon directly above us. Broad-shouldered, hands scarred from long years of hunting, dark hair tousled.

Arturo. My relief is bone deep.

"If you attack," Arturo cries, voice loud and ringing above the yelling of the men, "she will burn you!"

There's a sharp whirring noise as an arrow goes flying. The string snaps again, another arrow, gone. What fools.

A crackling noise rents the air. A burst of fire blazes past the window—both the men go up in flames, and their screams are terrible. The flapping draws nearer, and a great thud makes the carriage bounce. The sound of pattering boots grows loud and then louder.

The door snaps open, and Arturo fills the frame. He's dressed in black trousers and a matching tunic, a leather strap across his broad chest. On the opposite shoulder, he carries a medium-sized canvas bag.

He scowls at me. "There you are."

I laugh, tears streaming down my face. He came for me. Arturo climbs into the carriage, pulls a knife out of his boot, and cuts away my bindings. Then he lifts me off the floor and pulls me into his lap, presses his mouth against my throat. "Damn you, Zarela."

I let out a watery chuckle. And then a sudden thought seizes me. "How's my father?"

Arturo squeezes me, and I lean back, far enough to look into his face, but not far enough to not be in his arms. His gray eyes are the saddest I've ever seen them.

"No," I whisper. "*No.*"

"He's gone," he says in a gentle voice. "Died this afternoon. He took a turn quite suddenly and never recovered."

"He was poisoned by Hector." I let out a shuddering sob. Papá died alone. He's gone. How is that possible? His story can't be over. I was supposed to make it back to him in time. The tears keep coming, and a yawning pit stretches inside me, swallows me whole. I can't get enough air.

Arturo tightens his hold and his fingers draw circles against my back.

My breaths come out in short pants. I'm trying to climb out of a deep hole with my bare hands.

He presses a soft kiss against my temple. "Lola and Guillermo will be here any minute."

I turn my head so it's facing the doorway, the hill in the backdrop.

Sure enough, two figures run down the hill. Arturo helps me climb out of the carriage. His gaze drops to my raw wrists, and his mouth flattens into a thin line.

"Bastard," he hisses under his breath.

"Zarela, Zarela," Lola chants as she reaches us.

She throws her arms around me, and we hold on to each other tight. Her crying dampens my tunic, but I don't care. I pull away from her, and we're both a mess of tears and splotchy cheeks and runny noses. The dragon curls at the foot of the hill, watching us with mild interest. Lola pushes my hair away from my face and stares at me with bloodshot eyes.

"I don't understand," I say. "I heard so many people screaming. Who were they?"

"It was us," Guillermo says, tucking his chin toward his chest. "I used an encanto."

I stare at him, stunned. "Gracias."

"What do you want to do, Zarela?" Arturo asks.

I can't break down, no matter how much I want to. Anger swirls before me, burns through every thought. "Fly me back to Santivilla."

"Another dragon ride," Lola huffs, wiping her streaming eyes. "Ugh."

Arturo holds out his hand. "We might not make it in time."

"I have to try."

The corner of his lips kicks up. "Of course you do, mi amor."

Lola reaches for the bag and pulls out a red, glittering bundle. I gasp at the sight. The colorful, ornate stitching travels the length of the tunic arm sleeves, lined with gleaming brass buttons. Instead of pants, Lola designed a matching skirt with three layers of ruffles. The same ornate detail follows along the hem. The corresponding jacket has a thick, heavy hood with the same glittering stitching.

It's so beautiful, I don't want to touch it.

And when I lean closer, I realize what it's made of.

"Is that—dragon scales?" I let out a hoarse laugh. "This is what you two have been working on. All this time—it was to make me my own Dragonador outfit."

"Guillermo enchanted the hide, and I finished it." She purses her lips, thinking. "It's flame- and waterproof, repels noxious gas, and wards off smoke." Her face brightens. "The best part? The material doesn't stain!"

"Will it make me fly?"

Guillermo laughs. "That's a resounding no."

I pull her into a hug. Somehow, she made me smile. That's Lola, though. "You're the best damn seamstress living."

She sniffs. "I know."

"And the humblest," Arturo says wryly. "Señoritas, we need to go."

Lola drags me to the carriage, and she helps me change into the traje de luces that honors the traditional dress, but also fits the person I am. A flamenco dancer who can wield a capote like her father. We climb onto the back of the dragon, and Roja lifts off the ground with a great flap of her wings. Arturo pulls on the reins and guides her home.

I hope I'm not too late.

TREINTA Y CUATRO

The wind is an animal all on its own. At times gentle and murmuring, and in other moments loud and tempestuous. The breeze cuts my cheeks and whips my hair, hammering it into submission. It's freezing this high up above the roaming desert. Roja's wings cut mercilessly across the darkening sky. I lean forward, wanting to urge her faster. But she's already moving at a furious speed, chasing the last of the sun's rays. I bury my grief deep within me, let myself only feel the rage fueling my battered body.

I will not let Hector get away with this.

Santivilla's round outer walls come into view. We swoop lower, the four towers spread around, equally distant from one another and illuminated by guttering torches. Arturo sits behind me, one arm tight around my waist, holding me secure. The other grips a long leather strap tied around one of the dragon's ivory horns. Guillermo routinely yells out a curse with every dip and swerve, and Lola laughs in response.

The sun is near gone, and all that's left is a tiny sliver of light. The steady brightening of the moon and her many glimmering companions shines a way into the beating heart of the city. As we fly closer to Santivilla, my stomach clenches—there are protective measures taken against a dragon attack. But in general, the guards of the city usually wait to see what the beast will do first. If they attack, the dragon is sure to.

Arturo knows this, and he lets Roja swirl above the roofs, sweeping through the misty clouds and darkening sky. The bells ring, and I know we're being watched. Arturo guides the dragon toward La Giralda, and in the dying light, I catch sight of its turrets and red-gold banners whipping in the breeze. The arena is lit by dozens of torches—who made sure to light them?—and filled with a smattering of spectators.

More than I thought would show up.

Their sharp cries reach my ears, and I glance over my shoulder to Arturo. He winks at me and motions for me to take the reins. Lola peers down and bites her lip. Guillermo tightens his hold around her waist, a protective gesture that makes her smile softly to herself. The people below jump to their feet, and hoarse yells fill the night, drifting up to meet us in a riot of astonishment and horror.

Roja lowers onto the white sand, and the patrons stop running, shocked into silence at the sight of four people riding the elusive red dragon. The people of Santivilla haven't seen such a thing, not ever. The moment she has all four legs on the ground, a collective gasp makes a roaring sound in my ears.

The crowd is a blur of faces, but the Dragon Master stands out from the masses. He's dressed in his most somber ensemble befitting his status as a Master: ebony tunic with golden stitched flames racing up the sleeves, a heavy chain adorned with a single medallion. His white hair gleams a burnished gold from all the firelight.

A thrill sizzles through me.

The Dragon Master is on his feet, a look of pure astonishment etched into his weathered face. I wait for him to shout at me, to give the order for attack. But he does none of those things. He can't take his attention off the dragon and a tense silence settles over everyone.

Lola nudges my shoulder and gestures to the tunnel entrance where Hector waits, dressed in a resplendent Dragonador traje de luces in dark navy, adorned with coral and yellow flower embroidery. His white pants are lined with an enchanted shimmering thread stretching all the way down to the hem. On his feet are polished leather shoes with blue and white tassels.

He wears colors representative of *his* dragon ring.

"Zarela—" he growls, taking a step toward me.

Anger burns a path straight to my heart.

Arturo slides off the dragon and then turns to help me down. "Destroy him," he whispers.

Roja unfurls her great wings as Lola and Guillermo jump, landing on the white sand with loud thuds. Arturo is a steady presence next to me, his anger radiating off him as if he were a furnace. Hector takes a menacing step toward Roja, yanks his sword free, the metallic ring disturbing the sudden hush.

And then everything seems to happen at once.

The dragon lets out a bone-chilling snarl.

Don Eduardo shouts orders, calls me a fool.

I have seconds to act. I dart forward, stepping between the dragon and Hector, raising my hands. "Stay where you are, señor."

Hector stiffens at the cold formality in my voice. He takes another step forward, the metal in his hands glinting gold from the surrounding torches.

The man never listens to me.

"Don't move," Arturo snarls. "For your life."

Roja's hot breath curls around my back. I glance over my shoulder and shudder. Her rage is a tangible, scary thing. Ready to erupt, and I'm directly in her path. My knees lock and sweat drops down my back. Guards wearing the Gremio's color appear at the tunnel entrances, surrounding us. Another massacre at La Giralda.

"Zarela," Arturo says in a hoarse whisper.

I ignore him and move to lock eyes with the dragon, slowly raising my arms. Roja growls, not understanding. Saliva drips onto the white sand from her open jaw.

I need music.

"Zarela, move out of the way," Hector yells, furious.

"I need a guitar," Arturo says to the mago. "Quickly."

Guillermo reaches deep into his tunic pockets and pulls out a handful of wands, frantically reading the labels, and then finally settles on one of them. He breaks it in half and gold smoke mists from out of one end, shaping into a guitar. The mago tosses the instrument to Arturo and then leads Lola to one of the arena entrances.

Hector lunges forward—

The dragon roars, lifting its tail and crouching low, readying to leap.

"Now!" I scream with my hands twisted high above my head.

Arturo strikes commanding chords on the guitar, as if he were a general marching toward battle and death. The notes are loud and explosive, helped along by the magic of the encanto. Swallowing up all the other sounds: the screaming crowd, Hector's shouting, the dragon's snarl.

Roja and Hector startle, both jerking their heads toward Arturo.

I wait for the right beat, and the moment I hear it, I cock my hip and twirl my fingers.

Arturo's fingers dance along the strings, and the melody stirs the air, sinks into my bones, emboldens my feet. The notes roar and dance on the breeze. It's soothing and lovely and fills the hole in my heart where my grief seeks shelter.

Hector moves to grab me around the waist, but the dragon whips her tail and flings him backward. He lands on his side and immediately clutches his ribs.

Roja crouches, readying to leap.

But I twirl in front of her, blocking her path to Hector. I ought to let her have at him for what he's done to me, but I don't want to be responsible for one more death. My hips sway, rolling and beckoning and deliberate. I take a step forward with my right foot and stomp with my left. The notes blur together. They come faster, and I follow the song's lead, slamming my heels into the packed sand. I have to stomp twice as hard in order for the noise to carry. I lift the corner of my skirt, sweep it to the right and left.

I'm in this arena for my parents. Fighting for our name.

Dancing for our legacy.

I twirl closer and closer to Roja. She's on her feet and rocking forward and back, in tune with Arturo's playing. The crowd gasps as she slams her two front feet, the ground cracking under her claws. I twist my hands, curl each finger slower and dip low to the floor, and the dragon imitates me, neck bending, tail lifting high into the air.

Dimly I hear the roar of the crowd, the clapping and stomping of feet, the earsplitting whistles and exuberant cheering. All the cheering rushes into my head, and I think of my mother and what she might have thought of this performance. Would she be proud? As the music swells, my heart pounds faster. This dance is my own, but in the next moment, my feet move into familiar steps. A routine I've done a thousand times.

One that I love, one that is all my mother.

The noise coming from the crowd is deafening. They recognize this dance, have saved it in their hearts for years. The dragon follows me as I spin, moving from one end of the ring to the other. This show is exactly who I am. Half my mother, half my father. I carry both of their hearts within me. The music slows, and the dragon curls around me as the last notes slip away into the night.

No one shouts me out of the arena.

No one chants for my mother.

I pet Roja's side, and she huffs a great breath that tousles my hair, disgruntled by my touch. I hastily step away from her as Arturo strides toward me. He takes me in his arms and holds me tight. Brings his lips to the side of my neck and kisses the soft skin.

"Your father would have loved it," he whispers.

Tears cling to my eyelashes. I nod once and then take his hand. Everyone jumps to their feet, roaring and clapping. We walk to the spot right in front of the box where the Dragon Master waits with other prominent members of the Gremio.

I danced in the arena with a dragon and neither of us died. We co-existed, both drawn by something beautiful. We created something together, new and pure and lovely.

My mother would have loved it too.

Don Eduardo brings his hands up and claps. One, twice, a hundred times, and everyone follows suit. I never want to forget this moment, the feeling of having done something special, of standing on my own two feet after I've lost so much.

The Dragon Master lifts his arms and slowly lowers them, and the applause dies down. "You've surprised me, Zarela Zalvidar. I only wish your father had been able to see it."

A sob escapes me. "He did."

Movement catches the corner of my eye. Hector tries to take a step toward me, a peculiar expression on his face. For once, he's lost his calm, his rage. He gazes at me in stunned awe—as if realizing just how badly he's underestimated me.

Then Hector moves quickly toward Don Eduardo, who stands at the railing, gaze flickering between us. The rest of the crowd notices the discord, feels the tension twisting and tilting in the air, and they find their seats, waiting with a collective breath.

"Señorita Zarela," Don Eduardo says. "What you did was incredibly foolish. You could have died; you placed all of us in danger by coming here with a loose dragon."

Hector nods, a smug line in his posture, and I shift my attention to the ground.

"But," the Dragon Master continues, "I have never seen anything so marvelous in my entire life."

My shoulders sag, tears pricking my eyes as I lift my head. The Conde del Corte gazes down at me, a wistful smile on his weathered face.

"Don Eduardo—" Hector begins in an outraged tone.

"Hector only just finished telling us that tonight's performance is canceled due to the death of your father." Don Eduardo's attention swerves to Roja, who hasn't moved from her spot. "But you're here and you've danced"—he clears his throat, overcome—"with the Escarlata. Why do you look as if you've gone to battle?"

I'd forgotten about my torn-up wrists and windswept hair, my dirty training clothes.

"She's terribly distraught and obviously needs to see a healer," Hector says quickly. "Let me take care of her, and we'll visit the Gremio tomorrow."

The Dragon Master nods, accepting the words without hearing a word I have to say. They all expect me to accept the story they're writing for me. But I abhor the ending they've written. I will pen my own fate.

"You asked *me* why I look to have survived a battle? Because I have been held prisoner by Hector Valdiz and only just escaped," I say, my voice rising, and I imagine the words catch on fire, burning anyone who stands in my way.

At this, the arena bursts into loud whispering and chatter, but the noise dies down when Don Eduardo lifts a creased and weathered hand. Hector moves until we're standing side by side. I stiffen at the proximity.

"This child is obviously grieving over the loss of her parent and clearly imagining things," Hector exclaims. "She endangered all of our lives by bringing this monster here. Let me take her."

My body shakes with pent-up fury and disgust.

"I am distraught over the *murder* of my father," I say. "He was poisoned and died alone because I was kept a prisoner." I lift my arms. "Look at my wrists. See the burn marks where the rope bit into my skin. I'm here only because your nephew, my best friend, and the mago apprentice Guillermo rescued me with the help of this noble dragon behind me."

"She lies; she's hysterical," Hector cries. "This is only a desperate attempt to keep La Giralda."

I point to Hector. "This man held me against my will." A loud hum escalates at my declaration, and Don Eduardo rises and lowers his arms, demanding quiet. The crowd falls silent, but their eyes are on Hector.

Accusing. Shocked. Angry.

"He is also responsible for the massacre here in La Giralda on our five hundredth anniversary showcase," I say loud and clear. "I ask for justice."

"What do you have to say?" Don Eduardo exclaims to Hector. "Is this true?"

"All lies," Hector says, impervious. "Her father died, and Zarela wishes to blame someone. I'm afraid she's concocted this far-fetched tale to cope with the incredible amount of stress she's been experiencing. With her father gone, I am her guardian—and as dictated by law, responsible for her. While certainly embarrassing, I won't seek retribution for her outrageous claims."

I step forward, but Arturo places a gentle hand on my shoulder. Reminding me that I am not alone in this fight.

"Then how do you explain her wrists?" Arturo asks. "I planned her rescue, using that dragon." He points to Roja. "And if you take the north road, you'll find Hector's abandoned carriage and shorn bindings. How much more proof do you need?"

"You'll also find a dead sentry at the eastern gate—murdered by one of Hector's men," I add.

Hector scoffs. "He's clearly infatuated with her and will support her lies, whatever they may be!" he yells, gesturing to our clasped hands. "Look at them!"

Roja snarls, clearly annoyed by Hector's raised voice. She snaps her jaw and he falls quiet, eyeing her uneasily. The Dragon Master silently considers us, his eyes studying my wrists, then the legendary dragon. I wait with my heart in my throat. He beckons for two of his guards to come close and whispers something. They nod and immediately leave the box, no doubt to find the overturned carriage.

"If Señorita Zalvidar is lying, explain her injuries," the Dragon Master demands.

"Self-inflicted," Hector replies instantly. "As I said—"

"You think she hurt herself? Whatever for? Answer very carefully, Hector, for there are magical ways to prove you're lying. A simple encanto will reveal the effects of poison."

Hector stiffens, tension straightening his spine. "I stand by what I said."

"Then you are a fool." Don Eduardo sighs. "It's clear I didn't believe Zarela when I should, and Arturo has never lied to me. Hector Valdiz, you have betrayed the Gremio."

Triumph blazes within me. For once, the Dragon Master is looking at someone else in cold mistrust. Hector flinches.

"You have destroyed the life of Santiago Zalvidar, but I will not let you ruin his legacy or his place in the Gremio." The Dragon Master's raspy voice turns fiery hot, furious and eviscerating. I'm surprised Hector still stands. "Never again will you fight as a Dragonador. Your name will be stripped from our records." He leans forward, eyes menacing. "La Doña belongs to us now."

"Don Eduardo—" Hector begs.

But the Dragon Master raises his hand, and Hector falls silent. "You have no right to address me at all." The guards reappear at the arena entrance, and with a start, I realize Don Eduardo hadn't sent them to find the carriage after all.

The Dragon Master addresses me next. "I'm sorry for the ordeal you've gone through."

"Zarela," Hector says, reaching for me.

Don Eduardo motions to the sentries posted on either side of him. "Take him out of my sight. You'll await trial in the Gremio prison."

They drag him away as he rages my name, begging to speak with me. But his words aren't heard because the crowd lets out a collective cheer that threatens to shake every corner of Santivilla.

They whistle and clap, twirling their neckties in the air as a show of respect for Papá.

"I have something to say," Don Eduardo says when the whistling and stomping has died down. "I'd like to call for a vote as most of the ruling members of the Gremio are here. All in favor of reinstating the Zalvidar family and their descendants, and for La Giralda to forever remain in the care of this noble family, please raise your hand."

Everyone does. Even the people who aren't members of the guild. I let out a timid, happy laugh. Lola runs to where we stand together—dragging a mortified Guillermo—and she takes hold of my hand. We all lift our faces.

"By unanimous vote, it is my decision that La Giralda will forever belong to Zarela Zalvidar and her descendants. And I deem it proper that the Gremio help repair this magnificent dragon ring to its former glory," Don Eduardo says. "And Zarela?"

"Yes, Don Eduardo?"

"I invite you to become an official Dragonador among us."

I take Arturo's hand. "With respect, I will never fight a dragon, Don Eduardo. But if you'll permit it, I will dance with one."

Arturo squeezes my palm, looking at me with utter devotion.

The Dragon Master appears to consider this, thinking hard. "Well, it will make Martina Sanchez happy at least. One less dragon fighter in Santivilla. Who knows? Maybe the arenas will follow your example."

My jaw drops, hardly daring to believe. "Is that a yes?"

He nods. "It is, Señorita Zalvidar."

For the first time in three thousand years, there will be one arena where a dragon won't meet their end. It's a small step in the right direction. "Gracias, Don Eduardo."

Lola jumps up and down, half screaming, half crying. Arturo pulls us both into a tight embrace. I haul Guillermo into the fold, and he's surprised at first, but then smiles shyly. He leans down and kisses Lola on the cheek, near the curve of her mouth, and to my astonishment, she blushes. Surrounding us are the cheers of everyone in the arena, people clapping and hollering, their fans fluttering. Roja looks around, sniffs loudly, and expands her great wings, seemingly bored with the events. She glances at Arturo, who nods once, and then shoots up into the night. I watch her go, sure that I'll dance with her again.

As the noise reaches a crescendo, I tuck myself closer to my people, mi familia. Our lives will change, but we'll be together to face the rest. My heart wishes my father could be standing with us, and the grief I hold swarms close, demanding to be heard. Arturo wipes the sudden tears running down my chin, and he stares at me fiercely, reminding me that even in the worst days, he'll be with me.

EPILOGUE

I rest the bouquet of gardenias on Papá's tombstone and then settle onto the ground before it, as if I were preparing for a long visit with a friend. In a way, perhaps I am. My skirt bunches around my ankles, but the cemetery is near empty, and I've long since stopped comparing myself to Mamá's appearance, particularly in dress.

"We tried out a new dance with Roja," I begin conversationally. "She hated it, of course, but I think it was because she wanted to hold a sword instead of the cape. This made Arturo very grumpy, and Lola thought the dragon might actually use the sword on the costume. Have I told you that? Lola insists on all the dragons wearing costumes. I think it's adorable; Arturo thinks it's ridiculous. She's finally a member of the Gremio de los Sastres now, by the way. Her apprenticeship in sewing and design finally ended, and she's hoping to open up her own establishment. She's also forced Guillermo into becoming her beau. I think he's still figuring out exactly how that happened."

I clear my throat.

"Ignacio has been giving Arturo more responsibility every day, and between you and me, Arturo might be a ranch owner faster than he thinks." I break off, smiling. "We're in love, and I think you'd be pleased. He's kinder than most people think, hardworking and dedicated. My success doesn't intimidate him. He makes me laugh, even if I'm angry with him. I still don't know how he manages it."

The wind picks up furiously, and I glance around, bemused at the sudden sight of the leaves rustling and dancing in the air. The weather is crisp, and there's a bite to every morning. I pull my cloak around me tighter and then tap a finger against my lips. "What else can I tell you, dear Papá? Our shows continue to do well, and this week, I'll be dancing with not one dragon in the arena, but two. Don Eduardo is a frequent attender, but I don't think he comes to only view the performances," I muse. "He might be coming in order to repair the relationship with his nephew. Arturo has filled up our cellars with more dragons needing a temporary home before they're set free in the wild." I fall silent for a moment, staring at the stone, unable to get used to having a conversation with it. My gaze never drops to the ground—it still hurts too much to think of Papá buried under all that dirt.

My throat thickens. "I miss you terribly. So does Ofelia, by the way. She insists on continuing to lay out your clothes each day."

Slowly, I stand and brush the tips of my fingers to my lips. Then I gently press the stone and walk away, my heart heavy, but my mind clear. I walk out of the cemetery, past the wrought iron gates to where the other carriages are parked. Arturo leans against the side of ours, legs crossed at the ankles, leather hat at an angle over his windswept hair. When he sees me, a soft smile tugs the corners of his mouth. He seems to understand my mood instantly.

With one hand, Arturo opens the carriage door, and as he helps me inside, he asks, "How's your Papá?"

I think for a moment. "He wants to know if we're getting married."

Arturo climbs in after me and shuts the door behind me. He uses his fist to smack the ceiling twice. Then he glances at me. "What did you tell him?"

My brows quirk as I delicately shrug. "I told him I have many things to do first. Shows to perform, cities to visit, routines to dream up and practice."

He grins at me fondly. It's one of the things he loves about me, I think: my ambition and plans for the future, the desire to live up to my name in a way that makes *me* proud. He's built the same exact way. "You have a book to write," I add. "Dragons to save. And one day, a ranch to run." I smile shyly. "But maybe someday."

Arturo cradles my face in his hands. "I'd wait forever for you." He pulls me into a kiss, and it's like every other time.

We catch fire.

ACKNOWLEDGMENTS

My love of flamenco started when I was four, after my Tía Tere sent me a red, ruffled dress all the way from Seville. I'm not joking when I write that I never wanted to take it off. She died of breast cancer in 2012, and never got to read any of my books, but I like to think she'd especially love this one.

To my agent, Sarah Landis. You are a ray of sunshine in my publishing world and I'm so thankful for you! Thanks for the support and encouragement, especially during one of my meltdowns. You've kept me sane throughout this whole journey! ☺

I'm so thankful to everyone who helped shape *Together We Burn* into the story it is today. For the Wednesday Books team: Eileen Rothschild, Lisa Bonvissuto, Kerri Resnick, Melanie Sanders, Lexi Neuville, and Brant Janeway—a million thanks for falling in love with the world of Hispalia, and championing Zarela and Arturo. Eileen, thanks especially for pushing me to make this story as romantic as possible. All the kissing, all the time. Many thanks also to Christa Desir, and to the production manager, interior designer, and my publicist.

A heartfelt thanks to my writing friends: Rebecca Ross, Shelby Mahurin, Adrienne Young, Kristin Dwyer, Stephanie Garber, Rachel Griffin, Zoraida Córdova, Ashley Hearn, Emily Henry, Kerri Maniscalco, and Romina Garber. For the blurbs and critiques, long phone calls, group chats, and Zoom calls. You all are gems and I'm so thankful y'all are in my life. If I'm missing anyone, please blame my deadline brain!! Special shout-out to Stephanie for cutting words that didn't need to be there (you are brilliant! And ruthless! I love it!), to Kristin for making sure I nail emotion (it's so HARD! I don't understand how your brain works), and Rebecca for reading the sloppy first draft, chapter by chapter, and still finding nice things to say.

Elena Armas, mil gracias y besos por tu ayuda! Your voice memos on Whatsapp gave me so much life!

Thanks to my friends who have supported my dream from the be-ginning: Patricia Gray, Jessica Meyer, Elizabeth Sloan, Jessie Pierce, and Davey Olsen. Love you all so much. To my familia: Mamá, Papá, and Rodrigo, I love you! Thank you for the love and support. I wouldn't be here without any of you. (You don't have to buy twenty copies of all my books, promise.)

To Andrew, the love of my life, you are the reason for everything. Thanks for cooking and cleaning while I'm on deadline, for making me laugh when I want to cry, and for somehow knowing what I need before I do. You're the sriracha to my everything.

Lastly, to Jesus, for loving me exactly where I am.